ARE YOU READY TO:

Shake hands with an elf
Battle a troll
Enter a magic valley
Build your own Santa
Awaken a warlock
Slay a dragon
Dance with a fairy
Steal a dragon's treasure
Make a deal with a demon

And enjoy the thousand and one other adventures
awaiting all who dare to gaze upon these immortal

Treasures of Fantasy

WITH STORIES FROM:

Margaret Weis • Anne McCaffrey
Mercedes Lackey • Larry Niven
Poul Anderson • Roger Zelazny
Patricia A. McKillip • Andre Norton
Marion Zimmer Bradley • Orson Scott Card
R. A. Lafferty • Jennifer Roberson
John Jakes • Philip José Farmer • Joanna Russ
Lois Tilton • Alan Brennert • Robert Sheckley
C. J. Cherryh • Jane Yolen • Avram Davidson
Theodore Sturgeon • Philip K. Dick
Melanie Rawn • Ursula K. Le Guin
Tracy Hickman

CONTENTS

INTRODUCTION

It was one of those casual conversations on board an airplane. My companion asked me what type of work I did. I replied that I wrote fantasy novels.

"You know, books with elves and dwarves and dragons," I explained, having ruled out her initial concept of fantasies, which involved consenting adults, whips, and black leather.

"Isn't that nice," she said. "Any time you want, you can escape the real world."

I thought about that statement as I sat down to work. In my mind was the universal picture of fantasy readers and writers, fleeing the harsh realities of today's world by burying ourselves in realms of the imagination.

Imaginary realms in which the major theme is the conflict of good and evil.

Now there's something you don't see a lot in the real world.

Imaginary realms in which there is racial strife: dwarves, elves, and humans, orcs, and goblins, battling to survive, all of them convinced that their race deserves to dominate, all other races are inferior.

You never see prejudice like that here in the real world.

Imaginary realms in which young people come of age, struggle to understand themselves and their place in society. Realms in which people are willing to sacrifice their lives for causes in which they believe. Realms in which people work together to achieve their goals.

Pretty unrealistic, if you ask me.

Imaginary realms where wars ravage cities, innocents are slaughtered, atrocities committed. Realms where refugees flee, children starve, dictators rule.

How do fantasy writers come up with such wild ideas?

Fantasy tales are today's parables. They present problems

and issues of today in a manner that is enjoyable and therefore is often dismissed. Fantasy tales are not less powerful simply because they are entertaining. Sometimes we see so much evil around us that we become hardened, inured. Move the problems into a different setting and we suddenly see them more clearly. When we read about evil manifested in the form of a dragon setting fire to a city or a human butchering an elf, our eyes are opened. Hopefully, we will come to understand that, like Frodo, one person, no matter how small and insignificant, can make a difference.

So the next time someone accuses you of escaping today's problems by reading fantasy stories, make them a present of this book.

Fire-breathing dragons . . . napalm bombs . . .

One is more beautiful, but they're both just as horrifying.

Of the two genres, science fiction has been considered to be more serious, to take a more serious and scholarly approach to life. To prove that fantasy can achieve the same effect, we feature several stories in this fantasy anthology by novelists who are known for their work in science fiction: Anne McCaffrey, Andre Norton, and Ursula K. Le Guin. Men noted for their work in science fiction are also represented in this fantasy volume: Larry Niven, Poul Anderson, Philip K. Dick, Orson Scott Card.

Some personal favorites are included as well: Melanie Rawn, Marion Zimmer Bradley, Mercedes Lackey, Jennifer Roberson, C. J. Cherryh, Jane Yolen, Philip José Farmer, Theodore Sturgeon.

And here is at least one author, John Jakes, who is best known for his work in popular fiction.

Finally, I am so pleased that we were able to include a story by the late Roger Zelazny, whose life, as well as work, was an inspiration to us all.

—Margaret Weis

TREASURES
OF
FANTASY

THE BEST

MARGARET WEIS

Short story writing has always been very difficult for me. I sometimes spend more time agonizing over a short story plot than I do the plot for an entire novel. By contrast, the plot for this story came to me in a flash. No suffering. No screaming. No pain. An easy delivery. Perhaps that's why it's one of my favorites!

I knew the four would come. My urgent plea had brought them. Whatever their motives—and, among this diverse group, I knew those motives were mixed—they were here.

The best. The very best.

I stood in the door of the Bitter Ale Inn and, surveying them, my heart was easier than it had been in many, many days.

The four did not sit together. Of course, they didn't know each other, except perhaps by reputation. Each sat at his or her own table, eating, drinking quietly. Not making a show of themselves. They didn't need to. They were the best. But though they said nothing with their mouths—using them for the Bitter Ale so famous in these parts—they were putting their eyes to work: sizing each other up, taking each other's measure. I was thankful to see that each seemed to like what he or she saw. I wanted no bad blood between members of this group.

Sitting at the very front of the Inn, short in stature but large in courage—was Orin. The dwarf was renowned through these parts for his skill with his ax, but then so were most dwarves. His blade—Splithair—lay on the table before him, where he could keep both an eye and a loving hand on it. Orin's true talent lay beneath a mountain, as the saying went. He had traversed more dragon caves than any other dwarf who had ever lived. And he had never once lost his way, either there or (more important) back out again. Many a treasure-hunter owed his life—and about a third of the treasure—to his guide, Orin Dark-seer.

Seated near the dwarf, at the best table the Bitter Ale had to offer, was a woman of incredible beauty. Her hair was long and black as a moonless night, her eyes drank in men's souls like the dwarf was drinking ale. The tavern's regulars—a sorry lot of ne'er-do-wells— would have been nosing around her, their tongues hanging out, but for the marks on her clothes.

She was well-dressed, don't mistake me. The cloth she wore was the finest, most expensive velvet in all the land. Its blue color gleamed in the firelight. It was the silver embroidery on the cuffs of her robes and around the hemline that warned off the cheek-pinchers and kiss-snatchers—pentagrams and stars and intertwined circles and such like. Cabalistic marks. Her beautiful eyes met mine and I bowed to Ulanda, the sorceress, come all the way from her fabled castle hidden in the Blue Mist forest.

Seated near the door—as near the door as he could get and still remain in the Inn—was the one member of the four I knew well. I knew him because I was the one who had turned the key in his prison cell and set him free. He was thin and quick, with a mop of red hair and green roguish eyes that could charm a widow out of her life savings and leave her loving him for it. Those slender fingers of his could slide in and out of a pocket as fast as his knife could cut a purse from a belt. He was good, so good he wasn't often caught. Reynard Deft-hand had made one small mistake. He'd tried to lift a purse from me.

Directly across the room from Reynard—dark balancing light in the scales of creation—was a man of noble bearing and stern countenance. The regulars left him alone, too, out of respect for his long and shining sword and the white surcoat he wore, marked with the silver cross. Eric of Truestone, a holy paladin. I was as amazed to see him as I was pleased. I had sent my messengers to their headquarters, begging the knights for aid. I knew they would respond—they were honor-bound. But they had responded by sending me their best.

All four the best, the very best. I looked at them and I felt awed, humbled.

"You should be closing down for the night, Marian," I said, turning to the pretty lass who tended bar.

The four dragon-hunters looked at me and not one of them moved. The regulars, on the other hand, took the hint. They quaffed their ale and left without a murmur. I hadn't been in these parts long—newly come to my job—and, of course, they'd put me to the test. I'd been forced to teach them to respect me. That had been a week ago and one, so I heard, was still laid up. Several of the others winced and rubbed their cracked heads as they hurried past me, all politely wishing me good-night.

"I'll lock the door," I said to Marian.

She, too, left, also wishing me—with a saucy smile—a good night. I knew well she'd like to make my good night a better one, but I had business.

When she was gone, I shut and bolted the door. This clearly made Reynard nervous (he was already looking for another escape route), so I came quickly to the point.

"No need to ask why you're here. You've each

come in response to my plea for help. I am Gondar,
King Frederick's seneschal. I am the one who sent you
the message. I thank you for your quick response and I
welcome you, well, *most* of you"—I cast a stern glance
at Reynard, who grinned—"to Fredericksborough."

Sir Eric rose and made me a courteous bow. Ulanda
looked me over with her wonderful eyes. Orin grunted.
Reynard was jingling coins in his pocket. The regulars
would be out ale money tomorrow, I guessed.

"You all know why I sent for you," I continued. "At
least, you know part of the reason. The part I could
make public."

"Please be seated, Seneschal," said Ulanda, with a
graceful gesture. "And tell us the part you *couldn't*
make public."

The knight joined us, as did the dwarf. Reynard
was going to, but Ulanda warned him off with a look.
Not the least bit offended, he grinned again and leaned
against the bar.

The four waited politely for me to go on.

"I tell you this in absolute confidence," I said, lowering my voice. "As you know, our good king, Frederick, has journeyed to the north on invitation from his
half-brother, the Duke of Northhampton. There were
many in the court who advised His Majesty not to go.
None of us trust the twisting, covetous duke. But His
Majesty was ever a loving sibling and north he went.
Now, our worst fears have been realized. The duke is
holding the king hostage, demanding in ransom seven
coffers filled with gold, nine coffers filled with silver,
and twelve coffers filled with precious jewels."

"By the blood of our Savior, we should burn this
duke's castle to the ground," said Eric Truestone. His
hand clenched over his sword's hilt.

I shook my head. "We would never see His Majesty alive again."

"This is not why you brought us here," growled Orin. "Not to rescue your king. He may be a good king, for all I know, but . . ." The dwarf shrugged.

"Yes, but you don't care whether a human king lives or dies, do you, Orin?" I said, with a smile. "No reason you should. The dwarves have their own king."

"And there are some of us," said Ulanda softly, "who have no king at all."

I wondered if the rumors I'd heard about her were true, that she lured young men to her castle and kept them until she tired of them, then changed them into wolves, forced to guard her dwelling place. At night, it was said, you could hear their howls of anguish. Looking into those lovely eyes, I found myself thinking, *It might just be worth it!*

I wrenched myself back to the business at hand.

"I have not told you the worst," I said. "I collected the ransom. This is a wealthy kingdom. The nobles dipped into their treasuries. Their lady wives sacrificed their jewels. The treasure was loaded into a wagon, ready to be sent north when . . ." I paused, coughing.

Clearing my throat, wishing I had drawn myself a mug of ale, I continued, "A huge red dragon swept out of the sky and attacked the treasure caravan. I tried to stand and fight, but"—my face burned in shame—"I've never known such paralyzing fear. The next thing I knew, I was face-first on the ground, shivering in terror. The guard fled in panic.

"The great dragon settled down on the King's Highway. The dragon leisurely devoured the horses, then, lifting the wagon with all the treasure in its claws, the cursed beast flew away."

"Dragon-fear," said Orin, as one long experienced in such things.

"Though it has never happened to me, I've heard the dragon-fear can be devastating." Sir Eric rested his hand pityingly on mine. "It was foul magic that unmanned you, Seneschal. No need for shame."

"*Foul* magic," repeated Ulanda, casting the knight a dark look. Perhaps she was thinking what an excellent wolf he would make.

"I saw the treasure." Reynard heaved a gusty sigh. "It was a beautiful sight. And there must be more, lots more, in that dragon's lair."

"There is," said Orin. "Do you think yours is the only kingdom this dragon has robbed, Seneschal? My people were hauling a shipment of golden nuggets from our mines in the south when a red dragon—pull out my beard if it's not the same one—swooped out of the skies and made off with it!"

"Golden nuggets!" Reynard licked his lips. "How much were they worth, all told?"

Orin cast him a baleful glance. "Never you mind, Light-finger."

"The name is Deft-hand," Reynard said, but the dwarf ignored him.

"I have received word from my sisters in the east," Ulanda was saying, "that this same dragon is responsible for the theft of several of our coven's most powerful arcane artifacts. I would describe them to you, but they are very secret. And very dangerous, to the inexperienced," she added pointedly for Reynard's sake.

"We, too, have suffered by this wyrm," said Eric grimly. "Our brethren to the west sent us as a gift a holy relic—a finger-bone of our patron saint. The dragon attacked the escort, slaughtered them to a man, carried away our artifact."

Ulanda laughed, made a face. "I don't believe it! What would the dragon want with a moldy old finger-bone?"

The knight's face hardened. "The finger-bone was encased in a diamond, as big around as an apple. The diamond was carried in a chalice made of gold, encrusted with rubies and emeralds. The chalice was carried on a platter made of silver, set with a hundred sapphires . . ."

"I thought you holy knights took vows of poverty," Reynard insinuated slyly. "Maybe I should start going to church again."

Eric leapt to his feet. Glaring at the thief, the knight drew his sword. Reynard sidled over behind me.

"Hold, Sir Knight," I said, standing. "The route to the dragon's lair leads up a sheer cliff with nary a hand—or foot—hold in sight."

The knight eyed Reynard's slender fingers and wiry body. Sheathing his sword, the knight sat back down.

"You've discovered the lair!" Reynard cried. He was so excited I feared he might hug me.

"Is this true, Seneschal?" Ulanda leaned near me. I could smell musk and spice. Her fingertips were cool on my hand. "Have you found the dragon's lair?"

"I pray to Our Father you have! Gladly would I leave this life, spend eternity in the blessed realm of my God, if I could have a chance to fight this wyrm!" Eric vowed. Lifting a sacred medallion he wore around his neck to his lips, he kissed it to seal his holy oath.

"I lost my king's ransom," I said. "I took a vow neither to eat nor sleep until I had tracked the beast to its lair. Many weary days and nights I followed the trail—

a shining coin fallen to the ground, a jewel spilled from the wagon. The trail led straight to a peak known as Black Mountain. A day I waited, patient, watching. I was rewarded. I saw the dragon leave its lair. I know how to get inside."

Reynard began to dance around the tavern, singing and snapping his long fingers. Eric Truestone actually smiled. Orin Dark-Seer ran his thumb lovingly over his ax-blade. Ulanda kissed my cheek.

"You must come visit me some evening, Seneschal, when this adventure is ended," she whispered.

The four of them and I spent the night in the inn, were up well before dawn to begin our journey.

The Black Mountain loomed before us, its peak hidden by a perpetual cloud of gray smoke. The mountain is named for its shining black rock, belched up from the very bowels of the world. Sometimes the mountain still rumbles, just to remind us that it is alive, but none living could remember the last time it spewed flame.

We reached it by late afternoon. The sun's rays shone red on the cliff face we would have to climb. By craning the neck, one could see the gaping dark hole that was the entrance.

"Not a handhold in sight. By Our Lord, you weren't exaggerating, Seneschal," said Eric, frowning as he ran his hand over the smooth black rock.

Reynard laughed. "Bah! I've climbed castle walls that were as smooth as milady's— Well, let's just say they were smooth."

The thief looped a long length of rope over his shoulder. He started to add a bag full of spikes and a hammer, but I stopped him.

"The dragon might have returned. If so, the beast would hear you driving the spikes into the rock." I glanced upward. "The way is not far, just difficult. Once you make it, lower the rope down to us. We can climb it."

Reynard agreed. He studied the cliff face a moment, all seriousness now, no sign of a grin. Then, to the amazement of all of us watching, he attached himself to the rock like a spider and began to climb.

I had known Reynard was good, but I must admit, I had not known how good. I watched him crawl up that sheer cliff face, digging his fingers into minute cracks, his feet scrabbling for purchase, hanging on, sometimes, by effort of will alone. I was impressed. He was the best. No other man living could have climbed that cliff.

"The Gods are with us in our holy cause," said Eric reverently, watching Reynard scale the black rock like a lizard.

Ulanda stifled a yawn, covered her mouth with a dainty hand. Orin stomped his feet in impatience. I continued to watch Reynard, admiring his work. He had reached the entrance to the cavern, disappeared inside. In a moment, he came back out, indicated with a wave of his hand that all was safe.

Reynard lowered the rope down to us. Unfortunately, the rope he'd brought was far too short. We couldn't reach it. Orin began to curse loudly. Ulanda laughed, snapped her fingers, spoke a word. The rope shivered and suddenly it was exactly the right length.

Eric eyed the magicked rope dubiously, but it was his only way up. He took hold of it, then, appearing to think of something, he turned to the sorceress.

"My lady, I fear your delicate hands are not meant

for climbing ropes, nor are you dressed for scaling mountains. If you will forgive me the liberty, I will carry you up the cliff."

"Carry me!" Ulanda stared at him, then she laughed again.

Eric stiffened, his face went rigid and cold. "Your pardon, my lady—"

"Forgive me, Sir Knight," Ulanda interrupted smoothly. "But I am not a weak and helpless damsel. And it would be best if you remembered that. All of you."

So saying, Ulanda drew a lacy silken handkerchief from her pocket and spread the handkerchief upon the ground. Placing her feet upon the handkerchief, she spoke words that were like the sound of tinkling chimes. The handkerchief became hard as steel. It began to rise slowly into the air, bearing the sorceress with it.

Sir Eric's eyes widened. He made the sign against evil.

Ulanda floated calmly up the cliff face. Reynard was on hand to assist her with the landing at the mouth of the cave. I have excellent eyes and I could see their meeting. The thief's own eyes were bugged out of his head. He was practically drooling. We could all hear his words.

"What a second-story man you'd make! Lady, I'll give you half— Well, a fourth of my treasure share for that scrap of cloth."

Ulanda picked up the steel platform, snapped it in the air. Once again, the handkerchief was silk and lace. She placed it carefully in a pocket of her robes. The thief's eyes followed it all the way.

"It is not for sale," Ulanda said, and she shrugged. "You wouldn't find it of much value anyway. If anyone touches it, other than myself, the handkerchief will wrap itself around the unfortunate person's nose and mouth and will smother him to death."

She smiled at Reynard sweetly. He eyed her, decided she was telling the truth, gulped and turned hastily away.

"May Saint James preserve me," Eric said dourly. Laying his hand upon the rope, he started to climb.

He was strong, that knight. Encased in heavy plate armor and chain mail, his sword hanging from his side, he pulled himself up the cliff with ease. The dwarf was quick to follow, running up the rope nimbly. I took my time. It was nearly evening now, but the afternoon sun had warmed the rock. Hauling myself up that rope was hot work. I slipped once, giving myself the scare of a lifetime. I heaved a sign of relief when Eric pulled me up over the ledge and into the cool shadows of the cavern.

"Where's the dwarf?" I asked, noticing only three of my companions were around.

"He went ahead to scout the way," said Eric.

I nodded, glad for the chance to rest. Reynard drew up the rope and hid it beneath a rock for use on the way back. I glanced around. All along the sides of the cavern, I could see marks left by the dragon's massive body scraping against the rock. We were examining these when Orin returned, his bearded face split in a wide smile.

"You are right, Seneschal. This is the way to the dragon's lair. And this proves it."

Orin held up his find to the light. It was a golden nugget. Reynard eyed it covetously and I knew then and there it was going to cause trouble.

"This proves it!" Orin repeated, his eyes shining

bright as the gold. "This is the beast's hole. We've got him! Got him now!"

Eric Truestone, a grim look on his face, drew his sword and started for a huge tunnel that led from the cavern's entrance into the mountain. Shocked, Orin caught hold of the knight, pulled him back.

"Are you daft, man?" the dwarf demanded. "Will you go walking in the dragon's front door? Why don't you just ring the bell, let him know we're here?"

"What other way is there?" Eric asked, nettled at Orin's superior tone.

"The back way," said the dwarf cunningly. "The secret way. All dragons keep a back exit, just in case. We'll use that."

"You're saying we have to climb round to the other side of this bloody mountain?" Reynard protested. "After all this work it took to get here?"

"Naw, Light-finger!" Orin scoffed. "We'll go *through* the mountain. Safer, easier. Follow me."

He headed for what looked to me like nothing more than a crack in the wall. But once we had all squeezed through, we discovered a tunnel that led even deeper into the mountain.

"This place is blacker than the Evil One's heart," muttered Eric, as we took our first few tentative steps inside. Although he had spoken in a low voice, his words echoed alarmingly.

"Hush!" the dwarf growled. "What do you mean dark? *I* can see perfectly."

"But we humans can't! Do we dare risk a light?" I whispered.

"We won't get far without one," Eric grumbled. He'd already nearly brained himself on a low hanging rock. "What about a torch?"

"Torches smoke. And it's rumored there're other things living in this mountain besides the dragon!" Reynard said ominously.

"Will this do?" asked Ulanda.

Removing a jeweled wand from her belt, she held it up. She spoke no word, but—as if offended by the darkness—the wand began to shine with a soft, white light.

Orin shook his head over the frailty of humans and stumped off down the tunnel. We followed after.

The path led down and around and over and under and into and out of and up and sideways and across . . . a veritable maze. How Orin kept from getting lost or mixed up was beyond me. All of us had doubts (Reynard expressed his loudly), but Orin never wavered.

We soon lost track of time, wandering in the darkness beneath the mountain, but I would guess that we walked most of the night. If we had not found the coin, we would have known the dragon's presence just by the smell. It wasn't heavy or rank, didn't set us gagging or choking. It was a scent, a breath, a hint of blood and sulfur, gold and iron. The smell wasn't pervasive, but drifted through the narrow corridors like the dust, teasing, taunting. Just when Ulanda complained breathlessly that she couldn't stand another moment in this "stuffy hole," Orin brought us to a halt. Grinning slyly, he looked around at us.

"This is it," he said.

"This is what?" Eric asked dubiously, staring at yet another crack in the wall. (We'd seen a lot of cracks!)

"The dragon's other entrance," said the dwarf.

Squeezing through the crack, we found ourselves in another tunnel, this one far larger than any we'd found yet. We couldn't see daylight, but we could smell fresh air, so we knew the tunnel connected with the outside. Ulanda held her wand up to the wall and there again were the marks made by the dragon's body. To clinch the matter, a few red scales glittered on the ground.

Orin Dark-seer had done the impossible. He'd taken us clean through the mountain. The dwarf was pretty pleased with himself, but his pleasure was short-lived.

We stopped for a rest, to drink some water and eat a bite of food to keep up our energy. Ulanda was sitting beside me, telling me in a low voice of the wonders of her castle, when suddenly Orin sprang to his feet.

"Thief!" the dwarf howled. He leapt at Reynard. "Give it back!"

I was standing. So was Reynard, who managed to put me in between himself and the enraged dwarf.

"My gold nugget!" Orin shrieked.

"Share and share alike," Reynard said, bobbing this way and that to avoid the dwarf. "Finder's keepers."

Orin began swinging that damn ax of his a bit too near my knees for comfort.

"Shut them up, Seneschal!" Eric ordered me, as if I were one of his foot-soldiers. "They'll bring the dragon down us!"

"Fools! I'll put an end to this!" Ulanda reached her hand into a silken pouch she wore on her belt.

I think we may well have lost both thief and guide at that moment, but we suddenly had far greater problems.

"Orin! Behind you!" I shouted.

Seeing by the expression of sheer terror on my face that this was no trick, Orin whirled around.

A knight—or what had once been a knight—was walking toward us. His armor covered bone, not flesh. His helm rattled on a bare and blood-stained skull. He held a sword in his skeletal hand. Behind him, I saw what seemed an army of these horrors, though it was in reality only six or seven.

"I've heard tell of this!" Eric cried, awed. "These were once living men, who dared attack this dragon. The wyrm killed them and now forces their rotting corpses to serve him!"

"I'll put it out of its misery," Orin cried. Bounding forward the dwarf struck at the undead warrior with his ax.

The blade severed the knight's knees at the joint. The skeleton toppled. The dwarf laughed.

"No need to trouble yourselves over this lot," he told us. "Stand back."

The dwarf went after the second. But, at that moment, the first skeleton picked up it bones and began putting itself back together! Within moments, it was whole again. Swinging its bony arms, the skeleton knight brought its sword down on the dwarf's head. Fortunately for Orin, he was wearing a heavy steel helm. The sword did no damage, but the blow sent the dwarf reeling.

Ulanda already had her hand in her pouch. She drew out a noxious powder and tossed it onto the undead warrior nearest her. The skeleton went up in a whoosh of flame that nearly incinerated the thief, who had been attempting to lift a jeweled dagger from the undead warrior's belt. After that, Reynard very wisely took himself out of the way and watched the fight from a corner.

Eric Truestone drew his sword, but he did not

attack. Holding his blade by the hilt, he raised it in front of one of the walking skeletons. "I call on Saint James to free these noble knights of the curse that binds them to this wretched life."

The undead warrior dropped down into a pile of dust at the knight's feet. Orin, who had been exchanging blows with two corpses for some time and was now getting the worst of the battle, beat a strategic retreat. Between the two of them—Ulanda with her magic and Eric with his faith—they took care of the remainder of the skeletal warriors.

I had drawn my sword, but, seeing that my help wasn't needed, I watched in admiration. When the warriors were either reduced to dust or smoldering ash, the two returned. Ulanda's hair wasn't even mussed. Eric hadn't broken into a sweat.

"There are not two others in this land who could have done what you did," I said to them and I meant it.

"I am good at anything I undertake," Ulanda said. She wiped dust from her hands. "*Very* good," she added with a charming smile and a glance at me from beneath her long eyelashes.

"The Lord was with me," Eric said humbly.

The battered dwarf glowered. "Meaning to say my God Alberich wasn't?"

"The good knight means nothing of the sort." I was quick to end the argument. "Without you, Orin Dark-Seer, we would be food for the dragon right now. Why do you think the skeleton men attacked us? Because we are drawing too near the dragon's lair and that is due entirely to your expertise. No other dwarf in this land could have brought us this far safely, and we all know it."

At this, I glanced pointedly at Eric, who took the

hint and bowed courteously, if a bit stiffly, to the dwarf. Ulanda rolled her lovely eyes, but she muttered something gracious.

I gave Reynard a swift kick in the pants and the thief reluctantly handed over the golden nugget, which seemed to mean more to the dwarf than our words of praise. Orin thanked us all, of course, but his attention was for the gold. He examined it suspiciously, as if worried that Reynard might have tried to switch the real nugget with a fake. The dwarf bit down on it, polished it on his doublet. Finally certain the gold was real, Orin thrust it beneath his leather armor for safekeeping.

So absorbed was the dwarf in his gold that he didn't notice Reynard lifting his purse from behind. I did, but I took care not to mention it.

As I said, we were close to the dragon's lair.

We moved ahead, doubly cautious, keeping sharp watch for any foe. We were deep, deep inside the mountain now. It was silent, very silent. Too silent.

"You'd think we'd hear something," Eric whispered to me. "The dragon breathing, if nothing else. A beast that large would sound like a bellows down here."

"Perhaps this means he's not home!" Reynard said.

"Or perhaps it means we've come to a dead end," said Ulanda icily.

Rounding a corner of the tunnel, we all stopped and stared. The sorceress was right. Ahead of us, blocking our path, was a solid rock wall.

Orin's cheeks flushed. He tugged on his beard, cast us all a sidelong glance. "This *must* be the way," he muttered, kicking disconsolately at the rock.

"We'll have to go back," Eric said grimly. "Saint James is chastising me, telling me that I should have faced the wyrm in honorable battle. None of this skulking about like a—"

"Thief?" Reynard said brightly. "Very well, Sir Knight, you can go back to the front door if you want. I will sneak in by the window."

With this, Reynard closed his eyes and, flattening himself against the rock wall, he seemed—to all appearances—to be making love to it. His hands crawled over it, his fingers poking and prodding. He even whispered what sounded like cooing and coaxing words. Suddenly, with a triumphant grin, he placed his feet in two indentations in the bottom of the wall, put his hands in two cracks at the top, and pressed.

The rock wall shivered, then it began to slide to one side. A shaft of reddish light beamed out. The thief jumped off the wall and waved his hand at the opening he'd created.

"A secret door," Orin said, sniffing. "I knew it all along."

"You want to go around to the front now?" Reynard asked the knight slyly.

Eric glared at the thief, but he appeared to be having second thoughts about meeting the dragon face-to-face in an honorable fight. He drew his sword and waited for the wall to open completely so we could see inside.

The light pouring out from the doorway was extremely bright. All of us blinked and rubbed our eyes, trying to adjust them to the sudden brilliance after the darkness of the tunnels. We waited, listening for the dragon. None of us had a doubt but that we had discovered the beast's dwelling place.

We heard nothing. All was deathly quiet.

"The dragon's not home!" Reynard rubbed his hands. "Loki the Trickster is with me today!" He made a dash for the entrance, but Sir Eric's hand fell on his shoulder like doom.

"I will lead," he said. "It is my right."

Sword in hand, a prayer on his lips, the holy paladin walked into the dragon's lair.

Reynard crept right behind him. Orin, moving more cautiously, came behind the thief. Ulanda had taken a curious-looking scroll from her belt. Holding it fast, she entered the lair behind the dwarf. I drew my dagger. Keeping watch behind me, I entered last.

The door began to rumble shut.

I halted. "We're going to be trapped in here!" I called out loudly as I dared.

The others paid no attention to me. They had discovered the dragon's treasure room.

The bright light's source was a pit of molten rock, bubbling in a corner of the gigantic underground room. The floor of the cavern had been worn smooth, probably by the rubbing of the dragon's enormous body. A great, glittering heap, tall as His Majesty's castle, was piled together on the cavern floor.

Gathered here was every beautiful, valuable, and precious object in the kingdom. Gold shone red in the firelight; jewels of every color of the rainbow winked and sparkled. The silver reflected the smiles of the dragon-hunters. And, best of all, the cavern was uninhabited.

Sir Eric fell on his knees and began to pray.

Ulanda stared, open-mouthed.

Orin was weeping into his beard with joy.

But by now, the secret door had slammed shut.

Not one of them noticed.

"The dragon's not home!" Reynard shrieked and he made a dive for the treasure pile.

My treasure pile.

The thief began pawing through the gold.

My gold.

I walked up behind him.

"Never jump to conclusions," I said.

With my dagger, I gave him the death a thief deserves.

I stabbed him in the back.

"I thought you should at least have a look," I said to the dying Reynard kindly, gesturing to my horde. "Since you're the best."

Reynard slid off my dagger and fell to the floor. He was the most astonished looking corpse I'd ever seen. I still don't think he'd quite figured things out.

But Ulanda had. She was smart, that sorceress. She guessed the truth immediately, if a bit late—even before I took off my ring of shape-shifting.

Now, at last, after weeks of being cramped into that tiny form, I could stretch out. My body grew, slowly taking on its original, immense shape, almost filling the cavern. I held the ring up in front of her eyes.

"You were right," I told her, the jewel sparkling in what was now a claw. "Your coven *did* possess many powerful arcane objects. This is just one of them."

Ulanda stared at me in terror. She tried to use her scroll, but the dragon-fear was too much for her. The words of magic wouldn't come to her parched, pale lips.

She'd been sweet enough to invite me to spend the night, and so I did her a favor. I let her see, before she died, a demonstration of the magic now in my possession. Appropriately, one of my most prized artifacts—a necklace made out of magical wolf's teeth—encircled her lovely neck and tore out her throat.

All this time, Orin Dark-seer had been hacking at my hind leg with his ax. I let him get in a few licks. The dwarf hadn't been a bad sort, after all, and he'd done *me* a favor by showing me the weakness in my defenses. When he seemed likely to draw blood, however, I tired of the contest. Picking him up, I tossed him in the pool of molten lava. Eventually he'd become part of the mountain—a fitting end for a dwarf. I trust he appreciated it.

That left Sir Eric, who had wanted, all along, to meet me in honorable battle. I granted him his wish.

He faced me bravely, calling on Saint James to fight at his side.

Saint James must have busy with something else just then, for he didn't make an appearance.

Eric died in a blaze of glory.

Well, he died in a blaze.

I trust his soul went straight to Valhalla or wherever it is knights go, where it's my guess, his patron saint must have had some pretty fancy explaining to do.

They were dead now. All four.

I put out the fire and swept up the knight's ashes. Then I shoved the other two corpses out the secret door. The thief and the sorceress would take the place of the skeletal warriors I'd been forced to sacrifice to keep up appearances.

Crawling back to my treasure pile, I tidied up the gold a bit where the thief had disturbed it. Then I climbed on top, spread myself out, and burrowed deeply and luxuriously into the gold and silver and jewels. I spread my wings over my treasure protectively, even paused to admire the effect of the firelight shining on my red scales. I wrapped my long tail around the golden nuggets of the dwarves, stretched my body comfortably over the jewels of knights, lay my head down on the magical treasure of the coven.

I was tired, but satisfied. My plan had worked out wonderfully well.

I had rid myself of them. They'd been best. The very best.

Sooner or later, separately or together, they would have come after me. And they might have caught me napping.

I settled myself onto the treasure more comfortably and closed my eyes. I'd earned my rest.

I could sleep peacefully . . . now.

A PROPER
SANTA CLAUS

ANNE McCAFFREY

ANNE McCAFFREY is regarded as one of the best-selling science fiction writers in the world. Her Doona, Pern, and Rowan series have all won worldwide acclaim. A winner of both the Hugo and Nebula Awards, her recent novels include *Acorna: The Unicorn Girl,* co-written with Margaret Ball, and *Dragonseye.* She lives in Ireland. In "A Proper Santa Claus," she examines how the unfettered creativity of youth can clash with the rigid rules of adulthood, and the damage that can be inflicted.

Jeremy was painting. He used his fingers instead of the brush because he liked the feel of paint. Blue was soothing to the touch, red was silky, and orange had a gritty texture. Also he could tell when a color was "proper" if he mixed it with his fingers. He could hear his mother singing to herself, not quite on pitch, but it was a pleasant background noise. It went with the rhythm of his fingers stroking color onto the paper.

He shaped a cookie and put raisins on it, big, plump raisins. He attempted a sugar frosting but the white kind of disappeared into the orange of the cookie. So he globbed up chocolate brown and made an icing. Then he picked the cookie out of the paper and ate it. That left a hole in the center of the paper. It was an excellent cookie, though it made his throat very dry.

Critically he eyed the remaining unused space. Yes, there was room enough, so he painted a glass of Coke. He had trouble representing the bubbles that're supposed to bounce up from the bottom of the glass. That's why the Coke tasted flat when he drank it.

It was disappointing. He'd been able to make the cookie taste so good, why couldn't he succeed with the Coke? Maybe if he drew the bubbles in first . . . he was running out of paper.

"Momma, Momma?"

"What is it, honey?"

"Can I have more paper? Please?"

"Honest, Jeremy, you use up more paper. . . . Still, it does keep you quiet and out of my hair. . . . Why, whatever have you done with your paper? What are those holes?"

Jeremy pointed to the round one. "That was a cookie with raisins and choc'late icing. And that was a Coke only I couldn't make the bubbles bounce."

His mother gave him "the look," so he subsided.

"Jeremy North, you use more paper than— than a . . ."

"Newspaperman?" he suggested, grinning up at her. Momma liked happy faces best.

"Than a newspaperman."

"Can you paint on newspaper?"

His mother blinked. "I don't see why not. And there's pictures already. You can color them in." She obligingly rummaged in the trash and came up with several discarded papers. "There you are, love. Enough supplies to keep you in business a while. I hope."

Well, Jeremy hadn't planned on any business, and newsprint proved less than satisfactory. There wasn't enough white spaces to draw *his* paintings on, and the newspaper soaked up his paints when he tried to follow the already-pictures. So he carefully put the paints away, washed his hands, and went outside to play.

For his sixth birthday Jeremy North got a real school-type easel with a huge pad of paper that fastened onto it at the top and could be torn off, sheet by sheet. There was a rack of holes for his poster paint pots and a rack for his crayons and chalk and eraser. It was exactly what he wanted. He nearly cried for joy. He hugged his mother, and he climbed into his father's lap and kissed him despite his prickly beard.

"Okay, okay, da Vinci," his father laughed. "Go paint us a masterpiece."

Jeremy did. But he was so eager that he couldn't wait until the paint had completely dried. It smeared and blurred, brushing against his body as he hurried to find his dad. So the effect wasn't quite what Jeremy intended.

"Say, that's pretty good," said his father, casting a judicious eye on the proffered artwork. "What's it supposed to be?"

"Just what you wanted." Jeremy couldn't keep the disappointment out of his voice.

"I guess you're beyond me, young feller me lad. I can dig Andy Warhol when he paints tomato soup, but you're in Picasso's school." His father tousled his hair affectionately and even swung him up high so that, despite his disappointment, Jeremy was obliged to giggle and squeal in delight.

Then his father told him to take his painting back to his room.

"But it's your masterpiece, Daddy. I can fix it . . ."

"No, son. You painted it. You understand it." And his father went about some Sunday errand or other.

Jeremy did understand his painting. Even with the smears he could plainly see the car, just like the Admonsens', which Daddy had admired the previous week. It *had* been a proper car. If only Daddy had *seen* it . . .

His grandmother came, around lunchtime, and brought him a set of pastel crayons with special pastel paper and a simply superior picture book of North American animals and birds.

"Of course, he'll break every one of the pastels in the next hour," he heard his grandmother saying to his mother, "but you said he wants only drawing things."

"I like the book, too, Gramma," Jeremy said politely, but his fingers closed possessively around the pastels.

Gramma glanced at him and then went right on talking. "But I think it's about time he found out what animals really look like instead of those monstrosities he's forever drawing. His teacher's going to wonder about his home life when she sees those nightmares."

"Oh, c'mon, Mother. There's nothing abnormal about Jeremy. I'd far rather he daubed himself all over with paint than ran around like the Reckoffs' kids, slinging mud and sand everywhere."

"If you'd only *make* Jeremy . . ."

"Mother, you can't *make* Jeremy do anything. He slides away from you like . . . like a squeeze of paint."

Jeremy lost interest in the adults. As usual, they ignored his presence, despite the fact that he was the subject of their conversation. He began to leaf through the book of birds and animals. The pictures weren't proper. That brown wasn't a bird-brown. And the red of the robin had too much orange, not enough gray. He kept his criticism to himself, but by the time he'd catalogued the anatomical faults in the sketch of the mustang, he was thoroughly bored with the book. His animals might *look* like nightmares, but they were proper ones for all of that. They worked.

His mother and grandmother were engrossed in discussing the fixative that would have made the pictures "permanent." Gramma said she hadn't bought it because it would be dangerous for him to breathe the fumes. They continued to ignore him. Which was as well. He picked up the pastels and began to experiment. A green horse with pink mane and tail, however anatomically perfect, would arouse considerable controversy.

He didn't break a single one of the precious pastels. He even blew away the rainbow dust from the tray. But he didn't let the horse off the pad until after Gramma and his mother had wandered into the kitchen for lunch.

"I wish . . ."

The horse was lovely.

"I *wish* I had some . . ." Jeremy said.

The horse went cantering around the room, pink tail streaming out behind him and pink mane flying.

". . . Fixative, Green Horse!" But it didn't work. Jeremy knew it took more than just *wishing* to do it proper.

He watched regretfully as Green Horse pranced too close to a wall and brushed himself out of existence.

Miss Bradley, his first-grade teacher, evidently didn't find anything untoward about his drawings, for she constantly displayed them on the bulletin boards. She had a habit of pouncing on him when he had just about finished a drawing so that after all his effort, he hadn't much chance to see if he'd done it "proper" after all. Once or twice he managed to reclaim one from the board and use it, but Miss Bradley created so much fuss about the missing artwork that he diplomatically ceased to repossess his efforts.

On the whole he liked Miss Bradley, but about the first week in October she developed the distressing habit of making him draw to order: "class assignments," she called it. Well, that was all right for the ones who never knew what to draw anyhow, but "assignments" just did not suit Jeremy. While part of him wanted to do hobgoblins, and witches, and pumpkin moons, the other part obstinately refused.

"I'd really looked forward to *your* interpretations of Hallowe'en, Jeremy," Miss Bradley said sadly when he proffered another pedantic landscape with nothing but ticky-tacky houses. "This is very beautiful, Jeremy, but it isn't the assigned project. Now, look at Cynthia's witch and Mark's hobgoblin. I'm certain you could do something just as original."

Jeremy dutifully regarded Cynthia's elongated witch on an outsized broomstick apparently made from 2 ¥ 4s instead of broom reeds, and the hobgoblin Mark had created by splashing paint on the paper and folding, thus blotting the wet paint. Neither creation had any chance of working properly; surely Miss Bradley could see that. So he was obliged to tell her that his landscape was original, particularly if she would *look* at it properly.

"You're not getting the point, Jeremy," Miss Bradley said with unaccustomed sternness.

She wasn't either, but Jeremy thought he might better not say that. So he was the only student in the class who had no Hallowe'en picture for parents to admire on Back-to-School Night.

His parents were a bit miffed since they'd heard that Jeremy's paintings were usually prominently displayed.

"The assignment was Hallowe'en and Jeremy simply refused to produce something acceptable," Miss Bradley said with a slightly forced smile.

"Perhaps that's just as well," his mother said, a trifle sourly. "He used to draw the most frightening nightmares and say he 'saw' them."

"He's got a definite talent. Are either of you or Mr. North artistically inclined?"

"Not like he is," Mr. North replied, thinking that if he himself were artistically inclined he would use Miss Bradley as a model. "Probably he's used up all his Hallowe'en inspiration."

"Probably," Miss Bradley said with a laugh.

Actually Jeremy hadn't. Although he dutifully set out trick-or-treating, he came home early. His mother made him sort out his candy, apples, and money for UNICEF, and permitted him to stay up long past his regular bedtime to answer the door for other beggars. But, once safely in his room, he dove for his easel and drew frenetically, slathering black and blue poster paint across clean paper, dashing globs of luminescence for horrific accents. The proper ones took off or crawled obscenely around the room, squeaking and groaning until he released them into the night air for such gambols and aerial maneuvers as they were capable of. Jeremy was impressed. He hung over the windowsill, cheering them on by moonlight. (Around three o'clock there was a sudden shower. All the water solubles melted into the ground.)

For a while after that, Jeremy was not tempted to approach the easel at all, either in school or at home. At first, Miss Bradley was sincerely concerned lest she had inhibited her budding artist by arbitrary assignments. But he was only busy with a chemical garden, lumps of coal and bluing and ammonia and all that. Then she got the class involved in making candles out of plastic milk cartons for Thanksgiving, and Jeremy entered into the project with such enthusiasm that she was reassured.

She ought not to have been.

Three-dimensionality and a malleable substance fascinated Jeremy. He went in search of anything remotely pliable. He started with butter (his mother had a fit about a whole pound melted on his furry rug; he'd left the creature he'd created prancing around his room, but then the heat came up in the radiators). Then he tried mud (which set his mother screaming at him). She surrendered to the inevitable by supplying him with Play-Doh. However, now his creations thwarted him because as soon as the substance out of which the proper ones had been created hardened, they lost their mobility. He hadn't minded the ephemeral quality of his drawings, but he'd begun to count on the fact that sculpture lasted a while.

Miss Bradley introduced him to plasticine. And Christmas.

Success with three-dimensional figures, the availability of plasticine, and the sudden influx of all sorts of Christmas mail-order catalogues spurred Jeremy to unusual efforts. This time he did not resist the class assignment of a centerpiece to deck the Christmas festive tables. Actually, Jeremy scarcely heard what Miss Bradley was saying past her opening words.

"Here's a chance for you to create your very own Santa Claus and reindeer, or a sleigh full of presents. . . ."

Dancer, Prancer, Donner, Blitzen, and Dasher and Comet and Rudolph of the red nose, took form under his flying fingers. Santa's sack was crammed with full-color advertisements clipped from mail-order wishbooks. Indeed, the sleigh threatened to crumble on its runners from paper weight. He saved Santa Claus till the last. And once he had the fat and jolly gentleman seated in his sleigh, whip in hand, ready to urge his harnessed team, Jeremy was good and ready to make them proper.

Only they weren't; they remained obdurately immobile. Disconsolate, Jeremy moped for nearly a week, examining and re-examining his handiwork for the inhibiting flaw.

Miss Bradley had been enthusiastically complimentary and the other children sullenly envious of his success when the finished group was displayed on a special table, all red and white, with Ivory Snow snow and little evergreens in proportion to the size of the figures. There was even a convenient chimney for the good Santa to descend. Only Jeremy knew that that was not *his* Santa's goal.

In fact Jeremy quite lost interest in the whole Christmas routine. He refused to visit the Santa on tap at the big shopping center, although his mother suspected that his heart had been set on the Masterpiece Oil Painting Set with its enticing assortment of brushes and every known pigment in life-long-lasting color.

Miss Bradley, too, lost all patience with him and became quite stern with his inattentiveness, to the delight of his classmates.

As so often happens when people concentrate too hard on a problem, Jeremy almost missed the solution, inadvertently provided by the pert Cynthia, now basking in Miss Bradley's favor.

"He's naked, that's what. He's naked and ugly. Everyone knows Santa is red and white. And reindeers aren't gray-yecht. They're brown and soft and have fuzzy tails."

Jeremy had, of course, meticulously detailed the clothing on Santa and the harness on the animals, but they were still plasticine. It hadn't mattered with his other creations that they were the dull gray-brown of plasticene because that's how he'd envisaged them, being products of his imagination. But Santa wasn't, or so he thought.

To conform to a necessary convention was obviously, to Jeremy, the requirement that had prevented his Santa from being a proper one. He fabricated harness of string for the reindeer. And a new sleigh of balsa wood with runners of laboriously straightened bobby pins took some time and looked real tough. A judicious coat of paint smartened both reindeer and sleigh. However, the design and manufacture of the red Santa suit proved far more difficult and occupied every spare moment of Jeremy's time. He had to do it in the privacy of his room at home because, when Cynthia saw him putting harness on the reindeer, she twitted him so unmercifully that he couldn't work in peace at school.

He had had little practice with needle and thread, so he actually had to perfect a new skill in order to complete his project. Christmas was only a few days away before he was satisfied with his Santa suit.

He raced to school so he could dress Santa and make him proper. He was just as startled as Miss Bradley when he slithered to a stop inside his classroom door, and found her tying small gifts to the branches of the class tree. They stared at each other for a long moment, and then Miss Bradley smiled. She'd been so hard on poor Jeremy lately.

"You're awfully early, Jeremy. Would you like to help me . . . Oh! How adorable!" She spotted the Santa suit which he hadn't had the presence of mind to hide from her. "And you did them yourself? Jeremy, you never cease to amaze me." She took the jacket and pants and little hat from his unresisting hand, and examined them carefully. "They are simply beautiful. Just beautiful. But honestly, Jeremy, your Santa is lovely just as he is. No need to gild the lily."

"He isn't a proper Santa without a proper Santa suit."

Miss Bradley looked at him gravely, and then put her hands on his shoulders, making him look up at her.

"A *proper* Santa Claus is the one we have in our own hearts at this time of year, Jeremy. Not the ones in the department stores or on the street corners or on TV. They're just his helpers." You never knew which of your first-graders still did believe in Santa Claus in this cynical age, Miss Bradley thought. "A proper Santa Claus is the spirit of giving and sharing, of good fellowship. Don't let anyone tell you that there isn't a Santa Claus. The proper Santa Claus belongs to all of us."

Then, pleased with her eloquence and restraint, she handed him back the Santa suit and patted his shoulder encouragingly.

Jeremy was thunderstruck. *His* Santa Claus had only been made for Jeremy. But poor Miss Bradley's words rang in his ears. Miss Bradley couldn't know that she had improperly understood Jeremy's dilemma. Once again the blight of high-minded interpretation and ladylike good intentions withered primitive magic.

The little reindeer in their shrinking coats of paint would have pulled the sleigh only to Jeremy's house so that Santa could descend only Jeremy's chimney with the little gifts all bearing Jeremy's name.

There was no one there to tell him that it's proper for little boys and girls of his age to be selfish and acquisitive, to regard Santa as an exclusive property.

Jeremy took the garments and let Miss Bradley push him gently toward the table on which his figures were displayed.

She'd put tinsel about the scene, and glitter, but they didn't shine or glisten in the dull gray light filtering through the classroom windows. They weren't proper snow and icicles anyway.

Critically, he saw only string and the silver cake ornaments instead of harness and sleigh bells. He could see the ripples now in the unbent bobby pins which wouldn't ever draw the sleigh smoothly, even over Ivory Snow snow. Dully, he reached for the figure of his Santa Claus.

Getting on the clothes, he dented the plasticene a bit, but it scarcely mattered now. After he'd clasped Santa's malleable paw around the whip, the toothpick with a bright, thick, nylon thread attached to the top with glue, he stood back and stared.

A proper Santa Claus is the spirit of giving and sharing.

So overwhelming was Jeremy's sense of failure, so crushing his remorse for making a selfish Santa Claus instead of the one that belonged to everyone, that he couldn't imagine ever creating anything properly again.

WET
WINGS

❦

MERCEDES LACKEY

MERCEDES LACKEY was born in Chicago, and has worked as a lab assistant, security guard, and computer programmer before turning to fiction writing. Her first book, *Arrows of the Queen*, the first in the Valdemar series, was published in 1985. She won the Lambda Award for *Magic's Price* and Science Fiction Book Club Book of the Year for the *The Elvenbane*, co-authored with Andre Norton. Along with her husband, Larry Dixon, she is a federally licensed bird rehabilitator, specializing in wild birds. She shares her home with a menagerie of parrots, cats, and a Schutzhund-trained German shepherd. Her latest novel is *Firebird*. The story chosen here, "Wet Wings," deals with one of the basic problems writers may encounter in their career, the restriction of a person's imagination by a repressive society.

Katherine watched avidly, chin cradled in her old, arthritic hands, as the chrysalis heaved, and writhed, and finally split up the back. The crinkled, sodden wings of the butterfly emerged first, followed by the bloated body. She breathed a sigh of wonder, as she always did, and the butterfly tried to flap its useless wings in alarm as it caught her movement.

"Silly thing," she chided it affectionately. "You know you can't fly with wet wings!" Then she exerted a little of her magic; just a little, brushing the butterfly with a spark of calm that jumped from her trembling index finger to its quivering antenna.

The butterfly, soothed, went back to its real job, pumping the fluid from its body into the veins of its wings, unfurling them into their full glory. It was not a particularly rare butterfly, certainly not an endangered one; nothing but a common Buckeye, a butterfly so ordinary that no one even commented on seeing them when she was a child. But Katherine had always found the markings exquisite, and she had used this species and the Sulfurs more often than any other to carry her magic.

Magic. That was a word hard to find written anymore. No one approved of magic these days. Strange that in a country that gave the Church of Gaia equal rights with the Catholic Church, no one believed in magic.

But magic was not "correct." It was not given equally to all, nor could it be given equally to all. And that which could not be made equal, must be destroyed. . . .

"We always knew that there would be repression and a burning time again," she told the butterfly, as its wings unfolded a little more. "But we never thought that the ones behind the repression would come from our own ranks."

Perhaps she should have realized it would happen. So many people had come to her over the years, drawn by the magic in her books, demanding to be taught. Some had the talent and the will; most had only delusions. How they had cursed her when she told them the truth! They had wanted to be like the heroes and heroines of her stories: *special, powerful.*

She remembered them all; the boy she had told, regretfully, that his "telepathy" was only observation and the ability to read body language. The girl whose "psychic attacks" had been caused by potassium imbalances. The would-be "bardic mage" who had nothing other than a facility to delude himself. And the many who could not tell a tale, because they would not let themselves see the tales all around them. They were neither powerful nor special, at least not in terms either of the power of magic, nor the magic of story-telling. More often than not, they would go to someone else, demanding to be taught, unwilling to hear the truth.

Eventually, they found someone in one of the many movements that sprouted on the fringes like parasitic mushrooms. She, like the other mages of her time, had simply shaken her head and sighed for them. But what she had not reckoned on, nor had anyone else, was that these movements had gained strength and a life of their own—and had gone political.

Somehow, although the process had been so gradual she had never noticed when it had become unstoppable, those who cherished their delusions began to legislate some of those delusions. "Politically correct" they called it—and *some* of the things they had done she had welcomed, seeing them as the harbingers of more freedom, not less.

But they had gone from the reasonable to the unreasoning; from demanding and getting a removal of sexism to a denial of sexuality and the differences that should have been celebrated. From legislating the humane treatment of animals to making the possession of any animal or animal product without licenses and yearly inspections a crime. Fewer people bothered with owning a pet these days—no, not a pet, an "Animal Companion," and one did not "own" it, one "nurtured" it. Not when inspectors had the right to come into your home day or night, make certain that you were giving your Animal Companion all the rights to which it was entitled. And the rarer the animal, the more onerous the conditions. . . .

"That wouldn't suit you, would it, Horace?" she asked the young crow perched over the window. Horace was completely illegal; there was no way she could have gotten a license for him. She lived in an apartment, not on a farm; she could never give him the four-acre "hunting preserve" he required. Never mind that he had come to her, lured by her magic, and that he was free to come and go through her window, hunting and exercising at will. He also came and went with her little spell-packets, providing her with eyes on the world where she could not go, and bringing back the cocoons and chrysalises that she used for her butterfly-magics.

She shook her head, and sighed. They had sucked all the juice of life out of the world, that was what they had done. Outside, the gray overcast day mirrored the gray sameness of the world they had created. There were no bright colors anymore to draw the eye, only pastels. No passion, no fire, nothing to arouse any kind of emotions. They had decreed that everyone *must* be equal, and no one must be offended, ever. And they had begun the burning and the banning. . . .

She had become alarmed when the burning and banning started; she knew that her own world was doomed when it reached things like "Hansel and Gretel"—banned, not because there was a witch in it, but because the witch was evil, and that might offend witches. She had known that her own work was doomed when a book that had been lauded for its portrayal of a young gay hero was banned because the young gay hero was unhappy and suicidal. She had not even bothered to argue. She simply announced her retirement, and went into seclusion, pouring all her energies into the magic of her butterflies.

From the first moment of spring to the last of autumn, Horace brought her caterpillars and cocoons. When the young butterflies emerged, she gave them each a special burden and sent them out into the world again.

Wonder. Imagination. Joy. Diversity. Some she sent out to wake the gifts of magic in others. Some she sent to wake simple stubborn will.

Discontent. Rebellion. She sowed her seeds, here in this tiny apartment, of what she hoped would be the next revolution. She would not be here to see it—but the day would come, she hoped, when those who *were* different and special would no longer be willing or content with sameness and equality at the expense of diversity.

Her door buzzer sounded, jarring her out of her reverie.

She got up, stiffly, and went to the intercom. But the face there was that of her old friend Piet, the "Environmental Engineer" of the apartment building, and he wore an expression of despair.

"Kathy, the Psi-cops are coming for you," he said quickly, casting a look over his shoulder to see if there was anyone listening. "They made me let them in—"

The screen darkened abruptly.

Oh Gods—She had been so careful! But—in a way, she had expected it. She had been a world-renowned fantasy writer; she had made no secret of her knowledge of real-world magics. The Psi-cops had not made any spectacular arrests lately. Possibly they were running out of victims. She should have known they would start looking at people's pasts.

She glanced around at the apartment reflexively—

No. There was no hope. There were too many things she had that were contraband. The shelves full of books, the feathers and bones she used in her magics, the freezer full of meat that she shared with Horace and his predecessors, the wool blankets—

For that matter, they could arrest her on the basis of her jewelry alone, the fetish-necklaces she carved and made, the medicine-wheels and shields, and the prayer-feathers. She was not Native American; she had no right to make these things even for private use.

And she knew what would happen to her. The Psi-cops would take her away, confiscate all her property, and "re-educate" her.

Drugged, brainwashed, wired, and probed. There would be nothing left of her when they finished. They had "re-educated" Jim three years ago, and when he came out, everything, even his magic and his ability to tell a story, was gone. He had not even had the opportunity to gift it to someone else; they had simply crushed it. He had committed suicide less than a week after his release.

She had a few more minutes at most, before they zapped the lock on her door and broke in. She had to save something, anything!

Then her eyes lighted on the butterfly, his wings fully unfurled and waving gently, and she knew what she would do.

First, she freed Horace. He flew off, squawking indignantly at being sent out into the overcast. But there was no other choice. If they found him, they would probably cage him up and send him to a forest preserve somewhere. He did not know how to find food in a wilderness—let him at least stay here in the city, where he knew how to steal food from birdfeeders, and where the best Dumpsters were.

Then she cupped her hands around the butterfly, and gathered all of her magic. *All* of it this time; a great burden for one tiny insect, but there was no choice.

Songs and tales, magic and wonder; power, vision, will, strength—She breathed them into the butterfly's wings, and he trembled as the magic swirled around him, in a vortex of sparkling mist.

Pride. Poetry. Determination. Love. Hope—

She heard them at the door, banging on it, ordering her to open in the name of the Equal State. She ignored them. There was at least a minute or so left.

The gift of words. The gift of difference—

Finally she took her hands away, spent and exhausted, and feeling as empty as an old paper sack. The butterfly waved his wings, and though she could no longer see it, she knew that a drift of sparkling power followed the movements.

There was a whine behind her as the Psi-cops zapped the lock.

She opened the window, coaxed the butterfly onto her hand, and put him outside. An errant ray of sunshine broke through the overcast, gilding him with a glory that mirrored the magic he carried.

"Go," she breathed. "Find someone worthy."

He spread his wings, tested the breeze, and lifted off her hand, to be carried away.

And she turned, full of dignity and empty of all else, to face her enemies.

NOT LONG
BEFORE THE END

LARRY NIVEN

LARRY NIVEN has received the Hugo Award four times for his short fiction, and a Hugo and Nebula Award for his novel *Ringworld*. From his first story, "The Coldest Place," published in *If* in 1964, he has carved a wide niche for himself in the field of hard science fiction. In "Not Long Before the End," he hypothesizes a theory of how magic works, using science as a base. He takes a practical look at the dynamics of magic, and out comes a story as only he could tell it.

A swordsman battled a sorcerer, once upon a time.
In that age such battles were frequent. A natural antipathy exists between swordsmen and sorcerers, as between cats and small birds, or between rats and men. Usually the swordsman lost, and humanity's average intelligence rose some trifling fraction. Sometimes the swordsman won, and again the species was improved; for a sorcerer who cannot kill one miserable swordsman is a poor excuse for a sorcerer.

But this battle differed from the others. On one side, the sword itself was enchanted. On the other, the sorcerer knew a great and terrible truth.

We will call him the Warlock, as his name is both forgotten and impossible to pronounce. His parents had known what they were about. He who knows your name has power over you, but he must speak your name to use it.

The Warlock had found his terrible truth in middle age.

By that time he had traveled widely. It was not from choice. It was simply that he was a powerful magician, and he used his power, and he needed friends.

He knew spells to make people love a magician.

The Warlock had tried these, but he did not like the side effects. So he commonly used his great power to help those around him, that they might love him without coercion.

He found that when he had been ten to fifteen years in a place, using his magic as whim dictated, his powers would weaken. If he moved away, they returned. Twice he had had to move, and twice he had settled in a new land, learned new customs, made new friends. It happened a third time, and he prepared to move again. But something set him to wondering.

Why should a man's powers be so unfairly drained out of him?

It happened to nations too. Throughout history, those lands which had been richest in magic had been overrun by barbarians carrying swords and clubs. It was a sad truth, and one that did not bear thinking about, but the Warlock's curiosity was strong.

So he wondered, and he stayed to perform certain experiments.

His last experiment involved a simple kinetic sorcery set to spin a metal disc in midair. And when that magic was done, he knew a truth he could never forget.

So he departed. In succeeding decades he moved again and again. Time changed his personality, if not his body, and his magic became more dependable, if less showy. He had discovered a great and terrible truth, and if he kept it secret, it was through compassion. His truth spelled the end of civilization, yet it was of no earthly use to anyone.

So he thought. But some five decades later (the date was on the order of 12,000 B.C.) it occurred to him that all truths find a use somewhere, sometime.

And so he built another disc and recited spells over it, so that (like a telephone number already dialed but for one digit) the disc would be ready if ever he needed it.

The name of the sword was Glirendree. It was several hundred years old, and quite famous.

As for the swordsman, his name is no secret. It was Belhap Sattlestone Wirldess ag Miracloat roo Cononson. His friends, who tended to be temporary, called him Hap. He was a barbarian, of course. A civilized man would have had more sense than to touch Glirendree, and better morals than to stab a sleeping woman. Which was how Hap had acquired his sword. Or vice versa.

The Warlock recognized it long before he saw it. He was at work in the cavern he had carved beneath a hill, when an alarm went off. The hair rose up, tingling, along the back of his neck. "Visitors," he said.

"I don't hear anything," said Sharla, but there was an uneasiness to her tone. Sharla was a girl of the village who had come to live with the Warlock. That day she had persuaded the Warlock to teach her some of his simpler spells.

"Don't you feel the hair rising on the back of your neck? I set the alarm to do that. Let me just check . . ." He used a sensor like a silver hula hoop set on edge. "There's trouble coming. Sharla, we've got to get you out of here."

"But . . ." Sharla waved protestingly at the table where they had been working.

"Oh, that. We can quit in the middle. That spell

isn't dangerous." It was a charm against love-spells, rather messy to work, but safe and tame and effective. The Warlock pointed at the spear of light glaring through the hoop-sensor. "That's dangerous. An enormously powerful focus of mana power is moving up the west side of the hill. You go down the east side."

"Can I help? You've taught me *some* magic."

The magician laughed a little nervously. "Against that? That's Glirendree. Look at the size of the image, the color, the shape. No. You get out of here, and right now. The hill's clear on the eastern slope."

"Come with me."

"I can't. Not with Glirendree loose. Not when it's already got hold of some idiot. There are obligations."

They came out of the cavern together, into the mansion they shared. Sharla, still protesting, donned a robe and started down the hill. The Warlock hastily selected an armload of paraphernalia and went outside.

The intruder was halfway up the hill: a large but apparently human being carrying something long and glittering. He was still a quarter of an hour downslope. The Warlock set up the silver hula hoop and looked through it.

The sword was a flame of mana discharge, an eye-hurting needle of white light. Glirendree, right enough. He knew of other, equally powerful mana foci, but none were portable, and none would show as a sword to the unaided eye.

He should have told Sharla to inform the Brotherhood. She had that much magic. Too late now.

There was no colored borderline to the spear of light.

No green fringe effect meant no protective spells.

The swordsman had not tried to guard himself against what he carried. Certainly the intruder was no magician, and he had not the intelligence to get the help of a magician. Did he know *nothing* about Glirendree?

Not that that would help the Warlock. He who carries Glirendree was invulnerable to any power save Glirendree itself. Or so it was said.

"Let's test that," said the Warlock to himself. He dipped into his armload of equipment and came up with something wooden, shaped like an ocarina. He blew the dust off it, raised it in his fist and pointed it down the mountain. But he hesitated.

The loyalty spell was simple and safe, but it did have side effects. It lowered its victim's intelligence.

"Self-defense," the Warlock reminded himself, and blew into the ocarina.

The swordsman did not break stride. Glirendree didn't even glow; it had absorbed the spell that easily.

In minutes the swordsman would be here. The Warlock hurriedly set up a simple prognostics spell. At least he could learn who would win the coming battle.

No picture formed before him. The scenery did not even waver.

"Well, now," said the Warlock. "*Well*, now!" And he reached into his clutter of sorcerous tools and found a metal disc. Another instant's rummaging produced a double-edged knife, profusely inscribed in no known language, and very sharp.

At the top of the Warlock's hill was a spring, and the stream from that spring ran past the Warlock's house. The swordsman stood leaning on his sword, facing the

Warlock across that stream. He breathed deeply, for it had been a hard climb.

He was powerfully muscled and profusely scarred. To the Warlock it seemed strange that so young a man should have found time to acquire so many scars. But none of his wounds had impaired motor functions. The Warlock had watched him coming up the hill. The swordsman was in top physical shape.

His eyes were deep blue and brilliant, and half an inch too close together for the Warlock's taste.

"I am Hap," he called across the stream. "Where is she?"

"You mean Sharla, of course. But why is that your concern?"

"I have come to free her from her shameful bondage, old man. Too long have you—"

"Hey, hey, hey. Sharla's my *wife.*"

"Too long have you used her for your vile and lecherous purposes. Too—"

"She stays of her own free will, you nit!"

"You expect me to believe that? As lovely a woman as Sharla, could she love an old and feeble warlock?"

"Do I look feeble?"

The Warlock did not look like an old man. He seemed Hap's age, some twenty years old, and his frame and his musculature were the equal of Hap's. He had not bothered to dress as he left the cavern. In place of Hap's scars, his back bore a tattoo in red and green and gold, an elaborately curlicued penta-gramic design, almost hypnotic in its extradimen-sional involutions.

"Everyone in the village knows your age," said Hap. "You're two hundred years old, if not more."

"Hap," said the Warlock. "Belhap something-or-other roo Cononson. Now I remember. Sharla told me you tried to bother her last time she went to the village. I should have done something about it then."

"Old man, you lie. Sharla is under a spell. Everybody knows the power of a warlock's loyalty spell."

"I don't use them. I don't like the side effects. Who wants to be surrounded by friendly morons?" The Warlock pointed to Glirendree. "Do you know what you carry?"

Hap nodded ominously.

"Then you ought to know better. Maybe it's not too late. See if you can transfer it to your left hand."

"I tried that. I can't let go of it." Hap cut at the air, restlessly, with his sixty pounds of sword. "I have to sleep with the damned thing clutched in my hand."

"Well, it's too late then."

"It's worth it," Hap said grimly. "For now I can kill you. Too long has an innocent woman been subjected to your lecherous—"

"I know, I know." The Warlock changed languages suddenly, speaking high and fast. He spoke thus for almost a minute, then switched back to Rynaldese. "Do you feel any pain?"

"Not a twinge," said Hap. He had not moved. He stood with his remarkable sword at the ready, glowering at the magician across the stream.

"No sudden urge to travel? Attacks of remorse? Change of body temperature?" But Hap was grinning now, not at all nicely. "I thought not. Well, it had to be tried."

There was an instant of blinding light.

When it reached the vicinity of the hill, the meteorite had dwindled to the size of a baseball. It should have finished its journey at the back of Hap's head.

Instead, it exploded a millisecond too soon. When the light had died, Hap stood within a ring of craterlets.

The swordsman's unsymmetrical jaw dropped, and then he closed his mouth and started forward. The sword hummed faintly.

The Warlock turned his back.

Hap curled his lip at the Warlock's cowardice. Then he jumped three feet backward from a standing start. A shadow had pulled itself from the Warlock's back.

In a lunar cave with the sun glaring into its mouth, a man's shadow on the wall might have looked that sharp and black. The shadow dropped to the ground and stood up, a humanoid outline that was less a shape than a window view of the ultimate blackness beyond the death of the universe. Then it leapt.

Glirendree seemed to move of its own accord. It hacked the demon once lengthwise and once across, while the demon seemed to batter against an invisible shield, trying to reach Hap even as it died.

"Clever," Hap panted. "A pentagram on your back, a demon trapped inside."

"That's clever," said the Warlock, "but it didn't work. Carrying Glirendree works, but it's not clever. I ask you again, do you know what you carry?"

"The most powerful sword ever forged." Hap raised the weapon high. His right arm was more heavily muscled than his left, and inches longer, as if Glirendree had been at work on it. "A sword to make me the equal of any warlock or sorceress, and without the help of demons, either. I had to kill a woman who loved me to get it, but I paid that price gladly. When I have sent you to your just reward, Sharla will come to me—"

"She'll spit in your eye. Now will you listen to me?

Glirendree *is* a demon. If you had an ounce of sense, you'd cut your arm off at the elbow."

Hap looked startled. "You mean there's a demon imprisoned in the metal?"

"Get it through your head. *There is no metal.* It's a demon, a bound demon, and it's a parasite. It'll age you to death in a year unless you cut it loose. A warlock of the northlands imprisoned it in its present form, then gave it to one of his bastards, Jeery of Something-or-other. Jeery conquered half this continent before he died on the battlefield, of senile decay. It was given into the charge of the Rainbow Witch a year before I was born, because there never was a woman who had less use for people, especially men."

"That happens to have been untrue."

"Probably Glirendree's doing. Started her glands up again, did it? She should have guarded against that."

"A year," said Hap. "One year."

But the sword stirred restlessly in his hand. "It will be a glorious year," said Hap, and he came forward.

The Warlock picked up a copper disc. "Four," he said, and the disc spun in midair.

By the time Hap had sloshed through the stream, the disc was a blur of motion. The Warlock moved to keep it between himself and Hap, and Hap dared not touch it, for it would have sheared through anything at all. He crossed around it, but again the Warlock had darted to the other side. In the pause he snatched up something else: a silvery knife, profusely inscribed.

"Whatever that is," said Hap, "it can't hurt me. No magic can affect me while I carry Glirendree."

"True enough," said the Warlock. "The disc will lose its force in a minute anyway. In the meantime, I know a secret that I would like to tell, one I could never tell to a friend."

Hap raised Glirendree above his head and, two-handed, swung it down on the disc. The sword stopped jarringly at the disc's rim.

"It's protecting you," said the Warlock. "If Glirendree hit the rim now, the recoil would knock you clear down to the village. Can't you hear the hum?"

Hap heard the whine as the disc cut the air. The tone was going up and up the scale.

"You're stalling," he said.

"That's true. So? Can it hurt you?"

"No. You were saying you knew a secret." Hap braced himself, sword raised, on one side of the disc, which now glowed red at the edge.

"I've wanted to tell someone for such a long time. A hundred and fifty years. Even Sharla doesn't know." The Warlock still stood ready to run if the swordsman should come after him. "I'd learned a little magic in those days, not much compared to what I know now, but big, showy stuff. Castles floating in the air. Dragons with golden scales. Armies turned to stone, or wiped out by lightning, instead of simple death spells. Stuff like that takes a lot of power, you know?"

"I've heard of such things."

"I did it all the time, for myself, for friends, for whoever happened to be king, or whomever I happened to be in love with. And I found that after I'd been settled for a while, the power would leave me. I'd have to move elsewhere to get it back."

The copper disc glowed bright orange with the heat of its spin. It should have fragmented, or melted, long ago.

"Then there are the dead places, the places where a warlock dares not go. Places where magic doesn't work. They tend to be rural areas, farmlands and sheep ranges, but you can find the old cities, the castles built to float which now lie tilted on their sides, the unnaturally aged bones of dragons, like huge lizards from another age.

"So I started wondering."

Hap stepped back a bit from the heat of the disc. It glowed pure white now, and it was like a sun brought to earth. Through the glare Hap had lost sight of the Warlock.

"So I built a disc like this one and set it spinning. Just a simple kinetic sorcery, but with a constant acceleration and no limit point. You know what mana is?"

"What's happening to your voice?"

"Mana is the name we give to the power behind magic." The Warlock's voice had gone weak and high.

A horrible suspicion came to Hap. The Warlock had slipped down the hill, leaving his voice behind! Hap trotted around the disc, shading his eyes from its heat.

An old man sat on the other side of the disc. His arthritic fingers, half-crippled with swollen joints, played with a rune-inscribed knife. "What I found out—oh, there you are. Well, it's too late now."

Hap raised his sword, and his sword changed.

It was a massive red demon, horned and hooved, and its teeth were in Hap's right hand. It paused, deliberately, for the few seconds it took Hap to realize what had happened and to try to jerk away. Then it bit down, and the swordsman's hand was off at the wrist.

The demon reached out, slowly enough, but Hap in his surprise was unable to move. He felt the taloned fingers close his windpipe.

He felt the strength leak out of the taloned hand, and he saw surprise and dismay spread across the demon's face.

The disc exploded. All at once and nothing first, it disintegrated into a flat cloud of metallic particles and was gone, flashing away as so much meteorite dust. The light was as lightning striking at one's feet. The sound was its thunder. The smell was vaporized copper.

The demon faded, as a chameleon fades against its background. Fading, the demon slumped to the ground in slow motion, and faded further, and was gone. When Hap reached out with his foot, he touched only dirt.

Behind Hap was a trench of burnt earth.

The spring had stopped. The rocky bottom of the stream was drying in the sun.

The Warlock's cavern had collapsed. The furnishings of the Warlock's mansion had gone crashing down into that vast pit, but the mansion itself was gone without trace.

Hap clutched his messily severed wrist, and he said, "But what happened?"

"Mana," the Warlock mumbled. He spat out a complete set of blackened teeth. "Mana. What I discovered was that the power behind magic is a natural resource, like the fertility of the soil. When you use it up, it's gone."

"But—"

"Can you see why I kept it a secret? One day all the wide world's mana will be used up. No more mana, no more magic. Do you know that Atlantis is tectonically unstable? Succeeding sorcerer-kings renew the spells each generation to keep the whole continent from sliding into the sea. What happens when the spells don't work anymore? They couldn't possibly evacuate the whole continent in time. Kinder not to let them know."

"But . . . that disc."

The Warlock grinned with his empty mouth and ran his hands through snowy hair. All the hair came off in his fingers, leaving his scalp bare and mottled. "Senility is like being drunk. The disc? I told you. A kinetic sorcery with no upper limit. The disc keeps accelerating until all the mana in the locality has been used up."

Hap moved a step forward. Shock had drained half his strength. His foot came down jarringly, as if all the spring were out of his muscles.

"You tried to kill me."

The Warlock nodded. "I figured if the disc didn't explode and kill you while you were trying to go around it, Glirendree would strangle you when the constraint wore off. What are you complaining about? It cost you a hand, but you're free of Glirendree."

Hap took another step, and another. His hand was beginning to hurt, and the pain gave him strength. "Old man," he said thickly. "Two hundred years old. I can break your neck with the hand you left me. And I will."

The Warlock raised the inscribed knife.

"That won't work. No more magic." Hap slapped the Warlock's hand away and took the Warlock by his bony throat.

The Warlock's hand brushed easily aside, and came back, and up. Hap wrapped his arms around his belly and backed away with his eyes and mouth wide open. He sat down hard.

"A knife always works," said the Warlock.

"Oh," said Hap.

"I worked the metal myself, with ordinary black-smith's tools, so the knife wouldn't crumble when the magic was gone. The runes aren't magic. They only say—"

"Oh," said Hap. "Oh." He toppled sideways.

The Warlock lowered himself onto his back. He held the knife up and read the markings, in a language only the Brotherhood remembered.

AND THIS, TOO, SHALL PASS AWAY. It was a very old plat-itude, even then.

He dropped his arm back and lay looking at the sky.

Presently the blue was blotted by a shadow.

"I told you to get out of here," he whispered.

"You should have known better. What's *happened* to you?"

"No more youth spells. I knew I'd have to do it when the prognostics spell showed blank." He drew a ragged breath. "It was worth it. I killed Glirendree."

"Playing hero, at your age! What can I do? How can I help?"

"Get me down the hill before my heart stops. I never told you my true age—"

"I knew. The whole village knows." She pulled him to sitting position, pulled one of his arms around her neck. It felt dead. She shuddered, but she wrapped her own arm around his waist and gathered herself for the effort. "You're so thin! Come on, love. We're going to stand up." She took most of his weight onto her, and they stood up.

"Go slow. I can hear my heart trying to take off."

"How far do we have to go?"

"Just to the foot of the hill, I think. Then the spells will work again, and we can rest." He stumbled. "I'm going blind," he said.

"It's a smooth path, and all downhill."

"That's why I picked this place. I knew I'd have to use the disc someday. You can't throw away knowledge. Always the time comes when you use it, because you have to, because it's there."

"You've changed so. So—so ugly. And you smell."

The pulse fluttered in his neck, like a humming-bird's wings. "Maybe you won't want me, after seeing me like this."

"You can change back, can't you?"

"Sure. I can change to anything you like. What color eyes do you want?"

"I'll be like this myself someday," she said. Her voice held cool horror. And it was fading; he was going deaf.

"I'll teach you the proper spells, when you're ready. They're dangerous. Blackly dangerous."

She was silent for a time. Then: "What color were *his* eyes? You know, Belhap Sattlestone whatever."

"Forget it," said the Warlock, with a touch of pique.

And suddenly his sight was back.

But not forever, thought the Warlock as they stumbled through the sudden daylight. When the mana runs out, I'll go like a blown candle flame, and civilization will follow. No more magic, no more magic-based industries. Then the whole world will be barbarian until men learn a new way to coerce nature, and the swordsmen, the damned stupid swordsmen will win after all.

THE QUEEN OF AIR & DARKNESS

POUL ANDERSON

Mention the name POUL ANDERSON and instantly dozens of excellent science fiction novels and short stories spring to mind. However, like many authors, he has also tried his hand at fantasy fiction, with equally impressive results. Two of his novels that deserve mention are *Three Hearts and Three Lions* and *The Broken Sword,* the latter based on the Norse elven myths. He has also written in universes as diverse as Shakespeare's comedies and Robert E. Howard's Conan mythos. A seven-time winner of the Hugo Award, he has also been awarded three Nebulas and the Tolkien Memorial Award. "The Queen of Air and Darkness" shows us a glimpse of what happens when science and magic go head-to-head.

The last glow of the last sunset would linger almost until midwinter. But there would be no more day, and the northlands rejoiced. Blossoms opened, flamboyance on firethorn trees, steel-flowers rising blue from the brok and rainplant that cloaked all hills, shy whiteness of kiss-me-never down in the dales. Flitteries darted among them on iridescent wings; a crownbuck shook his horns and bugled. Between horizons the sky deepened from purple to sable. Both moons were aloft, nearly full, shining frosty on leaves and molten on waters. The shadows they made were blurred by an aurora, a great blowing curtain of light across half heaven. Behind it the earliest stars had come out.

A boy and a girl sat on Wolund's Barrow just under the dolmen it up-bore. Their hair, which streamed halfway down their backs, showed startlingly forth, bleached as it was by summer. Their bodies, still dark from that season, merged with earth and bush and rock, for they wore only garlands. He played on a bone flute and she sang. They had lately become lovers. Their age was about sixteen, but they did not know this, considering themselves Outlings and thus indifferent to time, remembering little or nothing of how they had once dwelt in the lands of men.

His notes piped cold around her voice:

Cast a spell,
weave it well
of dust and dew
and night and you.

A brook by the grave mound, carrying moonlight down to a hill-hidden river, answered with its rapids. A flock of hellbats passed black beneath the aurora.

A shape came bounding over Cloudmoor. It had two arms and two legs, but the legs were long and claw-footed and feathers covered it to the end of a tail and broad wings. The face was half human, dominated by its eyes. Had Ayoch been able to stand wholly erect, he would have reached to the boy's shoulder.

The girl rose. "He carries a burden," she said. Her vision was not meant for twilight like that of a north-land creature born, but she had learned how to use every sign her senses gave her. Besides the fact that ordinarily a pook would fly, there was a heaviness to his haste.

"And he comes from the south." Excitement jumped in the boy, sudden as a green flame that went across the constellation Lyrth. He sped down the mound. "Ohoi, Ayoch!" he called. "Me here, Mist-herd!"

"And Shadow-of-a-Dream," the girl laughed, following.

The pook halted. He breathed louder than the soughing in the growth around him. A smell of bruised yerba lifted where he stood.

"Well met in winterbirth," he whistled. "You can help me bring this to Carheddin."

He held out what he bore. His eyes were yellow lanterns above. It moved and whimpered.

"Why, a child," Mistherd said.

"Even as you were, my son, even as you were. Ho, ho, what a snatch!" Ayoch boasted. "They were a score in yon camp by Fallowwood, armed, and besides watcher engines they had big ugly dogs aprowl while they slept. I came from above, however, having spied on them till I knew that a handful of dazedust . . ."

"The poor thing." Shadow-of-a-Dream took the boy and held him to her small breasts. "So full of sleep yet, aren't you?" Blindly, he sought a nipple. She smiled through the veil of her hair. "No, I am still too young, and you already too old. But come, when you wake in Carheddin under the mountain, you shall feast."

"Yo-ah," said Ayoch very softly. "She is abroad and has heard and seen. She comes." He crouched down, wings folded. After a moment Mistherd knelt, and then Shadow-of-a-Dream, though she did not let go the child.

The queen's tall form blocked off the moons. For a while she regarded the three and their booty. Hill and moor sounds withdrew from their awareness until it seemed they could hear the northlights hiss.

At last Ayoch whispered, "Have I done well, Starmother?"

"If you stole a babe from a camp full of engines," said the beautiful voice, "then they were folk out of the far south who may not endure it as meekly as yeomen."

"But what can they do, Snowmaker?" the pook asked. "How can they track us?"

Mistherd lifted his head and spoke in pride. "Also, now they too have felt the awe of us."

"And he is a cuddly dear," Shadow-of-a-Dream

said. "And we need more like him, do we not, Lady Sky?"

"It had to happen in some twilight," agreed she who stood above. "Take him onward and care for him. By this sign," which she made, "is he claimed for the Dwellers."

Their joy was freed. Ayoch cartwheeled over the ground till he reached a shiverleaf. There he swarmed up the trunk and out on a limb, perched half hidden by unrestful pale foliage, and crowed. Boy and girl bore the child toward Carheddin at an easy distance-devouring lope which let him pipe and her sing:

> *Wahaii, wahaii!*
> *Wayala, laii!*
> *Wing on the wind*
> *high over heaven,*
> *shrilly shrieking,*
> *rush with the rainspears,*
> *tumble through tumult,*
> *drift to the moonhoar trees and*
> *   the dream-heavy shadows beneath them,*
> *and rock in, be one with the clinking*
> *   wavelets of lakes*
> *where the starbeams drown.*

As she entered, Barbro Cullen felt, through all grief and fury, stabbed by dismay. The room was unkempt. Journals, tapes, reels, codices, file boxes, bescribbled papers were piled on every table. Dust filmed most shelves and corners. Against one wall stood a laboratory setup, microscope and analytical equipment. She recognized it as compact and efficient, but it was not what you would expect in an office, and it gave the air a faint chemical reek. The rug was threadbare, the furniture shabby.

This was her final chance?

Then Eric Sherrinford approached. "Good day, Mrs. Cullen," he said. His tone was crisp, his handclasp firm. His faded gripsuit didn't bother her. She wasn't inclined to fuss about her own appearance except on special occasions. (And would she ever again have one, unless she got back Jimmy?) What she observed was a cat's personal neatness.

A smile radiated in crow's-feet from his eyes. "Forgive my bachelor housekeeping. On Beowulf we have—we had, at any rate, machines for that, so I never acquired the habit myself, and I don't want a hireling disarranging my tools. More convenient to work out of my apartment than keep a separate office. Won't you be seated?"

"No, thanks. I couldn't," she mumbled.

"I understand. But if you'll excuse me, I function best in a relaxed position."

He jackknifed into a lounger. One long shank crossed the other knee. He drew forth a pipe and stuffed it from a pouch. Barbro wondered why he took tobacco in so ancient a way. Wasn't Beowulf supposed to have the up-to-date equipment that they still couldn't afford to build on Roland? Well, of course old customs might survive anyhow. They generally did in colonies, she remembered reading. People had moved starward in the hope of preserving such outmoded things as their mother tongues or constitutional government or rational-technological civilization. . . .

Sherrinford pulled her up from the confusion of her weariness: "You must give me the details of your case, Mrs. Cullen. You've simply told me your son was kidnapped and your local constabulary did nothing. Otherwise, I know just a few obvious facts, such as your being widowed rather than divorced; and you're the daughter of outwayers in Olga Ivanoff Land, who nevertheless kept in close telecommunication with Christmas Landing; and you're trained in one of the biological professions; and you had several years' hiatus in field work until recently you started again."

She gaped at the high-cheeked, beak-nosed, black-haired and gray-eyed countenance. His lighter made a *scrit* and a flare which seemed to fill the room. Quietness dwelt on this height above the city, and winter dusk was seeping through the windows. "How in cosmos do you know that?" she heard herself exclaim.

He shrugged and fell into the lecturer's manner for which he was notorious. "My work depends on noticing details and fitting them together. In more than a hundred years on Roland, tending to cluster according to their origins and thought-habits, people have developed regional accents. You have a trace of the Olgan burr, but you nasalize your vowels in the style of this area, though you live in Portolondon. That suggests steady childhood exposure to metropolitan speech. You were part of Matsuyama's expedition, you told me, and took your boy along. They wouldn't have allowed any ordinary technician to do that; hence, you had to be valuable enough to get away with it. The team was conducting ecological research; therefore, you must be in the life sciences. For the same reason, you must have had previous field experience. But your skin is fair, showing none of the leatheriness one gets from prolonged exposure to this sun. Accordingly, you must have been mostly indoors for a good while before you went on your ill-fated trip. As for widowhood—you never mentioned a husband to me, but you have had a man whom you thought so highly of that you still wear both the wedding and the engagement ring he gave you."

Her sight blurred and stung. The last of those words had brought Tim back; huge, ruddy, laughterful and gentle. She must turn from this other person and stare outward. "Yes," she achieved saying, "you're right."

The apartment occupied a hilltop above Christmas Landing. Beneath it the city dropped away in walls, roofs, archaistic chimneys and lamplit streets, goblin lights of human-piloted vehicles, to the harbor, the sweep of Venture Bay, ships bound to and from the Sunward Islands and remoter regions of the Boreal Ocean, which glimmered like mercury in the afterglow of Charlemagne. Oliver was swinging rapidly higher, a mottled orange disk a full degree wide; closer to the zenith which it could never reach, it would shine the color of ice. Alde, half the seeming size, was a thin slow crescent near Sirius, which she remembered was near Sol, but you couldn't see Sol without a telescope. . . .

"Yes," she said around the pain in her throat, "my husband is about four years dead. I was carrying our first child when he was killed by a stampeding monocerus. We'd been married three years before. Met while we were both at the university—casts from School Central can only supply a basic education, you know. We founded our own team to do ecological studies under contract—you know, can a certain area be settled while maintaining a balance of nature, what crops will grow, what hazards, that sort of question. Well, afterward I did lab work for a fisher co-op in Portolondon. But the monotony, the . . . shut-in-ness . . . was eating me away.

Professor Matsuyama offered me a position on the team he was organizing to examine Commissioner Hauch Land. I thought, God help me, I thought Jimmy—Tim wanted him named James, once the tests showed it'd be a boy, after his own father and because of 'Timmy and Jimmy' and—oh, I thought Jimmy could safely come along. I couldn't bear to leave him behind for months, not at his age. We could make sure he'd never wander out of camp. What could hurt him inside it? *I* had never believed those stories about the Outlings stealing human children. I supposed parents were trying to hide from themselves the fact they'd been careless, they'd let a kid get lost in the woods or attacked by a pack of satans or—well, I learned better, Mr. Sherrinford. The guard robots were evaded and the dogs were drugged, and when I woke, Jimmy was gone."

He regarded her through the smoke from his pipe. Barbro Engdahl Cullen was a big woman of thirty or so (Rolandic years, he reminded himself, ninety-five percent of terrestrial, not the same as Beowulfan years), broad-shouldered, long-legged, full-breasted, supple of stride; her face was wide, straight nose, straightforward hazel eyes, heavy but mobile mouth; her hair was reddish brown, cropped below the ears, her voice husky, her garment a plain street robe. To still the writhing of her fingers, he asked skeptically, "Do you now believe in the Outlings?"

"No. I'm just not so sure as I was." She swung about with half a glare for him. "And we have found traces."

"Bits of fossils," he nodded. "A few artifacts of a neolithic sort. But apparently ancient, as if the makers died ages ago. Intensive search has failed to turn up any real evidence for their survival."

"How intensive can search be, in a summer-stormy, winter-gloomy wilderness around the North Pole?" she demanded. "When we are, how many, a million people on an entire planet, half of us crowded into this one city?"

"And the rest crowding this one habitable continent," he pointed out.

"Arctica covers five million square kilometers," she flung back. "The Arctic Zone proper covers a fourth of it. We haven't the industrial base to establish satellite monitor stations, build aircraft we can trust in those parts, drive roads through the damned darklands and establish permanent bases and get to know them and tame them. Good Christ, generations of lonely outwaymen told stories about Graymantle, and the beast was never seen by a proper scientist till last year!"

"Still, you continue to doubt the reality of the Outlings?"

"Well, what about a secret cult among humans, born of isolation and ignorance, lairing in the wilderness, stealing children when they can for . . ." She swallowed. Her head drooped. "But you're supposed to be the expert."

"From what you told me over the visiphone, the Portolondon constabulary questions the accuracy of the report your group made, thinks the lot of you were hysterical, claims you must have omitted a due precaution, and the child toddled away and was lost beyond your finding."

His dry words pried the horror out of her. Flushing, she snapped, "Like any settler's kid? No. I didn't simply yell. I consulted Data Retrieval. A few too many such cases are recorded for accident to be a very plausible explanation. And shall we totally ignore the frightened stories about reappearances? But when I went back to the constabulary with my facts, they brushed me off. I suspect that was not entirely because they're under-manned. I think they're afraid too. They're recruited from country boys, and Portolondon lies near the edge of the unknown."

Her energy faded. "Roland hasn't got any central police force," she finished drably. "You're my last hope."

The man puffed smoke into twilight, with which it blended, before he said in a kindlier voice than hitherto: "Please don't make it a high hope, Mrs. Cullen. I'm the solitary private investigator on this world, having no resources beyond myself, and a newcomer to boot."

"How long have you been here?"

"Twelve years. Barely time to get a little familiarity with the relatively civilized coastlands. You settlers of a century or more—what do you, even, know about Arc-tica's interior?"

Sherrinford sighed. "I'll take the case, charging no more than I must, mainly for the sake of the experi-ence," he said. "But only if you'll be my guide and assistant, however painful it will be for you."

"Of course! I dreaded waiting idle. Why me, though?"

"Hiring someone else as well qualified would be prohibitively expensive on a pioneer planet where every hand has a thousand urgent tasks to do. Besides, you have a motive. And I'll need that. As one who was born on another world altogether strange to this one, itself altogether strange to Mother Earth, I am too dauntingly aware of how handicapped we are."

Night gathered upon Christmas Landing. The air stayed mild, but glimmerlit tendrils of fog, sneaking through the streets, had a cold look, and colder yet was the aurora where it shuddered between the moons. The woman drew closer to the man in this darkening room, surely not aware that she did, until he switched on a fluoropanel. The same knowledge of Roland's aloneness was in both of them.

One light-year is not much as galactic distances go. You could walk it in about 270 million years, beginning at the middle of the Permian Era, when dinosaurs belonged to the remote future, and continuing to the present day when spaceships cross even greater reaches. But stars in our neighborhood average some nine light-years apart, and barely one percent of them have planets which are man-habitable, and speeds are limited to less than that of radiation. Scant help is given by relativistic time contraction and suspended animation en route. These made the journeys seem short, but history meanwhile does not stop at home.

Thus voyages from sun to sun will always be few. Colonists will be those who have extremely special reasons for going. They will take along germ plasm for exogenetic cultivation of domestic plants and animals—and of human infants, in order that population can grow fast enough to escape death through genetic drift. After all, they cannot rely on further immigration. Two or three times a century, a ship may call from some other colony. (Not from Earth. Earth has long ago sunk into alien concerns.) Its place of origin will be an old settlement. The young ones are in no position to build and man interstellar vessels.

Their very survival, let alone their eventual modernization, is in doubt. The founding fathers have had to take what they could get in a universe not especially designed for man.

Consider, for example, Roland. It is among the rare happy finds, a world where humans can live, breathe, eat the food, drink the water, walk unclad if they choose, sow their crops, pasture their beasts, dig their mines, erect their homes, raise their children and grandchildren. It is worth crossing three-quarters of a light-century to preserve certain dear values and strike new roots into the soil of Roland.

But the star Charlemagne is of type F9, 40 percent brighter than Sol, brighter still in the treacherous ultraviolet and wilder still in the wind of charged particles that seethes from it. The planet has an eccentric orbit. In the middle of the short but furious northern summer, which includes periastron, total insolation is more than double what Earth gets; in the depth of the long northern winter, it is barely less than terrestrial average.

Native life is abundant everywhere. But lacking elaborate machinery, not yet economically possible to construct for more than a few specialists, man can only endure the high latitudes. A 10-degree axial tilt, together with the orbit, means that the northern part of the Arctican continent spends half its year in unbroken sunlessness. Around the South Pole lies an empty ocean.

Other differences from Earth might superficially seem more important. Roland has two moons, small but close, to evoke clashing tides. It rotates once in thirty-two hours, which is endlessly, subtly disturbing to organisms evolved through gigayears of a quicker rhythm. The weather patterns are altogether unterrestrial. The globe is a mere 9,500 kilometers in diameter; its surface gravity is 0.42 É 980 cm/sec^2; the sea-level air pressure is slightly above one Earth atmosphere. (For actually, Earth is the freak, and man exists because a cosmic accident blew away most of the gas that a body its size ought to have kept, as Venus has done.)

However, Homo can truly be called sapiens when he practices his specialty of being unspecialized. His repeated attempts to freeze himself into an all-answering pattern or culture or ideology, or whatever he has named it, have repeatedly brought ruin. Give him the pragmatic business of making his living and he will usually do rather well. He adapts, within broad limits.

These limits are set by such factors as his need for sunlight and his being, necessarily and forever, a part of the life that surrounds him and a creature of the spirit within.

Portolondon thrust docks, boats, machinery, warehouses into the Gulf of Polaris. Behind them huddled the dwellings of its 5,000 permanent inhabitants: concrete walls, storm shutters, high-peaked tile roofs. The gaiety of their paint looked forlorn amid lamps; this town lay past the Arctic Circle.

Nevertheless Sherrinford remarked, "Cheerful place, eh? The kind of thing I came to Roland looking for."

Barbro made no reply. The days in Christmas Landing, while he made his preparations, had drained her. Gazing out the dome of the taxi that was whirring them downtown from the hydrofoil that brought them, she supposed he meant the lushness of forest and meadows along the road, brilliant hues and phosphorescence of flowers in gardens, clamor of wings overhead. Unlike terrestrial flora in cold climates, Arctican vegetation spends every daylit hour in frantic growth and energy storage. Not till summer's fever gives place to gentle winter does it bloom and fruit; and estivating animals rise from their dens and migratory birds come home.

The view was lovely, she had to admit: beyond the trees, a spaciousness climbing toward remote heights, silvery gray under a moon, an aurora, the diffuse radiance from a sun just below the horizon.

Beautiful as a hunting satan, she thought, and as terrible. That wilderness had stolen Jimmy. She wondered if she would at least be given to find his little bones and take them to his father.

Abruptly she realized that she and Sherrinford were at their hotel and that he had been speaking of the town. Since it was next in size after the capital, he must have visited here often before. The streets were crowded and noisy; signs flickered, music blared from shops, taverns, restaurants, sports centers, dance halls; vehicles were jammed down to molasses speed; the several-stories-high office buildings stood aglow. Portolondon linked an enormous hinterland to the outside world. Down the Gloria River came timber rafts, ores, harvest of farms whose owners were slowly making Rolandic life serve them, meat and ivory and furs gathered by rangers in the mountains beyond Troll Scarp. In from the sea came coastwise freighters, the fishing fleet, produce of the Sunward Islands, plunder of whole continents farther south where bold men adventured. It clanged in Portolondon, laughed, blustered, connived, robbed, preached, guzzled, swilled, toiled, dreamed, lusted, built, destroyed, died, was born, was happy, angry, sorrowful, greedy, vulgar, loving, ambitious, human. Neither the sun's blaze elsewhere nor the half-year's twilight here—wholly night around midwinter—was going to stay man's hand.

Or so everybody said.

Everybody except those who had settled in the darklands. Barbro used to take for granted that they were evolving curious customs, legends, and superstitions, which would die when the outway had been completely mapped and controlled. Of late, she had wondered. Perhaps Sherrinford's hints, about a change in his own attitude brought about by his preliminary research, were responsible.

Or perhaps she just needed something to think about besides how Jimmy, the day before he went, when she asked him whether he wanted rye or French bread for a sandwich, answered in great solemnity—he was becoming interested in the alphabet—"I'll have a slice of what we people call the F bread."

She scarcely noticed getting out of the taxi, registering, being conducted to a primitively furnished room. But after she unpacked, she remembered Sherrinford had suggested a confidential conference. She went down the hall and knocked on his door. Her knuckles sounded less loud than her heart.

He opened the door, finger on lips, and gestured her toward a corner. Her temper bristled until she saw the image of Chief Constable Dawson in the visiphone. Sherrinford must have chimed him up and must have a reason to keep her out of scanner range. She found a chair and watched, nails digging into knees.

The detective's lean length refolded itself. "Pardon the interruption," he said. "A man mistook the number. Drunk, by the indications."

Dawson chuckled. "We get plenty of those." Barbro recalled his fondness for gabbing. He tugged the beard which he affected, as if he were an outwayer instead of a townsman. "No harm in them as a rule. They only have a lot of voltage to discharge, after weeks or months in the backlands."

"I've gathered that that environment—foreign in a million major and minor ways to the one that created man—I've gathered that it does do odd things to the personality." Sherrinford tamped his pipe. "Of course, you know my practice has been confined to urban and suburban areas. Isolated garths seldom need private investigators. Now that situation appears to have changed. I called to ask you for advice."

"Glad to help," Dawson said. "I've not forgotten what you did for us in the de Tahoe murder case." Cautiously: "Better explain your problem first."

Sherrinford struck fire. The smoke that followed cut through the green odors—even here, a paved pair of kilometers from the nearest woods—that drifted past traffic rumble through a crepuscular window. "This is more a scientific mission than a search for an absconding debtor or an industrial spy," he drawled. "I'm looking into two possibilities: that an organization, criminal or religious or whatever, has long been active and steals infants; or that the Outlings of folklore are real."

"Huh?" On Dawson's face Barbro read as much dismay as surprise. "You can't be serious!"

"Can't I?" Sherrinford smiled. "Several generations' worth of reports shouldn't be dismissed out of hand. Especially not when they become more frequent and consistent in the course of time, not less. Nor can we ignore the documented loss of babies and small children, amounting by now to over a hundred, and never a trace found afterward. Nor the finds which demonstrate that an intelligent species once inhabited Arctica and may still haunt the interior."

Dawson leaned forward as if to climb out of the screen. "Who engaged you?" he demanded. "That Cullen woman? We were sorry for her, naturally, but she wasn't making sense, and when she got downright abusive . . ."

"Didn't her companions, reputable scientists, confirm her story?"

"No story to confirm. Look, they had the place ringed with detectors and alarms, and they kept mastiffs. Standard procedure in country where a hungry sauroid or whatever might happen by. Nothing could've entered unbeknownst."

"On the ground. How about a flyer landing in the middle of camp?"

"A man in a copter rig would've roused everybody."

"A winged being might be quieter."

"A living flyer that could lift a three-year-old boy? Doesn't exist."

"Isn't in the scientific literature, you mean, constable. Remember Graymantle; remember how little we know about Roland, a planet, an entire world. Such birds do exist on Beowulf—and on Rustum, I've read. I made a calculation from the local ratio of air density to gravity, and, yes, it's marginally possible here too. The child could have been carried off for a short distance before wing muscles were exhausted and the creature must descend."

Dawson snorted. "First it landed and walked into the tent where mother and boy were asleep. Then it walked away, toting him, after it couldn't fly farther. Does that sound like a bird of prey? And the victim didn't cry out, the dogs didn't bark!"

"As a matter of fact," Sherrinford said, "those inconsistencies are the most interesting and convincing features of the whole account. You're right, it's hard to see how a human kidnapper could get in undetected, and an eagle-type of creature wouldn't operate in that fashion. But none of this applies to a winged intelligent being. The boy could have been drugged. Certainly the dogs showed signs of having been."

"The dogs showed signs of having overslept. Nothing had disturbed them. The kid wandering by wouldn't do so. We don't need to assume one damn thing except, first, that he got restless and, second, that the alarms were a bit sloppily rigged—seeing as how no danger was expected from inside camp—and let him pass out. And, third, I hate to speak this way, but we must assume the poor tyke starved or was killed."

Dawson paused before adding: "If we had more staff, we could have given the affair more time. And would have, of course. We did make an aerial sweep, which risked the lives of the pilots, using instruments which would've spotted the kid anywhere in a fifty-kilometer radius, unless he was dead. You know how sensitive thermal analyzers are. We drew a complete blank. We have more important jobs than to hunt for the scattered pieces of a corpse."

He finished brusquely. "If Mrs. Cullen's hired you, my advice is you find an excuse to quit. Better for her, too. She's got to come to terms with reality."

Barbro checked a shout by biting her tongue.

"Oh, this is merely the latest disappearance of the series," Sherrinford said. She didn't understand how he could maintain his easy tone when Jimmy was lost.

"More thoroughly recorded than any before, thus more suggestive. Usually an outwayer family has given a tearful but undetailed account of their child who vanished and must have been stolen by the Old Folk. Sometimes, years later, they'd tell about glimpses of what they swore must have been the grown child, not really human any longer, flitting past in murk or peering through a window or working mischief upon them. As you say, neither the authorities nor the scientists have had personnel or resources to mount a proper investigation. But as I say, the matter appears to be worth investigating. Maybe a private party like myself can contribute."

"Listen, most of us constables grew up in the outway. We don't just ride patrol and answer emergency calls; we go back there for holidays and reunions. If any gang of . . . of human sacrificers was around, we'd know."

"I realize that. I also realize that the people you came from have a widespread and deep-seated belief in nonhuman beings with supernatural powers. Many actually go through rites and make offerings to propitiate them."

"I know what you're leading up to," Dawson fleered. "I've heard it before, from a hundred sensationalists. The aborigines are the Outlings. I thought better of you. Surely you've visited a museum or three, surely you've read literature from planets which do have natives—or damn and blast, haven't you ever applied that logic of yours?"

He wagged a finger. "Think," he said. "What have we in fact discovered? A few pieces of worked stone; a few megaliths that might be artificial; scratchings on rock that seem to show plants and animals, though not the way any human culture would ever have shown them; traces of fires and broken bones; other fragments of bone that seem as if they might've belonged to thinking creatures, as if they might've been inside fingers or around big brains. If so, however, the owners looked nothing like men. Or angels, for that matter. Nothing! The most anthropoid reconstruction I've seen shows a kind of two-legged crocagator.

"Wait, let me finish. The stories about the Outlings—oh, I've heard them too, plenty of them. I believed them when I was a kid—the stories tell how there're different kinds, some winged, some not, some half-human, some completely human except maybe for being too handsome . . . It's fairyland from ancient Earth all over again. Isn't it? I got interested once and dug into the Heritage Library microfiles, and be damned if I didn't find almost the identical yarns, told by peasants centuries before spaceflight.

"None of it squares with the scanty relics we have, if they are relics, or with the fact that no area the size of Arctica could spawn a dozen different intelligent species, or . . . hellfire, man, with the way your common sense tells you aborigines would behave when humans arrived!"

Sherrinford nodded. "Yes, yes," he said. "I'm less sure than you that the common sense of nonhuman beings is precisely like our own. I've seen so much variation within mankind. But, granted, your arguments are strong. Roland's too few scientists have more pressing tasks than tracking down the origins of what is, as you put it, a revived medieval superstition."

He cradled his pipe bowl in both hands and peered into the tiny hearth of it. "Perhaps what interests me most," he said softly, "is why—across that gap of centuries, across a barrier of machine civilization and its utterly antagonistic world view—no continuity of tradition whatsoever—why have hardheaded, technologically organized, reasonably well-educated colonists here brought back from its grave a belief in the Old Folk?"

"I suppose eventually, if the university ever does develop the psychology department they keep talking about, I suppose eventually somebody will get a thesis out of your question." Dawson spoke in a jagged voice, and he gulped when Sherrinford replied:

"I propose to begin now. In Commissioner Hauch Land, since that's where the latest incident occurred. Where can I rent a vehicle?"

"Uh, might be hard to do . . ."

"Come, come. Tenderfoot or not, I know better. In an economy of scarcity, few people own heavy equipment. But since it's needed, it can always be rented. I want a camper bus with a ground-effect drive suitable for every kind of terrain. And I want certain equipment installed which I've brought along, and the top canopy section replaced by a gun turret controllable from the driver's seat. But I'll supply the weapons. Besides rifles and pistols of my own, I've arranged to borrow some artillery from Christmas Landing's police arsenal."

"Hoy? Are you genuinely intending to make ready for . . . a war . . . against a myth?"

"Let's say I'm taking out insurance, which isn't terribly expensive, against a remote possibility. Now, besides the bus, what about a light aircraft carried piggyback for use in surveys?"

"No." Dawson sounded more positive than hitherto. "That's asking for disaster. We can have you flown to a base camp in a large plane when the weather report's exactly right. But the pilot will have to fly back at once, before the weather turns wrong again. Meteorology's underdeveloped on Roland; the air's especially treacherous this time of year, and we're not tooled up to produce aircraft that can outlive every surprise." He drew breath. "Have you no idea of how fast a whirly-whirly can hit, or what size hailstones might strike from a clear sky, or . . . ? Once you're there, man, you stick to the ground." He hesitated. "That's an important reason our information is so scanty about the outway, and its settlers are so isolated."

Sherrinford laughed ruefully. "Well, I suppose if details are what I'm after, I must creep along anyway."

"You'll waste a lot of time." Dawson said. "Not to mention your client's money. Listen, I can't forbid you to chase shadows, but . . ."

The discussion went on for almost an hour. When the screen finally blanked, Sherrinford rose, stretched, and walked toward Barbro. She noticed anew his peculiar gait. He had come from a planet with a fourth again of Earth's gravitational drag, to one where weight was less than half terrestrial. She wondered if he had flying dreams.

"I apologize for shuffling you off like that," he said. "I didn't expect to reach him at once. He was quite truthful about how busy he is. But having made contact, I didn't want to remind him overmuch of you. He can dismiss my project as a futile fantasy which I'll soon give up. But he might have frozen completely, might even have put up obstacles before us, if he'd realized through you how determined we are."

"Why should he care?" she asked in her bitterness.

"Fear of consequences, the worse because it is unadmitted—fear of consequences, the more terrifying because they are unguessable." Sherrinford's gaze went to the screen, and thence out the window to the aurora pulsing in glacial blue and white immensely far overhead. "I suppose you saw I was talking to a frightened man. Down underneath his conventionality and scoffing, he believes in the Outlings—oh, yes, he believes."

The feet of Mistherd flew over yerba and outpaced windblown driftweed. Beside him, black and misshapen, hulked Nagrim the nicor, whose earthquake weight left a swath of crushed plants. Behind, luminous blossoms of a firethorn shone through the twining, trailing outlines of Morgarel the wraith.

Here Cloudmoor rose in a surf of hills and thickets. The air lay quiet, now and then carrying the distance-muted howl of a beast. It was darker than usual at winterbirth, the moons being down and aurora a wan flicker above mountains on the northern world-edge. But this made the stars keen, and their numbers crowded heaven, and Ghost Road shone among them as if it, like the leafage beneath, were paved with dew.

"Yonder!" bawled Nagrim. All four of his arms pointed. The party had topped a ridge. Far off glimmered a spark. "Hoah, hoah! 'Ull we right off stamp dem flat, or pluck dem apart slow?"

We shall do nothing of the sort, bonebrain, Morgarel's answer slid through their heads. *Not unless they attack us, and they will not unless we make them aware of us, and her command is that we spy out their purposes.*

"Gr-r-rum-m-m. I know deir aim. Cut down trees, stick plows in land, sow deir cursed seed in de clods and in deir shes. 'Less we drive dem into de bitterwater, and soon, soon, dey'll wax too strong for us."

"Not too strong for the queen!" Mistherd protested, shocked.

Yet they do have new powers, it seems, Morgarel reminded him. *Carefully must we probe them.*

"Den carefully can we step on dem?" asked Nagrim.

The question woke a grin out of Mistherd's own uneasiness. He slapped the scaly back. "Don't talk, you," he said. "It hurts my ears. Nor think; that hurts your head. Come, run!"

Ease yourself, Morgarel scolded. *You have too much life in you, human-born.*

Mistherd made a face at the wraith, but obeyed to the extent of slowing down and picking his way through what cover the country afforded. For he traveled on behalf of the Fairest, to learn what had brought a pair of mortals questing hither.

Did they seek that boy whom Ayoch stole? (He continued to weep for his mother, though less and less often as the marvels of Carheddin entered him.) Perhaps. A bird-craft had left them and their car at the now-abandoned campsite, from which they had followed an outward spiral. But when no trace of the cub had appeared inside a reasonable distance, they did not call to be flown home. And this wasn't because weather forbade the farspeaker waves to travel, as was frequently the case. No, instead the couple set off toward the mountains of Moonhorn. Their course would take them past a few outlying invader steadings and on into realms untrodden by their race.

So this was no ordinary survey. Then what was it?

Mistherd understood now why she who reigned had made her adopted mortal children learn, or retain, the clumsy language of their forebears. He had hated that drill, wholly foreign to Dweller ways. Of course, you

obeyed her, and in time you saw how wise she had
been. . . .

Presently he left Nagrim behind a rock—the nicor
would only be useful in a fight—and crawled from
bush to bush until he lay within man-lengths of the
humans. A rainplant drooped over him, leaves soft on
his bare skin, and clothed him in darkness. Morgarel
floated to the crown of a shiverleaf, whose unrest
would better conceal his flimsy shape. He'd not be
much help either. And that was the most troublous,
the almost appalling thing here. Wraiths were among
those who could not just sense and send thought, but
cast illusions. Morgarel had reported that this time his
power seemed to rebound off an invisible cold wall
around the car.

Metal sheened faintly by the light of their campfire.
They sat on either side, wrapped in coats against a coolness that Mistherd, naked, found mild. The male drank
smoke. The female stared past him into a dusk which
her flame-dazzled eyes must see as thick gloom. The
dancing glow brought her vividly forth. Yes, to judge
from Ayoch's tale, she was the dam of the new cub.

Ayoch had wanted to come too, but the Wonderful
One forbade. Pooks couldn't hold still long enough for
such a mission.

The man sucked on his pipe. His cheeks thus
pulled into shadow while the light flickered across
nose and brow, he looked disquietingly like a shearbill
about to stoop on prey.

"—No, I tell you again, Barbro, I have no theories,"
he was saying. "When facts are insufficient, theorizing
is ridiculous at best, misleading at worst."

"Still, you must have some idea of what you're
doing," she said. It was plain that they had threshed

this out often before. No Dweller could be as persistent as she or as patient as he. "That gear you packed—that generator you keep running . . ."

"I have a working hypothesis or two, which suggested what equipment I ought to take."

"Why won't you tell me what the hypotheses are?"

"They themselves indicate that that might be inadvisable at the present time. I'm still feeling my way into the labyrinth. And I haven't had a chance yet to hook everything up. In fact, we're really only protected against so-called telepathic influence . . ."

"What?" She started. "Do you mean . . . those legends about how they can read minds too . . ." Her words trailed off and her gaze sought the darkness beyond his shoulders.

He leaned forward. His tone lost its clipped rapidity, grew earnest and soft. "Barbro, you're racking yourself to pieces. Which is no help to Jimmy if he's alive, the more so when you may well be badly needed later on. We've a long trek before us, and you'd better settle into it."

She nodded jerkily and caught her lip between her teeth for a moment before she answered, "I'm trying."

He smiled around his pipe. "I expect you'll succeed. You don't strike me as a quitter or a whiner or an enjoyer of misery."

She dropped a hand to the pistol at her belt. Her voice changed; it came out of her throat like knife from sheath. "When we find them, they'll know what I am. What humans are."

"Put anger aside also," the man urged. "We can't afford emotions. If the Outlings are real, as I told you I'm provisionally assuming, they're fighting for their homes." After a short stillness he added: "I like to think that if the first explorers had found live natives, men would not have colonized Roland. But it's too late now. We can't go back if we wanted to. It's a bitter-end struggle against an enemy so crafty that he's even hidden from us the fact that he is waging war."

"Is he? I mean, skulking, kidnapping an occasional child . . ."

"That's part of my hypothesis. I suspect those aren't harassments; they're tactics employed in a chillingly subtle strategy."

The fire sputtered and sparked. The man smoked awhile, brooding, until he went on:

"I didn't want to raise your hopes or excite you unduly while you had to wait on me, first in Christmas Landing, then in Portolondon. Afterward we were busy satisfying ourselves that Jimmy had been taken farther from camp than he could have wandered before collapsing. So I'm only now telling you how thoroughly I studied available material on the . . . Old Folk. Besides, at first I did it on the principle of eliminating every imaginable possibility, however absurd. I expected no result other than final disproof. But I went through everything, relics, analyses, histories, journalistic accounts, monographs; I talked to outwayers who happened to be in town and to what scientists we have who've taken any interest in the matter. I'm a quick study. I flatter myself I became as expert as anyone—though God knows there's little to be expert on. Furthermore, I, a comparative stranger to Roland, maybe looked on the problem with fresh eyes. And a pattern emerged for me.

"If the aborigines had become extinct, why hadn't they left more remnants? Arctica isn't enormous, and it's fertile for Rolandic life. It ought to have supported a population whose artifacts ought to have accumulated over millennia. I've read that on Earth, literally tens of thousands of paleolithic hand axes were found, more by chance than archaeology.

"Very well. Suppose the relics and fossils were deliberately removed, between the time the last survey party left and the first colonizing ships arrived. I did find some support for that idea in the diaries of the original explorers. They were too preoccupied with checking the habitability of the planet to make catalogues of primitive monuments. However, the remarks they wrote down indicate they saw much more than later arrivals did. Suppose what we have found is just what the removers overlooked or didn't get around to.

"That argues a sophisticated mentality, thinking in long-range terms, doesn't it? Which in turn argues that the Old Folk were not mere hunters or neolithic farmers."

"But nobody ever saw buildings or machines or any such thing," Barbro objected.

"No. Most likely the natives didn't go through our kind of metallurgic-industrial evolution. I can conceive of other paths to take. Their full-fledged civilization might have begun, rather than ended, in biological science and technology. It might have developed potentialities of the nervous system, which might be greater in their species than in man. We have those abilities to some degree ourselves, you realize. A dowser, for instance, actually senses variations in the local magnetic field caused by a water table. However, in us, these talents are maddeningly rare and tricky. So we took our business elsewhere. Who needs to be a telepath, say, when he has a visiphone? The Old Folk may have seen it the other way around. The artifacts of their civilization may have been, may still be, unrecognizable to men."

"They could have identified themselves to the men, though," Barbro said. "Why didn't they?"

"I can imagine any number of reasons. As, they could have had a bad experience with interstellar visitors earlier in their history. Ours is scarcely the sole race that has spaceships. However, I told you I don't theorize in advance of the facts. Let's say no more than that the Old Folk, if they exist, are alien to us."

"For a rigorous thinker, you're spinning a mighty thin thread."

"I've admitted this is entirely provisional." He squinted at her through a roil of campfire smoke. "You came to me, Barbro, insisting in the teeth of officialdom that your boy had been stolen, but your own talk about cultist kidnappers was ridiculous. Why are you reluctant to admit the reality of nonhumans?"

"In spite of the fact that Jimmy's being alive probably depends on it," she sighed. "I know."

A shudder. "Maybe I don't dare admit it."

"I've said nothing thus far that hasn't been speculated about in print," he told her. "A disreputable speculation, true. In a hundred years, nobody has found valid evidence for the Outlings being more than a superstition. Still, a few people have declared it's at least possible that intelligent natives are at large in the wilderness."

"I know," she repeated. "I'm not sure, though, what has made you, overnight, take those arguments seriously."

"Well, once you got me started thinking, it occurred to me that Roland's outwayers are not utterly isolated medieval crofters. They have books, telecommunications, power tools, motor vehicles; above all, they have a modern science-oriented education. Why *should* they turn superstitious? Something must be causing it." He stopped. "I'd better not continue. My ideas go further than this; but if they're correct, it's dangerous to speak them aloud."

Mistherd's belly muscles tensed. There was danger for fair, in that shearbill head. The Garland Bearer must be warned. For a minute he wondered about summoning Nagrim to kill these two. If the nicor jumped them fast, their firearms might avail them naught. But no. They might have left word at home, or . . . He came back to his ears. The talk had changed course. Barbro was murmuring, ". . . why you stayed on Roland."

The man smiled his gaunt smile. "Well, life on Beowulf held no challenge for me. Heorot is—or was; this was decades past, remember—Heorot was densely populated, smoothly organized, boringly uniform. That was partly due to the lowland frontier, a safety valve that bled off the dissatisfied. But I lack the carbon dioxide tolerance necessary to live healthily down there. An expedition was being readied to make a swing around a number of colony worlds, especially those which didn't have the equipment to keep in laser contact. You'll recall its announced purpose, to seek out new ideas in science, arts, sociology, philosophy, whatever might prove valuable. I'm afraid they found little on Roland relevant to Beowulf. But I, who had wangled a berth, I saw opportunities for myself and decided to make my home here."

"Were you a detective back there, too?"

"Yes, in the official police. We had a tradition of such work in our family. Some of that may have come from the Cherokee side of it, if the name means anything to you. However, we also claimed collateral descent from one of the first private inquiry agents on record, back on Earth before spaceflight. Regardless of how true that may be, I found him a useful model. You see, an archetype . . ."

The man broke off. Unease crossed his features. "Best we go to sleep," he said. "We've a long distance to cover in the morning."

She looked outward. "Here is no morning."

They retired. Mistherd rose and cautiously flexed limberness back into his muscles. Before returning to the Sister of Lyrth, he risked a glance through a pane in the car. Bunks were made up, side by side, and the humans lay in them. Yet the man had not touched her, though hers was a bonny body, and nothing that had passed between them suggested he meant to do so.

Eldritch, humans. Cold and claylike. And they would overrun the beautiful wild world? Mistherd spat in disgust. It must not happen. It would not happen. She who reigned had vowed that.

The lands of William Irons were immense. But this was because a barony was required to support him, his kin and cattle, on native crops whose cultivation was still poorly understood. He raised some terrestrial plants as well, by summerlight and in conservatories. However, these were a luxury. The true conquest of northern Arctica lay in yerba hay, in bathyrhiza wood, in pericoup and glycophyllon, and eventually, when the market had expanded with population and industry, in chalcanthemum for city florists and pelts of cage-bred rover for city furriers.

That was in a tomorrow Irons did not expect that he would live to see. Sherrinford wondered if the man really expected anyone ever would.

The room was warm and bright. Cheerfulness crackled in the fireplace. Light from fluoropanels gleamed off hand-carved chests and chairs and tables, off colorful draperies and shelved dishes. The outwayer sat solid in his high seat, stoutly clad, beard flowing down his chest. His wife and daughters brought coffee, whose fragrance joined the remnant odors of a hearty supper, to him, his guests, and his sons.

But outside, wind hooted, lightning flared, thunder bawled, rain crashed on roof and walls and roared down to swirl among the courtyard cobblestones. Sheds and barns crouched against hugeness beyond. Trees groaned, and did a wicked undertone of laughter run beneath the lowing of a frightened cow? A burst of hailstones hit the tiles like knocking knuckles.

You could feel how distant your neighbors were, Sherrinford thought. And nonetheless they were the people whom you saw oftenest, did daily business with by visiphone (when a solar storm didn't make gibberish of their voices and chaos of their faces) or in the flesh, partied with; gossiped and intrigued with, intermarried with; in the end, they were the people who would bury you. The lights of the coastal towns were monstrously farther away.

William Irons was a strong man. Yet when now he spoke, fear was in his tone. "You'd truly go over Troll Scarp?"

"Do you mean Hanstein Palisades?" Sherrinford responded, more challenge than question.

"No outwayer calls it anything but Troll Scarp," Barbro said.

And how had a name like that been reborn, light-years and centuries from Earth's Dark Ages?

"Hunters, trappers, prospectors—rangers, you call them—travel in those mountains," Sherrinford declared.

"In certain parts," Irons said. "That's allowed, by a pact once made 'tween a man and the queen after he'd done well by a jack-o'-the-hill that a satan had hurt. Wherever the plumablanca grows, men may fare, if they leave mangoods on the altar boulders in payment for what they take out of the land. Elsewhere"—one fist clenched on a chair arm and went slack again—"is not wise to go."

"It's been done, hasn't it?"

"Oh, yes. And some came back all right, or so they claimed, though I've heard they were never lucky afterward. And some didn't; they vanished. And some who returned babbled of wonders and horrors and stayed witlings the rest of their lives. Not for a long time has anybody been rash enough to break the pact and overtread the bounds." Irons looked at Barbro almost entreatingly. His woman and children stared likewise, grown still. Wind hooted beyond the walls and rattled the storm shutters. "Don't you."

"I've reason to believe my son is there," she answered.

"Yes, yes, you've told and I'm sorry. Maybe something can be done. I don't know what, but I'd be glad to, oh, lay a double offering on Unvar's Barrow this midwinter, and a prayer drawn in the turf by a flint knife. Maybe they'll return him." Irons sighed. "They've not done such a thing in man's memory, though. And he could have a worse lot. I've glimpsed them myself, speeding madcap through twilight. They seem happier than we are. Might be no kindness, sending your boy home again."

"Like in the Arvid song," said his wife.

Irons nodded. "M-hm. Or others, come to think of it."

"What's this?" Sherrinford asked. More sharply than before, he felt himself a stranger. He was a child of cities and technics, above all a child of the skeptical intelligence. This family *believed*. It was disquieting to see more than a touch of their acceptance in Barbro's slow nod.

"We have the same ballad in Olga Ivanoff Land," she told him, her voice less calm than the words. "It's one of the traditional ones—nobody knows who composed them—that are sung to set the measure of a ringdance in a meadow."

"I noticed a multilyre in your baggage, Mrs. Cullen," said the wife of Irons. She was obviously eager to get off the explosive topic of a venture in defiance of the Old Folk. A songfest could help. "Would you like to entertain us?"

Barbro shook her head, white around the nostrils. The oldest boy said quickly, rather importantly, "Well, sure, I can, if our guests would like to hear."

"I'd enjoy that, thank you." Sherrinford leaned back in his seat and stoked his pipe. If this had not happened spontaneously, he would have guided the conversation toward a similar outcome.

In the past he had had no incentive to study the folklore of the outway, and not much chance to read the scanty references on it since Barbro brought him her trouble. Yet more and more he was becoming convinced that he must get an understanding—not an anthropological study, but a feel from the inside out—of the relationship between Roland's frontiersmen and those beings which haunted them.

A bustling followed, rearrangement, settling down to

listen, coffee cups refilled and brandy offered on the side.
The boy explained, "The last line is the chorus. Everybody join in, right?" Clearly he too hoped thus to bleed
off some of the tension. Catharsis through music? Sherrinford wondered, and added to himself: no—exorcism.

A girl strummed a guitar. The boy sang to a melody
which beat across the storm noise:

> *It was the ranger Arvid*
> *rode homeward through the hills*
> *among the shadowy shiverleafs,*
> *along the chiming rills.*
> The dance weaves under the
> firethorn.
>
> *The night wind whispered around him*
> *with scent of brok and rue.*
> *Both moons rose high above him*
> *and hills aflash with dew.*
> The dance weaves under the
> firethorn.
>
> *And dreaming of that woman*
> *who waited in the sun,*
> *he stopped, amazed by starlight,*
> *and so he was undone.*
> The dance weaves under the
> firethorn.
>
> *For there beneath a barrow*
> *that bulked athwart a moon,*
> *the Outling folk were dancing*
> *in glass and golden shoon.*

The dance weaves under the
firethorn.

The Outling folk were dancing
like water, wind, and fire
to frosty-ringing harpstrings,
and never did they tire.
    The dance weaves under the
firethorn.

To Arvid came she striding
from where she watched the dance,
the Queen of Air and Darkness,
with starlight in her glance.
    The dance weaves under the
firethorn.

With starlight, love and terror
in her immortal eye,
the Queen of Air and Darkness . . .

"No!" Barbro leaped from her chair. Her fists were
clenched and tears flogged her cheekbones. "You
can't—pretend that—about the things that stole
Jimmy!"

She fled from the chamber, upstairs to her guest
bedroom.

But she finished the song herself. That was about sev-
enty hours later, camped in the steeps where rangers
dared not fare.

She and Sherrinford had not said much to the
Irons family, after refusing repeated pleas to leave the

forbidden country alone. Nor had they exchanged many remarks at first as they drove north. Slowly, however, he began to draw her out about her own life. After a while she almost forgot to mourn, in her remembering of home and old neighbors. Somehow this led to discoveries—that he, beneath his professional manner, was a gourmet and a lover of opera and appreciated her femaleness; that she could still laugh and find beauty in the wild land around her—and she realized, half guiltily, that life held more hope than even the recovery of the son Tim gave her.

"I've convinced myself he's alive," the detective said. He scowled. "Frankly, it makes me regret having taken you along, I expected this would be only a fact-gathering trip, but it's turning out to be more. If we're dealing with real creatures who stole him, they can do real harm. I ought to turn back to the nearest garth and call for a plane to fetch you."

"Like bottommost hell you will, mister," she said. "You need somebody who knows outway conditions, and I'm a better shot than average."

"M-m-m . . . it would involve considerable delay too, wouldn't it? Besides the added distance, I can't put a signal through to any airport before this current burst of solar interference has calmed down."

Next "night" he broke out his remaining equipment and set it up. She recognized some of it, such as the thermal detector. Other items were strange to her, copied to his order from the advanced apparatus of his birthworld. He would tell her little about them. "I've explained my suspicion that the ones we're after have telepathic capabilities," he said in apology.

Her eyes widened. "You mean it could be true, the queen and her people can read minds?"

"That's part of the dread which surrounds their legend, isn't it? Actually there's nothing spooky about the phenomenon. It was studied and fairly well defined centuries ago, on Earth. I daresay the facts are available in the scientific microfiles at Christmas Landing. You Rolanders have simply had no occasion to seek them out, any more than you've yet had occasion to look up how to build power-beamcasters or spacecraft."

"Well, how does telepathy work, then?"

Sherrinford recognized that her query asked for comfort as much as it did for facts, and he spoke with deliberate dryness: "The organism generates extremely longwave radiation which can, in principle, be modulated by the nervous system. In practice, the feebleness of the signals and their low rate of information transmission make them elusive, hard to detect and measure. Our prehuman ancestors went in for more reliable senses, like vision and hearing. What telepathic transceiving we do is marginal at best. But explorers have found extraterrestrial species that got an evolutionary advantage from developing the system further in their particular environments. I imagine such species could include one which gets comparatively little direct sunlight—in fact, appears to hide from broad day. It could even become so able in this regard that, at short range, it can pick up man's weak emissions and make man's primitive sensitivities resonate to its own strong sendings."

"That would account for a lot, wouldn't it?" Barbro said faintly.

"I've now screened our car by a jamming field," Sherrinford told her, "but it reaches only a few meters past the chassis. Beyond, a scout of theirs might get a warning from your thoughts, if you knew precisely what I'm trying to do. I have a well-trained subconscious which sees to it that I think about this in French when I'm outside. Communication has to be structured to be intelligible, you see, and that's a different enough structure from English. But English is the only human language on Roland and surely the Old Folk have learned it."

She nodded. He had told her his general plan, which was too obvious to conceal. The problem was to make contact with the aliens, if they existed. Hitherto, they had only revealed themselves, at rare intervals, to one or a few backwoodsmen at a time. An ability to generate hallucinations would help them in that. They would stay clear of any large, perhaps unmanageable expedition which might pass through their territory. But two people, braving all prohibitions, shouldn't look too formidable to approach. And . . . this would be the first human team which not only worked on the assumption that the Outlings were real, but possessed the resources of modern, off-planet police technology.

Nothing happened at that camp. Sherrinford said he hadn't expected it would. The Old Folk seemed cautious this near any settlement. In their own lands they must be bolder.

And by the following "night," the vehicle had gone well into yonder country. When Sherrinford stopped the engine in a meadow and the car settled down, silence rolled in like a wave.

They stepped out. She cooked a meal on the glower while he gathered wood, that they might later cheer themselves with a campfire. Frequently he glanced at his wrist. It bore no watch—instead, a radio-controlled dial, to tell what the instruments in the bus might register.

Who needed a watch here? Slow constellations wheeled beyond glimmering aurora. The moon Alde stood above a snowpeak, turning it argent, though this place lay at a goodly height. The rest of the mountains were hidden by the forest that crowded around. Its trees were mostly shiverleaf and feathery white plumablanca, ghostly amidst their shadows. A few firethorns glowed, clustered dim lanterns, and the underbrush was heavy and smelled sweet. You could see surprisingly far through the blue dusk. Somewhere nearby, a brook sang and a bird fluted.

"Lovely here," Sherrinford said. They had risen from their supper and not yet sat down again or kindled their fire.

"But strange," Barbro answered as low. "I wonder if it's really meant for us. If we can really hope to possess it."

His pipe stem gestured at the stars. "Man's gone to stranger places than this."

"Has he? I . . . oh, I suppose it's just something left over from my outway childhood, but do you know, when I'm under them I can't think of the stars as balls of gas whose energies have been measured, whose planets have been walked on by prosaic feet. No, they're small and cold and magical; our lives are bound to them; after we die, they whisper to us in our graves." Barbro glanced downward. "I realize that's nonsense."

She could see in the twilight how his face grew tight. "Not at all," he said. "Emotionally, physics may be a worse nonsense. And in the end, you know, after a sufficient number of generations, thought follows feeling. Man is not at heart rational. He could stop believing the stories of science if those no longer felt right."

He paused. "That ballad which didn't get finished

in the house," he said, not looking at her. "Why did it affect you so?"

"I couldn't stand hearing *them*, well, praised. Or that's how it seemed. Sorry for the fuss."

"I gather the ballad is typical of a large class."

"Well, I never thought to add them up. Cultural anthropology is something we don't have time for on Roland, or more likely it hasn't occurred to us, with everything else there is to do. But—now you mention it, yes, I'm surprised at how many songs and stories have the Arvid motif in them."

"Could you bear to recite it?"

She mustered the will to laugh. "Why, I can do better than that if you want. Let me get my multilyre and I'll perform."

She omitted the hypnotic chorus line, though, when the notes rang out, except at the end. He watched her where she stood against moon and aurora.

> *. . . the Queen of Air and Darkness*
> *cried softly under sky:*
>
> *"Light down, you ranger Arvid,*
> *and join the Outling folk.*
> *You need no more be human,*
> *which is a heavy yoke."*
>
> *He dared to give her answer:*
> *"I may do naught but run.*
> *A maiden waits me, dreaming*
> *in lands beneath the sun.*
>
> *"And likewise wait me comrades*
> *and tasks I would not shirk,*

for what is ranger Arvid
if he lays down his work?

"So wreak your spells, you Outling,
and cast your wrath on me.
Though maybe you can slay me,
you'll not make me unfree."

The Queen of Air and Darkness
stood wrapped about with fear
and northlight flares and beauty
he dared not look too near.

Until she laughed like harpsong
and said to him in scorn:
"I do not need a magic
to make you always mourn.

"I send you home with nothing
except your memory
of moonlight, Outling music,
night breezes, dew, and me.

"And that will run behind you,
a shadow on the sun,
and that will lie beside you
when every day is done.

"In work and play and friendship
your grief will strike you dumb
for thinking what you are—and—
what you might have become.

"You dull and foolish woman

treat kindly as you can.
Go home now, ranger Arvid,
set free to be a man!"
In flickering and laughter
the Outling folk were gone.
He stood alone by moonlight
and wept until the dawn.

    The dance weaves under the
firethorn.

She laid the lyre aside. A wind rustled leaves. After a long quietness Sherrinford said, "And tales of this kind are part of everyone's life in the outway?"

"Well, you could put it thus," Barbro replied. "Though they're not all full of supernatural doings. Some are about love or heroism. Traditional themes."

"I don't think your particular tradition has arisen of itself." His tone was bleak. "In fact, I think many of your songs and stories were not composed by human beings."

He snapped his lips shut and would say no more on the subject. They went early to bed.

Hours later, an alarm roused them.

The buzzing was soft, but it brought them instantly alert. They slept in gripsuits, to be prepared for emergencies. Skyglow lit them through the canopy. Sherrinford swung out of his bunk, slipped shoes on feet and clipped gun holster to belt. "Stay inside," he commanded.

"What's here?" Her pulse thuttered.

He squinted at the dials of his instruments and checked them against the luminous telltale on his wrist. "Three animals," he counted. "Not wild ones happening by. A large one, homeothermic, to judge from the infrared, holding still a short way off. Another . . . hm, low temperature, diffuse and unstable emission, as if it were more like a . . . a swarm of cells coordinated somehow . . . pheromonally? . . . hovering, also at a distance. But the third's practically next to us, moving around in the brush; and that pattern looks human."

She saw him quiver with eagerness, no longer seeming a professor. "I'm going to try to make a capture," he said. "When we have a subject for interrogation—stand ready to let me back in again fast. But don't risk yourself, whatever happens. And keep this cocked." He handed her a loaded big-game rifle.

His tall frame poised by the door, opened it a crack. Air blew in, cool, damp, full of fragrances and murmurings. The moon Oliver was now also aloft, the radiance of both unreally brilliant, and the aurora seethed in whiteness and ice blue.

Sherrinford peered afresh at his telltale. It must indicate the directions of the watchers, among those dappled leaves. Abruptly he sprang out. He sprinted past the ashes of the campfire and vanished under trees. Barbro's hand strained on the butt of her weapon.

Racket exploded. Two in combat burst onto the meadow. Sherrinford had clapped a grip on a smaller human figure. She could make out by streaming silver and rainbow flicker that the other was nude, male, long-haired, lithe, and young. He fought demoniacally, seeking to use teeth and feet and raking nails, and meanwhile he ululated like a satan.

The identification shot through her: a changeling, stolen in babyhood and raised by the Old Folk. This creature was what they would make Jimmy into.

"Ha!" Sherrinford forced his opponent around and drove stiffened fingers into the solar plexus. The boy gasped and sagged: Sherrinford manhandled him toward the car.

Out from the woods came a giant. It might itself have been a tree, black and rugose, bearing four great gnarly boughs; but earth quivered and boomed beneath its leg-roots, and its hoarse bellowing filled sky and skulls.

Barbro shrieked. Sherrinford whirled. He yanked out his pistol, fired and fired, flat whip-cracks through the half-light. His free arm kept a lock on the youth. The troll shape lurched under those blows. It recovered and came on, more slowly, more carefully, circling around to cut him off from the bus. He couldn't move fast enough to evade it unless he released his prisoner—who was his sole possible guide to Jimmy. . . .

Barbro leaped forth. "Don't!" Sherrinford shouted. "For God's sake, stay inside!" The monster rumbled and made snatching motions at her. She pulled the trigger. Recoil slammed her in the shoulder. The colossus rocked and fell. Somehow it got its feet back and lumbered toward her. She retreated. Again she shot and again. The creature snarled. Blood began to drip from it and gleam oilily amidst dewdrops. It turned and went off, breaking branches, into the darkness that laired beneath the woods.

"Get to shelter!" Sherrinford yelled. "You're out of the jammer field!"

A mistiness drifted by overhead. She barely glimpsed it before she saw the new shape at the meadow edge. "Jimmy!" tore from her.

"Mother." He held out his arms. Moonlight coursed in his tears. She dropped her weapon and ran to him.

Sherrinford plunged in pursuit. Jimmy flitted away

into the brush. Barbro crashed after, through clawing twigs. Then she was seized and borne away.

Standing over his captive, Sherrinford strengthened the fluoro output until vision of the wilderness was blocked off from within the bus. The boy squirmed beneath that colorless glare.

"You are going to talk," the man said. Despite the haggardness in his features, he spoke quietly.

The boy glared through tangled locks. A bruise was purpling on his jaw. He'd almost recovered ability to flee while Sherrinford chased and lost the woman. Returning, the detective had barely caught him. Time was lacking to be gentle, when Outling reinforcements might arrive at any moment. Sherrinford had knocked him out and dragged him inside. He sat lashed into a swivel seat.

He spat. "Talk to you, manclod?" But sweat stood on his skin, and his eyes flickered unceasingly around the metal which caged him.

"Give me a name to call you by."

"And have you work a spell on me?"

"Mine's Eric. If you don't give me another choice, I'll have to call you . . . m-m-m . . . Wuddikins."

"What?" However eldritch, the bound one remained a human adolescent. "Mistherd, then." The lilting accent of his English somehow emphasized its sullenness. "That's not the sound, only what it means. Anyway, it's my spoken name, naught else."

"Ah, you keep a secret name you consider to be real?"

"She does. I don't know myself what it is. She knows the real names of everybody."

Sherrinford raised his brows. "She?"

"Who reigns. May she forgive me, I can't make the reverent sign when my arms are tied. Some invaders call her the Queen of Air and Darkness."

"So." Sherrinford got pipe and tobacco. He let silence wax while he started the fire. At length he said, "I'll confess the Old Folk took me by surprise. I didn't expect so formidable a member of your gang. Everything I could learn had seemed to show they work on my race—and yours, lad—by stealth, trickery, and illusion."

Mistherd jerked a truculent nod. "She created the first nicors not long ago. Don't think she has naught but dazzlements at her beck."

"I don't. However, a steel-jacketed bullet works pretty well too, doesn't it?"

Sherrinford talked on, softly, mostly to himself: "I do still believe the, ah, nicors—all your half-humanlike breeds—are intended in the main to be seen, not used. The power of projecting mirages must surely be quite limited in range and scope as well as in the number of individuals who possess it. Otherwise she wouldn't have needed to work as slowly and craftily as she has. Even outside our mind-shield, Barbro—my companion—could have resisted, could have remained aware that whatever she saw was unreal . . . if she'd been less shaken, less frantic, less driven by need."

Sherrinford wreathed his head in smoke. "Never mind what I experienced," he said. "It couldn't have been the same as for her. I think the command was simply given us, 'You will see what you most desire in the world, running away from you into the forest.' Of course, she didn't travel many meters before the nicor waylaid her. I'd no hope of trailing them; I'm no Artican woodsman, and besides, it'd have been too easy to ambush me. I came back to you." Grimly: "You're my link to your overlady."

"You think I'll guide you to Starhaven or Carheddin? Try making me, clod-man."

"I want to bargain."

"I s'pect you intend more'n that." Mistherd's answer held surprising shrewdness. "What'll you tell after you come home?"

"Yes, that does pose a problem, doesn't it? Barbro Cullen and I are not terrified outwayers. We're of the city. We brought recording instruments. We'd be the first of our kind to report an encounter with the Old Folk, and that report would be detailed and plausible. It would produce action."

"So you see I'm not afraid to die," Mistherd declared, though his lips trembled a bit. "If I let you come in and do your man-things to my people, I'd have naught left worth living for."

"Have no immediate fears," Sherrinford said. "You're merely bait." He sat down and regarded the boy through a visor of calm. (Within, it wept in him: *Barbro, Barbro!*) "Consider. Your queen can't very well let me go back, bringing my prisoner and telling about hers. She has to stop that somehow. I could try fighting my way through—this car is better armed than you know—but that wouldn't free anybody. Instead, I'm staying put. New forces of hers will get here as fast as they can. I assume they won't blindly throw themselves against a machine gun, a howitzer, a fulgurator. They'll parley first, whether their intentions are honest or not. Thus I make the contact I'm after."

"What d'you plan?" The mumble held anguish.

"First, this, as a sort of invitation." Sherrinford reached out to flick a switch. "There. I've lowered my shield against mind reading and shape casting. I daresay the leaders, at least, will be able to sense that it's gone. That should give them confidence."

"And next?"

"Next we wait. Would you like something to eat or drink?"

During the time which followed, Sherrinford tried to jolly Mistherd along, find out something of his life. What answers he got were curt. He dimmed the interior lights and settled down to peer outward. That was a long few hours.

They ended at a shout of gladness, half a sob, from the boy. Out of the woods came a band of the Old Folk.

Some of them stood forth more clearly than moons and stars and northlights should have caused. He in the van rode a white crownbuck whose horns were garlanded. His form was manlike but unearthly beautiful, silver blond hair falling from beneath the antlered helmet, around the proud cold face. The cloak fluttered off his back like living wings. His frost-colored mail rang as he fared.

Behind him, to right and left, rode two who bore swords whereon small flames gleamed and flickered. Above, a flying flock laughed and trilled and tumbled in the breezes. Near them drifted a half-transparent mistiness. Those others who passed among trees after their chieftain were harder to make out. But they moved in quicksilver grace and as it were to a sound of harps and trumpets.

"Lord Luighaid." Glory overflowed in Mistherd's tone. "Her master Knower—himself."

Sherrinford had never done a harder thing than to sit at the main control panel, finger near the button of the shield generator, and not touch it. He rolled down a section of canopy to let voices travel. A gust of wind struck him in the face, bearing odors of the roses in his mother's garden. At his back, in the main body of the vehicle, Mistherd strained against his bonds till he could see the oncoming troop.

"Call to them," Sherrinford said. "Ask if they will talk with me."

Unknown, flutingly sweet words flew back and forth. "Yes," the boy interpreted. "He will, the Lord Luighaid. But I can tell you, you'll never be let go. Don't fight them. Yield. Come away. You don't know what 'tis to be alive till you've dwelt in Carheddin under the mountain."

The Outlings drew nigh.

Jimmy glimmered and was gone. Barbro lay in strong arms, against a broad breast, and felt the horse move beneath her. It had to be a horse, though only a few were kept any longer on the steadings, and they only for special uses or love. She could feel the rippling beneath its hide, hear a rush of parted leafage and the thud when a hoof struck stone; warmth and living scent welled up around her through the darkness.

He who carried her said mildly, "Don't be afraid, darling. It was a vision. But he's waiting for us, and we're bound for him."

She was aware in a vague way that she ought to feel terror or despair or something. But her memories lay behind her—she wasn't sure just how she had come to be here—she was borne along in a knowledge of being loved. At peace, at peace, rest in the calm expectation of joy . . .

After a while the forest opened. They crossed a lea

where boulders stood gray-white under the moons, their shadows shifting in the dim hues which the aurora threw across them. Flitteries danced, tiny comets, above the flowers between. Ahead gleamed a peak whose top was crowned in clouds.

Barbro's eyes happened to be turned forward. She saw the horse's head and thought, with quiet surprise: "Why, this is Sambo, who was mine when I was a girl." She looked upward at the man. He wore a black tunic and a cowled cape, which made his face hard to see. She could not cry aloud, here. "Tim," she whispered.

"Yes, Barbro."

"I buried you. . . ."

His smile was endlessly tender. "Did you think we're no more than what's laid back into the ground? Poor torn sweetheart. She who's called us is the All Healer. Now rest and dream."

"Dream," she said, and for a space she struggled to rouse herself. But the effort was weak. Why should she believe ashen tales about . . . atoms and energies, nothing else to fill a gape of emptiness . . . tales she could not bring to mind . . . when Tim and the horse her father gave her carried her on to Jimmy? Had the other thing not been the evil dream, and this her first drowsy awakening from it?

As if he heard her thoughts, he murmured, "They have a song in Outling lands. The Song of the Men:

> *The world sails*
> *to an unseen wind.*
> *Light swirls by the bows.*
> *The wake is night.*
> *But the Dwellers have no such sadness.*

"I don't understand," she said.

He nodded. "There's much you'll have to understand, darling, and I can't see you again until you've learned those truths. But meanwhile you'll be with our son."

She tried to lift her head and kiss him. He held her down. "Not yet," he said. "You've not been received among the queen's people. I shouldn't have come for you, except that she was too merciful to forbid. Lie back, lie back."

Time blew past. The horse galloped tireless, never stumbling, up the mountain. Once she glimpsed a troop riding down it and thought they were bound for a last weird battle in the west against . . . who? . . . one who lay cased in iron and sorrow. Later she would ask herself the name of him who had brought her into the land of the Old Truth.

Finally spires lifted splendid among the stars, which are small and magical and whose whisperings comfort us after we are dead. They rode into a courtyard where candles burned unwavering, fountains splashed and birds sang. The air bore fragrance of brok and pericoup, of ruse and roses, for not everything that man brought was horrible. The Dwellers waited in beauty to welcome her. Beyond their stateliness, pooks cavorted through the gloaming; among the trees darted children; merriment caroled across music more solemn.

"We have come—" Tim's voice was suddenly, inexplicably a croak. Barbro was not sure how he dismounted, bearing her. She stood before him and saw him sway on his feet.

Fear caught her. "Are you well?" She seized both

his hands. They felt cold and rough. Where had Sambo gone? Her eyes searched beneath the cowl. In this brighter illumination, she ought to have seen her man's face clearly. But it was blurred, it kept changing. "What's wrong, oh, what's happened?"

He smiled. Was that the smile she had cherished? She couldn't completely remember. "I—I must go," he stammered, so low she could scarcely hear. "Our time is not ready." He drew free of her grasp and leaned on a robed form which had appeared at his side. A haziness swirled over both their heads. "Don't watch me go . . . back into the earth," he pleaded. "That's death for you. Till our time returns— There, our son!"

She had to fling her gaze around. Kneeling, she spread wide her arms. Jimmy struck her like a warm, solid cannonball. She rumpled his hair; she kissed the hollow of his neck; she laughed and wept and babbled foolishness; and this was no ghost, no memory that had stolen off when she wasn't looking. Now and again, as she turned her attention to yet another hurt which might have come upon him—hunger, sickness, fear—and found none, she would glimpse their surroundings. The gardens were gone. It didn't matter.

"I missed you so, Mother. Stay?"

"I'll take you home, dearest."

"Stay. Here's fun. I'll show. But you stay."

A sighing went through the twilight. Barbro rose. Jimmy clung to her hand. They confronted the queen.

Very tall she was in her robes woven of north-lights, and her starry crown and her garlands of kiss-me-never. Her countenance recalled Aphrodite of Milos, whose picture Barbro had often seen in the realms of men, save that the queen's was more fair and more majesty dwelt upon it and in the nightblue eyes. Around her the gardens woke to new reality, the court of the Dwellers and the heaven-climbing spires.

"Be welcome," she spoke, her speaking a song, "forever."

Against the awe of her, Barbros said, "Moon-mother, let us go home."

"That may not be."

"To our world, little and beloved," Barbro dreamed she begged, "which we build for ourselves and cherish for our children."

"To prison days, angry nights, works that crumble in the fingers, loves that turn to rot or stone or driftweed, loss, grief, and the only sureness that of the final nothingness. No. You too, Wanderfoot who is to be, will jubilate when the banners of the Outworld come flying into the last of the cities and man is made wholly alive. Now go with those who will teach you."

The Queen of Air and Darkness lifted an arm in summons. It halted, and none came to answer.

For over the fountains and melodies lifted a grue-some growling. Fires leaped, thunders crashed. Her hosts scattered screaming before the steel thing which boomed up the mountainside. The pooks were gone in a whirl of frightened wings. The nicors flung their bodies against the unalive invader and were consumed, until their Mother cried to them to retreat.

Barbro cast Jimmy down and herself over him. Towers wavered and smoked away. The mountain stood bare under icy moons, save for rocks, crags, and farther off a glacier in whose depths the auroral light pulsed blue. A cave mouth darkened a cliff. Thither folk streamed, seeking refuge underground. Some were human of blood, some grotesques like the pooks and nicors and wraiths; but most were lean, scaly, long-tailed, long-beaked, not remotely men or Outlings.

For an instant, even as Jimmy wailed at her breast—perhaps as much because the enchantment had been wrecked as because he was afraid—Barbro pitied the queen who stood alone in her nakedness. Then that one also had fled, and Barbro's world shivered apart.

The guns fell silent; the vehicle whirred to a halt. From it sprang a boy who called wildly, "Shadow-of-a-Dream, where are you? It's me, Mistherd, oh, come, come!"—before he remembered that the language they had been raised in was not man's. He shouted in that until a girl crept out of a thicket where she had hidden. They stared at each other through dust, smoke and moonglow. She ran to him.

A new voice barked from the car, "Barbro, hurry!"

Christmas Landing knew day: short at this time of year, but sunlight, blue skies, white clouds, glittering water, salt breezes in busy streets and the sane disorder of Eric Sherrinford's living room.

He crossed and uncrossed his legs where he sat, puffed on his pipe as if to make a veil and said, "Are you certain you're recovered? You mustn't risk overstrain."

"I'm fine," Barbro Cullen replied, though her tone was flat. "Still tired, yes, and showing it, no doubt. One doesn't go through such an experience and bounce back in a week. But I'm up and about. And to be frank, I must know what's happened, what's going on, before I can settle down to regain my full strength. Not a word of news anywhere."

"Have you spoken to others about the matter?"

"No. I've simply told visitors I was too exhausted to talk. Not much of a lie. I assumed there's a reason for censorship."

Sherrinford looked relieved. "Good girl. It's at my urging. You can imagine the sensation when this is made public. The authorities agreed they need time to study the facts, think and debate in a calm atmosphere, have a decent policy ready to offer voters who're bound to become rather hysterical at first." His mouth quirked slightly upward. "Furthermore, your nerves and Jimmy's get their chance to heal before the journalistic storm breaks over you. How is he?"

"Quite well. He continues pestering me for leave to go play with his friends in the wonderful place. But at his age, he'll recover—he'll forget."

"He may meet them later anyhow."

"What? We didn't . . ." Barbro shifted in her chair. "I've forgotten too. I hardly recall a thing from our last hours. Did you bring back any kidnapped humans?"

"No. The shock was savage as it was, without throwing them straight into an . . . an institution. Mistherd, who's basically a sensible young fellow, assured me they'd get along, at any rate as regards survival necessities, till arrangements can be made." Sherrinford hesitated. "I'm not sure what the arrangements will be. Nobody is, at our present stage. But obviously they include those people—or many of them, especially those who aren't full-grown—rejoining the human race. Though they may never feel at home in civilization. Perhaps in a way that's best, since we will need some kind of mutually acceptable liaison with the Dwellers."

His impersonality soothed them both. Barbro

became able to say, "Was I too big a fool? I do remember how I yowled and beat my head on the floor."

"Why, no." He considered the big woman and her pride for a few seconds before he rose, walked over and laid a hand on her shoulder. "You'd been lured and trapped by a skillful play on your deepest instincts at a moment of sheer nightmare. Afterward, as that wounded monster carried you off, evidently another type of being came along, one that could saturate you with close-range neuropsychic forces. On top of this, my arrival, the sudden brutal abolishment of every hallucination, must have been shattering. No wonder if you cried out in pain. Before you did, you competently got Jimmy and yourself into the bus and you never interfered with me."

"What did you do?"

"Why, I drove off as fast as possible. After several hours, the atmospherics let up sufficiently for me to call Portolondon and insist on an emergency airlift. Not that that was vital. What chance had the enemy to stop us? They didn't even try—but quick transportation was certainly helpful."

"I figured that's what must have gone on." Barbro caught his glance. "No, what I meant was, how did you find us in the backlands?"

Sherrinford moved a little off from her. "My prisoner was my guide. I don't think I actually killed any of the Dwellers who'd come to deal with me. I hope not. The car simply broke through them, after a couple of warning shots, and afterward outpaced them. Steel and fuel against flesh wasn't really fair. At the cave entrance, I did have to shoot down a few of those troll creatures. I'm not proud of it."

He stood silent. Presently: "But you were a captive," he said. "I couldn't be sure what they might do to you, who had first claim on me." After another pause: "I don't look for any more violence."

"How did you make . . . the boy . . . cooperate?"

Sherrinford paced from her to the window, where he stood staring out at the Boreal Ocean. "I turned off the mind-shield," he said. "I let their band get close, in full splendor of illusion. Then I turned the shield back on, and we both saw them in their true shapes. As we went northward, I explained to Mistherd how he and his kind had been hoodwinked, used, made to live in a world that was never really there. I asked him if he wanted himself and whomever he cared about to go on till they died as domestic animals—yes, running in limited freedom on solid hills, but always called back to the dream kennel." His pipe fumed furiously. "May I never see such bitterness again. He had been taught to believe he was free."

Quiet returned above the hectic traffic. Charlemagne drew nearer to setting; already the east darkened.

Finally Barbro asked, "Do you know why?"

"Why children were taken and raised like that? Partly because it was in the pattern the Dwellers were creating; partly in order to study and experiment on members of our species—minds, that is, not bodies; partly because humans have special strengths which are helpful, like being able to endure full daylight."

"But what was the final purpose of it all?"

Sherrinford paced the floor. "Well," he said, "of course the ultimate motives of the aborigines are obscure. We can't do more than guess at how they think, let alone how they feel. But our ideas do seem to fit the data.

"Why did they hide from man? I suspect they, or

rather their ancestors—for they aren't glittering elves, you know; they're mortal and fallible too—I suspect the natives were only being cautious at first, more cautious than human primitives, though certain of those on Earth were also slow to reveal themselves to strangers. Spying, mentally eavesdropping, Roland's Dwellers must have picked up enough language to get some idea of how different man was from them, and how powerful; and they gathered that more ships would be arriving, bringing settlers. It didn't occur to them that they might be conceded the right to keep their lands. Perhaps they're still more fiercely territorial than we. They determined to fight, in their own way. I daresay, once we begin to get insight into that mentality, our psychological science will go through its Copernican revolution."

Enthusiasm kindled in him. "That's not the sole thing we'll learn, either," he went on. "They must have science of their own, a nonhuman science born on a planet that isn't Earth. Because they did observe us as profoundly as we've ever observed ourselves; they did mount a plan against us, one that would have taken another century or more to complete. Well, what else do they know? How do they support their civilization without visible agriculture or above-ground buildings or mines or anything? How can they breed whole new intelligent species to order? A million questions, ten million answers!"

"*Can* we learn from them?" Barbro asked softly. "Or can we only overrun them as you say they fear?"

Sherrinford halted, leaned elbow on mantel, hugged his pipe and replied, "I hope we'll show more charity than that to a defeated enemy. It's what they are. They tried to conquer us and failed, and now in a sense we are bound to conquer them, since they'll have to make their peace with the civilization of the machine rather than see it rust away as they strove for. Still, they never did us any harm as atrocious as what we've inflicted on our fellow men in the past. And, I repeat, they could teach us marvelous things; and we could teach them, too, once they've learned to be less intolerant of a different way of life."

"I suppose we can give them a reservation," she said, and didn't know why he grimaced and answered so roughly:

"Let's leave them the honor they've earned! They fought to save the world they'd always known from that"—he made a chopping gesture at the city—"and just possibly we'd be better off ourselves with less of it."

He sagged a trifle and sighed, "However, I suppose if Elfland had won, man on Roland would at last— peacefully, even happily—have died away. We live with our archetypes, but can we live in them?"

Barbro shook her head. "Sorry, I don't understand."

"What?" He looked at her in a surprise that drove out melancholy. After a laugh: "Stupid of me. I've explained this to so many politicians and scientists and commissioners and Lord knows what, these past days, I forgot I'd never explained to you. It was a rather vague idea of mine, most of the time we were traveling, and I don't like to discuss ideas prematurely. Now that we've met the Outlings and watched how they work, I do feel sure."

He tamped down his tobacco. "In limited measure," he said, "I've used an archetype throughout my own working life. The rational detective. It hasn't been a conscious pose—much—it's simply been an image which fitted my personality and professional style. But it draws an appropriate response from most people, whether or not they've ever heard of the original. The phenomenon is not uncommon. We meet persons who, in varying degrees, suggest Christ or Buddha or the Earth Mother or, say, on a less exalted plane, Hamlet or d'Artagnan. Historical, fictional, and mythical, such figures crystallize basic aspects of the human psyche, and when we meet them in our real experience, our reaction goes deeper than consciousness."

He grew grave again: "Man also creates archetypes that are not individuals. The anima, the shadow—and, it seems, the outworld. The world of magic, of glamour—which originally meant enchantment—of half-human beings, some like Ariel and some like Caliban, but each free of mortal frailties and sorrows—therefore, perhaps, a little carelessly cruel, more than a little tricksy; dwellers in dusk and moonlight, not truly gods but obedient to rulers who are enigmatic and powerful enough to be . . . Yes, our Queen of Air and Darkness knew well what sights to let lonely people see, what illusions to spin around them from time to time, what songs and legends to set going among them. I wonder how much she and her underlings gleaned from human fairy tales, how much they made up themselves, and how much men created all over again, all unwittingly, as the sense of living on the edge of the world entered them."

Shadows stole across the room. It grew cooler and the traffic noises dwindled. Barbro asked mutedly, "But what could this do?"

"In many ways," Sherrinford answered, "the outwayer *is* back in the Dark Ages. He has few neighbors, hears scanty news from beyond his horizon, toils to survive in a land he only partly understands, that may any night raise unforeseeable disasters against him and is bounded by enormous wildernesses. The machine civilization which brought his ancestors here is frail at best. He could lose it as the Dark Ages nations had lost Greece and Rome, as the whole of Earth seems to have lost it. Let him be worked on, long, strongly, cunningly, by the archetypical outworld, until he has come to believe in his bones that the magic of the Queen of Air and Darkness is greater than the energy of engines; and first his faith, finally his deeds will follow her. Oh, it wouldn't happen fast. Ideally, it would happen too slowly to be noticed, especially by self-satisfied city people. But when in the end a hinterland gone back to the ancient way turned from them, how could they keep alive?"

Barbro breathed, "She said to me, when their banners flew in the last of our cities, we would rejoice."

"I think we would have, by then," Sherrinford admitted. "Nevertheless, I believe in choosing one's destiny."

He shook himself, as if casting off a burden. He knocked the dottle from his pipe and stretched, muscle by muscle. "Well," he said, "it isn't going to happen."

She looked straight at him. "Thanks to you."

A flush went up his thin cheeks. "In time, I'm sure, somebody else would have . . . What matters is what we do next, and that's too big a decision for one individual or one generation to make."

She rose. "Unless the decision is personal, Eric," she suggested, feeling heat in her own face.

It was curious to see him shy. "I was hoping we might meet again."

"We will."

• • •

Ayoch sat on Wolund's Barrow. Aurora shuddered so brilliant, in such vast sheaves of light, as almost to hide the waning moons. Firethorn blooms had fallen; a few still glowed around the tree roots, amid dry brok which crackled underfoot and smelled like wood smoke. The air remained warm, but no gleam was left on the sunset horizon.

"Farewell, fare lucky," the pook called. Mistherd and Shadow-of-a-Dream never looked back. It was as if they didn't dare. They trudged on out of sight, toward the human camp whose lights made a harsh new star in the south.

Ayoch lingered. He felt he should also offer good-by to her who had lately joined him that slept in the dolmen. Likely none would meet here again for loving or magic. But he could only think of one old verse that might do. He stood and trilled:

> *Out of her breast*
> *a blossom ascended.*
> *The summer burned it.*
> *The song is ended.*

Then he spread his wings for the long flight away.

COMES NOW THE POWER

ROGER ZELAZNY

ROGER ZELAZNY (1937–1995) burst onto the speculative fiction writing scene as part of the "New Wave" group of writers in the mid to late 1960s. His books *This Immortal* and *Lord of Light* met universal praise, the latter winning a Hugo Award for best novel. His work is notable for his lyrical style and innovative use of language both in description and dialogue. His most recognized series is the Amber novels, about a parallel universe which is the true world with all others, Earth included, being mere shadows of Amber. Besides the Hugo, he was also awarded three Nebulas, three more Hugos, and two Locus awards. "Comes Now the Power" is a quietly moving story about the price of freedom and the kinds of people who are willing to pay it.

It was into the second year now, and it was maddening. Everything which had worked before failed this time. Each day he tried to break it, and it resisted his every effort.

He snarled at his students, drove recklessly, bloodied his knuckles against many walls. Nights, he lay awake cursing.

But there was no one to whom he could turn for help. His problem would have been nonexistent to a psychiatrist, who doubtless would have attempted to treat him for something else.

So he went away that summer, spent a month at a resort: nothing. He experimented with several hallucinogenic drugs; again, nothing. He tried free-associating into a tape recorder, but all he got when he played it back was a headache.

To whom does the holder of a blocked power turn, within a society of normal people?

. . . To another of his own kind, if he can locate one.

Milt Rand had known four other persons like himself: his cousin Gary, now deceased; Walker Jackson, a Negro preacher who had retired to somewhere down South; Tatya Stefanovich, a dancer, currently somewhere behind the Iron Curtain; and Curtis Legge, who, unfortunately, was suffering a schizoid reaction, paranoid type, in a state institution for the criminally insane. Others he had brushed against in the night, but had never met and could not locate now.

There had been blockages before, but Milt had always worked his way through them inside of a month. This time was different and special, though. Upsets, discomforts, disturbances, can dam up a talent, block a power. An event which seals it off completely for over a year, however, is more than a mere disturbance, discomfort, or upset.

The divorce had beaten hell out of him.

It is bad enough to know that somewhere someone is hating you; but to have known the very form of that hatred and to have proven ineffectual against it, to have known it as the hater held it for you, to have lived with it growing around you, this is more than distasteful circumstance. Whether you are offender or offended, when you are hated and you live within the circle of that hate, it takes a thing from you: it tears a piece of spirit from your soul, or, if you prefer, a way of thinking from your mind; it cuts and does not cauterize.

Milt Rand dragged his bleeding psyche around the country and returned home.

He would sit and watch the woods from his glassed-in back porch, drink beer, watch the fireflies in the shadows, the rabbits, the dark birds, an occasional fox, sometimes a bat.

He had been fireflies once, and rabbits, birds, occasionally a fox, sometimes a bat.

The wildness was one of the reasons he had moved beyond suburbia, adding an extra half-hour to his commuting time.

Now there was a glassed-in back porch between

him and these things he had once been part of. Now he was alone.

Walking the streets, addressing his classes at the institute, sitting in a restaurant, a theater, a bar, he was vacant where once he had been filled.

There are no books which tell a man how to bring back the power he has lost.

He tries everything he can think of, while he is waiting. Walking the hot pavements of a summer noon, crossing against the lights because traffic is slow, watching kids in swimsuits play around a gurgling hydrant, filthy water sluicing the gutter about their feet, as mothers and older sisters in halters, wrinkled shirts, bermudas, and sunburnt skins watch them, occasionally, while talking to one another in entranceways to buildings or the shade of a storefront awning. Milt moves across town, heading nowhere in particular, growing claustrophobic if he stops for long, his eyebrows full of perspiration, sunglasses streaked with it, shirt sticking to his sides and coming loose, sticking and coming loose as he walks.

Amid the afternoon, there comes a time when he has to rest the two fresh-baked bricks at the ends of his legs. He finds a tree-lawn bench flanked by high maples, eases himself down into it and sits there thinking of nothing in particular for perhaps twenty-five minutes.

Hello.

Something within him laughs or weeps.

Yes, hello, I am here! Don't go away! Stay! Please!

You are—like me. . . .

Yes, I am. You can see it in me because you are what you are. But you must read here and send here, too. I'm frozen. I—Hello? Where are you?

Once more, he is alone.

He tries to broadcast. He fills his mind with the

thoughts and tries to push them outside his skull.

Please come back! I need you. You can help me. I am desperate. I hurt. Where are you?

Again, nothing.

He wants to scream. He wants to search every room in every building on the block.

Instead, he sits there.

At 9:30 that evening they meet again, inside his mind.

Hello?

Stay! Stay, for God's sake! Don't go away this time! Please don't! Listen, I need you! You can help me.

How? What is the matter?

I'm like you. Or was, once. I could reach out with my mind and be other places, other things, other people. I can't do it now, though. I have a blockage. The power will not come. I know it is there. I can feel it. But I can't use . . . Hello?

Yes, I am still here. I can feel myself going away, though. I will be back. I . . .

Milt waits until midnight. She does not come back. It is a feminine mind which has touched his own. Vague, weak, but definitely feminine, and wearing the power. She does not come back that night, though. He paces up and down the block, wondering which window, which door . . .

He eats at an all-night café, returns to his bench, waits, paces again, goes back to the café for cigarettes, begins chain-smoking, goes back to the bench.

Dawn occurs, day arrives, night is gone. He is alone, as birds explore the silence, traffic begins to swell, dogs wander the lawns.

Then, weakly, the contact:

I am here. I can stay longer this time, I think. How can I help you? Tell me.

All right. Do this thing: Think of the feeling, the feeling of the out-go, out-reach, out-know that you have now. Fill your mind with that feeling and send it to me as hard as you can.

It comes upon him then as once it was: the knowledge of the power. It is earth and water, fire and air to him. He stands upon it, he swims in it, he warms himself by it, he moves through it.

It is returning! Don't stop now!

I'm sorry. I must. I'm getting dizzy. . . .

Where are you?

Hospital . . .

He looks up the street to the hospital on the corner, at the far end, to his left.

What ward? He frames the thought but knows she is already gone, even as he does it.

Doped-up or feverish, he decides, and probably out for a while now.

He takes a taxi back to where he had parked, drives home, showers and shaves, makes breakfast, cannot eat.

He drinks orange juice and coffee and stretches out on the bed.

Five hours later he awakens, looks at his watch, curses.

All the way back into town, he tries to recall the power. It is there like a tree, rooted in his being, branching behind his eyes, all bud, blossom, sap, and color, but no leaves, no fruit. He can feel it swaying within him, pulsing, breathing; from the tips of his toes to the roots of his hair he feels it. But it does not bend to his will, it does not branch within his consciousness, furl there it leaves, spread the aromas of life.

He parks in the hospital lot, enters the lobby, avoids the front desk, finds a chair beside a table filled with magazines.

Two hours later he meets her.

He is hiding behind a copy of *Holiday* and looking for her.

I am here.

Again, then! Quickly! The power! Help me to rouse it!

She does this thing.

Within his mind, she conjures the power. There is a movement, a pause, a movement, a pause. Reflectively, as though suddenly remembering an intricate dance step, it stirs within him, the power.

As in a surfacing bathyscaphe, there is a rush of distortions, then a clear, moist view without.

She is a child who has helped him.

A mind-twisted, fevered child, dying . . .

He reads it all when he turns the power upon her.

Her name is Dorothy and she is delirious. The power came upon her at the height of her illness, perhaps because of it.

Has she helped a man come alive again, or dreamed that she helped him? she wonders.

She is thirteen years old and her parents sit beside her bed. In the mind of her mother a word rolls over and over, senselessly, blocking all other thoughts, though it cannot keep away the feelings:

Methotrexate, methotrexate, methotrexate, meth . . .

In Dorothy's thirteen-year-old breastbone there are needles of pain. The fevers swirl within her, and she is all but gone to him.

She is dying of leukemia. The final stages are already arrived. He can taste the blood in her mouth.

Helpless within his power, he projects:

You have given me the end of your life and your final strength. I did not know this. I would not have asked it of you if I had.

Thank you, she says, *for the pictures inside you.*

Pictures?

Places, things I saw . . .

There is not much inside me worth showing. You could have been elsewhere, seeing better.

I am going again . . .

Wait!

He calls upon the power that lives within him now, fused with his will and his sense, his thoughts, memories, feelings. In one great blaze of life, he shows her Milt Rand.

Here is everything I have, all I have ever been that might please. Here is swarming through a foggy night, blinking on and off. Here is lying beneath a bush as the rains of summer fall about you, drip from the leaves upon your fox-soft fur. Here is the moon-dance of the deer, the dream drift of the trout beneath the dark swell, blood cold as the waters about you.

Here is Tatya dancing and Walker preaching; here is my cousin Gary, as he whittles, contriving a ball within a box, all out of one piece of wood. This is my New York and my Paris. This, my favorite meal, drink, cigar, restaurant, park, road to drive on late at night; this is where I dug tun-

nels, built a lean-to, went swimming; this, my first kiss;
these are the tears of loss; this is exile and alone, and recov-
ery, awe, joy; these, my grandmother's daffodils; this her
coffin, daffodils about it; these are the colors of the music I
love, and this is my dog who lived long and was good. See
all the things that heat the spirit, cool within the mind, are
encased in memory and one's self. I give them to you, who
have no time to know them.

He sees himself standing on the far hills of her
mind. She laughs aloud then, and in her room somewhere high away a hand is laid upon her and her wrist
is taken between fingers and thumb as she rushes
toward him suddenly grown large. His great black
wings sweep forward to fold her wordless spasm of life,
then are empty.

Milt Rand stiffens within his power, puts aside a
copy of *Holiday* and stands, to leave the hospital, full
and empty, empty, full, like himself, now, behind.

Such is the power of the power.

LADY OF
THE SKULLS

PATRICIA A. MCKILLIP

Ever since PATRICIA A. MCKILLIP's first book, *The Forgotten Beasts of Eld,* was published, she has been a rising name in fantasy fiction. Writing about the costs of acquiring and using power, she brings the usual tenets of fantasy to life with conviction and a poetic style all her own. She was awarded the World Fantasy Award in 1975. Her most recent novel is *The Book of Atrix Wolfe.* The "Lady of the Skulls" guards a object which doesn't need protection, but is the most valuable thing in the universe. See if you can guess what it is before the end of the story.

LADY OF
THE SKULLS

The Lady saw them ride across the plain: a company
of six. Putting down her watering can, which was
the bronze helm of some unfortunate knight, she
leaned over the parapet, chin on her hand. They were
all armed, their war-horses caparisoned; they glittered
under the noon sun with silver-edged shields, jeweled
bridles, and sword hilts. What, she wondered as always
in simple astonishment, did they imagine they had
come to fight? She picked up the helm, poured water
into a skull containing a miniature rose bush. The
water came from within the tower, the only source on
the entire barren, sun-cracked plain. The knights
would ride around the tower under the hot sun for
hours, looking for entry. At sunset, she would greet
them, carrying water.

She sighed noiselessly, troweling around the little
rose bush with a dragon's claw. If they were too blind
to find the tower door, why did they think they could
see clearly within it? They, she thought in sudden
impatience. They, they, they . . . they fed the plain
with their bleached bones; they never learned. . . .

A carrion-bird circled above her, counting heads.
She scowled at it; it cried back at her, mocking. *You,* its
black eye said, *never die. But you bring the dead to me.*

"They never listen to me," she said, looking over
the plain again, her eyes prickling dryly. In the dis-

tance, lightning cracked apart the sky; purple clouds rumbled. But there was no rain in them, never any rain; the sky was as tearless as she. She moved from skull to skull along the parapet wall, watering things she had grown stubbornly from seeds that blew from distant, placid gardens in peaceful kingdoms. Some were grasses, weeds, or wildflowers. She did not care; she watered anything that grew.

The men below began their circling. Their mounts kicked up dust, snorting; she heard cursing, bewildered questions, then silence as they paused to rest. Sometimes they called her, pleading. But she could do nothing for them. They churned around the tower, bright, powerful, richly armed. She read the devices on their shields: three of Grenelief, one of Stoney Head, one of Dulcis Isle, one of Carnelaine. After a time, one man dropped out of the circle, stood back. His shield was simple: a red rose on white. Carnelaine, she thought, looking down at him, and then realized he was looking up at her.

He would see a puff of airy sleeve, a red geranium in an upside-down skull. Lady of the Skulls, they called her, clamoring to enter. Sometimes they were more courteous, sometimes less. She watered, waiting for this one to call her. He did not; he guided his horse into the tower's shadow and dismounted. He took his helm off, sat down to wait, burrowing idly in the ground and flicking stones as he watched her sleeve sometimes, and sometimes the distant storm.

Drawn to his calm, the others joined him finally, flinging off pieces of armor. They cursed the hard ground and sat, their voices drifting up to her in the windless air as she continued her watering.

Like others before them, they spoke of what the

most precious thing of the legendary treasure might be, besides elusive. They had made a pact, she gathered: If one obtained the treasure, he would divide it among those left living. She raised a brow. The one of Dulcis Isle, a dark-haired man wearing red jewels in his ears, said,

"Anything of the dragon for me. They say it was a dragon's hoard, once. They say that dragon bones are worm-holed with magic, and if you move one bone the rest will follow. The bones will bring the treasure with them."

"I heard," said the man from Stoney Head, "there is a well and a fountain rising from it, and when the drops of the fountain touch ground they turn to diamonds."

"Don't talk of water," one of the three thick-necked, nut-haired men of Grenelief pleaded. "I drank all mine."

"All we must do is find the door. There's water within."

"What are you going to do?" the man of Carnelaine asked. "Hoist the water on your shoulder and carry it out?"

The straw-haired man from Stoney Head tugged at his long moustaches. He had a plain, blunt, energetic voice devoid of any humor. "I'll carry it out in my mouth. When I come back alive for the rest of it, there'll be plenty to carry it in. Skulls, if nothing else. I heard there's a sorceress' cauldron, looks like a rusty old pot—"

"May be that," another of Grenelief said.

"May be, but I'm going for the water. What else could be most precious in this heat-blasted place?"

"That's a point," the man of Dulcis Isle said. Then: "But no, it's dragon-bone for me."

"More to the point," the third of Grenelief said, aggrieved, "how do we get in the cursed place?"

"There's a lady up there watering plants," the man of Carnelaine said, and there were all their faces staring upward; she could have tossed jewels into their open mouths. "She knows we're here."

"It's the Lady," they murmured, hushed.

"Lady of the Skulls."

"Does she have hair, I wonder."

"She's old as the tower. She must be a skull."

"She's beautiful," the man of Stoney Head said shortly. "They always are, the ones who lure, the ones who guard, the ones who give death."

"Is it her tower?" the one of Carnelaine asked. "Or is she trapped?"

"What's the difference? When the spell is gone, so will she be. She's nothing real, just a piece of the tower's magic."

They shifted themselves as the tower shadow shifted. The Lady took a sip of water out of the helm, then dipped her hand in it and ran it over her face. She wanted to lean over the edge and shout at them all: Go home, you silly, brainless fools. If you know so much, what are you doing here sitting on bare ground in front of a tower without a door waiting for a woman to kill you? They moved to one side of the tower, she to the other, as the sun climbed down the sky. She watched the sun set. Still the men refused to leave, though they had not a stick of wood to burn against the dark. She sighed her noiseless sigh and went down to greet them.

The fountain sparkled in the midst of a treasure she had long ceased to notice. She stepped around gold armor, black, gold-rimmed dragon bones, the white bones of princes. She took the plain silver goblet beside the rim of the well, and dipped it into the water, feeling the cooling mist from the little fountain. The man of Dulcis Isle was right about the dragon bones. The doorway was the dragon's open yawning maw, and it was invisible by day.

The last ray of sunlight touched the bone, limned a black, toothed opening that welcomed the men. Mute, they entered, and she spoke.

"You may drink the water, you may wander throughout the tower. If you make no choice, you may leave freely. Having left, you may never return. If you choose, you must make your choice by sunset tomorrow. If you choose the most precious thing in the tower, you may keep all that you see. If you choose wrongly, you will die before you leave the plain."

Their mouths were open again, their eyes stunned at what hung like vines from the old dragon's bones, what lay heaped upon the floor. Flicking, flicking, their eyes came across her finally, as she stood patiently holding the cup. Their eyes stopped at her: a tall, broad-shouldered, barefoot woman in a coarse white linen smock, her red hair bundled untidily on top of her head, her long skirt still splashed with the wine she had spilled in the tavern so long ago. In the torchlight it looked like blood.

They chose to sleep, as they always did, tired by the long journey, dazed by too much rich, vague color in the shadows. She sat on the steps and watched them for a little. One cried in his sleep. She went to the top of the tower after a while, where she could watch the stars. Under the moon, the flowers turned odd, secret colors, as if their true colors blossomed in another land's daylight, and they had left their pale shadows behind by night. She fell asleep naming the moon's colors.

In the morning, she went down to see who had had sense enough to leave.

They were all still there, searching, picking, discarding among the treasures on the floor, scattered along the spiraling stairs. Shafts of light from the narrow windows sparked fiery colors that constantly caught their eyes, made them drop what they had, reach out again. Seeing her, the one from Dulcis Isle said, trembling, his eyes stuffed with riches, "May we ask questions? What is this?"

"Don't ask her, Marlebane," the one from Stoney Head said brusquely. "She'll lie. They all do."

She stared at him. "I will only lie to you," she promised. She took the small treasure from the hand of the man from Dulcis Isle. "This is an acorn made of gold. If you swallow it, you will speak all the languages of humans and animals."

"And this?" one of Grenelief said eagerly, pushing next to her, holding something of silver and smoke.

"That is a bracelet made of a dragon's nostril bone. The jewel in it is its petrified eye. It watches for danger when you wear it."

The man of Carnelaine was playing a flute made from a wizard's thigh bone. His eyes, the odd gray-green of the dragon's eye, looked dream-drugged with the music. The man of Stoney Head shook him roughly.

"Is that your choice, Ran?"

"No." He lowered the flute, smiling. "No, Corbeil."

"Then drop it before it seizes hold of you and you choose it. Have you seen yet what you might take?"

"No. Have you changed your mind?"

"No." He looked at the fountain, but, prudent, did not speak.

"Bram, look at this," said one brother of Grenelief to another. "Look!"

"I am looking, Yew."

"Look at it! Look at it, Ustor! Have you ever seen such a thing? Feel it! And watch: It vanishes, in light."

He held a sword; its hilt was solid emerald, its blade like water falling in clear light over stone. The Lady left them, went back up the stairs, her bare feet sending gold coins and jewels spinning down through the cross-hatched shafts of light. She stared at the place on the horizon where the flat dusty gold of the plain met the parched dusty sky. Go, she thought dully. Leave all this and go back to the places where things grow. Go, she willed them, go, go, go, with the beat of her heart's blood. But no one came out the door beneath her. Someone, instead, came up the stairs.

"I have a question," said Ran of Carnelaine.

"Ask."

"What is your name?"

She had all but forgotten; it came to her again, after a beat of surprise. "Amaranth." He was holding a black rose in one hand, a silver lily in the other. If he chose one, the thorns would kill him; the other, flashing its pure light, would sear through his eyes into his brain.

"Amaranth. Another flower."

"So it is," she said indifferently. He laid the magic flowers on the parapet, picked a dying geranium leaf, smelled the miniature rose. "It has no smell," she said. He picked another dead leaf. He seemed always on the verge of smiling; it made him look sometimes wise and sometimes foolish. He drank out of the bronze watering helm; it was the color of his hair.

"This water is too cool and sweet to come out of such a barren plain," he commented. He seated himself on the wall, watching her. "Corbeil says you are not real. You look real enough to me." She was silent, picking dead clover out of the clover pot. "Tell me where you came from."

She shrugged. "A tavern."

"And how did you come here?"

She gazed at him. "How did you come here, Ran of Carnelaine?"

He did smile then, wryly. "Carnelaine is poor; I came to replenish its coffers."

"There must be less chancy ways."

"Maybe I wanted to see the most precious thing there is to be found. Will the plain bloom again, if it is found? Will you have a garden instead of skull-pots?"

"Maybe," she said levelly. "Or maybe I will disappear. Die when the magic dies. If you choose wisely, you'll have answers to your questions."

He shrugged. "Maybe I will not choose. There are too many precious things."

She glanced at him. He was trifling, wanting hints from her, answers couched in riddles. Shall I take rose or lily? Or wizard's thigh bone? Tell me. Sword or water or dragon's eye? Some had questioned her so before.

She said simply, "I cannot tell you what to take. I do not know myself. As far as I have seen, everything kills." It was as close as she could come, as plain as she could make it: Leave. But he said only, his smile gone, "Is that why you never left?" She stared at him again. "Walked out the door, crossed the plain on some dead king's horse and left?"

She said, "I cannot." She moved away from him, tending some wildflower she called wind-bells, for she imagined their music as the night air tumbled down from the mountains to race across the plain. After a while, she heard his steps again, going down.

A voice summoned her: "Lady of the Skulls!" It was the man of Stoney Head. She went down, blinking in the thick, dusty light. He stood stiffly, his face hard. They all stood still, watching.

"I will leave now," he said. "I may take anything?"

"Anything," she said, making her heart stone against him, a ghost's heart, so that she would not pity him. He went to the fountain, took a mouthful of water. He looked at her, and she moved to show him the hidden lines of the dragon's mouth. He vanished through the stones.

They heard him scream a moment later. The three of Grenelief stared toward the sound. They each wore pieces of a suit of armor that made the wearer invisible: one lacked an arm, another a thigh, the other his hands. Subtly their expressions changed, from shock and terror into something more complex. Five, she saw them thinking. Only five ways to divide it now.

"Anyone else?" she asked coldly. The man of Dulcis Isle slumped down onto the stairs, swallowing. He stared at her, his face gold-green in the light. He swallowed again. Then he shouted at her.

She had heard every name they could think of to shout before she had ever come to the tower. She walked up the stairs past him; he did not have the courage to touch her. She went to stand among her plants. Corbeil of Stoney Head lay where he had fallen, a little brown patch of wet earth beside his open mouth. As she looked, the sun dried it, and the first of the carrion-birds landed.

She threw bones at the bird, cursing, though it

looked unlikely that anyone would be left to take his body back. She hit the bird a couple of times, then another came. Then someone took the bone out of her hand, drew her back from the wall.

"He's dead," Ran said simply. "It doesn't matter to him whether you throw bones at the birds or at him."

"I have to watch," she said shortly. She added, her eyes on the jagged line the parapet made against the sky, like blunt worn dragon's teeth, "You keep coming, and dying. Why do you all keep coming? Is treasure worth being breakfast for the carrion crows?"

"It's worth many different things. To the brothers of Grenelief it means adventure, challenge, adulation if they succeed. To Corbeil it was something to be won, something he would have that no one else could get. He would have sat on top of the pile, and let men look up to him, hating and envying."

"He was a cold man. Cold men feed on a cold fire. Still," she added, sighing, "I would have preferred to see him leave on his feet. What does the treasure mean to you?"

"Money." He smiled his vague smile. "It's not in me to lose my life over money. I'd sooner walk empty-handed out the door. But there's something else."

"What?"

"The riddle itself. That draws us all, at heart. What is the most precious thing? To see it, to hold it, above all to recognize it and choose it—that's what keeps us coming and traps you here." She stared at him, saw, in his eyes, the wonder that he felt might be worth his life.

She turned away; her back to him, she watered bleeding heart and columbine, stonily ignoring what the crows were doing below. "If you find the thing itself," she asked dryly, "what will you have left to wonder about?"

"There's always life."

"Not if you are killed by wonder."

He laughed softly, an unexpected sound, she thought, in that place. "Wouldn't you ride across the plain, if you heard tales of this tower, to try to find the most precious thing in it?"

"Nothing's precious to me," she said, heaving a cauldron of dandelions into shadow. "Not down there, anyway. If I took one thing away with me, it would not be sword or gold or dragon bone. It would be whatever is alive."

He touched the tiny rose. "You mean, like this? Corbeil would never have died for this."

"He died for a mouthful of water."

"He thought it was a mouthful of jewels." He sat beside the rose, his back to the air, watching her pull pots into shade against the noon light. "What makes him twice a fool, I suppose. Three times a fool: for being wrong, for being deluded, and for dying. What a terrible place this is. It strips you of all delusions and then it strips your bones."

"It is terrible," she said somberly. "Yet those who leave without choosing never seem to get the story straight. They must always talk of the treasure they didn't take, not of the bones they didn't leave."

"It's true. Always, they take wonder with them out of this tower and they pass it on to every passing fool." He was silent a little, still watching her. "Amaranth," he said slowly. "That's the flower in poetry that never dies. It's apt."

"Yes."

"And there is another kind of Amaranth, that's

fiery and beautiful and it dies. . . ." Her hands stilled, her eyes widened, but she did not speak. He leaned against the hot, crumbling stones, his dragon's eyes following her like a sunflower following the sun. "What were you," he asked, "when you were the Amaranth that could die?"

"I was one of those faceless women who brought you wine in a tavern. Those you shout at, and jest about, and maybe give a coin to and maybe not, depending how we smile."

He was silent, so silent she thought he had gone, but when she turned, he was still there; only his smile had gone. "Then I've seen you," he said softly, "many times, in many places. But never in a place like this."

"The man from Stoney Head expected someone else, too."

"He expected a dream."

"He saw what he expected: Lady of the Skulls." She pulled wild mint into a shady spot under some worn tapestry. "And so he found her. That's all I am now. You were better off when all I served was wine."

"You didn't build this tower."

"How do you know? Maybe I got tired of the laughter and the coins and I made a place for myself where I could offer coins and give nothing."

"Who built this tower?"

She was silent, crumbling a mint leaf between her fingers. "I did," she said at last. "The Amaranth who never dies."

"Did you?" He was oddly pale; his eyes glittered in the light as if at the shadow of danger. "You grow roses out of thin air in this blistered plain; you try to beat back death for us with our own bones. You curse our stupidity and our fate, not us. Who built this tower for you?"

She turned her face away, mute. He said softly, "The other Amaranth, the one that dies, is also called Love-lies-bleeding."

"It was the last man," she said abruptly, her voice husky, shaken with sudden pain, "who offered me a coin for love. I was so tired of being touched and then forgotten, of hearing my name spoken and then not, as if I were only real when I was looked at, and just something to forget after that, like you never remember the flowers you toss away. So I said to him: no, and no, and no. And then I saw his eyes. They were like amber with thorns of dark in them: sorcerer's eyes. He said, 'Tell me your name.' And I said, 'Amaranth,' and he laughed and laughed and I could only stand there, with the wine I had brought him overturned on my tray, spilling down my skirt. He said, 'Then you shall make a tower of your name, for the tower is already built in your heart.'"

"Love-lies-bleeding," he whispered.

"He recognized that Amaranth."

"Of course he did. It was what died in his own heart."

She turned then, wordless, to look at him. He was smiling again, though his face was still blanched under the hard, pounding light, and the sweat shone in his hair. She said, "How do you know him?"

"Because I have seen this tower before and I have seen in it the woman we all expected, the only woman some men ever know. . . . And every time we come expecting her, the woman who lures us with what's most precious to us and kills us with it, we build the tower around her again and again and again. . . ."

She gazed at him. A tear slid down her cheek, and

then another. "I thought it was my tower," she whispered. "The Amaranth that never dies but only lives forever to watch men die."

"It's all of us," he sighed. In the distance, thunder rumbled. "We all build towers, then dare each other to enter. . . ." He picked up the little rose in its skull pot and stood abruptly; she followed him to the stairs.

"Where are you going with my rose?"

"Out."

She followed him down, protesting. "But it's mine!"

"You said we could choose anything."

"It's just a worthless thing I grew, it's nothing of the tower's treasure. If you must take after all, choose something worth your life!"

He glanced back at her, as they rounded the tower stairs to the bottom. His face was bone-white, but he could still smile. "I will give you back your rose," he said, "if you will let me take the Amaranth."

"But I am the only Amaranth."

He strode past his startled companions, whose hands were heaped with *this, no this,* and *maybe this.* As if the dragon's magical eye had opened in his own eye, he led her himself into the dragon's mouth.

THE LONG NIGHT
OF WAITING

ANDRE NORTON

ANDRE NORTON has written and collaborated on over one hundred novels in her sixty years as a writer, working with such authors as Robert Bloch, Marion Zimmer Bradley, Mercedes Lackey, and Julian May. Her best known creation is the Witch World, which has been the subject of several novels and anthologies. She has received the Nebula Grand Master Award, the Fritz Leiber Award, and the Daedalus Award. Her most recent project is the creation of High Hallack, a writer's retreat in Monterey, Tennessee. In "The Long Night of Waiting" a most amazing discovery is made, as a lot of them are, by children.

"W hat—what are we going to do?" Lesley squeezed her hands so tightly together they hurt. She really wanted to run, as far and as fast as she could.

Rick was not running. He stood there, still holding to Alex's belt, just as he had grabbed his brother to keep him from following Matt. Following him where?

"We won't do anything," Rick answered slowly.

"But people'll ask—all kinds of questions. You only have to look at that—" Lesley pointed with her chin to what was now before them.

Alex still struggled for freedom. "Want Matt!" he yelled at the top of his voice. He wriggled around to beat at Rick with his fists.

"Let me go! Let me go—with Matt!"

Rick shook him. "Now listen here, shrimp. Matt's gone. You can't get to him now. Use some sense—look there. Do you see Matt? Well, do you?"

Lesley wondered how Rick could be so calm— accepting all of this just as if it happened every day—like going to school, or watching a tel-cast, or the regular, safe things. How could he just stand there and talk to Alex as if he were grown up and Alex was just being pesty as he was sometimes? She watched Rick wonderingly, and tried not to think of what had just happened.

"Matt?" Alex had stopped fighting. His voice sounded as if he were going to start bawling in a minute or two. And when Alex cried—! He would keep on and on, and they would have questions to answer. If they told the real truth—Lesley drew a deep breath and shivered.

No one, no one in the whole world would ever believe them! Not even if they saw what was right out here in this field now. No one would believe—they would say that she, Lesley, and Rick, and Alex were all mixed up in their minds. And they might even be sent away to a hospital or something! No, they could never tell the truth! But Alex, he would blurt out the whole thing if anyone asked a question about Matt. What could they do about Alex?

Her eyes questioned Rick over Alex's head. He was still holding their young brother, but Alex had turned, was gripping Rick's waist, looking up at him demandingly, waiting, Lesley knew, for Rick to explain as he had successfully most times in Alex's life. And if Rick couldn't explain this time?

Rick hunkered down on the ground, his hands now on Alex's shoulders.

"Listen, shrimp, Matt's gone. Lesley goes, I go, to school—"

Alex sniffed. "But the bus comes then, and you get on while I watch—then you come home again—" His small face cleared. "Then Matt—he'll come back? He's gone to school? But this is Saturday! You an' Lesley don't go on Saturday. How come Matt does? An' where's the bus? There's nothin' but that mean old dozer that's chewin' up things. An' now all these vines and stuff—and the dozer tipped right over an'—" He screwed around a little in Rick's grip to stare over his brother's hunched shoulder at the disaster area beyond.

"No." Rick was firm. "Matt's not gone to school. He's gone home—to his own place. You remember back at Christmas time, Alex, when Peter came with Aunt Fran and Uncle Porter? He came for a visit. Matt came with Lizzy for a visit—now he's gone back home—just like Peter did."

"But Matt said—he said *this* was his home!" countered Alex. "He didn't live in Cleveland like Peter."

"It was his home once," Rick continued still in that grown-up way. "Just like Jimmy Rice used to live down the street in the red house. When Jimmy's Dad got moved by his company, Jimmy went clear out to St. Louis to live."

"But Matt was sure! He said *this* was his home!" Alex frowned. "He said it over and over, that he had come home again."

"At first he did," Rick agreed. "But later, you know that Matt was not so sure, was he now? You think about that, shrimp."

Alex was still frowning. At least he was not screaming as Lesley feared he would be. Rick, she was suddenly very proud and a little in awe of Rick. How had he known how to keep Alex from going into one of his tantrums?

"Matt—he did say funny things. An' he was afraid of cars. Why was he afraid of cars, Rick?"

"Because where he lives they don't have cars."

Alex's surprise was open. "Then how do they go to the store? An' to Sunday School, an' school, an' every place?"

"They have other ways, Alex. Yes, Matt was afraid of a lot of things, he knew that this was not his home, that he had to go back."

"But—I want him—he—" Alex began to cry, not

with the loud screaming Lesley had feared, but in a way now which made her hurt a little inside as she watched him butt his head against Rick's shoulder, making no effort to smear away the tears as they wet his dirty cheeks.

"Sure you want him," Rick answered. "But Matt— he was afraid, he was not very happy here, now was he, shrimp?"

"With me, he was. We had a lot of fun, we did!"

"But Matt wouldn't go in the house, remember? Remember what happened when the lights went on?"

"Matt ran an' hid. An' Lizzy, she kept telling him an' telling him they had to go back. Maybe if Lizzy hadn't all the time told him that—"

Lesley thought about Lizzy. Matt was little—he was not more than Alex's age—not really, in spite of what the stone said. But Lizzy had been older and quicker to understand. It had been Lizzy who had asked most of the questions and then been sick (truly sick to her stomach) when Lesley and Rick answered them. Lizzy had been sure of what had happened then—just like she was sure about the other—that the stone must never be moved, nor that place covered over to trap anybody else. So that nobody would fall through—

Fall through into what? Lesley tried to remember all the bits and pieces Lizzy and Matt had told about where they had been for a hundred and ten years—a *hundred* and *ten* just like the stone said.

She and Rick had found the stone when Alex had run away. They had often had to hunt Alex like that. Ever since he learned to open the Safe-tee gate he would go off about once a week or so. It was about two months after they moved here, before all the new houses had been built and the big apartments at the end of the street. This was all more like real country then. Now it was different, spoiled—just this one open place left and that (unless Lizzy was right in thinking she'd stopped it all) would not be open long. The men had started to clear it off with the bulldozer the day before yesterday. All the ground on that side was raw and cut up, the trees and bushes had been smashed and dug out.

There had been part of an old orchard there, and a big old lilac bush. Last spring it had been so pretty. Of course, the apples were all little and hard, and had worms in them. But it had been pretty and a swell place to play. Rick and Jim Bowers had a house up in the biggest tree. Their sign said "No girls allowed," but Lesley had sneaked up once when they were playing Little League ball and had seen it all.

Then there was the stone. That was kind of scary. Yet they had kept going to look at it every once in a while, just to wonder.

Alex had found it first that day he ran away. There were a lot of bushes hiding it and tall grass. Lesley felt her eyes drawn in that direction now. It *was* still there. Though you have to mostly guess about that, only one teeny bit of it showed through all those leaves and things.

And when they had found Alex he had been working with a piece of stick, scratching at the words carved there which were all filled up with moss and dirt. He had been so busy and excited he had not tried to dodge them as he usually did, instead he wanted to know if those were real words, and then demanded that Rick read them to him.

Now Lesley's lips silently shaped what was carved there.

A long night of waiting.
To the Memory of our dear children,
Lizzy and Matthew Mendal,
Who disappeared on this spot
June 23, 1861.
May the Good Lord return them
to their loving parents and this
world in His Own reckoned time.
Erected to mark our years of watching,
June 23, 1900.

It had sounded so queer. At first Lesley had thought it was a grave and had been a little frightened. But Rick had pointed out that the words did not read like those on the stones in the cemetery where they went on Memorial Day with flowers for Grandma and Grandpa Targ. It was different because it never said "dead" but "disappeared."

Rick had been excited, said it sounded like a mystery. He had begun to ask around, but none of the neighbors knew anything—except this had all once been a farm. Almost all the houses on the street were built on that land. They had the oldest house of all. Dad said it had once been the farm house, only people had changed it and added parts like bathrooms.

Lizzy and Matt—

Rick had gone to the library and asked questions, too. Miss Adams, she got interested when Rick kept on wanting to know what this was like a hundred years ago (though of course he did not mention the stone, that was their own secret, somehow from the first they knew they must keep quiet about that). Miss Adams had shown Rick how they kept the old newspapers on film tapes. And when he did his big project for social

studies, he had chosen the farm's history, which gave
him a good chance to use those films to look things up.

That was how he learned all there was to know
about Lizzy and Matt. There had been a lot in the old
paper about them. Lizzy Mendal, Matthew Mendal,
aged eleven and five—Lesley could almost repeat it
word for word she had read Rick's copied notes so
often. They had been walking across this field, carrying
lunch to their father who was ploughing. He had been
standing by a fence talking to Doctor Levi Morris who
was driving by. They had both looked up to see Lizzy
and Matthew coming and had waved to them. Lizzy
waved back and then—she and Matthew—they were
just gone! Right out of the middle of an open field they
were gone!

Mr. Mendal and the Doctor, they had been so surprised they couldn't believe their eyes, but they had
hunted and hunted. And the men from other farms
had come to hunt too. But no one ever saw the children again.

Only about a year later, Mrs. Mendal (she had kept
coming to stand here in the field, always hoping, Lesley guessed, they might come back as they had gone)
came running home all excited to say she heard Matt's
voice, and he had been calling "Ma! Ma!"

She got Mr. Mendal to go back with her. And he
heard it, too, when he listened, but it was very faint.
Just like someone a long way off calling "Ma!" Then it
was gone and they never heard it again.

It was all in the papers Rick found, the story of
how they hunted for the children and later on about
Mrs. Mendal hearing Matt. But nobody ever was able to
explain what had happened.

So all that was left was the stone and a big mystery.

Rick started hunting around in the library, even after he finished his report, and found a book with other stories about people who disappeared. It was written by a man named Charles Fort. Some of it had been hard reading, but Rick and Lesley had both found the parts which were like what happened to Lizzy and Matt. And in all those other disappearances there had been no answers to what had happened, and nobody came back.

Until Lizzy and Matt. But suppose she and Rick and Alex told people now, would any believe them? And what good would it do, anyway? Unless Lizzy was right and people should know so they would not be caught. Suppose someone built a house right over where the stone stood, and suppose some day a little boy like Alex, or a girl like Lesley, or even a mom or dad, disappeared? She and Rick, maybe they ought to talk and keep on talking until someone believed them, believed them enough to make sure such a house was never going to be built, and this place was made safe.

"Matt—he kept sayin' he wanted his mom." Alex's voice cut through her thoughts. "Rick, where was his mom that she lost him that way?"

Rick, for the first time, looked helpless. How could you make Alex understand?

Lesley stood up. She still felt quite shaky and a little sick from the left-over part of her fright. But the worst was past now, she had to be as tough as Rick or he'd say that was just like a girl.

"Alex," she was able to say that quite naturally, and her voice did not sound too queer, "Matt, maybe he'll find his mom now, he was just looking in the wrong place. She's not here any more. You remember last Christmas when you went with Mom to see Santy

Claus at the store and you got lost? You were hunting mom and she was hunting you, and at first you were looking in the wrong places. But you did find each other. Well, Matt's mom will find him all right."

She thought that Alex wanted to believe her. He had not pushed away from Rick entirely, but he looked as if he was listening carefully to every word she said.

"You're sure?" he asked doubtfully. "Matt—he was scared he'd never find his mom. He said he kept calling an' calling an' she never came."

"She'll come, moms always do." Lesley tried to make that sound true. "And Lizzy will help. Lizzy," Lesley hesitated, trying to choose the right words, "Lizzy's very good at getting things done."

She looked beyond to the evidence of Lizzy's getting things done and her wonder grew. At first, just after it had happened, she had been so shocked and afraid, she had not really understood what Lizzy had done before she and Matt had gone again. What—what had Lizzy learned during that time when she had been in the other place? And how had she learned it? She had never answered all their questions as if she was not able to tell them what lay on the other side of that door, or whatever it was which was between here and there.

Lizzy's work was hard to believe, even when you saw it right before your eyes.

The bulldozer and the other machines which had been parked there to begin work again Monday morning—Well, the bulldozer was lying over on its side, just as if it were a toy Alex had picked up and thrown as he did sometimes when he got over-tired and cross. And the other machines—they were all pushed over, some even broken! Then there were the growing things. Lizzy had rammed her hands into the pockets of her dress-like apron and brought them out with seeds trickling between her fingers. And she had just thrown those seeds here and there, all over the place.

It took a long time for plants to grow—weeks— Lesley knew. But look—these were growing right while you watched. They had already made a thick mat over every piece of the machinery they had reached, like they had to cover it from sight quickly. And there were flowers opening—and butterflies—Lesley had never seen so many butterflies as were gathering about those flowers, arriving right out of nowhere.

"Rick—how—?" She could not put her wonder into a full question, she could only gesture toward what was happening there.

Her brother shrugged. It was as if he did not want to look at what was happening. Instead he spoke to both of them sharply.

"Listen, shrimp, Les, it's getting late. Mom and Dad will be home soon. We'd better get there before they do. Remember, we left all the things Matt and Lizzy used out in the summer house. Dad's going to work on the lawn this afternoon. He'll want to get the mower out of there. If he sees what we left there he'll ask questions for sure and we might have to talk. Not that it would do any good."

Rick was right. Lesley looked around her regretfully now. She was not frightened any more—she, well, she would like to just stay awhile and watch. But she reached for Alex's sticky hand. To her surprise he did not object or jerk away, he was still hiccuping a little as he did after he cried. She was thankful Rick had been able to manage him so well.

They scraped through their own private hole in the fence into the backyard, heading to the summer house which Rick and Dad had fixed up into a rainy day place to play and a storage for the outside tools. The camping bags were there, even the plates and cups. Those were still smeared with jelly and peanut butter. Just think, Matt had never tasted jelly and peanut butter before, he said. But he had liked it a lot. Lesley had better sneak those in and give them a good washing. And the milk—Lizzy could not understand how you got milk from a bottle a man brought to your house and not straight from a cow. She seemed almost afraid to drink it. And she had not liked Coke at all— said it tasted funny.

"I wish Matt was here." Alex stood looking down at the sleeping bag, his face clouding up again. "Matt was fun—"

"Sure he was. Here, shrimp, you catch ahold of that and help me carry this back. We've got to get it into the camper before Dad comes."

"Why?"

Oh, dear, was Alex going to have one of his stubborn question-everything times? Lesley had put the plates and cups back into the big paper bag in which she had smuggled the food from the kitchen this morning, and was folding up the extra cover from Matt's bed.

"You just come along and I'll tell you, shrimp," she heard Rick say. Rick was just wonderful today. Though Mom always said that Rick could manage Alex better than anyone else in the whole family when he wanted to make the effort.

There, she gave a searching look around as the boys left (one of the bags between them) this was cleared. They would take the other bag, and she would do the dishes. Then Dad could walk right in and never know that Lizzy and Matt had been here for two nights and a day.

Two nights and a day—Lizzy had kept herself and Matt out of sight yesterday when Lesley and Rick had been at school. She would not go near the house, nor let Matt later when Alex wanted him to go and see the train Dad and Rick had set up in the family room. All she had wanted were newspapers. Lesley had taken those to her and some of the magazines Mom had collected for the Salvation Army. She must have read a lot, because when they met her after school, she had a million questions to ask.

It was then that she said she and Matt had to go away, back to where they had come from, that they could not stay in this mixed up horrible world which was not the right one at all! Rick told her about the words on the stones and how long it had been. First she called him a liar and said that was not true. So after dark he had taken a flashlight and went back to show her the stone and the words.

She had been the one to cry then. But she did not for long. She got to asking what was going to happen in the field, looking at the machines. When Rick told her, Lizzy had said quick and hot, no, they mustn't do that, it was dangerous—a lot of others might go through. And they, those in the other world, didn't want people who did bad things to spoil everything.

When Rick brought her back she was mad, not at him, but at everything else. She made him walk her down to the place from which you could see the intercity thruway, with all the cars going whizz. Rick said he was sure she was scared. She was shaking, and she held onto his hand so hard it hurt. But she made herself watch. Then, when they came back, she said Matt and she—they had to go. And she offered to take Alex, Lesley, and Rick with them. She said they couldn't want to go on living here.

That was the only time she talked much of what it was like there. Birds and flowers, no noise or cars rushing about, nor bulldozers tearing the ground up, everything pretty. It was Lesley who had asked then:

"If it was all that wonderful, why did you want to come back?"

Then she was sorry she had asked because Lizzy's face looked like she was hurting inside when she answered:

"There was Ma and Pa. Matt, he's little, he misses Ma bad at times. Those others, they got their own way of life, and it ain't much like ours. So, we've kept a-tryin' to get back. I brought somethin'—just for Ma." She showed them two bags of big silvery leaves pinned together with long thorns. Inside each were seeds, all mixed up big and little together.

"Things grow there," she nodded toward the field, "they grow strange-like. Faster than seeds hereabouts. You put one of these," she ran her finger tip in among the seeds, shifting them back and forth, "in the ground, and you can see it grow. Honest-Injun-cross-my-heart-an'-hope-to-die if that ain't so. Ma, she hankers for flowers, loves 'em truly. So I brought her some. Only, Ma, she ain't here. Funny thing—those over there, they have a feelin' about these here flowers and plants. They tell you right out that as long as they have these growin' 'round they're safe."

"Safe from what?" Rick wanted to know.

"I dunno—safe from somethin' as they think may change 'em. See, we ain't the onlyest ones gittin' through to there. There's others, we've met a couple.

Susan—she's older 'n me and she dresses funny, like one of the real old time ladies in a book picture. And there's Jim—he spends most of his time off in the woods, don't see him much. Susan's real nice. She took us to stay with her when we got there. But she's married to one of them, so we didn't feel comfortable most of the time. Anyway they had some rules—they asked us right away did we have anything made of iron. Iron is bad for them, they can't hold it, it burns them bad. And they told us right out that if we stayed long we'd change. We ate their food and drank their drink stuff—that's like cider and it tastes good. That changes people from here. So after awhile anyone who comes through is like them. Susan mostly is by now, I guess. When you're changed you don't want to come back."

"But you didn't change," Lesley pointed out. "You came back."

"And how come you didn't change?" Rick wanted to know. "You were there long enough—a hundred and ten years!"

"But," Lizzy had beat with her fists on the floor of the summer house then as if she were pounding a drum. "It weren't that long, it couldn't be! Me, I counted every day! It's only been ten of 'em, with us hunting the place to come through on every one of 'em, calling for Ma and Pa to come and get us. It weren't no hundred and ten years—"

And she had cried again in such a way as to make Lesley's throat ache. A moment later she had been bawling right along with Lizzy. For once Rick did not look at her as if he were disgusted, but instead as if he were sorry, for Lizzy, not Lesley, of course.

"It's got to be that time's different in that place," he said thoughtfully. "A lot different. But, Lizzy, it's true, you know—this is 1971, not 1861. We can prove it."

Lizzy wiped her eyes on the hem of her long apron. "Yes, I got to believe. 'Cause what you showed me ain't my world at all. All those cars shootin' along so fast, lights what go on and off when you press a button on the wall—all these houses built over Pa's good farmin' land—what I read today. Yes, I gotta believe it—but it's hard to do that, right hard!

"And Matt 'n' me, we don't belong here no more, not with all this clatter an' noise an' nasty smelling air like we sniffed down there by that big road. I guess we gotta go back there. Leastwise, we know what's there now."

"How can you get back?" Rick wanted to know.

For the first time Lizzy showed a watery smile. "I ain't no dunce, Rick. They got rules, like I said. You carry something outta that place and hold on to it, an' it pulls you back, lets you in again. I brought them there seeds for Ma. But I thought maybe Matt an' me—we might want to go visitin' there. Susan's been powerful good to us. Well, anyway, I got these too."

She had burrowed deeper in her pocket, under the packets of seeds and brought out two chains of woven grass, tightly braided. Fastened to each was a small arrowhead, a very tiny one, no bigger than Lesley's little fingernail.

Rick held out his hand. "Let's see."

But Lizzy kept them out of his reach.

"Them's no Injun arrowheads, Rick. Them's what they use for their own doin's. Susan, she calls them 'elf-shots.' Anyway, these here can take us back if we wear 'em. And we will tomorrow, that's when we'll go."

They had tried to find out more about there, but Lizzy would not answer most of their questions. Lesley thought she could not for some reason. But she remained firm in her decision that she and Matt would be better off there than here. Then she had seemed sorry for Lesley and Rick and Alex that they had to stay in such a world, and made the suggestion that they link hands and go through together.

Rick shook his head. "Sorry—no. Mom and Dad—well, we belong here."

Lizzy nodded. "Thought you would say that. But—it's so ugly now, I can't see as how you want to." She cupped the tiny arrowheads in her hand, held them close. "Over there it's so pretty. What are you goin' to do here when all the ground is covered up with houses and the air's full of bad smells, an' those cars go rush-rush all day and night too? Looky here—" She reached for one of the magazines. "I'm the best reader in the school house. Miss Jane, she has me up to read out loud when the school board comes visitin'." She did not say that boastfully, but as if it were a truth everyone would know. "An' I've been readin' pieces in here. They've said a lot about how bad things are gittin' for you all—bad air, bad water—too many people—everything like that. Seems like there's no end but bad here. Ain't that so now?"

"We've been studying about it in school," Lesley agreed, "Rick and me, we're on the pick-up can drive next week. Sure we know."

"Well, this ain't happening over there, you can bet you! They won't let it."

"How do they stop it?" Rick wanted to know.

But once more Lizzy did not answer. She just shook her head and said they had their ways. And then she had gone on:

"Me an' Matt, we have to go back. We don't belong here now, and back there we do, sorta. At least it's more like what we're used to. We have to go at the same hour as before—noon time—"

"How do you know?" Rick asked.

"There's rules. We were caught at noon then, we go at noon now. Sure you don't want to come with us?"

"Only as far as the field," Rick had answered for them. "It's Saturday, we can work it easy. Mom has a hair appointment in the morning, Dad is going to drive her 'cause he's seeing Mr. Chambers, and they'll do the shopping before they come home. We're supposed to have a picnic in the field, like we always do. Being Saturday the men won't be working there either."

"If you have to go back at noon," Lesley was trying to work something out, "how come you didn't get here at noon? It must have been close to five when we saw you. The school bus had let us off at the corner and Alex had come to meet us—then we saw you—"

"We hid out," Lizzy had said then. "Took a chance on you 'cause you were like us—"

Lesley thought she would never forget that first meeting, seeing the fair haired girl a little taller than she, her hair in two long braids, but such a queer dress on—like a "granny" one, yet different, and over it a big coarse-looking checked apron. Beside her Matt, in a checked shirt and funny looking pants, both of them barefooted. They had looked so unhappy and lost. Alex had broken away from Lesley and Rick and had run right over to them to say "Hi" in the friendly way he always did.

Lizzy had been turning her head from side to side as if hunting for something which should be right there before her. And when they had come up she had spoken almost as if she were angry (but Lesley guessed she was really frightened) asking them where the Mendal house was.

If it had not been for the stone and Rick doing all that hunting down of the story behind it, they would not have known what she meant. But Rick had caught on quickly. He had said that they lived in the old Mendal house now, and they had brought Lizzy and Matt along with them. But before they got there they had guessed who Lizzy and Matt were, impossible as it seemed.

Now they were gone again. But Lizzy, what had she done just after she had looped those grass strings around her neck and Matt's and taken his hand? First she had thrown out all those seeds on the ground. And then she had pointed her finger at the bulldozer, and the other machines which were tearing up the rest of the farm she had known.

Lesley, remembering, blinked and shivered. She had expected Lizzy and Matt to disappear, somehow she had never doubted that they would. But she had not foreseen that the bulldozer would flop over at Lizzy's pointing, the other things fly around as if they were being thrown, some of them breaking apart. Then the seeds sprouting, vines and grass, and flowers, and small trees shooting up—just like the time on TV when they speeded up the camera somehow so you actually saw a flower opening up. What had Lizzy learned there that she was able to do all that?

Still trying to remember it all, Lesley wiped the dishes. Rick and Alex came in.

"Everything's put away," Rick reported. "And Alex, he understands about not talking about Matt."

"I sure hope so, Rick. But—how did Lizzy do that—make the machines move by just pointing at them? And how can plants grow so quickly?"

"How do I know?" he demanded impatiently. "I didn't see any more than you did. We've only one thing to remember, we keep our mouths shut tight. And we've got to be just as surprised as anyone else when somebody sees what happened there—"

"Maybe they won't see it—maybe not until the men come on Monday," she said hopefully. Monday was a school day, and the bus would take them early. Then she remembered.

"Rick, Alex won't be going to school with us. He'll be here with Mom. What if somebody says something and he talks?"

Rick was frowning. "Yeah, I see what you mean. So—we'll have to discover it ourselves—tomorrow morning. If we're here when people get all excited we can keep Alex quiet. One of us will have to stay with him all the time."

But in the end Alex made his own plans. The light was only gray in Lesley's window when she awoke to find Rick shaking her shoulder.

"What—what's the matter?"

"Keep it low!" he ordered almost fiercely. "Listen, Alex's gone—"

"Gone where?"

"Where do you think? Get some clothes on and come on!"

Gone to there? Lesley was cold with fear as she pulled on jeans and a sweatshirt, thrust her feet into shoes. But how could Alex—? Just as Matt and Lizzy had gone the first time. They should not have been afraid of being disbelieved, they should have told Dad and Mom all about it. Now maybe Alex would be gone for a hundred years. No—not Alex!

She scrambled downstairs. Rick stood at the back door waving her on. Together they raced across the backyard, struggled through the fence gap and—

The raw scars left by the bulldozer were gone. Rich foliage rustled in the early morning breeze. And the birds—! Lesley had never seen so many different kinds of birds in her whole life. They seemed so tame, too, swinging on branches, hopping along the ground, pecking a fruit. Not the sour old apples but golden fruit. It hung from bushes, squashed on the ground from its own ripeness.

And there were flowers—and—

"Alex!" Rick almost shouted.

There he was. Not gone, sucked into there where they could never find him again. No, he was sitting under a bush where white flowers bloomed. His face was smeared with juice as he ate one of the fruit. And he was patting a bunny! A real live bunny was in his lap. Now and then he held the fruit for the bunny to take a bite too. His face, under the smear of juice, was one big smile. Alex's happy face which he had not worn since Matt left.

"It's real good," he told them.

Scrambling to his feet he would have made for the fruit bush but Lesley swooped to catch him in a big hug.

"You're safe, Alex!"

"Silly!" He squirmed in her hold. "Silly Les. This is a good place now. See, the bunny came 'cause he knows that. An' all the birds. This is a good place. Here—" he struggled out of her arms, went to the bush and pulled off two of the fruit. "You eat—you'll like them."

"He shouldn't be eating those. How do we know it's good for him?" Rick pushed by to take the fruit from his brother.

Alex readily gave him one, thrust the other at Lesley.

"Eat it! It's better'n anything!"

As if she had to obey him, Lesley raised the smooth yellow fruit to her mouth. It smelled—it smelled good—like everything she liked. She bit into it.

And the taste—it did not have the sweetness of an orange, nor was it like an apple or a plum. It wasn't like anything she had eaten before. But Alex was right, it was good. And she saw that Rick was eating, too.

When he had finished her elder brother turned to the bush and picked one, two, three, four—

"You are hungry," Lesley commented. She herself had taken a second. She broke it in two, dropped half to the ground for two birds. Their being there, right by her feet, did not seem in the least strange. Of course one shared. It did not matter if life wore feathers, fur, or plain skin, one shared.

"For Mom and Dad," Rick said. Then he looked around.

They could not see the whole of the field, the growth was too thick. And it was reaching out to the boundaries. Even as Lesley looked up a vine fell like a hand on their own fence, caught fast, and she was sure that was only the beginning.

"I was thinking, Les," Rick said slowly. "Do you remember what Lizzy said about the fruit from there changing people. Do you feel any different?"

"Why no." She held out her finger. A bird fluttered up to perch there, watching her with shining beads of eyes. She laughed. "No, I don't feel any different."

Rick looked puzzled. "I never saw a bird that tame before. Well, I wonder— Come on, let's take these to Mom and Dad."

They started for the fence where two green runners now clung. Lesley looked at the house, down the street to where the apartment made a monstrous outline against the morning sky.

"Rick, why do people want to live in such ugly places. And it smells bad—"

He nodded. "But all that's going to change. You know it, don't you?"

She gave a sigh of relief. Of course she knew it. The change was beginning and it would go on and on until here was like there and the rule of iron was broken for all time.

The rule of iron? Lesley shook her head as if to shake away a puzzling thought. But, of course, she must have always known this. Why did she have one small memory that this was strange? The rule of iron was gone, the long night of waiting over now.

A DOZEN OF EVERYTHING

MARION ZIMMER BRADLEY

MARION ZIMMER BRADLEY is known for retelling the Arthurian legend from the point of view of the female characters in *The Mists of Avalon,* which has become an international bestseller. Her long-running Darkover series, which combines fantasy with science fiction, has generated popular and critical acclaim, as well as several anthologies set in that world. Currently, she lives in Berkeley, California, still writing and editing the *Sword and Sorceress* anthology series and her own magazine, *Marion Zimmer Bradley's Fantasy Magazine.* Here, she puts a new spin on the adage, "Be careful what you wish for."

When Marcie unwrapped the cut-glass bottle, she thought it was perfume. "Oh, fine," she said to herself sardonically, "Here I am, being married in four days, and without a rag to wear, and Aunt Hepsibah sends me perfume!"

It wasn't that Marcie was mercenary. But Aunt Hepsibah was, as the vulgar expression puts it, rolling in dough; and she spent about forty dollars a year. She lived in Egypt, in a little mud hut, because, as she said, she wanted to Soak Up the Flavor of the East . . . in large capitals. She wrote Marcie, who was her only living relative, long incoherent letters about the Beauty of the Orient, and the Delights of Contemplation; letters which Marcie dutifully read and as dutifully answered with "Dear Aunt Hepsibah; I hope you are well . . ."

She sighed, and examined the label. Printed in a careful, vague Arabic script, it read "Djinn Number Seven." Marcie shrugged.

Oh well, she thought, it's probably very chi-chi and expensive. If I go without lunch this week, I can manage to get myself a fancy negligee, and maybe a pair of new gloves to wear to the church. Greg will like the perfume, and if I keep my job for a few months after we're married, we'll get along. Of course, Emily Post says that a bride should have a dozen of everything, but we can't *all* be lucky.

She started to put the perfume into her desk drawer—for her lunch hour was almost over—then, on an impulse, she began carefully to work the stopper loose. "I'll just take a tiny sniff—" she thought . . .

The stopper stuck; Marcie twitched, pulled—choked at the curious, pervasive fragrance which stole out. "It sure is strong—" she thought, holding the loosened stopper in her hand . . . then she blinked and dropped it to the floor, where the precious cut-glass shattered into a million pieces.

Marcie was a normal child of her generation, which is to say, she went to the movies regularly. She had seen *Sinbad the Sailor,* and *The Thief of Bagdad,* so, of course, she knew immediately what was happening, as the pervasive fragrance rolled out and coalesced into a huge, towering figure with a vaguely oriental face. "My gosh," she breathed, then, as she noticed imminent peril to the office ceiling, directed, "Hey, stick your head out the window—quick!"

"To hear is to obey," said the huge figure sibilantly, "but, O mistress, if I might venture to make a suggestion, that might attract attention. Permit me—" and he promptly shrank to a less generous proportion. "They don't make palaces as big these days, do they?" he asked confidentially.

"They certainly do not," gulped Marcie, "Are you—are you a genie?"

"I am not," the figure said with asperity. "Can't you read? I am a djinn—Djinn Number Seven to be exact."

"Er—you mean you have to grant me my wish?"

The djinn scowled. "Now, there is a strange point of ethics," he murmured. "Since the stopper on the bottle is broken, I can't ever be shut up again. At the same time, since you so generously let me out, I shall gladly grant you one wish. What will it be?"

Marcie didn't even hesitate. Here was a chance to make a good wedding present out of Aunt Hepsibah's nutty old bottle, and after all, she wasn't a greedy girl. She smiled brilliantly. "I'm being married in a few days—" she started.

"You want an elixir of love? Of eternal beauty?"

"No, sir-eee!" Marcie shuddered, she had read the Arabian Nights when she was a little girl; she knew you could not make a magical bargain with a genie—er—djinn. "No, as a matter of fact, I just want—well, a household trousseau. Nice things to be married in, and that kind of thing—just to start us off nicely."

"I'm afraid I don't quite understand." The djinn frowned. "Trousseau? That word has come in since my time. Remember, I haven't been out of this bottle since King Solomon was in diapers."

"Well—sheets, and towels, and slips, and night-gowns—" Marcie began, then dismissed it. "Oh well, just give me a dozen of everything," she told him.

"To hear is to obey," the djinn intoned. "Where shall I put it, O mistress?"

"Oh, in my room," Marcie told him, then, remembering her five-dollar-a-week hall bedroom. "Maybe you'll have to enlarge the room a little, but you can do that, can't you?"

"Oh, sure," said the djinn casually. "A djinn, my dear mistress, can do anything. And now, farewell forever, and thank you for letting me out."

He vanished so swiftly that Marcie rubbed her eyes, and the little cut-glass bottle fell to the floor. After a moment, Marcie picked it up, sniffing at the empty bottle. A curious faint fragrance still clung to it, but it was otherwise empty.

"Did I dream this whole thing?" she asked herself dizzily.

The buzzer rang, and the other typists in the office came back to their desks. "Gosh," someone asked, "have you been sitting here all during lunch hour, Marcie?"

"I—I took a little nap—" Marcie answered, and carefully palmed the cut-glass bottle into her desk drawer.

That afternoon seemed incredibly long to Marcie. The hands of the clock lagged as they inched around the dial, and she found herself beginning one business letter "Dear Djinn—" She ripped it out angrily, typed the date on a second letterhead, and started over; "Djinntlemen; we wish to call your attention—"

Finally, the hands reached five, and Marcie, whisking a cover over her typewriter, clutched her handbag and literally ran from the office. "There won't be anything there—" she kept telling herself, as she walked rapidly down the block, "there won't be anything—but suppose there was, suppose . . ."

The hall of the rooming-house was ominously quiet. Marcie ascended the stairs, wondering at the absence of the landlady, the lack of noise from the other boarders. A curious reluctance dragged at her hands as she thrust her key into the lock.

"It's all nonsense," she said aloud. "Here goes—"

She shut her eyes and opened the door. She walked in . . .

There was a dozen of everything. The room extended into gray space, and Marcie, opening her eyes, caught her hands to her throat to stifle a scream. There were a dozen of her familiar bed; a dozen gray cats snoozing on the pillow; a dozen dainty negligees, piled carefully by it; a dozen delicate packages labelled "Nylon stockings," and a dozen red apples rolling slightly beside them. Before her staring eyes a dozen elephants lumbered through the gray space, and beyond, her terrified vision focused on a dozen white domes that faded into the dim spaces of the expanded room, and a dozen tall cathedrals as well.

A dozen of *everything* . . .

"Marcie—Marcie, where are you?" she heard a man's voice shouting from the hall. Marcie whirled. Greg! And he was outside—outside this nightmare! She fled blindly, stumbling over a dozen rolled-up Persian carpets, grazing the edge of one of a dozen grand pianos; she screamed, visualizing a dozen rattlesnakes somewhere . . .

"Greg!" she shrieked.

Twelve doors were flung violently open.

"Marcie, sweetheart, what's the matter?" pleaded a jumble of tender voices, and twelve of Greg, pushing angrily at one another, rushed into the room.

SANDMAGIC

ORSON SCOTT CARD

Although best known for his Nebula and Hugo Award–
winning science fiction novels *Ender's Game* and *Speaker
for the Dead*, ORSON SCOTT CARD is also an accomplished
fantasy and horror writer. Among his other achievements
are two Locus Awards, a Hugo Award for nonfiction, and
a World Fantasy Award. Currently he is working on the
Tales of Alvin Maker series, which chronicles the history
of an alternate 19th century America where magic works.
The Alvin Maker series, like the majority of his work, deals
with messianic characters and their influence on the
world around them. His short fiction has been collected
in the anthology *Maps in a Mirror*. "Sandmagic" shows
what can be both gained and lost when one lives only for
revenge.

The great domes of the city of Gyree dazzled blue and red when the sun shone through a break in the clouds, and for a moment Cer Cemreet thought he saw some of the glory the uncles talked about in the late night tales of the old days of Greet. But the capital did not look dazzling up close, Cer remembered bitterly. Now dogs ran in the streets and rats lived in the wreckage of the palace, and the King of Greet lived in New Gyree in the hills far to the north, where the armies of the enemy could not go. Yet.

The sun went back behind a cloud and the city looked dark again. A Nefyr patrol was riding briskly on the Hetterwee Road far to the north. Cer turned his gaze to the lush grass on the hill where he sat. The clouds meant rain, but probably not here, he thought. He always thought of something else when he saw a Nefyr patrol. Yes, it was too early in Hrickan for rains to fall here. This rain would fall in the north, perhaps in the land of the King of the High Mountains, or on the vast plain of Westwold where they said horses ran free but were tame for any man to ride at need. But no rain would fall in Greet until Doonse, three weeks from now. By then the wheat would all be stored and the hay would be piled in vast ricks as tall as the hill Cer sat on.

In the old days, they said, all during Doonse the great wagons from Westwold would come and carry off the hay to last them through the snow season. But not now, Cer remembered. This year and last year and the year before the wagons had come from the south and east, two-wheeled wagons with drivers who spoke, not High Westil, but the barbarian Fyrd language. Fyrd or firt, thought Cer, and laughed, for firt was a word he could not say in front of his parents. They spoke firt.

Cer looked out over the plain again. The Nefyr patrol had turned from the highway and were on the road to the hills.

The road to the hills. Cer leaped to his feet and raced down the track leading home. A patrol heading for the hills could only mean trouble.

He stopped to rest only once, when the pain in his side was too bad to bear. But the patrol had horses, and he arrived home only to see the horses of the Nefyrre gathered at his father's gate.

Where are the uncles? Cer thought. The uncles must come.

But the uncles were not there, and Cer heard a terrible scream from inside the garden walls. He had never heard his mother scream before, but somehow he knew it was his mother, and he ran to the gate. A Nefyr soldier seized him and called out, "Here's the boy!" in a thick accent of High Westil, so that Cer's parents could understand. Cer's mother screamed again, and now Cer saw why.

His father had been stripped naked, his arms and legs held by two tall Nefyrre. The Nefyr captain held his viciously curved short-sword, point up, pressing against Cer's father's hard-muscled stomach. As Cer and his mother watched, the sword drew blood, and the captain pushed it in to the hilt, then pulled it up to the ribs. Blood gushed. The captain had been careful not to touch the heart, and now they thrust a spear into the huge wound, and lifted it high, Cer's father dangling from the end. They lashed the spear to the gatepost, and the blood and bowels stained the gates and the walls.

For five minutes more Cer's father lived, his chest heaving in the agony of breath. He may have died of pain, but Cer did not think so, for his father was not the kind to give in to pain. He may have died of suffocation, for one lung was gone and every breath was excruciating, but Cer did not think so, for his father kept breathing to the end. It was loss of blood, Cer decided, weeks later. It was when his body was dry, when the veins collapsed, that Cer's father died.

He never uttered a sound. Cer's father would never let the Nefyrre hear him so much as sigh in pain.

Cer's mother screamed and screamed until blood came from her mouth and she fainted.

Cer stood in silence until his father died. Then when the captain, a smirk on his face, walked near Cer and looked in his face, Cer kicked him in the groin.

They cut off Cer's great toes, but like his father, Cer made no sound.

Then the Nefyrre left and the uncles came.

Uncle Forwin vomited. Uncle Erwin wept. Uncle Crune put his arm around Cer's shoulder as the servants bound his maimed feet and said, "Your father was a great, a brave man. He killed many Nefyrre, and burned many wagons. But the Nefyrre are strong."

Uncle Crune squeezed Cer's shoulder. "Your father was stronger. But he was one, and they were many."

Cer looked away.

"Will you not look at your uncle?" Uncle Crune asked.

"My father," Cer said, "did not think that he was alone."

Uncle Crune got up and walked away. Cer never saw the uncles again.

He and his mother had to leave the house and the fields, for a Nefyr farmer had been given the land to farm for the King of Nefyryd. With no money, they had to move south, across the River Greebeck into the drylands near the desert, where no rivers flowed and so only the hardiest plants lived. They lived the winter on the charity of the desperately poor. In the summer, when the heat came, so did the Poor Plague which swept the drylands. The cure was fresh fruits, but fresh fruits came from Yffyrd and Suffyrd and only the rich could buy them, and the poor died by the thousands, Cer's mother was one of them.

They took her out on the sand to burn her body and free her spirit. As they painted her with tar (tar, at least, cost nothing, if a man had a bucket), five horsemen came to the brow of a dune to watch. At first Cer thought they were Nefyrre, but no. The poor people looked up and saluted the strangers, which Greetmen never do the enemy. These, then, were desert men, the Abadapnur nomads, who raided the rich farms of Greet during dry years, but who never harmed the poor.

We hated them, Cer thought, when we were rich. But now we are poor, and they are our friends.

His mother burned as the sun set.

Cer watched until the flames went out. The moon was high for the second time that night. Cer said a prayer to the moonlady over his mother's bones and ashes and then he turned and left.

He stopped at their hut and gathered the little food they had, and put on his father's tin ring, which the Nefyrre had thought was valueless, but which Cer knew was the sign of the Cemreet family's authority since forever ago.

Then Cer walked north.

He lived by killing rats in barns and cooking them. He lived by begging at poor farmer's doors, for the rich farmers had servants to turn away beggars. That, at least, Cer remembered, his father had never done. Beggars always had a meal at his father's house.

Cer also lived by stealing when he could hunt or beg no food. He stole handfuls of raw wheat. He stole carrots from gardens. He stole water from wells, for which he could have lost his life in this rainless season. He stole, one time, a fruit from a rich man's food wagon.

It burned his mouth, it was so cold and the acid so strong. It dribbled down his chin. As a poor man and a thief, Cer thought, I now eat a thing so dear that even my father, who was called wealthy, could never buy it.

And at last he saw the mountains in the north. He walked on, and in a week the mountains were great cliffs and steep slopes of shale. The Mitherkame, where the king of the High Mountains reigned, and Cer began to climb.

He climbed all one day and slept in a cleft of a rock. He moved slowly, for climbing in sandals was clumsy, and without his great toes Cer could not climb barefoot. The next morning he climbed more. Though he nearly fell one time when falling would have meant crashing a mile down onto the distant plain, at last he reached the knifelike top of the Mitherkame, and heaven.

For of a sudden the stone gave way to soil. Not the pale sandy soil of the drylands, nor the red soil of

Greet, but the dark black soil of the old songs from the north, the soil that could not be left alone for a day or it would sprout plants that in a week would be a forest.

And there *was* a forest, and the ground was thick with grass. Cer had seen only a few trees in his life, and they had been olive trees, short and gnarled, and fig sycamores, that were three times the height of a man. These were twenty times the height of a man and ten steps around, and the young trees shot up straight and tall so that not a sapling was as small as Cer, who for twelve years old was not considered small.

To Cer, who had known only wheat and hay and olive orchards, the forest was more magnificent than the mountain or the city or the river or the moon.

He slept under a huge tree. He was very cold that night. And in the morning he realized that in a forest he would find no farms, and where there were no farms there was no food for him. He got up and walked deeper into the forest. There were people in the High Mountains, else there would be no king, and Cer would find them. If he didn't, he would die. But at least he would not die in the realms of the Nefyrre.

He passed many bushes with edible berries, but he did not know they could be eaten so he did not eat. He passed many streams with slow stupid fish that he could have caught, but in Greet fish was never eaten, because it always carried disease, and so Cer caught no fish.

And on the third day, when he began to feel so weak from hunger that he could walk no longer, he met the treemage.

He met him because it was the coldest night yet,

and at last Cer tore branches from a tree to make a fire. But the wood did not light, and when Cer looked up he saw that the trees had moved. They were coming closer, surrounding him tightly. He watched them, and they did not move as he watched, but when he turned around the ones he had not been watching were closer yet. He tried to run, but the low branches made a tight fence he could not get through. He couldn't climb, either, because the branches all stabbed downward. Bleeding from the twigs he had scraped, Cer went back to his camping place and watched as the trees at last made a solid wall around him.

And he waited. What else could he do in his wooden prison?

In the morning he heard a man singing, and he called for help.

"Oh ho," he heard a voice say in a strange accent. "Oh ho, a tree cutter and a firemaker, a branch killer and a forest hater."

"I'm none of those," Cer said. "It was cold, and I tried to build a fire only to keep warm."

"A fire, a fire," the voice said. "In this small part of the world there are no fires of wood. But that's a young voice I hear, and I doubt there's a beard beneath the words."

"I have no beard," Cer answered. "I have no weapon, except a knife too small to harm you."

"A knife? A knife that tears sap from living limbs, Redwood says. A knife that cuts twigs like soft manfingers, says Elm. A knife that stabs bark till it bleeds, says Sweet Aspen. Break your knife," said the voice outside the trees, "and I will open your prison."

"But it's my only knife," Cer protested, "and I need it."

"You need it here like you need fog on a dark night. Break it or you'll die before these trees move again."

Cer broke his knife.

Behind him he heard a sound, and he turned to see a fat old man standing in a clear space between the trees. A moment before there had been no clear space.

"A child," said the man.

"A fat old man," said Cer, angry at being considered as young as his years.

"An illbred child at that," said the man. "But perhaps he knows no better, for from the accent of his speech I would say he comes from Greetland, and from his clothing I would say he was poor, and it's well known in Mitherwee that there are no manners in Greet."

Cer snatched up the blade of his knife and ran at the man. Somehow there were many sharp-pointed branches in the way, and his hand ran into a hard limb, knocking the blade to the ground.

"Oh, my child," said the man kindly. "There is death in your heart."

The branches were gone, and the man reached out his hands and touched Cer's face. Cer jerked away.

"And the touch of a man brings pain to you." The man sighed. "How inside-out your world must be."

Cer looked at the man coldly. He could endure taunting. But was that kindness in the old man's eyes?

"You look hungry," said the old man.

Cer said nothing.

"If you care to follow me, you may. I have food for you, if you like."

Cer followed him.

They went through the forest, and Cer noticed that the old man stopped to touch many of the trees.

And a few he pointedly snubbed, turning his back or taking a wider route around them. Once he stopped and spoke to a tree that had lost a large limb—recently, too, Cer thought, because the tar on the stump was still soft. "Soon there'll be no pain at all," the old man said to the tree. Then the old man sighed again. "Ah, yes, I know. And many a walnut in the falling season."

Then they reached a house. If it could be called a house, Cer thought. Stones were the walls, which was common enough in Greet, but the roof was living wood—thick branches from nine tall trees, interwoven and heavily leaved, so that Cer was sure no drop of rain could ever come inside.

"You admire my roof?" the old man asked. "So tight that even in the winter, when the leaves are gone, the snow cannot come in. But *we* can," he said, and led the way through a low door into a single room.

The old man kept up a constant chatter as he fixed breakfast: berries and cream, stewed acorns, and thick slices of cornbread. The old man named all the foods for Cer, because except for the cream it was all strange to him. But it was good, and it filled him.

"Acorn from the Oaks," said the old man. "Walnuts from the trees of that name. And berries from the bushes, the neartrees. Corn, of course, comes from an untree, a weak plant with no wood, which dies every year."

"The trees don't die every year, then, even though it snows?" Cer asked, for he had heard of snow.

"Their leaves turn bright colors, and then they fall, and perhaps that's a kind of death," said the old man. "But in Eanan the snow melts and by Blowan there are leaves again on all the trees."

Cer did not believe him, but he didn't disbelieve him either. Trees were strange things.

"I never knew that trees in the High Mountains could move."

"Oh ho," laughed the old man. "And neither can they, except here, and other woods that a treemage tends."

"A treemage? Is there magic then?"

"Magic. Oh ho," the man laughed again. "Ah yes, magic, many magics, and mine is the magic of trees."

Cer squinted. The man did not look like a man of power, and yet the trees had penned an intruder in. "You rule the trees here?"

"Rule?" the old man asked, startled. "What a thought. Indeed no. I serve them. I protect them. I give them the power in me, and they give me the power in them, and it makes us all a good deal more powerful. But rule? That just doesn't enter into magic. What a thought."

Then the old man chattered about the doings of the silly squirrels this year, and when Cer was through eating the old man gave him a bucket and they spent the morning gathering berries. "Leave a berry on the bush for every one you pick," the old man said. "They're for the birds in the fall and for the soil in the Kamesun, when new bushes grow."

And so Cer, quite accidentally, began his life with the treemage, and it was as happy a time as Cer ever had in his life, except when he was a child and his mother sang to him and except for the time his father took him hunting deer in the hills of Wetfell.

And after the autumn when Cer marveled at the colors of the leaves, and after the winter when Cer tramped through the snow with the treemage to tend to ice-splintered branches, and after the spring when Cer thinned the new plants so the forest did not become overgrown, the treemage began to think that the dark places in Cer's heart were filled with light, or at least put away where they could not be found.

He was wrong.

For as he gathered leaves for the winter's fires Cer dreamed he was gathering the bones of his enemies. And as he tramped the snow he dreamed he was marching into battle to wreak death on the Nefyrre. And as he thinned the treestarts Cer dreamed of slaying each of the uncles as his father had been slain, because none of them had stood by him in his danger.

Cer dreamed of vengeance, and his heart grew darker even as the wood was filled with the bright light of the summer sun.

One day he said to the treemage, "I want to learn magic."

The treemage smiled with hope. "You're learning it," he said, "and I'll gladly teach you more."

"I want to learn things of power."

"Ah," said the treemage, disappointed. "Ah, then, you can have no magic."

"You have power," said Cer. "I want it also."

"Oh, indeed," said the treemage. "I have the power of two legs and two arms, the power to heat tar over a peat fire to stop the sap flow from broken limbs, the power to cut off diseased branches to save the tree, the power to teach the trees how and when to protect themselves. All the rest is the power of the trees, and none of it is mine."

"But they do your bidding," said Cer.

"Because I do theirs!" the treemage said, suddenly angry. "Do you think that there is slavery in this wood? Do you think I am a king? Only men allow men to rule them. Here in this wood there is only love, and on that love and by that love the trees and I have the magic of the wood."

Cer looked down, disappointed. The treemage misunderstood, and thought that Cer was contrite.

"Ah, my boy," said the treemage. "You haven't learned it, I see. The root of magic is love, the trunk is service. The treemages love the trees and serve them and then they share treemagic with the trees. Lightmages love the sun and make fires at night, and the fire serves them as they serve the fire. Horsemages love and serve horses, and they ride freely whither they will because of the magic in the herd. There is field magic and plain magic, and the magic of rocks and metals, songs and dances, the magic of winds and weathers. All built on love, all growing through service."

"I must have magic," said Cer.

"Must you?" asked the treemage. "Must you have magic? There are kinds of magic, then, that you might have. But I can't teach them to you."

"What are they?"

"No," said the treemage, and he wouldn't speak again.

Cer thought and thought. What magic could be demanded against anyone's will?

And at last, when he had badgered and nagged the treemage for weeks, the treemage angrily gave in. "Will you know then?" the treemage snapped. "I will tell you. There is sea-magic, where the wicked sailors serve the monsters of the deep by feeding them living flesh. Would you do that?" But Cer only waited for more.

"So that appeals to you," said the treemage. "Then you will be delighted at desertmagic."

And now Cer saw a magic he might use. "How is that performed?"

"*I* know not," said the treemage icily. "It is the blackest of the magics to men of *my* kind, though your dark heart might leap to it. There's only one magic darker."

"And what is that?" asked Cer.

"What a fool I was to take you in," said the treemage. "The wounds in your heart, you don't want them to heal; you love to pick at them and let them fester."

"What is the darkest magic?" demanded Cer.

"The darkest magic," said the treemage, "is one, thank the moon, that you can never practice. For to do it you have to love men and love the love of men more than your own life. And love is as far from you as the sea is from the mountains, as the earth is from the sky."

"The sky touches the earth," said Cer.

"Touches, but never do they meet," said the treemage.

Then the treemage handed Cer a basket, which he had just filled with bread and berries and a flagon of streamwater. "Now go."

"Go?" asked Cer.

"I hoped to cure you, but you won't have a cure. You clutch at your suffering too much to be healed."

Cer reached out his foot toward the treemage, the crusty scars still a deep red where his great toe had been.

"As well you might try to restore my foot."

"Restore?" asked the treemage. "I restore nothing. But I staunch, and heal, and I help the trees forget their lost limbs. For if they insist on rushing sap to the limb as if it were still there, they lose all their sap; they dry, they wither, they die."

Cer took the basket.

"Thank you for your kindness," said Cer. "I'm sorry that you don't understand. But just as the tree can never forgive the ax or the flame, there are those that must die before I can truly live again."

"Get out of my wood," said the treemage. "Such darkness has no place here."

And Cer left, and in three days came to the edge of the Mitherkame, and in two days reached the bottom of the cliffs, and in a few weeks reached the desert. For he would learn desertmagic. He would serve the sand, and the sand would serve him.

On the way the soldiers of Nefyryd stopped him and searched him. When they saw that he had no great toes, they beat him and shaved off his young and scraggly beard and sent him on his way with a kick.

Cer even stopped where his father's farm had been. Now all the farms were farmed by Nefyrre, men of the south who had never owned land before. They drove him away, afraid that he might steal. So he snuck back in the night and from his father's storehouse stole meat and from his father's barn stole a chicken.

He crossed the Greebeck to the drylands and gave the meat and the chicken to the poor people there. He lived with them for a few days. And then he went out into the desert.

He wandered in the desert for a week before he ran out of food and water. He tried everything to find the desertmagic. He spoke to the hot sand and the burning rocks as the treemage had spoken to the trees. But the sand was never injured and did not need a healing touch, and the rocks could not be harmed and so they needed no protection. There was no answer when Cer talked, except the wind which cast sand in his eyes.

And at last Cer lay dying on the sand, his skin

caked and chafed and burnt, his clothing long since tattered away into nothing, his flagon burning hot and filled with sand, his eyes blind from the whiteness of the desert.

He could neither love nor serve the desert, for the desert needed nothing from him and there was neither beauty nor kindness to love.

But he refused to die without having vengeance. Refused to die so long that he was still alive when the Abadapnu tribesmen found him. They gave him water and nursed him back to health. It took weeks, and they had to carry him on a sledge from waterhole to water-hole.

And as they traveled with their herds and their horses, the Abadapnur carried Cer farther and farther away from the Nefyrre and the land of Greet.

Cer regained his senses slowly, and learned the Abadapnu language even more slowly. But at last, as the clouds began to gather for the winter rains, Cer was one of the tribe, considered a man because he had a beard, considered wise because of the dark look on his face that remained even on those rare times when he laughed.

He never spoke of his past, though the Abadapnur knew well enough what the tin ring on his finger meant and why he had only eight toes. And they, with the perfect courtesy of the incurious, asked him nothing.

He learned their ways. He learned that starving on the desert was foolish, that dying of thirst was unnecessary. He learned how to trick the desert into yielding up life. "For," said the tribemaster, "the desert is never willing that anything should live."

Cer remembered that. The desert wanted nothing to live. And he wondered if that was a key to desertmagic. Or was it merely a locked door that he could never open? How can you serve and be served by the sand that wants only your death? How could he get vengeance if he was dead? "Though I would gladly die if my dying could kill my father's killers," he said to his horse one day. The horse hung her head, and would only walk for the rest of the day, though Cer kicked her to try to make her run.

Finally one day, impatient that he was doing nothing to achieve his revenge, Cer went to the tribemaster and asked him how one learned the magic of the sand.

"Sandmagic? You're mad," said the tribemaster. For days the tribemaster refused to look at him, let alone answer his questions, and Cer realized that here on the desert the sandmagic was hated as badly as the treemage hated it. Why? Wouldn't such power make the Abadapnur great?

Or did the tribemaster refuse to speak because the Abadapnur did not know the sandmagic?

But they knew it.

And one day the tribemaster came to Cer and told him to mount and follow.

They rode in the early morning before the sun was high, then slept in a cave in a rocky hill during the heat of the day. In the dusk they rode again, and at night they came to the city.

"Ettuie," whispered the tribemaster, and then they rode their horses to the edge of the ruins.

The sand had buried the buildings up to half their height, inside and out, and even now the breezes of evening stirred the sand and built little dunes against the walls. The buildings were made of stone, rising not to domes like the great cities of the Greetmen but to spires, tall towers that seemed to pierce the sky.

"Ikikietar," whispered the tribemaster. "Ikikiaiai re dapii. O ikikiai etetur o abadapnur, ikikiai re dapii."

"What are the 'knives'?" asked Cer. "And how could the sand kill them?"

"The knives are these towers, but they are also the stars of power."

"What power?" asked Cer eagerly.

"No power for you. Only power for the Etetur, for they were wise. They had the manmagic."

Manmagic. Was that the darkest magic spoken of by the treemage?

"Is there a magic more powerful than manmagic?" Cer asked.

"In the mountains, no," said the tribemaster. "On the well-watered plain, in the forest, on the sea, no."

"But in the desert?"

"A huu par eiti ununura," muttered the tribemaster, making the sign against death. "Only the desert power. Only the magic of the sand."

"I want to know," said Cer.

"Once," the tribemaster said, "once there was a mighty empire here. Once a great river flowed here, and rain fell, and the soil was rich and red like the soil of Greet, and a million people lived under the rule of the King of Ettue Dappa. But not all, for far to the west there lived a few who hated Ettue and the manmagic of the kings, and they forged the tool that undid this city.

"They made the wind blow from the desert. They made the rains run off the earth. By their power the river sank into the desert sand, and the fields bore no fruit, and at last the King of Ettue surrendered, and half his kingdom was given to the sandmages. To the dapinur. That western kingdom became Dapnu Dap."

"A kingdom?" said Cer, surprised. "But now the great desert bears that name."

"And once the great desert was no desert, but a land of grasses and grains like your homeland to the north. The sandmages weren't content with half a kingdom, and they used their sandmagic to make a desert of Ettue, and they covered the lands of rebels with sand, until at last the victory of the desert was complete, and Ettue fell to the armies of Greet and Nefyryd—they were allies then—and we of Dapnu Dap became nomads, living off that tiny bit of life that even the harshest desert cannot help but yield."

"And what of the sandmages?" asked Cer.

"We killed them."

"All?"

"All," said the tribemaster. "And if any man will practice sandmagic, today, we will kill him. For what happened to us we will let happen to no other people."

Cer saw the knife in the tribemaster's hand.

"I will have your vow," said the tribemaster. "Swear before these stars and this sand and the ghosts of all who lived in this city that you will seek no sandmagic."

"I swear," said Cer, and the tribemaster put his knife away.

The next day Cer took his horse and a bow and arrows and all the food he could steal and in the heat of the day when everyone slept he went out into the desert. They followed him, but he slew two with arrows and the survivors lost his trail.

Word spread through the tribes of the Abadapnur that a would-be sandmage was loose in the desert, and all were ready to kill him if he came. But he did not come.

For he knew now how to serve the desert, and how

to make the desert serve him. For the desert loved death, and hated grasses and trees and water and the things of life.

So in service of the sand Cer went to the edge of the land of the Nefyrre, east of the desert. There he fouled wells with the bodies of diseased animals. He burned fields when the wind was blowing off the desert, a dry wind that pushed the flames into the cities. He cut down trees. He killed sheep and cattle. And when the Nefyrre patrols chased him he fled onto the desert where they could not follow.

His destruction was annoying, and impoverished many a farmer, but alone it would have done little to hurt the Nefyrre. Except that Cer felt his power over the desert growing. For he was feeding the desert the only thing it hungered for: death and dryness.

He began to speak to the sand again, not kindly, but of land to the east that the sand could cover. And the wind followed his words, whipping the sand, moving the dunes. Where he stood the wind did not touch him, but all around him the dunes moved like waves of the sea.

Moving eastward.

Moving onto the lands of the Nefyrre.

And now the hungry desert could do in a night a hundred times more than Cer could do alone with a torch or a knife. It ate olive groves in an hour. The sand borne on the wind filled houses in a night, buried cities in a week, and in only three months had driven the Nefyrre across the Greebeck and the Nefyr River, where they thought the terrible sandstorms could not follow.

But the storms followed. Cer taught the desert almost to fill the river, so that the water spread out a foot deep and miles wide, flooding some lands that had been dry, but also leaving more water surface for the sun to drink from; and before the river reached the sea it was dry, and the desert swept across into the heart of Nefyryd.

The Nefyrre had always fought with the force of arms, and cruelty was their companion in war. But against the desert they were helpless. They could not fight the sand. If Cer could have known it, he would have gloried in the fact that, untaught, he was the most powerful sandmage who had ever lived. For hate was a greater teacher than any of the books of dark lore, and Cer lived on hate.

And on hate alone, for now he ate and drank nothing, sustaining his body through the power of the wind and the heat of the sun. He was utterly dry, and the blood no longer coursed through his veins. He lived on the energy of the storms he unleashed. And the desert eagerly fed him, because he was feeding the desert.

He followed his storms, and walked through the deserted towns of the Nefyrre. He saw the refugees rushing north and east to the high ground. He saw the corpses of those caught in the storm. And he sang at night the old songs of Greet, the war songs. He wrote his father's name with chalk on the wall of every city he destroyed. He wrote his mother's name in the sand, and where he had written her name the wind did not blow and the sand did not shift, but preserved the writing as if it had been incised on rock.

Then one day, in a lull between his storms, Cer saw a man coming toward him from the east. Abadapnu, he wondered, or Nefyrre? Either way he drew his knife, and fit the nock of an arrow on his bowstring.

But the man came with his hands extended, and he called out, "Cer Cemreet."

It had never occurred to Cer that anyone knew his name.

"Sandmage Cer Cemreet," said the man when he was close. "We have found who you are."

Cer said nothing, but only watched the man's eyes.

"I have come to tell you that your vengeance is full. Nefyryd is at its knees. We have signed a treaty with Greet and we no longer raid into Hetterwee. Driplin has seized our westernmost lands."

Cer smiled. "I care nothing for your empire."

"Then for our people. The deaths of your father and mother have been avenged a hundred thousand times, for over two hundred thousand people have died at your hands."

Cer chuckled. "I care nothing for your people."

"Then for the soldiers who did the deed. Though they acted under orders, they have been arrested and killed, as have the men who gave them those orders, even our first general, all at the command of the King so that your vengeance will be complete. I have brought you their ears as proof of it," said the man, and he took a pouch from his waist.

"I care nothing for soldiers, nor for proof of vengeance," said Cer.

"Then what do you care for?" asked the man quietly.

"Death," said Cer.

"Then I bring you that, too," said the man, and a knife was in his hand, and he plunged the knife into Cer's breast where his heart should have been. But when the man pulled the knife out no blood followed, and Cer only smiled.

"Indeed you brought it to me," said Cer, and he stabbed the man where his father had been stabbed, and drew the knife up as it had been drawn through his father's body, except that he touched the man's heart, and he died.

As Cer watched the blood soaking into the sand, he heard in his ears his mother's screams, which he had silenced for these years. He heard her screams and now, remembering his father and his mother and himself as a child he began to cry, and he held the body of the man he had killed and rocked back and forth on the sand as the blood clotted on his clothing and his skin. His tears mixed with the blood and poured into the sand and Cer realized that this was the first time since his father's death that he had shed any tears at all.

I am not dry, thought Cer. There is water under me still for the desert to drink.

He looked at his dry hands, covered with the man's blood, and tried to scrub off the clotted blood with sand. But the blood stayed, and the sand could not clean him.

He wept again. And then he stood and faced the desert to the west, and he said, "Come."

A breeze began.

"Come," he said to the desert, "come and dry my eyes."

And the wind came up, and the sand came, and Cer Cemreet was buried in the sand, and his eyes became dry, and the last life passed from his body, and the last sandmage passed from the world.

Then came the winter rains, and the refugees of Nefyryd returned to their land. The soldiers were called home, for the wars were over, and now their weapons were the shovel and the plow. They redug the trench of the Nefyr and the Greebeck, and the river soon flowed deep again to the sea. They scattered grass seed and cleaned their houses of sand. They carried water into the ruined fields with ditches and aqueducts.

Slowly life returned to Nefyryd.

And the desert, having lost its mage, retreated quietly to its old borders, never again to seek death where there was life. Plenty of death already where nothing lived, plenty of dryness to drink where there was no water.

In a wood a little way from the crest of the Mitherkame, a treemage heard the news from a wandering tinker.

The treemage went out into the forest and spoke softly to the Elm, to the Oak, to the Redwood, to the Sweet Aspen. And when all had heard the news, the forest wept for Cer Cemreet, and each tree gave a twig to be burned in his memory, and shed sap to sink into the ground in his name.

NARROW VALLEY

R. A. LAFFERTY

Humor and hope for the future are two hallmarks of the stories of R. A. LAFFERTY. Outrageous yet believable characters, transformation, and the eternal war between Heaven and Hell also appear in his work. He has been writing fiction unlike anything else for more than twenty-five years, and has been rewarded with a Hugo award and a World Fantasy Lifetime Achievement award in 1990. He lives in Tulsa, Oklahoma. The old ways of the Native Americans meet with the hardheaded practicality of the American immigrants, with unpredictably strange results, in "Narrow Valley."

In the year 1893, land allotments in severalty were made to the remaining eight hundred and twenty-one Pawnee Indians. Each would receive one hundred and sixty acres of land and no more, and thereafter the Pawnees would be expected to pay taxes on their land, the same as the White-Eyes did.

"Kitkehahke!" Clarence Big-Saddle cussed. "You can't kick a dog around proper on a hundred and sixty acres. And I sure am not hear before about this pay taxes on land."

Clarence Big-Saddle selected a nice green valley for his allotment. It was one of the half-dozen plots he had always regarded as his own. He sodded around the summer lodge that he had there and made it an all-season home. But he sure didn't intend to pay taxes on it.

So he burned leaves and bark and made a speech:

"That my valley be always wide and flourish and green and such stuff as that!" he orated in Pawnee chant style, "But that it be narrow if an intruder come."

He didn't have any balsam bark to burn. He threw on a little cedar bark instead. He didn't have any elder leaves. He used a handful of jack-oak leaves. And he forgot the word. How you going to work it if you forget the word?

"Petahauerat!" he howled out with the confidence he hoped would fool the fates.

"That's about the same long of a word," he said in a low aside to himself. But he was doubtful. "What am I, a White Man, a burr-tailed jack, a new kind of nut to think it will work?" he asked. "I have to laugh at me. Oh well, we see."

He threw the rest of the bark and the leaves on the fire, and he hollered the wrong word out again.

And he was answered by a dazzling sheet of summer lightning.

"Skidi!" Clarence Big-Saddle swore. "It worked. I didn't think it would."

Clarence Big-Saddle lived on his land for many years, and he paid no taxes. Intruders were unable to come down to his place. The land was sold for taxes three times, but nobody ever came down to claim it. Finally, it was carried as open land on the books. Homesteaders filed on it several times, but none of them fulfilled the qualification of living on the land.

Half a century went by. Clarence Big-Saddle called his son.

"I've had it, boy," he said. "I think I'll just go in the house and die."

"Okay, Dad," the son, Clarence Little-Saddle, said. "I'm going in to town to shoot a few games of pool with the boys. I'll bury you when I get back this evening."

So the son Clarence Little-Saddle inherited. He also lived on the land for many years without paying taxes.

There was a disturbance in the courthouse one day. The place seemed to be invaded in force, but actually there were but one man, one woman, and five children. "I'm Robert Rampart," said the man, "and we want the Land Office."

"I'm Robert Rampart, Junior," said a nine-year-old

gangler, "and we want it pretty blamed quick."

"I don't think we have anything like that," the girl at the desk said. "Isn't that something they had a long time ago?"

"Ignorance is no excuse for inefficiency, my dear," said Mary Mabel Rampart, an eight-year-old who could easily pass for eight and a half. "After I make my report, I wonder who will be sitting at your desk tomorrow?"

"You people are either in the wrong state or the wrong century," the girl said.

"The Homestead Act still obtains," Robert Rampart insisted. "There is one tract of land carried as open in this country. I want to file on it."

Cecilia Rampart answered the knowing wink of a beefy man at a distant desk. "Hi," she breathed as she slinked over. "I'm Cecilia Rampart, but my stage name is Cecilia San Juan. Do you think that seven is too young to play ingenue roles?"

"Not for you," the man said. "Tell your folks to come over here."

"Do you know where the Land Office is?" Cecilia asked.

"Sure. It's the fourth left-hand drawer of my desk. The smallest office we got in the whole courthouse. We don't use it much anymore."

The Ramparts gathered around. The beefy man started to make out the papers.

"This is the land description—" Robert Rampart began, "—why, you've got it down already. How did you know?"

"I've been around here a long time," the man answered.

They did the paperwork, and Robert Rampart filed on the land.

"You won't be able to come onto the land itself, though," the man said.

"Why won't I?" Rampart demanded. "Isn't the land description accurate?"

"Oh, I suppose so. But nobody's ever been able to get to the land. It's become a sort of joke."

"Well, I intend to get to the bottom of that joke," Rampart insisted. "I will occupy the land, or I will find out why not."

"I'm not sure about that," the beefy man said. "The last man to file on the land, about a dozen years ago, wasn't able to occupy the land. And he wasn't able to say why he couldn't. It's kind of interesting, the look on their faces after they try it for a day or two, and then give it up."

The Ramparts left the courthouse, loaded into their camper, and drove out to find their land. They stopped at the house of a cattle and wheat farmer named Charley Dublin. Dublin met them with a grin which indicated he had been tipped off.

"Come along if you want to, folks," Dublin said. "The easiest way is on foot across my short pasture here. Your land's directly west of mine."

They walked the short distance to the border.

"My name is Tom Rampart, Mr. Dublin." Six-year-old Tom made conversation as they walked. "But my name is really Ramires, and not Tom. I am the issue of an indiscretion of my mother in Mexico several years ago."

"The boy is a kidder, Mr. Dublin," said the mother, Nina Rampart, defending herself. "I have never been in Mexico, but sometimes I have the urge to disappear there forever."

"Ah yes, Mrs. Rampart. And what is the name of

the youngest boy here?" Charles Dublin asked.

"Fatty," said Fatty Rampart.

"But surely that is not your given name?"

"Audifax," said five-year-old Fatty.

"Ah well, Audifax, Fatty, are you a kidder too?"

"He's getting better at it, Mr. Dublin," Mary Mabel said. "He was a twin till last week. His twin was named Skinny. Mama left Skinny unguarded while she was out tippling, and there were wild dogs in the neighborhood. When Mama got back, do you know what was left of Skinny? Two neck bones and an ankle bone. That was all."

"Poor Skinny," Dublin said. "Well, Rampart, this is the fence and the end of my land. Yours is just beyond."

"Is that ditch on my land?" Rampart asked.

"That ditch *is* your land."

"I'll have it filled in. It's a dangerous deep cut even if it is narrow. And the other fence looks like a good one, and I sure have a pretty plot of land beyond it."

"No, Rampart, the land beyond the second fence belongs to Holister Hyde," Charley Dublin said. "That second fence is the *end* of your land."

"Now, just wait a minute, Dublin! There's something wrong here. My land is one hundred and sixty acres, which would be a half mile on a side. Where's my half-mile width?"

"Between the two fences."

"That's not eight feet."

"Doesn't look like it, does it, Rampart? Tell you what—there's plenty of throwing-sized rocks around. Try to throw one across it."

"I'm not interested in any such boys' games," Rampart exploded. "I want my land."

But the Rampart children *were* interested in such games. They got with it with those throwing rocks. They winged them out over the little gully. The stones acted funny. They hung in the air, as it were, and diminished in size. And they were small as pebbles when they dropped down, down into the gully. None of them could throw a stone across that ditch, and they were throwing kids.

"You and your neighbor have conspired to fence open land for your own use," Rampart charged.

"No such thing, Rampart," Dublin said cheerfully. "My land checks perfectly. So does Hyde's. So does yours, if we knew how to check it. It's like one of those trick topological drawings. It really is a half mile from here to there, but the eye gets lost somewhere. It's your land. Crawl through the fence and figure it out."

Rampart crawled through the fence, and drew himself up to jump the gully. Then he hesitated. He got a glimpse of just how deep that gully was. Still, it wasn't five feet across.

There was a heavy fence post on the ground, designed for use as a corner post. Rampart up-ended it with some effort. Then he shoved it to fall and bridge the gully. But it fell short, and it shouldn't have. An eight-foot post should bridge a five-foot gully.

The post fell into the gully, and rolled and rolled and rolled. It spun as though it were rolling outward, but it made no progress except vertically. The post came to rest on a ledge of the gully, so close that Rampart could almost reach out and touch it, but it now appeared no bigger than a match stick.

"There is something wrong with that fence post, or with the world, or with my eyes," Robert Rampart said. "I wish I felt dizzy so I could blame it on that."

"There's a little game that I sometimes play with my neighbor Hyde when we're both out," Dublin said. "I've a heavy rifle and I train it on the middle of his forehead as he stands on the other side of the ditch apparently eight feet away. I fire it off then (I'm a good shot), and I hear it whine across. It'd kill him dead if things were as they seem. But Hyde's in no danger. The shot always bangs into that little scuff of rocks and boulders about thirty feet below him. I can see it kick up the rock dust there, and the sound of it rattling into those little boulders comes back to me in about two and a half seconds."

A bull-bat (poor people call it the night-hawk) raveled around in the air and zoomed out over the narrow ditch, but it did not reach the other side. The bird dropped below ground level and could be seen against the background of the other side of the ditch. It grew smaller and hazier as though at a distance of three or four hundred yards. The white bars on its wings could no longer be discerned; then the bird itself could hardly be discerned; but it was far short of the other side of the five-foot ditch.

A man identified by Charley Dublin as the neighbor Hollister Hyde had appeared on the other side of the little ditch. Hyde grinned and waved. He shouted something, but could not be heard.

"Hyde and I both read mouth," Dublin said, "so we can talk across the ditch easy enough. Which kid wants to play chicken? Hyde will barrel a good-sized rock right at your head, and if you duck or flinch you're chicken."

"Me! Me!" Audifax Rampart challenged. And Hyde, a big man with big hands, did barrel a fearsome jagged rock right at the head of the boy. It would have killed him if things had been as they appeared. But the rock diminished to nothing and disappeared into the ditch. Here was a phenomenon—things seemed real-sized on either side of the ditch, but they diminished coming out over the ditch either way.

"Everybody game for it?" Robert Rampart Junior asked.

"We won't get down there by standing here," Mary Mabel said.

"Nothing wenchered, nothing gained," said Cecilia. "I got that from an ad for a sex comedy."

Then the five Rampart kids ran down into the gully. Ran *down* is right. It was almost as if they ran down the vertical face of a cliff. They couldn't do that. The gully was no wider than the stride of the biggest kids. But the gully diminished those children, it ate them alive. They were doll-sized. They were acorn-sized. They were running for minute after minute across a ditch that was only five feet across. They were going deeper in it, and getting smaller. Robert Rampart was roaring his alarm, and his wife Nina was screaming. Then she stopped. "What am I carrying on so loud about?" she asked herself. "It looks like fun. I'll do it too."

She plunged into the gully, diminished in size as the children had done, and ran at a pace to carry her a hundred yards away across a gully only five feet wide.

That Robert Rampart stirred things up for a while then. He got the sheriff there, and the highway patrolmen. A ditch had stolen his wife and five children, he said, and maybe had killed them. And if anybody laughs, there may be another killing. He got the colonel of the State National Guard there, and a command post set up. He got a couple of airplane pilots. Robert Rampart had one quality: when he hollered, people came.

He got the newsmen out from T-Town, and the eminent scientists, Dr. Velikof Vonk, Arpad Arkabaranan, and Willy McGilly. That bunch turns up every time you get on a good one. They just happen to be in that part of the country where something interesting is going on.

They attacked the thing from all four sides and the top, and by inner and outer theory. If a thing measures a half mile on each side, and the sides are straight, there just has to be something in the middle of it. They took pictures from the air, and they turned out perfect. They proved that Robert Rampart had the prettiest hundred and sixty acres in the country, the larger part of it being a lush green valley, and all of it being a half mile on a side, and situated just where it should be. They took ground-level photos then, and it showed a beautiful half-mile stretch of land between the boundaries of Charley Dublin and Holister Hyde. But a man isn't a camera. None of them could see that beautiful spread with the eyes in their heads. Where was it?

Down in the valley itself everything was normal. It really was a half mile wide and no more than eighty feet deep with a very gentle slope. It was warm and sweet, and beautiful with grass and grain.

Nina and the kids loved it, and they rushed to see what squatter had built that little house on their land. A house, or a shack. It had never known paint, but paint would have spoiled it. It was built of split timbers dressed near smooth with axe and draw knife, chinked with white clay, and sodded up to about half its height. And there was an interloper standing by the little lodge.

"Here, here, what are you doing on our land?"

Robert Rampart Junior demanded of the man. "Now you just shamble off again wherever you came from. I'll bet you're a thief, too, and those cattle are stolen."

"Only the black-and-white calf," Clarence Little-Saddle said. "I couldn't resist him, but the rest are mine. I guess I'll just stay around and see that you folks get settled all right."

"Is there any wild Indians around here?" Fatty Rampart asked.

"No, not really. I go on a bender about every three months and get a little bit wild, and there's a couple Osage boys from Gray Horse that get noisy sometimes, but that's about all," Clarence Little-Saddle said.

"You certainly don't intend to palm yourself off on us as an Indian," Mary Mabel challenged. "You'll find us a little too knowledgeable for that."

"Little girl, you as well tell this cow there's no room for her to be a cow since you're so knowledgeable. She thinks she's a short-horn cow named Sweet Virginia. I think I'm a Pawnee Indian named Clarence. Break it to us real gentle if we're not."

"If you're an Indian where's your war bonnet? There's not a feather on you anywhere."

"How you be sure? There's a story that we got feathers instead of hair on— Aw, I can't tell a joke like that to a little girl! How come you're not wearing the Iron Crown of Lombardy if you're a white girl? How you expect me to believe you're a little white girl and your folks came from Europe a couple hundred years ago if you don't wear it? There were six hundred tribes, and only one of them, the Oglala Sioux, had the war bonnet and only the big leaders, never more than two or three of them alive at one time, wore it."

"Your analogy is a little strained," Mary Mabel

said. "Those Indians we saw in Florida and the ones at Atlantic City had war bonnets, and they couldn't very well have been the kind of Sioux you said. And just last night on the TV in the motel, those Massachusetts Indians put a war bonnet on the President and called him the Great White Father. You mean to tell me that they were all phonies? Hey, who's laughing at who here?"

"If you're an Indian where's your bow and arrow?" Tom Rampart interrupted. "I bet you can't even shoot one."

"You're sure right there," Clarence admitted. "I never shot one of those things but once in my life. They used to have an archery range in Boulder Park over in T-Town, and you could rent the things and shoot at targets tied to hay bales. Hey, I barked my whole forearm and nearly broke my thumb when the bowstring thwacked home. I couldn't shoot that thing at all. I don't see how anybody ever could shoot one of them."

"Okay, kids," Nina Rampart called to her brood. "Let's start pitching this junk out of the shack so we can move in. Is there any way we can drive our camper down here, Clarence?"

"Sure, there's a pretty good dirt road, and it's a lot wider than it looks from the top. I got a bunch of green bills in an old night charley in the shack. Let me get them, and then I'll clear out for a while. The shack hasn't been cleaned out for seven years, since the last time this happened. I'll show you the road to the top, and you can bring your car down it."

"Hey, you old Indian, you lied!" Cecilia Rampart shrilled from the doorway of the shack. "You *do* have a war bonnet. Can I have it?"

"I didn't mean to lie, I forgot about that thing," Clarence Little-Saddle said. "My son Clarence Bare-Back sent that to me from Japan for a joke a long time ago. Sure, you can have it."

All the children were assigned tasks carrying the junk out of the shack and setting fire to it. Nina Rampart and Clarence Little-Saddle ambled up to the rim of the valley by the vehicle road that was wider than it looked from the top.

"Nina, you're back! I thought you were gone forever," Robert Rampart jittered at seeing her again. "What—where are the children?"

"Why, I left them down in the valley, Robert. That is, ah, down in that little ditch right there. Now you've got me worried again. I'm going to drive the camper down there and unload it. You'd better go on down and lend a hand too, Robert, and quit talking to all these funny-looking men here."

And Nina went back to Dublin's place for the camper.

"It would be easier for a camel to go through the eye of a needle than for that intrepid woman to drive a car down into that narrow ditch," the eminent scientist Dr. Velikof Vonk said.

"You know how that camel does it?" Clarence Little-Saddle offered, appearing of a sudden from nowhere. "He just closes one of his own eyes and flops back his ears and plunges right through. A camel is mighty narrow when he closes one eye and flops back his ears. Besides, they use a big-eyed needle in the act."

"Where'd this crazy man come from?" Robert Rampart demanded, jumping three feet in the air. "Things are coming out of the ground now. I want my land! I want my children! I want my wife! Whoops, here she comes driving it. Nina, you can't drive a loaded camper into a little ditch like that! You'll be killed or collapsed!"

Nina Rampart drove the loaded camper into the little ditch at a pretty good rate of speed. The best of belief is that she just closed one eye and plunged right through. The car diminished and dropped, and it was smaller than a toy car. But it raised a pretty good cloud of dust as it bumped for several hundred yards across a ditch that was only five feet wide.

"Rampart, it's akin to the phenomenon known as looming, only in reverse," the eminent scientist Arpad Arkabaranan explained as he attempted to throw a rock across the narrow ditch. The rock rose very high in the air, seemed to hang at its apex while it diminished to the size of a grain of sand, and then fell into the ditch not six inches of the way across. There isn't anybody going to throw across a half-mile valley even if it looks five feet. "Look at a rising moon sometime, Rampart. It appears very large, as though covering a great sector of the horizon, but it only covers one half of a degree. It is hard to believe that you could set seven hundred and twenty of such large moons side by side around the horizon, or that it would take one hundred and eighty of the big things to reach from the horizon to a point overhead. It is also hard to believe that your valley is five hundred times as wide as it appears, but it has been surveyed, and it is."

"I want my land. I want my children. I want my wife," Robert chanted dully. "Damn, I let her get away again."

"I tell you, Rampy," Clarence Little-Saddle squared on him, "a man that lets his wife get away twice doesn't deserve to keep her. I give you till nightfall; then you forfeit. I've taken a liking to the brood. One of us is going to be down there tonight."

After a while a bunch of them were off in that little tavern on the road between Cleveland and Osage. It was only a half mile away. If the valley had run in the other direction, it would have been only six feet away.

"It is a psychic nexus in the form of an elongated dome," said the eminent scientist Dr. Velikof Vonk. "It is maintained subconsciously by the concatenation of at least two minds, the stronger of them belonging to a man dead for many years. It has apparently existed for a little less than a hundred years, and in another hundred years it will be considerably weakened. We know from our checking out of folk tales of Europe as well as Cambodia that these ensorcelled areas seldom survive for more than two hundred and fifty years. The person who first set such a thing in being will usually lose interest in it, and in all worldly things, within a hundred years of his own death. This is a simple thanatopsychic limitation. As a short-term device, the thing has been used several times as a military tactic.

"This psychic nexus, as long as it maintains itself, causes group illusion, but it is really a simple thing. It doesn't fool birds or rabbits or cattle or cameras, only humans. There is nothing meteorological about it. It is strictly psychological. I'm glad I was able to give a scientific explanation to it or it would have worried me."

"It is the continental fault coinciding with a noospheric fault," said the eminent scientist Arpad Arkabaranan. "The valley really is a half mile wide, and at the same time it really is only five feet wide. If we measured correctly, we would get these dual measurements. Of course it is meteorological! Everything including dreams is meteorological. It is the animals and cameras which are fooled, as lacking a true dimension; it is only humans who see the true duality. The phenomenon should be common along the whole continental fault where the earth gains or loses a half mile that has to go somewhere. Likely it extends through the whole sweep of the Cross Timbers. Many of those trees appear twice, and many do not appear at all. A man in the proper state of mind could farm that land or raise cattle on it, but it doesn't really exist. There is a clear parallel in the Luftspiegelungthal sector in the Black Forest of Germany which exists, or does not exist, according to the circumstances and to the attitude of the beholder. Then we have the case of Mad Mountain in Morgan County, Tennessee, which isn't there all the time, and also the Little Lobo Mirage south of Presidio, Texas, from which twenty thousand barrels of water were pumped in one two-and-a-half-hour period before the mirage reverted to mirage status. I'm glad I was able to give a scientific explanation to this or it would have worried me."

"I just don't understand how he worked it," said the eminent scientist Willy McGilly. "Cedar bark, jack-oak leaves, and the word 'Petahauerat.' The thing's impossible! When I was a boy and we wanted to make a hideout, we used bark from the skunk-spruce tree, the leaves of a box-elder, and the word was 'Boadicea.' All three elements are wrong here. I cannot find a scientific explanation for it, and it does worry me."

They went back to Narrow Valley. Robert Rampart was still chanting dully: "I want my land. I want my children. I want my wife."

Nina Rampart came chugging up out of the narrow ditch in the camper and emerged through that little gate a few yards down the fence row.

"Supper's ready and we're tired of waiting for you,

Robert," she said. "A fine homesteader you are! Afraid to come onto your own land! Come along now, I'm tired of waiting for you."

"I want my land! I want my children! I want my wife!" Robert Rampart still chanted. "Oh, there you are, Nina. You stay here this time. I want my land! I want my children! I want an answer to this terrible thing."

"It is time we decided who wears the pants in this family," Nina said stoutly. She picked up her husband, slung him over her shoulder, carried him to the camper and dumped him in, slammed (as it seemed) a dozen doors at once, and drove furiously down into Narrow Valley, which already seemed wider.

Why, that place was getting normaler and normaler by the minute! Pretty soon it looked almost as wide as it was supposed to be. The psychic nexus in the form of an elongated dome had collapsed. The continental fault that coincided with the noospheric fault had faced facts and decided to conform. The Ramparts were in effective possession of their homestead, and Narrow Valley was as normal as any place anywhere.

"I have lost my land," Clarence Little-Saddle moaned. "It was the land of my father Clarence Big-Saddle, and I meant it to be the land of my son Clarence Bare-Back. It looked so narrow that people did not notice how wide it was, and people did not try to enter it. Now I have lost it."

Clarence Little-Saddle and the eminent scientist Willy McGilly were standing on the edge of Narrow Valley, which now appeared its true half-mile extent. The moon was just rising, so big that it filled a third of the sky. Who would have imagined that it would take 180 of such monstrous things to reach from the horizon to a point overhead, and yet you could sight it with sighters and figure it so.

"I had the little bear-cat by the tail and I let go," Clarence groaned. "I had a fine valley for free, and I have lost it. I am like that hard-luck guy in the funny-paper or Job in the Bible. Destitution is my lot."

Willy McGilly looked around furtively. They were alone on the edge of the half-mile-wide valley.

"Let's give it a booster shot," Willy McGilly said.

Hey, those two got with it! They started a snapping fire and began to throw the stuff onto it. Bark from the dog-elm tree—how do you know it won't work?

It *was* working! Already the other side of the valley seemed a hundred yards closer, and there were alarmed noises coming up from the people in the valley.

Leaves from a black locust tree—and the valley narrowed still more! There was, moreover, terrified screaming of both children and big people from the depths of Narrow Valley, and the happy voice of Mary Mabel Rampart chanting "Earthquake! Earthquake!"

"That my valley be always wide and flourish and such stuff, and green with money and grass!" Clarence Little-Saddle orated in Pawnee chant style, "but that it be narrow if intruders come, smash them like bugs!"

People, that valley wasn't over a hundred feet wide now, and the screaming of the people in the bottom of the valley had been joined by the hysterical coughing of the camper car starting up.

Willy and Clarence threw everything that was left on the fire. But the word? The word? Who remembers the word?

"Corsicanatexas!" Clarence Little-Saddle howled out with confidence he hoped would fool the fates.

He was answered, not only by a dazzling sheet of summer lightning, but also by thunder and raindrops.

"Chahiksi!" Clarence Little-Saddle swore. "It worked.

I didn't think it would. It will be all right now. I can use the rain."

The valley was again a ditch only five feet wide.

The camper car struggled out of Narrow Valley through the little gate. It was smashed flat as a sheet of paper, and the screaming kids and people in it had only one dimension.

"It's closing in! It's closing in!" Robert Rampart roared, and he was no thicker than if he had been made out of cardboard.

"We're smashed like bugs," the Rampart boys intoned. "We're thin like paper."

"*Mort, ruine, écrasement!*" spoke-acted Cecilia Rampart like the great tragedienne she was.

"Help! Help!" Nina Rampart croaked, but she winked at Willy and Clarence as they rolled by. "This homesteading jag always did leave me a little flat."

"Don't throw those paper dolls away. They might be the Ramparts," Mary Mabel called.

The camper car coughed again and bumped along on level ground. This couldn't last forever. The car was widening out as it bumped along.

"Did we overdo it, Clarence?" Willy McGilly asked. "What did one flatlander say to the other?"

"Dimension of us never got around," Clarence said. "No, I don't think we overdid it, Willy. That car must be eighteen inches wide already, and they all ought to be normal by the time they reach the main road. The next time I do it, I think I'll throw wood-grain plastic on the fire to see who's kidding who."

GUINEVERE'S
TRUTH

JENNIFER ROBERSON

JENNIFER ROBERSON began her writing career with the Chronicles of the Cheysuli, which spanned eight books and brought her name to the forefront of the fantasy genre. She has also written excellent stand-alone novels, including *Lady of the Forest* and *Royal Captive*. She has also edited several anthologies, the most notable being a tribute to the work of Marion Zimmer Bradley, *Return to Avalon*. Her newest novel is *Highwayman*. "Guinevere's Truth" empowers one of the most scandal-ridden women in mythology and restores to her the dignity and power that all women should possess.

I am not what they say I am, these bitch-begotten myth-makers so adept at patching together occasional truths, and falsehoods into a wholly improper motley. They were not *there,* any of them, to say what did happen. Or also to say what did not.

They call it a tragedy now. I suppose it is; I suspect it was even then, when none of us knew. When none of us thought beyond what two of us imagined might be enough to preserve a realm. To preserve a man's dignity.

They make of it now a sacrament, some of them; others name it sin. To us, it was merely what *was.* We were never prescient, to know what would come of the moment. We were never wise, to consider consequences. We were what we were. Nothing more than that.

More, now, they would and will have us be. Great glyphs of human flesh, striding out of stories, tidbits of tales of others such as we: kings and queens and knights . . . and the follies of the flesh.

Was it folly? No. Not then. Not now. Was it flesh? Oh yes. Entirely the flesh. Wholly *of* the flesh, though they would have it be more: sacrament, or sin. The anvil upon which a realm was sundered, despite the tedious truth.

A man, first. A woman. A binding between them, magicked and ill-wrought, yet enough to get a child.

And that child, bred up to be a king despite his bastardy, was made to *be* a king—be it necessary, be it required that he kill another king to gain the crown. To break what was built of heart, mortared together by blood.

And yet they blame me.

Seductress? I was not raised so, nor was given to believe it could be so; men wanted me for what I was, not who. The daughter of a man judged to be of use, of some small power in the chess game of the realm, the patchwork of a place that was not, until he came, a nation in any wise.

But he came. Was born to come. Bred to come, to take up a people as he took up the sword, to preserve what might otherwise have fallen before it was truly built; bred and brought up to stitch together out of the fragile patchwork a whole and well-made quilt resilient enough to guard the limbs of his lady, his one true lady, his steadfast Lady whose name was Britain.

A man who is king needs nothing of a wife but that she be his queen, and bear him an heir.

Whore? Some name me so. And would have burned me for it.

Yet I will burn. The priests tell me so. Afterward. God will not tolerate an adulteress in His realm.

If that be so, if it be true of men as well as of women, then surely we will play this out again, this tragedy, this travesty, this humiliating dance. And none of us wanting it.

If that be hell, we have lived it.

Such stories, in their conception, in the truths of their births, are infinitely simple. Ours was no different. But they make of it now a grand entertainment, fit to cause people to weep.

We none of us wept.

It was what it *was*, not this great sweeping epic, not this literature of the soul, binding others to it. There was no immensity to it, no bard's brilliant embroidery to win him a month of meals. Our tapestry was naught but a square of clean, fine linen, hemmed on all the edges . . . only later was it used to sop and display the blood of Britain's broken heart.

His one true lady, undone. His wife, the queen, unmasked.

Seductress. Adulteress. And worse yet: barren.

Ah, but it *was* my lack. His seed was proven, though unknown by any save the woman who was his sister. His seed was sowed, was born, was bred up to be a king, even if it be necessary to kill another king.

Well, it is done.

All of it is done. And all of it also *un*done; there was no wisdom in the bastard who was inexplicably son and nephew, to see what might come of it. To see what has.

Lies. So many lies. The truth, you see, is plain, is prosaic beyond belief, and therefore tedious.

A man, and a woman. Stripped of all save the flesh, and the flesh freed of such constraints as crown, as armor. And the hearts stripped of all things save compassion for a king who needed a son, yet had none of his queen.

We did not know, then, what we came to know: that the king had bred a son. We knew only there was none and no promise of it, and a man growing older with no son to come after him, to life the great burden and don it himself, like the hair shirt of priests. It was known only that Britain had need of an heir, and that the king's wife, after so much time in the royal bed, offered nothing to prove his manhood.

It was a solution, we thought, that might prove least painful to a man who was king, and was of himself well worth the sacrifice: his wife and his liege man would between them, in his name and the name of his realm, make a child. And call it the king's.

But no child came of it. Only grief.

It is easier, I know, to make a myth of it, to commute us to legend. But the truth is small, and of less glory than what is sung: what we did was to comfort the king. To save what the king had wrought.

Practicality. Not undying, tragic love. Not this travesty of the truth.

But it is prettier, I admit, what they have made of it.

Such a small story, ours. And a world wrenched awry.

Blame me as you will for the folly, but not for the intent. Any more than you blame the bards for making magic of what was nothing more than necessity as we viewed it then, for and in the name of a simple, compassionate man.

For king that was, and king that shall be.

STORM IN
A BOTTLE

JOHN JAKES

The Kent Family Chronicles, a sweeping saga of American life from the Revolutionary War to the present, made their author, JOHN JAKES, a recognized name all over the world. He is also an accomplished western, fantasy, and science fiction writer. He has adapted several of his books for television and written several plays. He has also edited several anthologies, most notably the celebrated New Trails series. "Storm in a Bottle" is part of his earlier work, with his inimitable style on full display in this tale of Brak the Barbarian.

1

The train of seven two-wheeled carts creaked around another corner, and the big, yellow-haired barbarian still standing stubbornly upright in the fourth vehicle let out a growl of surprise.

His scarred hands reached automatically for the cart's side-rail, closed. Veins stood out; a long, clotted sword wound down his left forearm began to ooze scarlet again.

One of the small, pelt-clad men crowded into the same cart grumbled when the bigger man accidentally stepped on his foot. In response, the barbarian moved his wrists closer together. The hateful chain-links hanging between iron wrist-cuffs momentarily formed a sort of noose. The barbarian's eyes left no doubt about whose neck the iron noose would fit.

The little, foul-smelling complainer glanced away, looking for sympathy from his companions in the creaking vehicle. The barbarian paid no more attention. Standing tall, he was the only prisoner in all seven carts who did not wear scabrous-looking fur clothing, and whose body was not matted with dark, wiry hair.

For a moment the barbarian forgot his seething rage at being captured, subdued, chained out on the

arid plateau two days ago. He was diverted by the sight
revealed when the caravan rounded the corner, passing
from stifling shadow to the full glare of the sun.

The big man saw a broad avenue, imposingly
paved, heat-hazed. The avenue stretched into the distance past shops, public marts, fountained cul-de-sacs
where no water ran. At the avenue's far end rose massive
buildings of yellow stone, larger and higher than any
other structures in the walled city.

The barbarian took note of artfully-sculpted idols
lining both sides of the avenue at one-square intervals.
All the statues were identical; all were of the same trans-
parent crystal. The image was that of a seated human
figure with the head of a long-snouted animal. The
creature's open jaws held a thin disc. From the ferocity
of the expression, it was clear that the half-beast was
about to crunch the disc between its fangs. The image
was repeated endlessly, pedestal after crystal-topped
pedestal, up the sweltering avenue beneath the cloudless noon sky.

Soldiers of the lord to whose slaving party Brak the
barbarian had fallen prey jogged their mounts along
the line of seven carts, occasionally cracking short
whips. But listlessly. Their dust-covered faces and dust-
dulled armor were evidence of the long trek in across
the wasteland with the prisoners. On the left wrist of
each soldier, from the mounted leader and his sub-
commanders to the two dozen accompanying foot, a
simple bronze bracelet shot off red-gold glints.

Men and women of the city watched the little caravan from positions beneath awnings and on balconies.
Some of the watchers wore elegant robes, others more
common cloth.

A boy with one leg missing hobbled forward on a

crutch and lobbed a stone at the cart in which Brak rode. The big barbarian stiffened, then realized the stone was not for him, but for the pack of bent, sullen-eyed little men crouched at his calves like stunted trees surrounding one that had grown straight.

The rock struck a man near Brak. He yelped, jumped up, began to clash his chain and screech at the watchers. His guttural speech was incomprehensible, but not his fury.

Instantly, three mounted officers converged on the cart, began to arc their whips onto the backs of the prisoners. The little men cringed and shrieked. The tip of one lash flicked Brak's face. With a deep-chested yell, he caught the whip's end and yanked, all his humiliation and self-disgust surfacing as he hauled the surprised officer out of his saddle.

The officer swore, scrabbling in the street on hands and knees. He struggled to free his short-sword. But his fellow officers repaid the barbarian's outburst for him. They pressed their mounts in closer to the cart, whose driver had brought it to an abrupt halt and leaped down out of range of Brak's flailing chains. In a moment, the stifling air resounded with the methodical cracking of whips.

Brak made abortive grabs at one or two. Futile. He closed his eyes and gripped the cart rail, trying not to shudder at each new welt laid atop the others crisscrossing his back. He would show them he was not like these dog-men whimpering at his feet. Above all, he would not cry out.

And somehow, he would escape the accursed chains dangling between his wrists like the weight of the world—

"Enough."

The voice Brak had heard before sliced through the

cracking of the whips, and another sound—the murmurings of the city people as they surged forward to stare at the strange, savage figure of the hulk-shouldered man who wore a lion-hide around his middle and his hair in a long yellow braid down his back.

Brak took another lash as the commander shouted again, "*Enough!*"

The whips laid off. Brak opened his eyes to stare into the thin, leather-cheeked face of the young and dusty veteran to whom he had been presented—beaten to his knees—after his capture.

The commander sidled his mount nearer, shook his head wearily:

"You will cast your life away, then? I told you there was a chance for you, outlander—"

"A chance to wear your chains," Brak said, and spat.

The spittle struck the commander's breastplate, barely dampening the yellow dust. The commander straightened in his saddle, fingers closing tighter around the butt of his whip.

Then, as if from weariness, or fear, or both, he slumped, letting the insult pass.

"You have the strength to keep fighting back but I haven't the strength to keep fighting you," the commander sighed. "We'll let someone else drub you into line. Just be thankful you're not like the rest of the filth we caught. Then you wouldn't even have the opportunity of manful service. You'd be put three floors underground, turning the grind-wheels for the rest of your life."

"I have no part of this fight between you and your lice-ridden enemies!" Brak snarled, gesturing at the glare-eyed little men crouched around him. His chains clinked. "I was a traveler harming no one. I was set upon—!"

The commander shrugged. "We've gone over it before. I'll not debate. While the foes of Lord Magnus yap around his heels—" cruelly, he kicked one of the little men through the uprights of the cart side, "—our fighting companies need every recruit." He held up his left arm. The bronze bracelet flashed. "I've explained your choice. Wear one of these—or a grave-cloth."

He cracked his whip, shouting to the head of the caravan:

"Move on, damn you! We've had fourteen days of this sun!"

"And so have we, and more!" a woman cried from the crowd. "If the Children of the Smoke can't bring the Worldbreaker down with spears, they'll bring him down with magic."

The commander glanced down at the crone. "No rain, then?"

"Does it look like we've been cleansed with rain? Refreshed?" someone else yelled. "The Children of the Smoke have bewitched the sky!"

"*Ah!*" The commander gestured angrily. "They have no wizards—"

"Then why does the plain of Magnus burn?" another voice jeered. "Why do the reservoirs go dry? Tell us that, captain!"

Others joined the clamor. Brak thought a riot might erupt on the spot. Nearly a hundred people started shoving and jostling the cart. But the soldiers drove them back with cuts of their whips and jabs of their short-swords.

Wearily, Brak reflected that it all had the quality of a nightmare. The heat haze blurred everything, including the snowy ramparts of the Mountains of Smoke far eastward. Those mountains supposedly guarded the approaches to the world's rim, and hid the homes of whatever gods ruled these so-called civilized lands.

During the sweltering ride across the plateau to the city, Brak had seen once-fertile fields that were parched, their crops stunted. He had listened to grumbling conversations of the soldiers in the heat of evening and learned that his fellow prisoners, all sharp teeth and matted hair and hateful eyes, belonged to a large nomadic tribe from the foothills of those distant mountains. Every few years, the tribe tried to gain more lands belonging to the lord who ruled the plateau. It had been Brak's misfortune to be captured and cast among the enemy while he was continuing his long journey southward to golden Khurdisan, where he was bound to seek his fortune—

Some inquisitive soul in the crowd pointed at Brak. "Who is he? Where's he from?"

"He says the wild steppes of the north," a soldier answered.

"Kill him—his presence is another bad omen!" the cry rang back.

"No worse than no rain for a three-month," snarled the soldier, riding on.

The cart driver resumed his place and the caravan again moved down the dusty avenue between the crystal images of the man-beast with the disc in its mouth. Brak mastered his fury as best he could, though the new and old whip-wounds, a webwork on his muscled back, made it difficult. So did the scowls of the soldiers, the taunts of the crowd—

The soldiers had slain his pony in the capture. Broken his broadsword. And chained him. Again he looked yearningly east, toward the cool blue spires rising above the rooftops and the city wall. The Mountains of Smoke, white-crowned. Beyond that barrier, he'd been told, lay down-sloping passes that led into the south—

But he would never see them unless he escaped his chains. Kept his temper—and his life.

He clenched his upper teeth on his lower lip, tasting his own briny sweat, and squinted into the hellish glare of noonday, and saw certain curious things he had not seen before.

2

Most of the citizens abroad in this obviously prosperous city looked wan, frightened. Brak noted another curiosity as the cart rolled past one of the crystal statues. The disc in the mouth of the beast-headed figure had a horizontal crack across its center. He thought this a flaw until he perceived that the discs of several more statues were similarly designed.

He signaled a soldier. The man rode in, but not too close. Brak asked:

"Why is the round thing in the statute's mouth shown broken?"

"Because that is the god-image of Lord Magnus, idiot. Once he held all of creation in his possession—to break or preserve as he saw fit. Now he's an old man. And his wizard, Ool, has no spells against whatever damned magic is being worked on this land."

Brak wiped his sweat-running neck. "You mean no rain."

The soldier nodded. "Without it, the reservoirs go empty. The crops perish. It's never happened before. Not in a hundred years, or a hundred again. This was a green and pleasant land before the parching of the skies."

Brak jerked a hand to indicate the bent, hairy heads around his knees. "And the sorcerers of your enemies worked the enchantment?"

"They have no sorcerers!" the soldier rasped back. "Nothing but old medicine women who birth babies."

Or they had no sorcerers until now, Brak thought. But he kept the retort to himself—because the more closely he looked, the more clearly he could discern the tiredness and terror lurking in the eyes of military man and civilian alike.

Once more he stared down at his chained wrists while the carts lurched nearer the jumble of yellow buildings at the avenue's end. He understood one more thing now. In addition to a tribe of enemies and a magical blight that was decimating city and countryside alike, the kingdom was also burdened with a lord who thought mightily of himself. Enough, anyway, to build endless replicas of a savage image of himself, and plant in its jaws a representation of the World—

That was what it looked like, eh? Brak had never seen it depicted before.

All the emerging circumstances only heightened his determination to escape. But he would take his time, be cunning and careful—

If he survived this particular ride. He didn't care for the expressions of the men and women lining the avenue. They continued to murmur and point at him. He was an omen, and not a favorable one—

Under those hostile glares, a total weariness descended on him suddenly. Maybe this *was* the end after all. Maybe he was fated to die chained and helpless in a country whose strutting lord appeared close to defeat. Worldbreaker indeed! In all the land he'd traversed thus far, Brak had never heard the name.

Another jarring memory reinforced his new pessimism. What about the toll he had exacted for his capture? How would they settle with him for that?

Head lowered, he was staring at the dusty paving-stones rolling by when the shadow of the horse of an attending soldier suddenly vanished.

Shrieks, oaths from both sides of the avenue—

Sudden chittering barks of pleasure from the little prisoners in the carts—

And Brak jerked his head up to gasp while horror shivered his sweaty spine.

In the center of the sky, the sun was disappearing.

A smear of gray widened, dulling the light. Tendrils of the strange cloud reached toward all points on the horizon at once—and what had been noon became stifling twilight almost instantly.

The cart horses reacted to the uproar, neighed, pawed the air. One driver jumped down and fled into an alley, not looking back—

There was no wind, no roar of storm. Only that awesome gray cloud spreading and spreading from the apex of heaven. The commotion along the boulevard turned to hysterical tumult.

Darkening, the cloud seemed to race past the city's walls toward the mountains and the wasted plain in the other direction. A young woman fell to her knees, rent the garments over her breasts, shrieked—

Brak whirled. On his left, he saw a chilling sight: the gigantic statue of the lord with creation in his mouth began to fill with some dark red substance, translucent, *like blood*—

And the redness was rising in every statue along the avenue.

Kicking his horse, the harried young commander raced up and down the line, lashing his whip to keep the crowd back:

"There's no danger. No danger! It's only another of the enemy's magical apparitions—"

But the crystal images kept darkening, like the sky. The red climbed from the waist toward the head. Noon turned to night. All around Brak, the Children of the Smoke still barked and chittered—though many of them now looked fully as frightened as the citizens of the city.

The whipping and the oaths of the soldiers proved futile. The maddened crowds began to surge forward again. Suddenly Brak realized their objective. Another accusing hand pointed his way:

"You brought a polluted pagan through the gates. *That's the reason for all this—!*"

"Stand back, he's a military prisoner!" the commander yelled, just before being buffetted from his horse. The mob surged around the cart, all hateful eyes, clawing hands. Brak felt the left wheel lift.

The Children of the Smoke began to gibber and slaver as the cart tilted. Brak knew what would happen. Tumbled into that mob, he'd be torn apart—

As the cart tilted even more sharply, he jumped wide, heedless of where he landed. Both feet came down on a fat man's shoulder. As Brak continued his fall, hands tore at him. But his weight crashed him through to the pavement.

For a moment he was ringed by dirty feet, the hems of dusty robes. Then he glanced up from hands and knees and saw a ring of almost insane faces. Old, young, male, female—and above them, a sky turned nearly to ebony—

Peripherally, he saw one of the crystal statues. By now it was red to the tips of the beast-head's ears.

"Sacrifice the pagan to drive out the darkness!" a man screamed, lunging.

Brak had no weapon save the length of chain hanging between his hands. He fought to his feet, pressed his wrists together, began to swing them in a circle, whipping them around, faster and faster. The chain opened a man's cheek. Blood gushed. A knife raked Brak's shoulder. He darted away, keeping the chain swinging.

Another man ventured too close. The end of the chain pulped one eyeball. The man dropped, howling—

And then, it seemed, the splendid boulevard of Lord Magnus the Worldbreaker became utter bedlam.

The mob poured at Brak from all directions, a blur of distorted faces, yapping mouths, glazed eyes that promised murder. So this was to be the end, was it? Dying a victim of some accursed magic in which he had no hand, but for which he was being blamed and punished—

The crystal statues had filled completely, scarlet from pedestal to snout-tip. Even the cracked discs of creation were suffused with the evil-looking red. The arch of heaven was dark gray from end to end. Brak abandoned all his former resolve to preserve his life so that he might escape. Now he only wanted to sell his life expensively. If these deranged fools would kill him, they would not do so easily—

Whir and *crack,* the chain whirled. A forearm snapped; a scalp dripped gore. Brak kicked, snarled, spat, worked the chain until he could barely see, so thick was the sweat clogging on his eyelids. Although the sky had blackened, the air had not cooled. He fought in some dim, steaming inferno—

A hand grabbed his ankle. He stamped down, hard. His attacker shrieked, held up ruined, boneless fingers. Whir and *crack,* the chain sliced the air—and suddenly his tormenters began to retreat from his savage figure: from the whip of his long yellow braid; from the flying fur-puff at the end of the lion's tail at his waist; from that brain-spattered chain swinging, *scything*—

A way opened. He lunged through full speed, crashing into one of the statue pedestals. Behind him, the crowd bayed its anger. The crowd was growing larger as more and more citizens poured in from intersecting avenues. In a moment, backed against the pedestal, Brak was surrounded.

He whirled, leaped high, started to clamber upward, his thighs bloody from the nail-marks of hands that clawed him. He gained the top of the pedestal, teetered there, feeling the cool of the crystal against his back. To gain momentum for flailing the chain down at the enraged faces and the hands straining to reach him, he whipped the iron links back over his left shoulder—

The chain smashed against the statue. A prolonged glassy crackling modulated into a sudden loud thunderclap. Light smote Brak's eyes, blinding.

Noon light—

The illusion-cloud in the heavens was gone. Below him, terrorized people dropped to their knees, shielded their eyes—

The chain clinked down across Brak's shoulder. Panting, he curled his toes around the pedestal's edge and squinted across the avenue. There, another statue of Lord

Magnus the Worldbreaker was crystal-bright, empty of scarlet.

So was every similar image along the avenue.

"You cursed fools—!" Flaying about with his whip, the commander, on horseback again, rode through the mob. "We tried to tell you it was only a wizard's illusion!"

"From where?" someone screamed.

"From the enemy who will conquer!" another cried.

"And *he* dispelled it," the commander said, reining up just below an exhausted Brak leaning against the image. The commander had a puzzling, almost sad expression on his face. "The chain's blow did it—"

The officer gestured with his whip. Brak craned his buzzing head around, saw a crystalline webbing of cracks running through the bent left knee of the seated figure. Again he felt the clutch of inexplicable dread. The darkness and the rising red had indeed been potent mindspells. No scarlet ran out from the statue. It was solid.

The commander's smile was feeble. "The end of a short and glorious career," he said. "Now you must be taken to Lord Magnus himself. For the one crime of killing three of my men when you were captured—and the greater crime of profaning an image of the lord."

"*Profaning*—!" Brak screamed, gripping the statute to keep from falling. "The chain broke the statue and the spell and that's an *offense*?"

"Regrettably so. I have no choice but to present you to Lord Magnus for sentence of execution."

In the hot noon silence, while the kneeling, cringing throng peered at Brak through fingers or across the uplifted sleeves of robes, the commander looked sick at heart. For a moment his eyes locked with Brak's, as if begging understanding. Brak was too full of rage. He twisted his head around and spat on the webwork of the smashed crystal. He was done; he knew it. The defilement of the idol brought pleasure.

With another, somehow-sad gesture, the commander raised his whip to signal his stunned men forming up on the rim of the terrorized mob. He pointed to Brak and said:

"Drag him down."

3

In the largest of the immense buildings he'd glimpsed from afar, Brak the barbarian was conducted into an echoing hall and thrust to his knees by the tense commander. The vast, high-windowed chamber was an inferno of early afternoon shadows. The air was oppressive. Brak had great difficulty breathing.

On the journey to the great complex of yellow stone, Brak had several times entertained the idea of trying to break free. But each time, he'd decided to wait. Partly out of self-interest; partly from a sort of morbid curiosity. Before his life was taken away, he wanted to set eyes on this lord who styled himself Worldbreaker.

And there was always a faint, formless hope that if he were clever enough—though in what way, he couldn't yet say—he might save himself. The prospect made it seem sensible for him to check his impulse to fight and run.

"You may raise your head to the lord," whispered the decidedly nervous commander who stood next to the kneeling barbarian. Brak obeyed.

All he saw at first was a step. Then another; and eight more, each revealed as his gaze traveled up to a throne that had once been splendid, but was now all green-tinged bronze.

The lower portion of the throne was a massive chair. Its high, solid back rose upward and jutted out over the throne-seat to form the gigantic head and snout of the lord's image, complete with cracked disc in its jaws. In the shelter of this canopy sat the Worldbreaker.

A small, thick-chested man. So short his plain, worn soldier's boots barely touched the floor. He wore a military kilt and the familiar bronze bracelet of the army on his left wrist. He looked more like a member of the foot troops than he did a king.

He had a squarish, strong-featured face, much lined. Pure white hair hung to his shoulders. Prepared to be contemptuous, Brak found it hard somehow. The ruler did not adorn himself ostentatiously, though perhaps only because of the heat, which was causing the three or four dozen court officials and military men surrounding the throne's base to shift from foot to foot, mop their sweated cheeks with kerchiefs and sigh frequently.

Two things about Lord Magnus the Worldbreaker impressed Brak deeply—and alarmed him as well. One was the man's grave, pitiless stare. The other was his body. Calves and thighs, forearms and shoulders and trunk were a war-map of the past. Mountain ranges and valleys of scar tissue created a whole geography of battle on the flesh of the ruler. He was, Brak sensed, no commander who had sent his armies ahead to fight. He had led them.

"You may address the lord," said a man who glided into sight from the gloom at one side of the great throne.

"Thanks be to you, oh sexless one," returned the commander, genuflecting. Brak peered at this new personage who had taken a place at the lord's right hand.

The newcomer was a tall, heavily robed man of middle years. He looked overweight. He had an oval, curiously hairless head, opaque eyes, flesh as white as the belly of a new-caught fish. Under the man's basilisk stare, Brak shivered.

The commander spoke to the ruler on the throne:

"With great Ool's leave given, Lord Magnus, I beg to report a most unfortunate occurrence on the avenue—"

Ool, Brak thought. *So this gelded creature is the ruler's wizard?* An odd specimen indeed. While the others in the chamber were obviously suffering from the heat, Ool's pasty white jowls and ivory forehead remained dry. His hands were completely hidden within the voluminous linen of his crossed sleeves.

Lord Magnus gave a tired nod:

"I saw, Captain Xeraph. From the watch-roof I saw the dark heavens and the red-running idols. A footman brought word of the desecration of one of them." The little man's gaze hardened, raking Brak up and down. "This is the pagan slave who worked the damage?"

Suddenly Brak was on his feet. "No, lord. I'm no man's slave. I was set on by your human carrion, caught and trussed up with these—" He rattled his iron chainlinks.

Ool whispered, "Be silent, barbarian, or you will be slain where you stand."

"I'll be damned before I'll be silent!" Brak yelled.

The hairless wizard inclined his pale head. Three spearmen started clattering down the throne steps, weapons pointed at Brak's chest. The barbarian braced for the attack.

"*Hold.*"

The single, powerful syllable from Lord Magnus checked the spearmen's descent. They swung, looked upward for further instructions. Ool nodded acquiescence, but unhappily; he nibbled at his underlip and treated Brak to a baleful glare.

"You have a ready tongue for a captive," said Lord Magnus in a toneless voice that might have been threatening, or might not. Brak could not tell; nor read that old, scarred countenance. "And you have no knowledge, evidently, that my image is sacred?"

"But shattering it shattered the spell," Brak retorted, glancing pointedly at the pasty-jowled Ool. The man remained impassive. Brak finished, "No one else seemed able to do that."

"Aye, the darkness rolled back," Magnus agreed. "The darkness which cannot be—" his mouth wrenched, a quick, sour imitation of a smile, "—since our mortal enemies have no enchanters to work such spells. None at all! Therefore we cannot be plagued. What happened is impossible—*everything* is impossible!" he shouted, slamming a hornhard palm on the throne's curved arm.

At that moment Brak sensed just how much rage must be seething under that gnarled old exterior. It was a rage like his own. Although Brak did not care for this lord and never would, he did not precisely hate him, either. It was a puzzling circumstance he did not fully understand.

Lord Magnus went on, "The Children cannot work wizardries against us, therefore all I see is a deception. The water-channels dry and silted—a deception. The people maddened and near to revolt—deception. The noon heavens like midnight—and a chain that breaks the illusion—no, none of it's real. Perhaps not even you, eh, outlander?"

Brak rattled his chains. "Take these off and I'll show you my hands are real. You'll see how real when they close on the throats of your jackals."

The commander, Captain Xeraph, gulped audibly. Gasps and oaths rippled through the crowd clustered near the throne. Swords snicked out of scabbards. Abruptly, Lord Magnus laughed.

The sound was quick, harsh—and stunned everyone, including the big barbarian. With effort, he stared the ruler down. Neither man blinked.

"You seem determined to die quickly," Lord Magnus said.

"It appears I have no choice in the matter, lord." Mocking: "I violated your holy image—"

"And," put in the hairless Ool, his calm tone belying the animosity Brak saw in his eyes, "if our intelligence may be trusted, slew three of Captain Xeraph's best when they took you prisoner."

"Aye," Brak nodded. "Because they had no reason to seize me."

"The fact that you crossed my boundary-marker is reason enough," Lord Magnus advised.

"To you, lord. To a traveler bound to Khurdisan—no."

Magnus lifted one scar-crusted hand, scratched his sweaty chin where a beard stubble already showed white after the day's razoring. "Cease your glowering and grimacing, kindly! Don't you wonder why you're not dead by now? You apparently fail to recognize a chance to survive when it's presented to you."

In the little man's dark eyes, Brak saw nothing he

could comprehend. A plot was weaving. But what kind of plot, he could not tell. Still, something in him seized at the half-offered promise. He felt hope for the first time.

The ghoul-white face of Ool the sexless looked stark. *Careful,* Brak thought. *Do not appear over-eager—*

He licked his sweaty lips, said:

"I do not understand the lord's meaning, that's true. But I understand little or nothing of what has befallen me. I tell you again—there was no reason for me to be imprisoned. Or brought to your city in bondage."

"You deny that a man can be slain for killing three soldiers of a land through which he travels?" Magnus asked.

"I was attacked!"

"You deny a man can be punished for desecrating the sacred law of such a land?"

"I never broke your image on purpose. Only accidentally, while trying to save myself from the mob."

"And you broke the darkness too," Magnus mused. Suddenly a finger stabbed out, pointing down. Brak saw that the finger was a toughened stub at the end; lopped off at the first knuckle long ago.

"What is your name, outlander? Where did you journey from? Most important—how did you come by the power that broke the darkness?"

The big barbarian answered, "Lord, I'm called Brak. My home was once the northern steppes. My people cast me out for mocking their gods—"

"Ah, you make a habit of that!" said Magnus, the corners of his mouth twisting again.

"When the rules of such gods defy a man's own good sense, yes. I am bound south for Khurdisan—or I was," he added with a smoldering glance at the uncomfortable Captain Xeraph. "As to why and how I was able to rend the darkness in the sky—" *Careful!* He spaced the next words with deliberate slowness. "—I ask leave not to say."

Ool chuckled, a dry, reedy sound. "In other words, you confirm that you have no real powers."

Staring fiercely at the wizard, Brak replied, "I neither confirm it nor deny it, magician. After I am dead you may make up your own mind."

Again Magnus laughed. He studied Brak closely, said at last:

"But perhaps—as I hinted—there is another way. For the first time, I am besieged by forces against which my host and my chariots will not avail. You are a bold man, barbarian. Strong-looking to boot. You *seem* to have thaumaturgic skills—whether by training or by accident, you don't care to reveal. Very well—"

Magnus stood. Brak realized just how short the old man really was. But his ridged shoulders and scar-marked belly looked tough as iron.

"You cannot guess the extremes to which we have gone to overcome this plague of dryness. A plague that can destroy this kingdom as the pitiful clubs and daggers of the Children of the Smoke never could before. So despite your crimes, my rude friend—and because you staved off carnage in the streets—I will strike you a bargain."

Cold and shrewd, the eyes of the Worldbreaker pierced down from the sweaty gloom around the throne.

"You will not die. You will not wear chains—"

Brak's heart almost burst at the sudden, unexpected reprieve; then he heard the jarring conclusion:

"If you can bring down the rain."

"Bring down the—?"

He wanted to laugh. He couldn't. He was too appalled by the sudden snapping of the trap.

"Open the heavens!" Magnus exclaimed, his voice genuinely powerful now. "Darken the skies—but this time, so they flood the land with downpour. Unbind the spell of the Children of the Smoke—whatever it is, and from wherever it comes—and you'll neither die nor wear chains again. That is my concession and my promise, Brak barbarian. Whether you have true or only chance powers, we shall now discover, I warn you, none has succeeded so far in undoing the plague spell. My own wizard is helpless—" A lifted hand made Ool bristle; more softly, Magnus went on, "Though not through any lack of daily effort and industry, I must hasten to add. Now—"

He directed his gaze at the astounded young commander.

"While we test the barbarian, Captain Xeraph, you shall be his guardian and constant companion. Let him not out of your sight for a moment, or your own life is forfeit."

The commander went white. Brak started to protest that he had been lured into a hopeless snare, but Magnus gestured:

"I have already given you a great concession. Keep silent and ask for nothing more."

He turned his back, starting to leave by circling the throne. After a quick glance down the stairs at Brak, the eunuch Ool plucked his lord's forearm. Annoyed, Magnus stopped.

Ool leaned in, whispered. Magnus pondered. Then he wheeled around, said to Brak:

"One further condition—and a wise one, I think.

You have two days and two nights to make it rain, no more."

Again Brak sensed the old fighter's desperation; glimpsed it in his eyes just before the Worldbreaker vanished behind the throne, Ool gliding after him, a white specter—

Leaving Brak to reflect dismally that he would have been better off to have been killed outright.

4

"Balls of the gods, will you pick a piece and move it?" shouted Captain Xeraph, jumping up. He stalked through the arch to the little balcony overlooking the city and, a floor below, a courtyard shared by four barracks buildings.

Perched on a stool much too small for his bulk, Brak looked with bleary eyes at the out-of-humor officer pacing back and forth just beyond the arch. Xeraph was stripped down to his kilt. Both occupants of the tiny officer's apartment in the yellow stone complex were sticky with perspiration, even though the sun had simmered out of sight hours ago. But another light limned the officer's profile as he leaned on the balcony rail and gazed at the night city.

The rooftops were outlined by red glares from half a dozen locations. The roaring of mobs and the crashes of mass destruction carried through the still air. Xeraph's right hand strayed absently to the bracelet on his left wrist as he stared at the fires with something akin to longing.

The captain's apartment consisted of two narrow rooms. Both rooms were sparsely furnished. But the addition of a pallet for Xeraph's semiprisoner badly cramped the main room. The master of the quarters swung suddenly, glaring—another challenge for Brak to get on with his move.

The huge yellow-haired man picked up the tail of his lion-clout, used it to wipe sweat from his nose, then draped it over one muscled thigh so it hung between his legs. He reached down for the wine jar beside his bare feet.

He tilted the jug, drank deeply of the dry red wine, heedless of the way it dripped down his chin onto his massive chest. Putting the jar aside again, he peered fuzzily at the playing board set on a low block of stone.

The board featured a pattern of squares in two colors. On the squares sat oddly-carved wood pieces of different designs. Half the pieces were lacquered dark green. The others had been left unfinished.

For two hours, Captain Xeraph had been trying to teach him the confusing game. Eating little and drinking much after the disastrous interview with Magnus earlier in the day, Brak had no head for it. Even sober, he had decided, he probably couldn't comprehend it.

But Xeraph was so obviously upset by his enforced confinement with a prisoner that Brak made one more effort. He picked up one of his pieces, the one named— let's see, could he remember?—the fortress.

Xeraph watched him slide the piece to the adjoining square. With a curse, the captain stormed back into the room, snatched up the piece and shook it in Brak's face:

"This is the wizard, you idiot! The wizard cannot move in that pattern. I must have explained it ten times!"

Brak's temper let go. Growling, he lifted a corner of

the playing board. Several pieces fell off. With a sweep of his thick arm, he scattered the rest, then flung the board on the floor.

"Take your playthings and throw 'em in the pit!" Brak shouted, his eyes ugly. The hateful chains clinked between his wrists.

For a moment he thought Captain Xeraph would grab his short-sword from the scabbard hanging on a wall peg. Xeraph's neck muscles bunched. But he managed control. He sighed a long, disgusted sigh:

"I shouldn't expect some unlettered foreigner to master a game played by civilized gentlemen. But gods! I'm already sick of tending you—!"

"I didn't ask to be penned up here!" Brak screamed back, and again it seemed as if the two would go for each other's throat. Then, sighing again, Xeraph slumped, as if the heat, the effort of argumentation, were too much.

He sprawled on Brak's pallet while the latter stood glowering and fingering the chain.

"Well, one night's almost done," Xeraph said in a gloomy tone. "One more, and two days, and Magnus will take your head." His eyes sought Brak's. He almost sounded sorrowful: "You have no spells to bring rain, do you?"

Brak's answer was a terse, "Of course not. Why the darkness lifted when I smashed the idol, I don't know. Your lord's a desperate man—he admitted it himself. I have seen men in similar predicaments grow rash and foolish. That's what happened when your lord offered me that ridiculous bargain for my life."

Xeraph clucked his tongue. "The lord's too old— that's what they're all saying. Believe me, Magnus has no lack of courage—"

"His scars prove that."

"—but for once, the odds are too overwhelming. He can't cope with the magic with which the Children have cursed us."

"Nor, apparently, can his own wizard, despite those efforts to which Magnus referred. How does the eunuch try to bring down rain and end the drought?"

The officer shrugged. "To watch Ool do whatever he does—mix potions, wail at the sky—is forbidden to all but a few young boys who attend him. They are specially selected and, I might add, perverted." Xeraph's mouth quirked in distaste. "Every day, Ool rides out in his chariot, that much I know. He goes toward the channel that once brought sweet rainwater from the lower slopes of the Mountains of Smoke." Xeraph gestured eastward. "Somewhere out there, Ool tries to undo the curse—in secret." The captain concluded sarcastically, "Like to discover some of his methods, would you?"

"They sound worthless. On the other hand, since I have no powers of my own, I've thought of the idea. I don't intend to spend the rest of the allotted time pacing this room and drinking myself into oblivion."

That amused Xeraph. "Oh, you think you can improve upon Ool's performance, do you? Acquire magical skills like that?" He snapped his fingers.

Brak scowled. "I doubt it. But there must be an answer somewhere. And if it lies in magic, what better place to begin the search than with Ool?"

"You don't give up easily," Xeraph said, not without admiration. Brak simply stared at the litter of game pieces scattered around his thoroughly dirty feet. Xeraph harrumphed. "Brak, there is no answer! Except this. The rain won't come. And you'll die. Then the rest of us. This time—" Restless, he rose and wandered back to the balcony. "—This time I think the Worldbreaker himself will be broken. And all of his kingdom in the bargain."

Suddenly Xeraph's voice grew louder: "They're already going mad! Drinking, rioting, setting fires—"

"And you feel you should be out there helping to quell it."

Xeraph spun. "Yes! That duty, I understand. This—" His gesture swept the lamplit chamber resentfully. "It's fool's work."

Speaking out of genuine feeling, Brak said, "Captain, I am sorry the lot fell to you."

"No apologies," Xeraph cut him off. "I obey orders. It's a bad twist of fate's twine, that's all. We've had nothing else for months—why should I expect a change?"

Once more the young officer leaned on the railing, staring in dismay at the sullen scarlet silhouettes of the city's rooftops. His eyes picked up red reflections, simmered with frustration. Hopelessness.

Brak resumed his place on the stool. He picked up a wooden piece which, if his wine-buzzing head served him, represented a male ruler. He asked:

"Has Lord Magnus no trusted advisers to help point the way out of this difficult situation? No generals—?"

"He is the general," Xeraph returned. "He is the government, the chief judge—everything. Before, his shoulders have always been strong enough, his mind quick enough—"

The statement somehow fitted with Brak's appraisal of the tough little warrior. The barbarian studied the piece in his sweat-glistening palm a moment longer.

"The lord hasn't even a wife to counsel him?" he wanted to know.

"He did, many years ago—why go into all this?" Xeraph said irritably.

"I don't know," Brak admitted. "Except that I don't want to be killed."

Xeraph managed an exhausted smile. "That, at least, is something we have in common."

"We were talking of Magnus. He has no sons—?"

Xeraph shook his head. "No issue at all." Briefly, then, he narrated the story of Magnus's consort, a queen whose name he could not even recall because she had died forty years earlier, well before Xeraph himself had been born. But legend said the lord's wife had been exceedingly lovely and desirable.

Lord Magnus had been away on a campaign to harry the Children of the Smoke, who were making one of their abortive advances into his territory. A soldier in the small detachment left behind to garrison the city— "Name unknown, identity unknown," Xeraph commented—entered the apartment of the lord's wife by stealth one night. Presumably drunk, he raped her.

"The lady cried out and the terrified fool cut her throat. There was a great melee in the darkness. The soldier was pursued. Another captain who died only a six-month ago was on duty in the palace at the time, and swore he caught the offender for a moment. Claimed he ran him through with a spear. But the man ultimately escaped in the confusion—to perish of his wound in some back alley, presumably. His corpse was never found. And as I say, his name remains unknown to this day. Magnus was so exercised with grief, he could never take another woman to his side, except for serving girls for single nights of pleasure. Even that stopped five or six years ago," Xeraph finished unhappily.

Brak set the lord-piece aside in favor of the piece he had moved wrongly before: the wizard.

"And this court magician—do you think he serves the Worldbreaker well?"

Xeraph shrugged. "If not well, then faithfully and diligently, at least. You heard the lord say as much. Ool was a wandering shaman, I'm told. He came to court a long time ago, and stayed. Until now, he's always seemed proficient in minor spells and holy rituals. But this particular curse has proved too large for his powers—as it has for the lord's. And so we'll be destroyed—"

"Unless it rains."

Captain Xeraph glanced away.

Brak walked to the balcony, looking out into the flame-shot dark. Thinking aloud, he said, "Perhaps I would indeed do well to observe this Ool at work. It's possible I might find inspiration! Discover powers I never knew I had—"

At first Xeraph's expression showed surprise. This was quickly replaced by new annoyance:

"I told you, Brak—observance of the wizard's private mysteries is forbidden. Just as entering his quarters is forbidden."

Brak shook his head. The long yellow braid bobbed gently against his lash-marked back. "When my life is forfeit, nothing's forbidden."

Again Xeraph couldn't contain a half-admiring smile: "Gods, what a determined lout you are. In better times, Lord Magnus could use a hundred like you in his fighting companies."

"I mean to be free of these chains, captain, not serve your lord or any other."

"What about the lord who takes life?" Xeraph

retorted. "It's him you'll be serving at sunset the day after tomorrow! Look—why risk more trouble with Ool? You've admitted you have no arcane talents—"

"But I repeat, I won't sit and wait to be executed. If you can think of a better idea than observing the wizard, tell me and I'll do it."

"We'll do it," Xeraph corrected. "Remember, if I lose sight of you—" Matter-of-factly, he stroked an index finger across his sweat-blackened throat. In the distance, another huge crash rent the night. A column of flame and sparks shot heavenward. Somewhere a mob bayed like a beast.

Finally, Brak gave a crisp nod. "Well, then—tomorrow, when I'm rested—and sober—I mean to find this water channel where master Ool tries his futile spells. You can either let me blunder there alone, or you can go with me and fulfill the lord's charge that you keep watch on me."

"You could never pass the city gates without me."

"Don't be too sure, captain."

Slowly Xeraph wiped his palms down his lean thighs. He gave Brak a steady look. Not defying him. Testing:

"But what if I say no to your excursion, my friend?"

"I will go anyway."

"I might stop you."

"You might try," Brak replied softly.

In truth, he felt that the plan was exactly like all other plans afloat in the capital of Magnus the Worldbreaker: worthless. But he had no other alternative in mind.

He felt like an animal hunted by mounted men and dogs. With certain doom at his heels, he was still unwilling to stop and await death. He preferred motion—even though it was empty of solid hope or solid purpose. At least doing something might temporarily dispel the morbid thoughts of his future—besides, perhaps the scheme wasn't so foolish after all.

The wizard Ool presented curious contradictions. If he had entrenched himself at the court with his magical proficiency in the past, why had his talents suddenly proved wanting? Having experienced firsthand the abilities of both lesser and greater wizards, Brak could understand how Ool might not be competent to overcome the drought spell. Yet it was still odd that none around Lord Magnus raised the question of why Ool failed. They merely accepted it.

Perhaps they were too occupied with the tangible, pressing dangers of an advancing enemy and a populace in near-revolt. Perhaps the outside viewpoint of a stranger was required to see past distractions to simple, essential questions—

Such was the puzzle of Ool. Brak's hard, sweating face confirmed his resolve concerning the matter.

All at once, Captain Xeraph bowed to that, and laughed:

"Damn you for an insolent rogue, Brak—all right, we'll go. At sunrise." He kicked at the fallen playpieces and added, with a smile that bore no malice, "It can't be any more useless than trying to teach a thick-skulled foreigner this noble game."

Brak smiled a bleak smile in return and reached for the wine jar. Out in the city, more burning buildings began to fall, crashing—

5

The sun ate cruelly at Brak's body, promising painful burns by nightfall. With Captain Xeraph, he was crouched at the foot of a ridge some distance east of the city. The wall, some rooftops and columns of smoke could still be seen through clouds of dust blowing across empty, desiccated fields.

Like Brak, Captain Xeraph had cast aside the coarse cowled cloak each had worn to slip through the city gates shortly after dawn. Xeraph's presence had permitted them to leave with only a brief questioning. The discarded cloaks lay under a stone now, snapping and fluttering at their feet.

Xeraph wore a plain artisan's kilt. Except for his short-sword and the bronze bracelet which could not be removed, there was nothing to mark him as a military man.

He looked fearful as Brak peered toward the jumbled boulders along the ridge-top. Both men could clearly hear the strange sounds coming from the far side.

Brak knew why Xeraph was upset. What they were about to do was forbidden. Yet as Brak listened, the sounds seemed more odd than alarming; a mystery more than a menace.

He heard the creak of wheels, the rattle of hoofs. Now louder, then fading—exactly like the furious thudding of beaten drumheads. A voice chanted an incomprehensible singsong.

"I am going up to look, captain," Brak said.

Xeraph swallowed. "Very well, we'll—" Abruptly: "No, I'll stay here."

He shoved the point of his sword against Brak's throat. The barbarian edged away quickly but carefully. Xeraph's trembling hand might cause an accident.

"Don't get out of sight, understand?"

Xeraph darted a nervous glance around the sere

horizon. Further east stood a farmstead, abandoned in the blowing dust. Hoofs and wheels, drums and chanting grew louder again. Brak gave a tight nod, turned and began to clamber up the hillside.

He moved cautiously, with the craft of the steppe-born hunter. Twice he stopped still and cursed, as the damnable chains between his wrists clinked too loudly.

He turned once to see Captain Xeraph staring up at him with an absolutely terrified expression. Brak hardened his heart and continued his climb. Whatever lay on the other side of the ridge was not sacred to him. And in his travels toward Khurdisan's golden crescent in the far south, he had encountered many marvels and enchantments. He did not precisely fear the sight of an inept wizard.

At length he worked himself between two boulders, his lips already dry and cracked from the heat. He looked out and down—

And blinked in astonishment.

As Xeraph had said, an immense, stone-lined channel lay below. It stretched east toward the mountains, west toward the city. The channel was filled with blowing dust.

Along a track on the far side, an imposing gold-chased chariot drawn by four white horses raced at furious speed. Brak counted five people in the oversized car, in addition to the driver.

Gripping the car's front rail, his voluminous robes flying behind him, stood Ool the magician, head thrown back. It was Ool uttering that weird, ululating chant.

Behind him, swaying and knocking against one another, was a quartet of boys with pudgy pink legs, ringleted hair, soft hands and generally feminine appearance. One had a pair of drums suspended on a strap around his neck. Another pounded the skin drumhead with padded beaters. A third picked up lengths of wood from the floor of the car and set them afire with a torch. The fourth threw the fresh-lit firebrands out of the car while Ool continued to chant.

Brak swore a foul oath. The whole expedition had been wasted. He had seen a similar ceremony in his youth in the wild lands of the north—and if this was all Ool could muster to open the heavens and relieve the drought, he was a poor wizard indeed.

The chariot continued to race along beside the channel, traveling a short way eastward before wheeling back again. Ool kept up his singsong chant. The drums pounded. The torches arched out of the car every which way—

Despairing, Brak watched only a few moments longer. Just as the chariot completed its course away on his left and turned back toward his vantage point, he prepared to rejoin Xeraph. The chariot swept along beside the channel—and a gust of wind caught the magician's gown, flattened his sleeves back against his forearms. Suddenly Brak's belly flip-flopped. He stared through the sweat running off his eyebrows. Stared and stared as the chariot raced nearer, boiling dust out behind—

Firebrands scattered sparks. The drums *thud-thudded*. Brak squinted against the sun-glare, watching Ool's hands gripping the rail of the car—

As the chariot swept past, a thin suspicion became an alarming possibility.

The chariot thundered on, the drum-throbs and hoof-rattles and wheel-creaks diminishing again. Brak scrambled up, avoiding Captain Xeraph's anxious gaze from the bottom of the ridge.

What should he do? Go instantly to Lord Magnus?

No, he'd never be believed. He was an outlander with no status except the useless one of prisoner. Automatically, he would be counted a liar.

And if Ool heard of an accusation, he would probably move against the barbarian in some secret way. Have him slain before the time limit expired—

Yet Brak knew he had to act. Gazing into the dusty sunlight, he let his mind cast up images of the magician in the chariot. White cheeks. Jowls jiggling, soft and flabby. And the hands; the momentarily bared hands and forearms—those Brak saw most vividly of all.

Not a little frightened, he clambered down. Xeraph clutched his arm:

"What did you see?"

"Trumpery," Brak said with a curt wave, wanting no hint of his suspicion to show on his face. "Magic such as the pathetic shamans of my own land practiced in hopes of changing the weather—"

Briefly he described the sights he'd observed— except for Ool's revealed hands.

Captain Xeraph was baffled by the details Brak reported. He asked for further explanation.

"They beat drums and throw torches helter-skelter to simulate thunder and lightning. Along with that, Ool howls some spell or other. The idea is to summon storms by imitating them. I've never seen it work before and I venture it won't work now."

Because, whispered a cold little serpent voice in his mind, *it is not meant to work.*

"Captain Xeraph," he said, "we must immediately—"

He stopped. Would this plain soldier who dealt in

simple, fundamental concepts such as marching formations and use of weapons understand what he did not fully understand himself? Certainly he could not prove so much as one jot of his suspicion—yet. An accusation now, even presented to one such as Xeraph who, Brak felt, half-trusted him, would only bring ridicule.

Brow furrowed, Xeraph stared at him. "Must what, outlander? Finish what you started to say."

At last Brak knew what he must do. *Tonight.* Tonight would provide the only hours of darkness left.

But as he realized what he had to do—and do alone—he felt dismayed. If he took the risk, followed out the sketchy plan already in mind, he might put Captain Xeraph's life in jeopardy. And while he would never be fond of any captor, Xeraph was at least more agreeable than most.

Still, his own life was in jeopardy too. That made the difference.

"We must immediately return to the city," Brak concluded, a hasty lie. He felt the shame of a betrayer, the dread of the night's work waiting. "I saw nothing but a eunuch doing child's magic."

Xeraph looked relieved. They crept away from the ridge. The drumming and chanting and the chariot-clatter faded.

Cloaked again, they trudged west in the heat. Each was silent, but for different reasons.

6

A night and a day. Like some drunken balladeer's refrain, the words kept coming to Brak's thoughts as he lay tensely on his pallet, counting time. *A night and a day—*

Outside, steamy darkness; his final night was perhaps half gone already. On the morrow, he would have no more chance. The light of the simmering sky would make his desperate gamble impossible. *A night and a day to make it rain—*

No, he amended in the grim silence of his thoughts, *a night—this night—to discover why it does* not *rain.*

At last, the stertorous breathing of Captain Xeraph subsided in the adjoining room. Brak rolled over, raised himself on an elbow, then bunched his legs beneath him.

Slowly he rose to a standing position. His body was already slicked with perspiration. The fall of the sun had brought no relief, no coolness. Through the arch that led to the apartment's regular bedchamber, the sounds of Xeraph thrashing came again.

As he stole barefoot toward the peg where Xeraph's sword-scabbard hung, Brak tried to remember the position of the hilt—about half way up the wall, wasn't it? He kept moving, cautiously—

Another pace.

Another.

Three more to go.

Then two.

He froze.

Soldiers were crossing the courtyard below the balcony. Three or four of them, he couldn't be certain. They were singing an obscene barracks ditty.

At last a heavy door closed. Brak moved again, wondering that the men of Lord Magnus had the heart to sing while the red of last night's fires still flickered throughout one quarter of the sky. A vast tenement section had been set ablaze, Xeraph had reported after the evening meal. The flaming devastation had yet to be contained—

Well, perhaps the soldiers of Magnus drank heaviest and sang loudest when they were powerless against certain defeat.

He listened. The courtyard was silent.

He lifted his hand, groping for the hilt of the short-sword. But somehow, while his attention had been distracted by the noises below, he had lost his precise sense of distances in the dark. Reaching out, he felt the back of his right hand collide suddenly with the hilt while his fingers closed on empty air. The scabbard knocked the wall. Loudly—

For a moment he held absolutely still, breath sucked in. But the damage was done. Wakened by the noisy thump against the intervening wall, Xeraph muttered a questioning monosyllable.

Brak didn't debate with himself for long. There would be no arguing with Xeraph. The captain would forbid what he'd planned. He jerked the short-sword from the scabbard, heedless of the racket of his chain. He pivoted and plunged toward the balcony.

Behind him he heard Xeraph thrash, call out. Then Brak caught the *slap-slap* of running feet.

One thick, scarred leg hooked over the low balcony wall as Xeraph rushed from the darkened apartment. Both hands on the hilt, Brak whipped up the short-sword, turning the blade just so and hammering it down in what he hoped would be a felling but not wounding blow.

Again he cursed his bad luck. He could tell the blow was mis-aimed. Xeraph was moving too fast, cursing him as a damned trickster—

The sword-flat thwacked and slid away. Captain

Xeraph let out a loud, hurt cry as he crumpled.

Brak listened again, hoping that the doorkeeper on the floor below was drowsing in his booth. But again luck eluded him. The distant rapping of boots signaled the doorkeeper climbing the inner stairs to investigate the cry.

Brak faced a terrible decision. Remain—and fail. Or go on, and leave Xeraph to be discovered. Minus his prisoner. The barbarian knew what Xeraph's punishment would be—

In the hot darkness, Brak's face hardened. He would try to complete his night errand swiftly. Come back to Xeraph in time.

But if he failed—

Well, better not to think of that.

Xeraph was a decent, kindly jailer. But something deeper and darker within the huge barbarian swept that consideration aside. Something deeper, darker— and as heavy as the chains between his wrists.

The doorkeeper hammered outside Xeraph's apartment. A querulous voice inquired whether something was amiss. Xeraph, a fallen lump, stirred. Groaned. Brak's face was pitiless, a mask for his regret as he swung his other leg over and dropped toward the courtyard.

He would save Xeraph if he could. But above all, he would not live in chains.

7

Infuriated by the series of unlucky circumstances that had so far wrecked all but the basic thrust of his plan, Brak landed in a jarring crouch. He did his best to muffle the clinking links against his naked belly, at the same time maneuvering to keep from being cut by the sword.

He heard the doorkeeper knocking more insistently now. He bolted for the far side of the quadrangle, and a passage that would lead to a second, larger yard in the palace complex.

The knocking and shouting continued. Brak dodged into the passage just as a lamp was lit in another officer's apartment. The whole area would be awake soon. Damn and damn again!

Racing down the passage, he checked where the wall ended. He flattened his naked back against stone that still radiated heat. Behind him, more lamps bobbed. Shouts of genuine alarm were being raised.

He forced his concentration ahead. Saw a tired, limping soldier crossing the dark square on guard duty. The man walked with infernal slowness. Would he hear the commotion—?

Brak's breath hissed in and out of his lungs, a low, bestial sound. His eyes picked up some of the scarlet glare in the cloudless sky. Like a preying animal, he watched and counted time's destructive passage. If the soldier reacted to the distant noise from the officer's quarters— or if he about-faced to recross the square instead of proceeding on rounds elsewhere, Brak intended to kill him.

But the man did vanish inside a lantern-hung doorway. Perhaps he'd heard the racket and didn't care. Perhaps he wanted a drink of cool wine to break the night's sticky monotony. Whatever the reason, he was gone.

Whipping his head left and right, Brak checked for anyone else who might be observing him. He saw no one. He broke from cover, dashed toward the outer staircase of the two-story yellow building directly opposite.

On the second floor of that structure, he had learned via a casual inquiry to Xeraph, Ool the eunuch had his quarters. The floor below was occupied by the two dozen pink-lipped boys who served him. No one else was permitted to enter the building, Xeraph said. No other servants. Not even Lord Magnus.

Panting, Brak reached the exterior steps, crouched at the bottom, peering upward. He expected to see a guard posted on the terrace entrance to Ool's apartment. He saw no one.

Taking a tight grip on the sword's hilt, he began to climb, muffling the clinking chain as best he could. Time was running too fast for complete caution—

He still had no clear notion of what he expected to find, should he be lucky enough to penetrate Ool's private quarters. Evidence of treachery—but in what form? He couldn't predict.

Still, he was convinced his suspicions had some foundation. So he took the stairs three at a time.

By the time he neared the top, he wondered whether Ool's position was so secure, and his powers so feared, that he needed no personal guards. Somehow, Brak couldn't believe that. Yet, conscious of Xeraph's peril, he didn't pause to ponder the question—

He reached the terrace, immediately turned right toward a doorless arch where thin hangings stirred slowly. Deep in the dark of the apartment beyond, he saw white light flicker. He heard a small, hollow rumbling, mysterious and inexplicable, that somehow made his spine crawl.

A slithering noise spun him around.

He sucked in a startled breath at the sight of one— no, two—gods, *three* of the plump-faced boys rising from the shadow of the terrace railing. Had they been squatted there all along? Because of his haste and the darkness, Brak had missed them.

Their peculiar bright eyes glistened with red reflec-

tions from the sky. One boy giggled, shuffled a san-
daled foot forward. Pressed against him, his companions followed suit.

The three advanced another step with those glee-
ful, half-mad expressions on their faces. *Were they
drugged assassins—?*

Wary, awaiting attack, Brak was in one way reassured. Ool's quarters were, in fact, guarded. Because he
had something to conceal?

In a wet, lisping voice, one of the round-faced trio
said, "No one may enter to disturb the slumber of the
sexless one."

"I think this says otherwise," Brak growled, giving
the short-sword a flourish.

From the apartment he heard that preternatural
rumbling again. The white-fleshed boys interlocked
their hands and laughed at him. High-pitched, feminine giggles—

They were not armed. *But they were laughing at him!*

He backed up a pace, dread grabbing at his bowels.
The trio kept mincing toward him, hands clutching
hands. The faces suddenly glowed paste-white, illuminated by that strange radiance flaring inside the apartment—

Somehow, Brak's eyes misted. He blinked. No, the
trouble was not in his eyes. A fog seemed to be forming
around the boys.

The middle boy opened his mouth to laugh again.
And Brak's brain shrieked nameless terror as that
mouth began to *grow*—

Began to stretch upward, downward, to both
sides simultaneously, becoming a huge, spectral mon-
strosity with sharp, filed teeth that gleamed wet with
spittle. *Teeth the size of Brak's own head*—

Suddenly there were three giant, slavering mouths, each swollen outward from the head of a boy. There was a mouth on his left, another on his right, one directly ahead—all three arching forward to bite his skull and crack it—

Enchantments! Brak's mind screamed. *Illusions! They need no weapons because Ool taught them to guard with spells—*

Yet his own terror was real. So was the horrendous *craack* as the gigantic, disembodied central mouth clashed its teeth together, almost taking off his left arm.

Brak could see nothing of the trio of boys now. Only the formless mist in which the distended mouths were the sole perverted reality. Huge pink-lipped maws, clicking and grimacing and coming closer, left and right and ahead, *closer*—

The left mouth clashed its teeth three times. Then an immense, serpentine tongue shot from the maw and licked the lower lip in anticipation. A spittle-gob the size of fist dripped from the tongue's end—

Mesmerized with dread, Brak barely heard the noise on his right. He jerked his head around just in time to see the mouth arching over him, the gigantic teeth straining apart in preparation for the death-bite. Brak's brain howled his mortal fear. Yet something else within him still cried out:

Spells! Mind-dreams! You have seen them before! FIGHT THEM—

Both hands on the blade-hilt, he somehow found strength to hurl himself beneath the closing jaws— *CRAACK*—and stab into the mist as far as his chained arms would permit. Somewhere in that ghostly whorl of mind-smoke, the tip of his sword struck solid flesh—

A human shriek, bubbling and wild, roiled the smoke suddenly. The grinding mouth that had almost closed on him vanished.

The images of the other two began to shimmer and grow dim. Through the smoke he perceived a dying boy sprawled on the terrace flags, black-looking blood pouring out of his stabbed throat.

The mouth facing Brak flew at him, sharp-filed teeth wide open. But this time Brak fought his own hysteria more successfully, braced his legs and stabbed into the mist beneath the apparition—

And it too vanished, simultaneously with a cry of mortal hurt.

One phantom left—and that image was feeble. Through the vile, immense tongue, Brak glimpsed the reddened heavens of the city. He tossed his sword to his left hand, extended both arms as far as he could, and killed the unseen boy behind the snapping mouth—

Which shrank and puffed away, leaving three sad, suetlike bodies in a bloodied heap.

Gasping, Brak wiped sweat from his eyes. His heart pounded so heavily that it almost brought physical pain. Surely the cries of the boy-guards with their devilish mind projections had wakened the sleeper in the apartment. And others near the square—

Brak peered over the stone railing, saw the lone soldier pacing listlessly again. The only sounds the big barbarian heard were the drag of the soldier's boots and—behind him—that strange, hollow crashing that reverberated into stillness.

He leaned down, prodded one of the forlorn corpses. His fingers came away sticky with warm blood. No, the obscene mouths had not been real. But the briefly-invisible bodies that had tasted his iron had been real. That in itself was a reassurance of sanity, giving him the courage to turn, take three steps, raise his short-sword to touch the edge of one of the hangings and lift it—

Again that eerie white light flickered and danced deep in the apartment's gloom.

Brak tried to discern the light's source. It seemed to radiate from behind another drapery. But he couldn't be sure.

He listened again.

Silence. Where was Ool?

If Brak had somehow slain the evil boys without a sound, perhaps the wizard had not been awakened. Perhaps all the noises he'd heard during the struggle had been illusions too. The thought emboldened him to the point of taking one step past the hanging. From the concealment of the distant drapery, the hollow booming sounded once more.

Brak's backbone crawled as a sibilant voice spoke:

"Even in sleep, my mind is linked with those of my protectors. Their power comes from my thoughts, you see. When they died, I awakened. To give you a fitting reception, my curious outlander."

On the last word spoken by the unseen Ool, the short-sword in Brak's right hand burned. He screamed and let go.

The blade flew toward the ceiling, lighting the whole splendidly-furnished apartment for one bizarre instant. The sword turned molten, dripping. Dollops of glowing fire struck the apartment's tiles and burned smoking pits into them.

Brak dodged back from the fire-shower, seeing

eyond it the hairless body of Ool standing beside his canopied bed, naked save for a loin-wrapping of linen that matched the whiteness of his flesh.

The last droplets of the destroyed sword struck the tiles and hissed out. But not before Brak had glimpsed the damning evidence again:

Ool's left wrist did bear the mark Brak thought he had seen when the wind blew back the wizard's sleeves in the chariot—

The mark was a scarred ridge of tissue circling the left wrist. Once, the man's flesh had been bound by a tight bracelet.

"You have come to perish, then," smiled Ool. "I shan't disappoint you—"

Immense, invisible hands created with no more than a blink of Ool's basilisk eyes lifted Brak and hurled him to the floor. His ears rang as he hit. His body went numb with pain.

Slowly, the pale wizard advanced toward the place where the big barbarian lay writhing, trying to regather his strength. With a little purse of his lips, Ool lifted one bare foot and placed it on Brak's sweating chest. With his right hand he made a quick mesmeric pass.

Instantly, Brak felt as though the weight of a building pressed down on him. He clenched his teeth, lashed his head from side to side, growled savagely—

But he could not move. He was held by the magical weight of Ool's soft, clammy foot.

From where he sprawled, Brak saw the magician's obscenely white shine in the glare from behind the far curtain. Ool the sexless one lifted his left forearm, displayed the scarred wrist almost mockingly.

"Is this what you came to see, outlander? Well—" An exquisite shrug. "Look your last."

8.

Brak the barbarian lay helpless under that pasty white foot, his arms and legs and trunk tingling faintly. The pain of his hard fall was diminishing. But he was still unable to move. He was prisoned not by visible weight, but by the weight of Ool's arcane talents.

From what Brak could see of Ool, whenever the white light-source flared behind the distant curtain, the wizard continued to act amused. At length he gave voice to that amusement:

"You played boldly before my Lord Magnus, that I'll put to your credit. But you were foredoomed. Consider it an act of mercy on my part when I suggested you be allowed only two days and nights to work your nonexistent magic. No one can draw down the rain because I have gathered and held it. There."

A supple, almost boneless gesture with the left hand—toward the rumbling light-source.

"For the Children of the Smoke," Brak gasped out.

"Ultimately," Ool agreed. "But in chief, for myself. You see—" the whitish lips hardened into a cruel line, "—years ago, the Worldbreaker took something from me that represented irredeemable loss. Not by his own hand did he take it from me. But the hand which did the deed was his instrument. So I fled west to the lands of Shend, and for several years I discipled myself to their great wizards. I had some natural talent, I discovered—most humans do. Perhaps even you. But such talents lie dormant for lack of training and development. Had I not been so blessed, however, I would have sought another means of revenging myself. In any case, when my preparations were complete, I returned to his court as a different man. Unrecognized. My plan was to gain the confidence of Lord Magnus. Thus I served him well and faithfully for years—"

"Until the time when you were ready to strike against him."

Ool nodded. "You have a sharper wit than the few northlanders I've encountered. You have brains you put to use—guessing, puzzling out answers—yes, you're right. I waited. Always maintaining secret communication with the Children. Always urging *them* to wait until their numbers were great enough—and Lord Magnus was old, his powers failing. The hour came finally, as I knew it would," Ool said with another purse of the moist lips. "In a few weeks—a month or two—but soon, the Children will sweep out of the east. By then, the maddened people within these walls will have no more heart or strength to resist. Even the army will rise, I imagine. Such is the miraculous power of nature's rain—and the lack thereof."

"Was—" Brak thrashed again. But the supernatural weight seemed to restrain every part of him. "—Was it you, then, who blackened the sky and filled the crystal idols with what looked like blood?"

"Of course." Ool smiled. "There will be additional—ah—demonstrations of that sort before I send my last signal to the Children. Alas, you spoiled that particular illusion. The blow from your chain, I think. Breaking the idol, it broke the projective trance. I was lying yonder—" he indicated the rumpled bedclothes that exuded a sweet but somehow foul perfume, "—arranging it all with my mind. Of a sudden, I was jolted awake. Much the same thing happened when you killed my dear little guards. But enough of that. Although you are the loser and I am the winner in this small contest—"

He smiled again, seeing the glare in Brak's eyes.

Again the big barbarian tried to move; futile. The naked foot held him. He could do nothing but clench and unclench his fists.

"—I respect certain of your qualities. I would like to know this much. What brought you here? These rooms are forbidden, even to the lord. I made sure of that long ago, so I could pursue my—private ventures undisturbed."

"The sight of the scar brought me," Brak said. "And certain things repeated by Captain Xeraph—"

Ool's hairless brows quirked, the back and sides of his oval head illuminated by another glare from behind the drape. "But when did you see the scar, pray? In public, I keep my hands forever hid in full sleeves."

"I spied on your so-called spell-working at the water-channel yesterday. While you were in the chariot, the wind blew your gown aside as the car went by the rocks where I was watching."

Ool was genuinely amused.

"I don't doubt your own people cast you out, my friend. No spellworker of small talent could abide a man of your perceptions observing his mummery."

"But the holding back of the rain is no mummery—"

"I told you, I have not held it back," Ool corrected, crooking one pudgy finger in an almost schoolmasterish way. "I have imprisoned it. That, too, I learned in Shend, and thought it an excellent major weapon at the proper time. That time, mercifully, has come."

"Will—" Again Brak forced out each word. "Will you rule the Children when they take over the Worldbreaker's kingdom?"

After a thoughtful pause, Ool replied, "I think not.

I'll advise them, no doubt. Influence them. But the real savor of this victory will come long before I find myself in such a position." The white-oval face wrenched. "My only desire is to bring down that swilling, posturing little war-cock!"

"At least—" Brak struggled to breathe. "—at least he'll die a man. Which is more than you can ever claim."

Ool's pale face contorted. He shrilled an almost feminine scream, leaning over. One wrathful hand slapped Brak's face. The blow was sharp, vicious. But the big barbarian hardly felt it; he felt something more important. Something for which he'd hoped and gambled with the gasped insult—

He felt the shift in weight on his chest. The pressure lessened ever so little. Still bent over, Ool was prey now. If he could strike fast enough—

Brak's chained hands came up. An inch. Another. Faster, rising—

By leaning to strike Brak's face, Ool had somehow weakened the occult weight. Brak could shift his trunk a little, raise one shoulder up in the same instant he seized Ool's left ankle with both hands, and wrenched.

Heaving against the phantom power holding him down, Brak managed to hurl the wizard off balance. Ool toppled backwards, linen wrap flying.

The wizard reeled into a taboret, collapsed it as he fell, floundering and shrieking. Brak struggled to his feet, his huge, rope-muscled body washed by the white glare from behind the drapery. The hollow boom rolled through the chamber as Brak drove himself toward that curtain and the secret it concealed—

Behind him, Ool squealed and gibbered in rage. At any moment Brak expected some ensorcelled bolt of fire to strike him, char the flesh off his bones, burn him dead. His leaping strides were long, fear-driven—

Ool still flopped about on hands and knees, not yet fully recovered from his upsetting. Brak's hands closed on the white-shimmering drapery, coarse stuff. He tugged. Rings clattered. Fabric tore—

With a cry of terror, Brak flung up an arm to shield his eyes.

On a low stone pedestal in an alcove stood a flask of strangely opalescent glass. The flask, stoppered, was no more than four hands high. Inside—*inside*—

Brak's skin crawled. His mouth tasted the bile of nauseous terror as he watched miniature stormclouds whirl and tumble within the flask.

The clouds moved with incredible speed, smashing the side of the glass prison, turning under and smashing again. Tiny lightning bolts sizzled and spat within the flask, spending themselves against the sides in unearthly fire-showers—

As Ool had said: the storms of heaven, magically imprisoned.

Noise behind him. The wizard scrambling up—

Terrified almost witless, Brak grabbed at the awful flask, heard Ool shriek:

"Do not touch it—!"

The flask vibrated in Brak's hand, shooting off its white glare of prisoned lightnings, booming the sound of captured thunder. The flask cast a sickly white aura between the barbarian and the sorcerer, who was framed against the terrace where his dead guardians lay. Ool's supple white hands rose in the beginning of what Brak knew would be a last, death-bringing spell-cast—

He hurled the flask with all his strength.

Ool saw it flying at him, white and thundering. The motions of his spell dissolved into frantic, fending gestures. He managed to hit the flask, deflect it. But when he saw the direction, he screamed and screamed—

The flask fell toward the floor.

Struck the tiles.

Shattered—

A cataclysm of lightbursts and thunderclaps smote Brak's brain and body. Unleashed winds picked him up, tossed him toward the splitting ceiling, tumbled him and bounced him off a wall while noise drummed, glare burned, shrieking gale-winds funneled skyward—

The whirlwind dropped Brak through white-glaring darkness, smashing the sense out of him an instant after he heard Ool's final scream drowned in the roar of furious, downpouring rain.

9

Bloodied, only half in possession of his senses, wracked with pain yet forcing himself to drag the flaccid white corpse by its ankle, Brak the barbarian sought the hall of Lord Magnus the Worldbreaker.

It was not hard to find. Drums hammered. Pipes skirled. Joyous, almost hysterical voices whooped and sang as he came limping up a long, empty corridor where torches blew and sheeting rain gusted in through high slot windows.

Staggering, Brak dropped to one knee. He released Ool's ankle, held both palms against his eyelids, fighting back the pain.

He had wakened in the apartment, finding half the ceiling caved away. The snapped end of a beam had crushed Ool's skull. Behind him along the ghostly corridor, Brak could see a trail of red and gray paste where Ool's head had dragged.

For his part, Brak had been prisoned beneath a rubble-heap, badly knocked and gashed, but with no detectable damage besides general pain and a sharper one that might indicate a shattered bone somewhere in his left leg. He could barely support himself on that side.

Some of Ool's boy guardians had come creeping upstairs fearfully. At the sight of their dead master, they fled into the night. Brak had pulled himself up and out of the ruins of the ceiling from which the prisoned storm-forces had escaped to spread and deluge the land with the rain; rain that even now rivered loudly off the palace rooftop. He'd hauled Ool's shattered body through empty squares and courtyards while his pain-dulled mind perceived cries of jubilation from streets and palace buildings alike.

Now he gained his feet again. He saw a turning in the corridor just ahead. He clutched Ool's ankle, shambled on, drenched by a gust of rain through a window he passed. Cold, clean rain pouring down on the kingdom of Lord Magnus the Worldbreaker—

Weaving on his feet, struggling against the agony that seared his whole left side, Brak limped to the entrance of the huge hall, and waited.

A thousand people thronged there, it seemed, reveling. They axed open wine casks, lay beneath the pouring red streams, bathing in them. Others whooped and danced impromptu steps: soldiers and courtiers, ladies and serving-maids alike—

One wine-drenched bawd saw Brak slouched in the great doorway and screamed.

The merrymaking ended. Heads turned. Mouths gaped.

Like some great wounded animal, Brak the barbarian dragged his victim on, up through a long, quickly-opened aisle of faces to the foot of the beast-throne where Magnus the Worldbreaker sat, wine cup in hand.

The rain drummed and hammered in the dark night outside. Magnus's lined face bore a disbelieving look as he stared down at the grim, bloodied hulk of a man who, with his good right foot, rolled the wizard's corpse to the base of the throne stairs and then simply stared upward.

"Was it you who brought the rain—at the price of my wizard's life?" Magnus asked, as if he couldn't quite countenance it. Ripples of amazement noised through the crowd, stilled suddenly by the lord's upraised hand.

At first Brak could manage no more than a single, pain-wracked shake of his head. Then he said:

"I only freed what your treacherous magician prisoned inside a flask with a powerful spell—to bring this kingdom down. Many—"

Brak saw three lords seated on the throne. Then two. He rubbed his eyes; fought the hurt spearing up his left side; stiffened his injured leg so he wouldn't totter and fall.

"—many years ago, I was told, a soldier ravished your wife, and escaped. But not before a spear gave him a wound. Look at the wizard's arm, which he has kept concealed from you—from everyone—since the first day he came to your court. Once he wore your bracelet. Pull away his waist linen—" This Brak had already done, back in the apartment, to verify his suspicion. "A spear that struck in darkness robbed him of what a man can afford to lose least of all—"

He swayed, dizzy, as soldiers and courtiers ran forward to strip the corpse and expose the sexless, scarred ruin at the joining of Ool's pale legs.

A woman fainted. The linen was hastily replaced.

Lord Magnus gazed down in wonder and loathing. Brak forced out more hoarse words:

"He escaped to the land of Shend, and there learned sorceries. He returned and gained your favor under the name by which you knew him. For years he conspired with the Children of the Smoke, until the arrival of the hour he deemed opportune to—" A wracking cough that started deep in his belly nearly spilled Brak over. "—to bring you down. All this I will repeat in detail at—some better time." Glowering, he swung his head left and right. He missed the one face he sought: "Where is Captain Xeraph?"

"In the dungeons, being drawn on the wheel for permitting your escape."

"I struck him by surprise. He had no chance—let him go."

Silence.

"I said let him go!"

Lord Magnus signaled. Two senior officers dashed for a portal as Brak went on:

"Before I make my departure, I will explain fully how I destroyed the man who would have destroyed you, lord. But I want your leave—" Again a terrible, sick spell of dizziness swept him. The pain climbed through his left leg and his torso to eat at his brain. He braced his gashed left leg, dug horny nails into his palms: fresh pain, to sting his senses alive again.

"—to claim what you promised me if the rain came down in two days and two nights. That I will be free of your bondage."

Suddenly, horrifyingly, in the small, scarred face of Lord Magnus the Worldbreaker whose booted feet did not reach the floor in front of his throne, there was both cheerfulness and cunning. In the rain-hissing silence, the lord said:

"Barbarian, you heard me amiss. I spoke exactly this. *You will not die. You will not wear chains.* I never said you would go free. In fact I never intended that at all—and chose my words accordingly. I am ever in need of stout, quick-witted fighters—and will number you among such from this day forward. Instead of chains, you will only wear the bronze bracelet of my army."

10

From somewhere deep in his hurt body, Brak's cry of betrayal bellowed out:

"The gods damn you for deception—*I will escape!*"

Looking down on his new thrall with scarcely-concealed admiration, Lord Magnus gave a tired, pleased nod.

"Accepted. I will prevent it, if I can."

It made no difference to Brak the barbarian that he knew why Lord Magnus had deceived him, and would impress him into service. In his terrible pain, he felt only hatred. Faces, forms, firelight from socketed torches swam together and melted into darkness as he threw his head back and let out one long, baying howl of animal rage.

Lunging, he tried to climb the throne stairs to his captor. But he was too weak. He fell back, sprawling over the corpse of Ool. His mind darkened swiftly—

There was sudden stillness except for the hammer of the rain. The unconscious barbarian's right arm slipped off the dead magician's shoulder where it had rested, and struck the floor with a last faint clattering of chain.

SAIL ON! SAIL ON!

PHILIP JOSÉ FARMER

PHILIP JOSÉ FARMER has written more than fifty novels and numerous short stories in the past five decades, garnering three Hugo Awards along the way. His stories are always thought-provoking, speculating on alien reproduction, religion, and the transformation of mankind under any and all conditions, from the horrors of vampires and werewolves to reincarnation and the afterlife. Best known for the Riverworld novels and short stories, in which everyone that ever lived populates a ten-million-mile long river, he uses famous personalities to quest for truth, whether it be religious, physical, or mortal. He lives in Illinois. "Sail On! Sail On!" rewrites history with a sly nod to the beliefs of the fifteenth century.

Friar Sparks sat wedged between the wall and the realizer. He was motionless except for his forefinger and his eyes. From time to time his finger tapped rapidly on the key upon the desk, and now and then his irises, gray-blue as his native Irish sky, swiveled to look through the open door of the *toldilla* in which he crouched, the little shanty on the poop deck. Visibility was low.

Outside was dusk and a lantern by the railing. Two sailors leaned on it. Beyond them bobbed the bright lights and dark shapes of the *Niña* and the *Pinta*. And beyond them was the smooth horizon-brow of the Atlantic, edged in black and blood by the red dome of the rising moon.

The single carbon filament bulb above the monk's tonsure showed a face lost in fat—and in concentration.

The luminiferous ether crackled and hissed tonight, but the phones clamped over his ears carried, along with them, the steady dots and dashes sent by the operator at the Las Palmas station on the Grand Canary.

"*Zziss!* So you are out of sherry already. . . . *Pop!* . . . Too bad . . . *Crackle* . . . you hardened old winebutt . . . *Zzz* . . . May God have mercy on your sins. . . .

"Lots of gossip, news, et cetera . . . *Hisses!* . . . Bend

your ear instead of your neck, impious one . . . The Turks are said to be gathering . . . *crackle* . . . an army to march on Austria. It is rumored that the flying sausages, said by so many to have been seen over the capitals of the Christian world, are of Turkish origin. The rumor goes they have been invented by a renegade Rogerian who was converted to the Muslim religion. . . . I say . . . *zziss* . . . to that. No one of us would do that. It is a falsity spread by our enemies in the Church to discredit us. But many people believe that. . . .

"How close does the Admiral calculate he is to Cipangu now?

"Flash! Savonarola today denounced the Pope, the wealthy of Florence, Greek art and literature, and the experiments of the disciples of Saint Roger Bacon. . . . *Zzz!* . . . The man is sincere but misguided and dangerous. . . . I predict he'll end up on the stake he's always prescribing for us. . . .

"*Pop.* . . . This will kill you. . . . Two Irish mercenaries by the name of Pat and Mike were walking down the street of Granada when a beautiful Saracen lady leaned out of a balcony and emptied a pot of . . . *hiss!* . . . and Pat looked up and . . . *Crackle* . . . Good, hah? Brother Juan told that last night. . . .

"PV . . . PV . . . Are you coming in? . . . PV . . . PV . . . Yes, I know it's dangerous to bandy such jests about, but nobody is monitoring us tonight. . . . *Zzz* . . . I think they're not, anyway. . . ."

And so the ether bent and warped with their messages. And presently Friar Sparks tapped out the PV that ended their talk—the "*Pax vobiscum.*" Then he pulled the plug out that connected his earphones to the set and, lifting them from his ears, clamped them down forward over his temples in the regulation manner.

After sidling bent-kneed from the *toldilla*, punishing his belly against the desk's hard edge as he did so, he walked over to the railing. De Salcedo and de Torres were leaning there and talking in low tones. The big bulb above gleamed on the page's red-gold hair and on the interpreter's full black beard. It also bounced pinkishly off the priest's smooth-shaven jowls and the light scarlet robe of the Rogerian order. His cowl, thrown back, served as a bag for scratch paper, pens, an ink bottle, tiny wrenches and screwdrivers, a book on cryptography, a slide rule, and a manual of angelic principles.

"Well, old rind," said young de Salcedo familiarly, "what do you hear from Las Palmas?"

"Nothing now. Too much interference from that." He pointed to the moon riding the horizon ahead of them. "What an orb!" bellowed the priest. "It's as big and red as my revered nose!"

The two sailors laughed, and de Salcedo said, "But it will get smaller and paler as the night grows, Father. And your proboscis will, on the contrary, become larger and more sparkling in inverse proportion according to the square of the ascent—"

He stopped and grinned, for the monk had suddenly dipped his nose, like a porpoise diving into the sea, raised it again, like the same animal jumping from a wave, and then once more plunged it into the heavy currents of their breath. Nose to nose, he faced them, his twinkling little eyes seeming to emit sparks like the realizer in his *toldilla*.

Again, porpoiselike, he sniffed and snuffed several times, quite loudly. Then, satisfied with what he had gleaned from their breaths, he winked at them. He did not, however, mention his findings at once, preferring to sidle toward the subject.

He said, "This Father Sparks on the Grand Canary is so entertaining. He stimulates me with all sorts of philosophical notions, both valid and fantastic. For instance, tonight, just before we were cut off by that"— he gestured at the huge bloodshot eye in the sky—"he was discussing what he called worlds of parallel time tracks, an idea originated by Dysphagius of Gotham. It's his idea there may be other worlds in coincident but not contacting universes, that God, being infinite and of unlimited creative talent and ability, the Master Alchemist, in other words, has possibly—perhaps necessarily—created a plurality of continua in which every probable event has happened."

"Huh?" grunted de Salcedo.

"Exactly. Thus, Columbus was turned down by Queen Isabella, so this attempt to reach the Indies across the Atlantic was never made. So we would not now be standing here plunging ever deeper into Oceanus in our three cockleshells, there would be no booster buoys strung out between us and the Canaries, and Father Sparks at Las Palmas and I on the *Santa Maria* would not be carrying on our fascinating conversations across the ether.

"Or, say, Roger Bacon was persecuted by the Church, instead of being encouraged and giving rise to the order whose inventions have done so much to insure the monopoly of the Church on alchemy and its divinely inspired guidance of that formerly pagan and hellish practice."

De Torres opened his mouth, but the priest silenced him with a magnificent and imperious gesture and continued.

"Or, even more ridiculous, but thought-provoking, he speculated just this evening on universes with different physical laws. One, in particular, I thought very droll. As you probably don't know, Angelo Angelei has proved, by dropping objects from the Leaning Tower of Pisa, that different weights fall at different speeds. My delightful colleague on the Grand Canary is writing a satire which takes place in a universe where Aristotle is made out to be a liar, where all things drop with equal velocities, no matter what their size. Silly stuff, but it helps to pass the time. We keep the ether busy with our little angels."

De Salcedo said, "Uh, I don't want to seem too curious about the secrets of your holy and cryptic order, Friar Sparks. But these little angels your machine realizes intrigue me. Is it a sin to presume to ask about them?"

The monk's bull roar slid to a dove cooing. "Whether it's a sin or not depends. Let me illustrate, young fellows. If you were concealing a bottle of, say, very scarce sherry on you, and you did not offer to share it with a very thirsty old gentleman, that would be a sin. A sin of omission. But if you were to give that desert-dry, that pilgrim-weary, that devout, humble, and decrepit old soul a long, soothing, refreshing, and stimulating draught of lifegiving fluid, daughter of the vine, I would find it in my heart to pray for you for that deed of loving-kindness, of encompassing charity. And it would please me so much I might tell you a little of our realizer. Not enough to hurt you, just enough so you might gain more respect for the intelligence and glory of my order."

De Salcedo grinned conspiratorially and passed the monk the bottle he'd hidden under his jacket. As the friar tilted it, and the chug-chug-chug of vanishing sherry became louder, the two sailors glanced meaningfully at each other. No wonder the priest, reputed to be so brilliant in his branch of the alchemical mysteries, had yet been sent off on this half-baked voyage to devil-knew-where. The Church had calculated that if he survived, well and good. If he didn't, then he would sin no more.

The monk wiped his lips on his sleeve, belched loudly as a horse, and said, "*Gracias,* boys. From my heart, so deeply buried in this fat, I thank you. An old Irishman, dry as a camel's hoof, choking to death with the dust of abstinence, thanks you. You have saved my life."

"Thank rather that magic nose of yours," replied de Salcedo. "Now, old rind, now that you're well greased again, would you mind explaining as much as you are allowed about that machine of yours?"

Friar Sparks took fifteen minutes. At the end of that time, his listeners asked a few permitted questions.

". . . and you say you broadcast on a frequency of eighteen hundred k.c.?" the page asked. "What does 'k.c.' mean?"

"*K* stands for the French *kilo,* from a Greek word meaning thousand. And *c* stands for the Hebrew *cherubim,* the 'little angels.' Angel comes from the Greek *angelos,* meaning messenger. It is our concept that the ether is crammed with these cherubim, these little messengers. Thus, when we Friar Sparkses depress the key of our machine, we are able to realize some of the infinity of 'messengers' waiting for just such a demand for service.

"So, eighteen hundred k.c. means that in a given unit of time one million, eight hundred thousand cherubim line up and hurl themselves across the ether, the nose of one being brushed by the feathertips of the cherub's wings ahead. The height of the wing crests of each little creature is even, so that if you were to draw an outline of the whole train, there would be nothing to distinguish one cherub from the next, the whole column forming that grade of little angels known as C.W."

"C.W.?"

"Continuous wingheight. My machine is a C.W. realizer."

Young de Salcedo said, "My mind reels. Such a concept! Such a revelation! It almost passes comprehension. Imagine, the aerial of your realizer is cut just so long, so that the evil cherubim surging back and forth on it demand a predetermined and equal number of good angels to combat them. And this seduction coil on the realizer crowds 'bad' angels into the left-hand, the sinister, side. And when the bad little cherubim are crowded so closely and numerously that they can't bear each other's evil company, they jump the spark gap and speed around the wire to the 'good' plate. And in this racing back and forth they call themselves to the attention of the 'little messengers,' the yea-saying cherubim. And you, Friar Sparks, by manipulating your machine thus and so, and by lifting and lowering your key, you bring these invisible and friendly lines of carriers, your etheric and winged postmen, into reality. And you are able, thus, to communicate at great distances with your brothers of the order."

"Great God!" said de Torres.

It was not a vain oath but a pious exclamation of wonder. His eyes bulged; it was evident that he suddenly saw that man was not alone, that on every side, piled on top of each other, flanked on every angle, stood a host. Black and white, they presented a solid chessboard of the seemingly empty cosmos, black for the nay-sayers, white for the yea-sayers, maintained by a Hand in delicate balance and subject as the fowls of the air and the fish of the sea to exploitation by man.

Yet de Torres, having seen such a vision as has made a saint of many a man, could only ask, "Perhaps you could tell me how many angels may stand on the point of a pin?"

Obviously, de Torres would never wear a halo. He was destined, if he lived, to cover his bony head with the mortarboard of a university teacher.

De Salcedo snorted. "I'll tell you. Philosophically speaking, you may put as many angels on a pinhead as you want to. Actually speaking, you may put only as many as there is room for. Enough of that. I'm interested in facts, not fancies. Tell me, how could the moon's rising interrupt your reception of the cherubim sent by the Sparks at Las Palmas?"

"Great Caesar, how would I know? Am I a repository of universal knowledge? No, not I! A humble and ignorant friar, I! All I can tell you is that last night it rose like a bloody tumor on the horizon, and that when it was up I had to quit marshaling my little messengers in their short and long columns. The Canary station was quite overpowered, so that both of us gave up. And the same thing happened tonight."

"The moon sends messages?" asked de Torres.

"Not in a code I can decipher. But it sends, yes."

"Santa Maria!"

"Perhaps," suggested de Salcedo, "there are people on that moon, and they are sending."

Friar Sparks blew derision through his nose. Enormous as were his nostrils, his derision was not small-bore. Artillery of contempt laid down a barrage that would have silenced any but the strongest of souls.

"Maybe—" de Torres spoke in a low tone—"maybe, if the stars are windows in heaven, as I've heard said, the angels of the higher hierarchy, the big ones, are real-izing—uh—the smaller? And they only do it when the moon is up so we may know it is a celestial phenome-non?"

He crossed himself and looked around the vessel.

"You need not fear," said the monk gently. "There is no Inquisitor leaning over your shoulder. Remember, I am the only priest on this expedition. Moreover, your conjecture has nothing to do with dogma. However, that's unimportant. Here's what I don't understand: How can a heavenly body broadcast? Why does it have the same frequency as the one I'm restricted to? Why—"

"I could explain," interrupted de Salcedo with all the brashness and impatience of youth. "I could say that the Admiral and the Rogerians are wrong about the earth's shape. I could say the earth is not round but is flat. I could say the horizon exists, not because we live upon a globe, but because the earth is curved only a lit-tle ways, like a greatly flattened-out hemisphere. I could also say that the cherubim are coming, not from Luna, but from a ship such as ours, a vessel which is hanging in the void off the edge of the earth."

"What?" gasped the other two.

"Haven't you heard," said de Salcedo, "that the King of Portugal secretly sent out a ship after he turned down Columbus's proposal? How do we know he did not, that the messages are from our predecessor, that he sailed off the world's rim and is now suspended in the air and becomes exposed at night because it follows the moon around Terra—is, in fact, a much smaller and unseen satellite?"

The monk's laughter woke many men on the ship. "I'll have to tell the Las Palmas operator your tale. He can put it in that novel of his. Next you'll be telling me those messages are from one of those fire-shooting sausages so many credulous laymen have been seeing flying around. No, my dear de Salcedo, let's not be ridiculous. Even the ancient Greeks knew the earth was round. Every university in Europe teaches that. And we Rogerians have measured the circumference. We know for sure that the Indies lie just across the Atlantic. Just as we know for sure, through mathematics, that heavier-than-air machines are impossible. Our Friar Ripskulls, our mind doctors, have assured us these flying creations are mass hallucinations or else the tricks of heretics or Turks who want to panic the populace.

"That moon radio is no delusion, I'll grant you. What it is, I don't know. But it's not a Spanish or Portuguese ship. What about its different code? Even if it came from Lisbon, that ship would still have a Rogerian operator. And he would, according to our policy, be of a different nationality from the crew so he might the easier stay out of political embroilments. He wouldn't break our laws by using a different code in order to communicate with Lisbon. We disciples of Saint Roger do not stoop to petty boundary intrigues. Moreover, that realizer would not be powerful enough to reach Europe, and must, therefore, be directed at us."

"How can you be sure?" said de Salcedo. "Distressing though the thought may be to you, a priest could be subverted. Or a layman could learn your secrets and invent a code. I think that a Portuguese ship is sending to another, a ship perhaps not too distant from us."

De Torres shivered and crossed himself again. "Perhaps the angels are warning us of approaching death? Perhaps?"

"Perhaps? Then why don't they use our code? Angels would know it as well as I. No, there is no perhaps. The order does not permit perhaps. It experiments and finds out; nor does it pass judgment until it knows."

"I doubt we'll ever know," said de Salcedo gloomily. "Columbus has promised the crew that if we come across no sign of land by evening tomorrow, we shall turn back. Otherwise—" he drew a finger across his throat—"*kkk!* Another day, and we'll be pointed east and getting away from that evil and bloody-looking moon and its incomprehensible messages."

"It would be a great loss to the order and to the Church," sighed the friar. "But I leave such things in the hands of God and inspect only what He hands me to look at."

With which pious statement Friar Sparks lifted the bottle to ascertain the liquid level. Having determined in a scientific manner its existence, he next measured its quantity and tested its quality by putting all of it in that best of all chemistry tubes, his enormous belly.

Afterward, smacking his lips and ignoring the pained and disappointed looks on the faces of the sailors, he went on to speak enthusiastically of the water screw and the engine which turned it, both of which had been built recently at the St. Jonas College at Genoa. If Isabella's three ships had been equipped with those, he declared, they would not have to depend upon the wind. However, so far, the fathers had forbidden its extended use because it was feared the engine's fumes might poison the air and the terrible speeds it made possible might be fatal to the human body. After which he plunged into a tedious description of the life of his patron saint, the inventor of the first cherubim realizer and receiver, Jonas of Carcassonne, who had been martyred when he grabbed a wire he thought was insulated.

The two sailors found excuses to walk off. The

monk was a good fellow, but hagiography bored them. Besides, they wanted to talk of women. . . .

If Columbus had not succeeded in persuading his crews to sail one more day, events would have been different.

At dawn the sailors were very much cheered by the sight of several large birds circling their ships. Land could not be far off; perhaps these winged creatures came from the coast of fabled Cipangu itself, the country whose houses were roofed with gold.

The birds swooped down. Closer, they were enormous and very strange. Their bodies were flattish and almost saucer-shaped and small in proportion to the wings, which had a spread of at least thirty feet. Nor did they have legs. Only a few sailors saw the significance of that fact. These birds dwelt in the air and never rested upon land or sea.

While they were meditating upon that, they heard a slight sound as of a man clearing his throat. So gentle and far off was the noise that nobody paid any attention to it, for each thought his neighbor had made it.

A few minutes later, the sound had become louder and deeper, like a lute string being twanged.

Everybody looked up. Heads were turned west.

Even yet they did not understand that the noise like a finger plucking a wire came from the line that held the earth together, and that the line was stretched to its utmost, and that the violent finger of the sea was what had plucked the line.

It was some time before they understood. They had run out of horizon.

When they saw that, they were too late.

The dawn had not only come up *like* thunder, it *was* thunder. And though the three ships heeled over at once and tried to sail close-hauled on the port tack, the suddenly speeded-up and relentless current made beating hopeless.

Then it was the Rogerian wished for the Genoese screw and the wood-burning engine that would have made them able to resist the terrible muscles of the charging and bull like sea. Then it was that some men prayed, some raved, some tried to attack the Admiral, some jumped overboard, and some sank into a stupor.

Only the fearless Columbus and the courageous Friar Sparks stuck to their duties. All that day the fat monk crouched wedged in his little shanty, dot-dashing to his fellow on the Grand Canary. He ceased only when the moon rose like a huge red bubble from the throat of a dying giant. Then he listened intently all night and worked desperately, scribbling and swearing impiously and checking cipher books.

When the dawn came up again in a roar and a rush, he ran from the *toldilla,* a piece of paper clutched in his hand. His eyes were wild, and his lips were moving fast, but nobody could understand that he had cracked the code. They could not hear him shouting, "It is the Portuguese! It is the Portuguese!"

Their ears were too overwhelmed to hear a mere human voice. The throat clearing and the twanging of the string had been the noises preliminary to the concert itself. Now came the mighty overture; as compelling as the blast of Gabriel's horn was the topple of Oceanus into space.

MY DEAR
EMILY

JOANNA RUSS

JOANNA RUSS is another author who gained prominence in the New Wave of the 1960s, writing fanciful, thought-provoking fantasy and science fiction. Her work combines fantasy and the supernatural, with a theme of oblique feminism and empowerment in the background, as in "My Dear Emily." Educated at Cornell University, she has been teaching English for the past twenty-five years, and is currently Professor of English at the University of Washington—Seattle. She has won two Nebulas and one Hugo Award, and lives in Seattle. One of the most ancient creatures of the night, the vampire, faces the unbridled emotions of a 19th century woman in the following story.

San Francisco, 188—

I am so looking forward to seeing my dear Emily at
last, now she is grown, a woman, although I'm sure I
will hardly recognize her. She must not be proud (as if
she could be!) but will remember her friends, I know,
and have patience with her dear Will who cannot help
but remember the girl she was, and the sweet influence she had in her old home. I talk to your father
about you every day, dear, and he longs to see you as I
do. Think! a learned lady in our circle! But I know you
have not changed. . . .

Emily came home from school in April with her
bosom friend Charlotte. They had loved each
other in school, but they didn't speak much on the
train. While Emily read Mr. Emerson's poems, Charlotte examined the scenery through opera-glasses. She
expressed her wish to see "savages."

"That's foolish," says Emily promptly.

"If we were carried off," says Charlotte, "I don't
think you would notice it in time to disapprove."

"That's very foolish," says Emily, touching her
round lace collar with one hand. She looks up from Mr.
Emerson to stare Charlotte out of countenance, prop-

erly, morally, and matter-of-course young lady. It has always been her style.

"The New England look," Charlotte snaps resentfully. She makes her opera-glasses slap shut.

"I should like to be carried off," she proposes; "but then I don't have an engagement to look forward to. A delicate affair."

"You mustn't make fun," says Emily. Mr. Emerson drops into her lap. She stares unseeing at Charlotte's opera-glasses.

"Why do they close?" she asks helplessly.

"I beg your pardon?" blankly, from Charlotte.

"Nothing. You're much nicer than I am," says Emily.

"Look," urges Charlotte kindly, pressing the toy into her friend's hand.

"For savages?"

Charlotte nods, Emily pushes the spring that will open the little machine, and a moment later drops them into her lap where they fall on Mr. Emerson. There is a cut across one of her fingers and a blue pinch darkening the other.

"They hurt me," she says without expression, and as Charlotte takes the glasses up quickly, Emily looks with curious sad passivity at the blood from her little wound, which has bled an incongruous passionate drop on Mr. Emerson's cloth-bound poems. To her friend's surprise (and her own, too) she begins to cry, heavily, silently, and totally without reason.

He wakes up slowly, mistily, dizzily, with a vague memory of having fallen asleep on plush. He is intensely miserable, bound down to his bed with hoops of steel, and the memory adds nausea to his misery, solidifying ticklishly around his bare hands and the back of his neck as he drifts toward wakefulness. His stomach turns over with the dry brushy filthiness of it. With the caution of the chronically ill, he opens his eyelids, careful not to move, careful even to keep from focusing his gaze until—he thinks to himself—his bed stops holding him with the force of Hell and this intense miserable sickness goes down, settles . . . Darkness. No breath. A glimmer of light, a stone wall. He thinks: *I'm dead and buried, dead and buried, dead and—* With infinite care he attempts to breathe, sure that this time it will be easy; he'll be patient, discreet, sensible, he won't do it all at once—

He gags. Spasmodically, he gulps, cries out, and gags again, springing convulsively to his knees and throwing himself over the low wall by his bed, laboring as if he were breathing sand. He starts to sweat. His heartbeat comes back, then pulse, then seeing, hearing, swallowing . . . High in the wall a window glimmers, a star is out, the sky is pale evening blue. Trembling with nausea, he rises to his feet, sways a little in the gloom, then puts out one arm and steadies himself against the stone wall. He sees the window, sees the door ahead of him. In his tearing eyes the star suddenly blazes and lengthens like a knife; his hands over his face, longing for life and strength to come back, the overwhelming flow of force that will crest at sunrise, leaving him raging at the world and ready to kill anyone, utterly proud and contemptuous, driven to sleep as the last resort of a balked assassin. But it's difficult to stand, difficult to breathe: *I wish I were dead and buried, dead and buried, dead and buried— But there!* he whispers to himself like a charm, *There, it's going, it's going away.* He smiles slyly round at his companionable, merciful stone walls. With an involuntarily silent, gliding gait he moves toward the door, opens the iron gate, and goes outside. Life is coming back. The trees are black against the sky, which yet holds some light; far away in the West lie the radiant memories of a vanished sun. An always vanished sun.

"Alive!" he cries, in triumph. It is—as usual—his first word of the day.

Dear Emily, sweet Emily, met Martin Guevara three days after she arrived home. She had been shown the plants in the garden and the house plants in stands and had praised them; she had been shown the sun-pictures and had praised *them;* she had fingered antimacassars, promised to knit, exclaimed at gaslights, and passed two evenings at home, doing nothing. Then in the hall that led to the pantry Sweet Will had taken her hand and she had dropped her eyes because you were supposed to and that was her style. Charlotte (who slept in the same room as her friend) embraced her at bedtime, wept over the handtaking, and then Emily said to her dear, dear friend (without thinking):

"Sweet William."

Charlotte laughed.

"It's not a joke!"

"It's so funny."

"I love Will dearly." She wondered if God would strike her dead for a hypocrite. Charlotte was looking at her oddly, and smiling.

"You mustn't be full of levity," said Emily, peeved. It was then that Sweet William came in and told them of tomorrow's garden-party, which was to be composed of her father's congregation. They were lucky, he said, to have acquaintances of such position and character. Charlotte slipped out on purpose, and Will, seeing they were alone, attempted to take Emily's hand again.

"Leave me alone!" Emily said angrily. He stared.

"I said leave me alone!"

And she gave him such a look of angry pride that, in fact, he did.

Emily sees Guevara across the parlor by the abominable cherry-red sofa, talking animatedly and carelessly. In repose he is slight, undistinguished, and plain, but no one will ever see him in repose; Emily realizes this. His strategy is never to rest, to bewilder, he would (she thinks) slap you if only to confuse you, and when he can't he's always out of the way and attacking, making one look ridiculous. She knows nobody and is bored; she starts for the door to the garden.

At the door his hand closes over her wrist; he has somehow gotten there ahead of her.

"The lady of the house," he says.

"I'm back from school."

"And you've learned—?"

"Let me go, please."

"Never." He drops her hand and stands in the doorway. She says:

"I want to go outside."

"Never."

"I'll call my father."

"Do." She tries and can't talk; I wouldn't *bother*, she thinks to herself, loftily. She goes out into the garden with him. Under the trees his plainness vanishes like smoke.

"You want lemonade," he says.

"I'm not going to talk to you," she responds. "I'll talk to Will. Yes! I'll make him—"

"In trouble," says Mr. Guevara, returning silently with lemonade in a glass cup.

"No thank you."

"She wants to get away," says Martin Guevara. "I know."

"If I had your trick of walking like a cat," she says, "I could get out of anything."

"I *can* get out of anything," says the gentleman, handing Emily her punch, "out of an engagement, a difficulty. I can even get *you* out of anything."

"I loathe you," whispers Emily suddenly. "You walk like a cat. You're ugly."

"Not out here," he remarks.

"Who has to be afraid of lights?" cries Emily energetically. He stands away from the paper lanterns strung between the trees, handsome, comfortable and collected, watching Emily's cut-glass cup shake in her hand.

"I can't move," she says miserably.

"Try." She takes a step toward him. "See; you can."

"But I wanted to go *away!*" With sudden hysteria she flings the lemonade (cup and all) into his face, but he is no longer there.

"What are you doing at a church supper, you hypocrite!" she shouts tearfully at the vacancy.

Sweet William has to lead her in to bed.

"You thought better of it," remarks Martin, head framed in an evening window, sounds of footsteps outside, ladies' heels clicking in the streets.

"I don't know you," she says miserably, "I just don't." He takes her light shawl, a pattern in India cashmere.

"That will come," he says, smiling. He sits again, takes her hand, and squeezes the skin on the wrist.

"Let me go, please?" she says like a child.

"I don't know."

"You talk like the smart young gentlemen at Andover; they were all fools."

"Perhaps you overawed them." He leans forward and puts his hand around the back of her neck for a moment. "Come on, dear."

"What are you talking about!" Emily cries.

"San Francisco is a lovely city. I had ancestors here three hundred years ago."

"Don't think that because I came here—"

"She doesn't," he whispers, grasping her shoulder, "she doesn't know a thing."

"God damn you!"

He blinks and sits back. Emily is weeping. The confusion of the room—an over-stuffed, over-draped hotel room—has gotten on her nerves. She snatches for her shawl, which is still in his grasp, but he holds it out of her reach, darting his handsome, unnaturally young face from side to side as she tries to reach round him. She falls across his lap and lies there, breathless with terror.

"You're cold," she whispers, horrified, "you're cold as a corpse." The shawl descends lightly over her head and shoulders. His frozen hands help her to her feet. He is delighted; he bares his teeth in a smile.

"I think," he says, tasting it, "that I'm going to visit your family."

"But you don't—" she stumbles—"you don't want to . . . sleep with me. I know it."

"I can be a suitor like anyone else," he says.

That night Emily tells it all to Charlotte, who, afraid of the roué, stays up and reads a French novel as the light drains from the windows and the true black dark takes its place. It is almost dawn and Charlotte has been dozing, when Emily shakes her friend awake, kneeling by the bed with innocent blue eyes reflecting the dying night.

"I had a terrible dream," she complains.

"Hmmmm?"

"I dreamed," says Emily tiredly. "I had a night-mare. I dreamed I was walking by the beach and I decided to go swimming and then a . . . a thing, I don't know . . . it took me by the neck."

"Is that all?" says Charlotte peevishly.

"I'm sick," says Emily with childish satisfaction. She pushes Charlotte over in the bed and climbs in with her. "I won't have to see that man again if I'm sick."

"Pooh, why not?" mumbles Charlotte.

"Because I'll have to stay home."

"He'll visit you."

"William won't let him."

"Sick?" says Charlotte then, suddenly waking up. She moves away from her friend, for she has read more bad fiction than Emily and less moral poetry.

"Yes, I feel awful," says Emily simply, resting her head on her knees. She pulls away in tired irritation when her friend reaches for the collar of her nightdress. Charlotte looks and jumps out of bed.

"Oh," says Charlotte. "Oh—goodness—oh—" holding out her hands.

"What on earth's the matter with you?"

"He's—" whispers Charlotte in horror, "he's—"

In the dim light her hands are black with blood.

"You've come," he says. He is lying on his hotel sofa, reading a newspaper, his feet over one arm and a hand trailing on the rug.

"Yes," she answers, trembling with resolution.

"I never thought this place would have such a good use. But I never know when I'll manage to pick up money—"

With a blow of her hand, she makes a fountain of the newspaper; he lies on the sofa, mildly amused.

"Nobody knows I came," she says rapidly. "But I'm going to finish you off. I know how." She hunts feverishly in her bag.

"I wouldn't," he remarks quietly.

"Ah!" Hauling out her baby cross (silver), she confronts him with it like Joan of Arc. He is still amused, still mildly surprised.

"In your hands?" he says delicately. Her fingers are loosening, her face pitiful.

"My dear, the significance is in the feeling, the faith, not the symbol. You use that the way you would use a hypodermic needle. Now in your father's hands—"

"I dropped it," she says in a little voice. He picks it up and hands it to her.

"You can touch—" she says, her face screwing up for tears.

"I can."

"Oh my God!" she cries in despair.

"My dear." He puts one arm around her, holding her against him, a very strong man for she pushes frantically to free herself. "How many times have *I* said that! But you'll learn. Do I sound like the silly boys at Andover?" Emily's eyes are fixed and her throat contracts; he forces her head between her knees. "The way you go on, you'd think I was bad luck."

"I—I—"

"And you without the plentiful lack of brains that characterizes your friend. She'll be somebody's short work and I think I know whose."

Emily turns white again.

"I'll send her around to you afterwards. Good God! What do you think will happen to her?"

"She'll die," says Emily clearly. He grasps her by the shoulders.

"Ah!" he says with immense satisfaction. "And after that? Who lives forever after that? Did you know that?"

"Yes, people like you don't die," whispers Emily. "But you're not people—"

"No," he says intently, "no. We're not." He stands Emily on her feet. "We're a passion!" Smiling triumphantly, he puts his hands on each side of her head, flattening the pretty curls, digging his fingers into the hair, in a grip Emily can no more break than she could break a vise.

"We're passion," he whispers, amused. "Life is passion. Desire makes life."

"Ah, let me go," says Emily.

He smiles ecstatically at the sick girl.

"Desire," he says dreamily, "lives; *that* lives when nothing else does, and we're desire made purely, desire walking the Earth. Can a dead man walk? Ah! If you want, want, want . . ."

He throws his arms around her, pressing her head to his chest and nearly suffocating her, ruining her elaborate coiffure and crushing the lace at her throat. Emily breathes in the deadness about him, the queer absence of odor, or heat, or presence; her mouth is pressed against the cloth of his fashionable suit, expensive stuff, a good dollar a yard, gotten by—what? But his hands are strong enough to get anything.

"You see," he says gently. "I enjoy someone with intelligence, even with morals; it adds a certain— And besides—" here he releases her and holds her face up to his— "we like souls that come to us; these visits to the bedrooms of unconscious citizens are rather like frequenting a public brothel."

"I abhor you," manages Emily. He laughs. He's delighted.

"Yes, yes, dear," he says, "but don't imagine we're callous parasites. Followers of the Marquis de Sade, perhaps—you see Frisco has evening hours for its bookstores!—but sensitive souls, really, and apt to long for a little conscious partnership." Emily shuts her eyes. "I said," he goes on, with a touch of hardness, "that I am a genuine seducer. I flatter myself that I'm not an animal."

"You're a monster," says Emily, with utter conviction. Keeping one hand on her shoulder, he steps back a pace.

"Go." She stands, unable to believe her luck, then makes what seems to her a rush for the door; it carries her into his arms.

"You see?" He's pleased; he's proved a point.

"I can't," she says, with wide eyes and wrinkled forehead . . .

"You will." He reaches for her and she faints.

Down in the dark where love and some other things make their hiding place, Emily drifts aimlessly, quite alone, quite cold, like a dead woman without a passion in her soul to make her come back to life.

She opens her eyes and finds herself looking at his face in the dark, as if the man carried his own light with him.

"I'll die," she says softly.

"Not for a while," he drawls, sleek and content.

"You've killed me."

"I've loved."

"Love!"

"Say 'taken' then, if you insist."

"I do! I do!" she cried bitterly.

"You decided to faint."

"Oh the hell with you!" she shouts.

"Good girl!" And as she collapses, weeping hysterically, "Now, now, come here, dear . . . " nuzzling her abused little neck. He kisses it in the tenderest fashion with an exaggerated, mocking sigh; she twists away, but is pulled closer and as his lips open over the teeth of inhuman, dead desire, his victim finds—to her surprise—that there is no pain. She braces herself and then, unexpectedly, shivers from head to foot.

"Stop it!" she whispers, horrified. "Stop it! Stop it!"

But a vampire who has found a soul-mate (even a temporary one) will be immoderate. There's no stopping them.

Charlotte's books have not prepared her for this.

"You're to stay in the house, my dear, because you're ill."

"I'm not," Emily says, pulling the sheet up to her chin.

"Of course you are." The Reverend beams at her, under the portrait of Emily's dead mother which hangs in Emily's bedroom. "You've had a severe chill."

"But I have to get out!" says Emily, sitting up. "Because I have an appointment, you see."

"Not now," says the Reverend.

"But I *can't* have a severe chill in the *summer*!"

"You look so like your mother," says the Reverend, musing. After he has gone away, Charlotte comes in.

"I have to stay in the damned bed," says Emily forcefully, wiggling her toes under the sheet. Charlotte, who has been carrying a tray with tea and a posy on it, drops it on the washstand.

"Why, Emily!"

"I have to stay in the damned bed the whole damned day," Emily adds.

"Dear, why do you use those words?"

"Because the whole world's damned!"

After the duties of his employment were completed at six o'clock on Wednesday, William came to the house with a doctor and introduced him to the Reverend and Emily's bosom friend. The street lamps would not be lit for an hour but the sun was just down and a little party congregated in the garden under remains of Japanese paper lanterns. No one ever worried that these might set themselves on fire. Lucy brought tea—they were one of the few civilized circles in Frisco—and over the tea, in the darkening garden, to the accompaniment of sugar-tongs and plopping cream (very musical) they talked.

"Do you think," says the Reverend, very worried, "that it might be consumption?"

"Perhaps the lungs are affected," says the doctor.

"She's always been such a robust girl." This is William, putting down the teapot which has a knitted tube about the handle, for insulation. Charlotte is stirring her tea with a spoon.

"It's very strange," says the doctor serenely, and he repeats "It's very strange" as shadows advance in the garden. "But young ladies, you know—especially at twenty—young ladies often take strange ideas into their heads; they do, they often do; they droop; they worry."

His eyes are mild, his back sags, he hears the pleasant gurgle of more tea. A quiet consultation, good people, good solid people, a little illness, nothing serious—

"No," says Charlotte. Nobody hears her.

"I knew a young lady once—" ventures the doctor mildly.

"No," says Charlotte, more loudly. Everyone turns to her, and Lucy, taking the opportunity, insinuates a plate of small-sized muffins in front of Charlotte.

"I can tell you all about it," mutters Charlotte, glancing up from under her eyebrows. "But you'll *laugh.*"

"Now, dear—" says the Reverend.

"Now, miss—" says the doctor.

"As a friend—" says William.

Charlotte begins to sob.

"Oh," she says, "I'll—I'll tell you about it."

Emily meets Mr. Guevara at the Mansion House at seven, having recovered an appearance of health (through self-denial) and a good solid record of spending the evenings at home (through self-control). She stands at the hotel's wrought-iron gateway, her back rigid as a stick, drawing on white gloves. Martin materializes out of the blue evening shadows and takes her arm.

"I shall like living forever," says Emily, thoughtfully.

"God deliver me from Puritans," says Mr. Guevara.

"What?"

"You're a lady. You'll swallow me up."

"I'll do anything I please," remarks Emily severely, with a glint of teeth.

"Ah."

"I will." They walk through the gateway. "You don't care two pins for me."

"Unfortunately," says he, bowing.

"It's not unfortunate as long as *I* care for me," says Emily, smiling with great energy. "Damn them all."

"You proper girls would overturn the world." Along they walk in the evening, in a quiet, respectable rustle of clothes. Halfway to the restaurant she stops and says breathlessly:

"Let's go—somewhere else!"

"My dear, you'll ruin your health!"

"You know better. Three weeks ago I was sick as a dog and much you cared; I haven't slept for days and I'm fine."

"You look fine."

"Ah! You mean I'm beginning to look dead, like you." She tightens her hold on his arm, to bring him closer.

"Dead?" says he, slipping his arm around her.

"Fixed. Bright-eyed. Always at the same heat and not a moment's rest."

"It agrees with you."

"I adore you," she says.

When Emily gets home, there's a reckoning. The Reverend stands in the doorway and sad William, too, but not Charlotte, for she is on the parlor sofa, having had hysterics.

"Dear Emily," says the Reverend. "We don't know how to tell you this—"

"Why, Daddy, *what?*" exclaims Emily, making wide-eyes at him.

"Your little friend told us—"

"Has something happened to Charlotte?" cries Emily. "Oh tell me, tell me, what happened to Charlotte?" And before they can stop her she has flown into the parlor and is kneeling beside her friend, wondering if she dares pinch her under cover of her shawl. William, quick as a flash, kneels on one side of her and Daddy on the other.

"Dear Emily!" cries William with fervor.

"Oh, sweetheart!" says Charlotte, reaching down and putting her arms around her friend.

"You're well!" shouts Emily, sobbing over Charlotte's hand and thinking perhaps to bite her. But the Reverend's arms lift her up.

"My dear," says he, "you came home unaccompanied. You were not at the Society."

"But," says Emily, smiling dazzlingly, "two of the girls took all my hospital sewing to their house because we must finish it right away and I have not—"

"You have been lying to us," the Reverend says. *Now,* thinks Emily, *Sweet William will cover his face.* Charlotte sobs.

"She can't help it," Charlotte brokenly. "It's the spell."

"Why, I think everyone's gone out of their minds," says Emily, frowning. Sweet William takes her from Daddy, leading her away from Charlotte.

"Weren't you with a gentleman tonight?" says Sweet Will firmly. Emily backs away.

"For shame!"

"She doesn't remember it," explains Charlotte; "it's part of his spell."

"I think you ought to get a doctor for *her,*" observes Emily.

"You were with a gentleman named Guevara," says Will, showing less tenderness than Emily expects. "Weren't you? Well—weren't you?"

"Bad cess to you if I was!" snaps Emily, surprised at herself. The other three gasp. "I won't be questioned," she goes on, "and I won't be spied upon. And I think you'd better take some of Charlotte's books away from her; she's getting downright silly."

"You have too much color," says Will, catching her hands. "You're ill but you don't sleep. You stay awake all night. You don't eat. But look at you!"

"I don't understand you. Do you want me to be ugly?" says Emily, trying to be pitiful. Will softens; she sees him do it.

"My dear Emily," he says. "My dear girl—we're afraid for you."

"Me?" says Emily, enjoying herself.

"We'd better put you to bed," says the Reverend kindly.

"You're so kind," whispers Emily, blinking as if she held back tears.

"That's a good girl," says Will, approving. "We know you don't understand. But we'll take care of you, Em."

"*Will* you?"

"Yes, dear. You've been near very grave danger, but luckily we found out in time, and we found out what to do; we'll make you well, we'll keep you safe, we'll—"

"Not with *that* you won't," says Emily suddenly, rooting herself to the spot, for what William takes out of his vest pocket (where he usually keeps his watch) is a broad-leaved, prickle-faced dock called wolfsbane; it must distress any vampire of sense to be so enslaved to pure superstition. But enslaved they are, nonetheless.

"Oh, no!" says Emily swiftly. "That's silly, perfectly silly!"

"Common sense must give way in such a crisis," remarks the Reverend gravely.

"You bastard!" shouts Emily, turning red, attempting to tear the charm out of her fiancé's hand and jump up and down on it. But the Reverend holds one arm and Charlotte the other and between them they pry her fingers apart and William puts his property gently in his vest pocket again.

"She's far gone," says the Reverend fearfully, at his angry daughter. Emily is scowling, Charlotte stroking her hair.

"Ssssh" says Will with great seriousness. "We must get her to bed," and between them they half-carry Emily up the stairs and put her, dressed as she is, in the big double bed with the plush headboard that she has shared so far with Charlotte. Daddy and fiancé confer in the room across the long, low rambling hall, and Charlotte sits by her rebellious friend's bed and attempts to hold her hand.

"I won't permit it; you're a damned fool!" says Emily.

"Oh, Emmy!"

"Bosh."

"It's true!"

"Is it?" With extraordinary swiftness, Emily turns round in the bed and rises to her knees. "Do you know anything about it?"

"I know it's horrid, I—"

"Silly!" Playfully Emily puts her hands on Charlotte's shoulders. Her eyes are narrowed, her nostrils widened to breathe; she parts her lips a little and looks archly at her friend. "You don't know anything about it," she says insinuatingly.

"I'll call your father," says Charlotte quickly.

Emily throws an arm around her friend's neck.

"Not yet! Dear Charlotte!"

"We'll save you," says Charlotte doubtfully.

"Sweet Charrie; you're my friend, aren't you?"

Charlotte begins to sob again.

"Give me those awful things, those leaves."

"Why, Emily, I *couldn't*!"

"But he'll come for me and I have to protect myself, don't I?"

"I'll call your father," says Charlotte firmly.

"No, I'm *afraid*." And Emily wrinkles her forehead sadly.

"Well—"

"Sometimes I—I—" falters Emily. "I can't move or run away and everything looks so—so strange and *horrible*—"

"Oh, here!" Covering her face with one hand, Charlotte holds out her precious dock leaves in the other.

"Dear, dear! Oh, sweet! Oh thank you! Don't be afraid. He isn't after you."

"I hope not," says the bosom friend.

"Oh no, he told me. It's me he's after."

"How awful," says Charlotte, sincerely.

"Yes," says Emily. "Look." And she pulls down the collar of her dress to show the ugly marks, white dots unnaturally healed up, like the pockmarks of a drug addict.

"Don't!" chokes Charlotte.

Emily smiles mournfully. "We really ought to put the lights out," she says.

"Out!"

"Yes, you can see him better that way. If the lights are on, he could sneak in without being seen; he doesn't mind lights, you know."

"I don't know, dear—"

"I do." (Emily is dropping the dock leaves into the washstand, under cover of her skirt.) "I'm afraid. Please."

"Well—"

"Oh, you must!" And leaping to her feet, she turns down the gas to a dim glow; Charlotte's face fades into the obscurity of the deepening shadows.

"So. The lights are out," says Emily quietly.

"I'll ask Will—" Charlotte begins . . .

"No, dear."

"But, Emily—"

"He's coming, dear."

"You mean Will is coming."

"No, not Will."

"Emily, you're a—"

"I'm a sneak," says Emily, chuckling. "Sssssh!" And, while her friend sits paralyzed, one of the windows swings open in the night breeze, a lead-paned window that opens on a hinge, for the Reverend is fond of culture and old architecture. Charlotte lets out a little noise in her throat; and then—with the smash of a pistol shot—the gaslight shatters and the flame goes out. Gas hisses into the air, quietly, insinuatingly, as if explaining the same thing over and over. Charlotte screams with her whole heart. In the dark a hand clamps like a vise on Emily's wrist. A moment passes.

"Charlotte?" she whispers.

"Dead," says Guevara.

Emily has spent most of the day asleep in the rubble, with his coat rolled under her head where he threw it the moment before sunrise, the moment before he staggered to his place and plunged into sleep. She has watched the dawn come up behind the rusty barred gate, and then drifted into sleep herself with his face before her closed eyes—his face burning with a rigid, constricted, unwasting vitality. Now she wakes aching and bruised, with the sun of late afternoon in her face.

Sitting against the stone wall, she sneezes twice and tries, ineffectually, to shake the dust from her silk skirt.

Oh, how—she thinks vaguely—*how messy.* She gets to her feet. *There's something I have to do.* The iron gate swings open at a touch. *Trees and gravestones tilted every which way. What did he say? Nothing would disturb it but a Historical Society.*

Having tidied herself as best she can, with his coat over her arm and the address of his tailor in her pocket, she trudges among the erupted stones, which tilt crazily to all sides as if in an earthquake. Blood (Charlotte's, whom she does not think about) has spread thinly on to her hair and the hem of her dress, but her hair is done up with fine feeling, despite the absence of a mirror, and her dress is dark gray; the spot looks like a spot of dust. She folds the coat into a neat package and uses it to wipe the dust off her shoes, then lightens her step past the cemetery entrance, trying to look healthy and respectable. She aches all over from sleeping on the ground.

Once in town and having ascertained from a shop window that she will pass muster in a crowd, Emily trudges up hills and down hills to the tailor, the evidence over her arm. She stops at other windows, to look or to admire herself; thinks smugly of her improved coloring; shifts the parcel on her arm to show off her waist. In one window there is a display of religious objects—beads and crosses, books with fringed gilt bookmarks, a colored chromo of Madonna and Child. In this window Emily admires herself.

"It's Emily, dear!"

A Mrs. L—— appears in the window beside her, with Constantia, Mrs. L——'s twelve-year-old offspring.

"Why, dear, whatever happened to you?" Mrs. L——, noticing no hat, no gloves, and no veil.

"Nothing: whatever happened to you?" says Emily cockily. Constantia's eyes grow wide with astonishment at the fine, free audacity of it.

"Why, you look as if you'd been—"

"Picnicking," says Emily, promptly. "One of the gentlemen spilled beer on his coat." And she's in the shop now and hanging over the counter, flushed, counting the coral and amber beads strung around a crucifix.

Mrs. L—— knocks doubtfully on the window-glass. Emily waves and smiles.

Your father—form Mrs. L——'s lips in the glass. Emily nods and waves cheerfully.

They do go away, finally.

"A fine gentleman," says the tailor earnestly, "a very fine man." He lisps a little.

"Oh very fine," agrees Emily, sitting on a stool and kicking the rungs with her feet. "Monstrous fine."

"But very careless," says the tailor fretfully, pulling Martin's coat nearer the window so he can see it, for the shop is a hole-in-the-wall and dark. "He shouldn't send a lady to this part of the town."

"I was a lady once," says Emily.

"Mmmmmm."

"It's fruit stains—something awful, don't you think?"

"I cannot have this ready by tonight," looking up.

"Well, you must, that's all," says Emily calmly. "You always have and he has a lot of confidence in you, you know. He'd be awfully angry if he found out."

"Found out?" sharply.

"That you can't have it ready by tonight."

The tailor ponders.

"I'll positively stay in the shop while you work," says Emily flatteringly.

"Why, Reverend, I saw her on King Street as dirty as a gypsy, with her hair loose and the wildest eyes and I *tried* to talk to her, but she dashed into a shop—"

The sun goes down in a broad belt of gold, goes down over the ocean, over the hills and the beaches, makes shadows lengthen in the street near the quays where a lisping tailor smooths and alters, working against the sun (and very uncomfortable he is, too), watched by a pair of unwinking eyes that glitter a little in the dusk inside the stuffy shop. (*I think I've changed,* meditates Emily.)

He finishes, finally, with relief, and sits with an *ouf!* handing her the coat, the new and beautiful coat that will be worn as soon as the eccentric gentleman comes out to take the evening air. The eccentric gentleman, says Emily incautiously, will do so in an hour by the Mansion House when the last traces of light have faded from the sky.

"Then, my dear Miss," sayd the tailor unctuously, "I think a little matter of pay—"

"You don't think," says Emily softly, "or you wouldn't have gotten yourself into such a mess as to be this eccentric gentleman's tailor." And out she goes.

Now nobody can see the stains on Emily's skirt or in her hair; street lamps are being lit, there are no more carriages, and the number of people in the streets grows— San Francisco making the most of the short summer nights. It is perhaps fifteen minutes back to the fashionable part of the town where Emily's hatless, shawlless state will be looked on with disdain; here nobody notices. Emily dawdles through the streets, fingering her throat, yawning, looking at the sky, thinking: *I love, I love, I love—*

She has fasted for the day but she feels fine; she feels busy, busy inside as if the life inside her is flowering and bestirring itself, populated as the streets. She remembers—

I love you, I hate you. You enchantment, you degrading necessity, you foul and filthy life, you promise of endless love and endless time . . .

What words to say with Charlotte sleeping in the same room, no, the same bed, with her hands folded under her face! Innocent sweetheart, whose state must now be rather different.

Up the hills she goes, where the view becomes wider and wider, and the lights spread out like sparkles on a cake, out of the section which is too dangerous, too low, and too furtive to bother with a lady (or is it something in her eyes?), into the broader bystreets where shore-leave sailors try to make her acquaintance by falling into step and seizing her elbow; she snakes away with unbounded strength, darts into shadows; laughs in their faces: "I've got what I want!"

"Not like me!"

"Better!"

This is the Barbary Coast, only beginning to become a tourist attraction; there are barkers outside the restaurants advertising pretty waiter girls, dance halls, spangled posters twice the height of a man, crowds upon crowds of people, one or two guides with tickets in their hats, and Emily—who keeps to the shadows. She nearly chokes with laughter: *What a field of ripe wheat!* One of the barkers hoists her by the waist onto his platform.

"Do you see this little lady? Do you see this—"

"Let me go, God damn you!" she cries indignantly.

"This angry little lady—" pushing her chin with one sunburned hand to make her face the crowd. "This—" But here Emily hurts him, slashing his palm with her teeth, quite pleased with herself, but surprised, too, for the man was holding his hand cupped and the whole thing seemed to happen of itself. She escapes instantly into the crowd and continues up through the Coast, through the old Tenderloin, drunk with self-confidence, slipping like a shadow through the now genteel streets and arriving at the Mansion House gate having seen no family spies and convinced that none has seen her.

But nobody is there.

Ten by the clock, and no one is there, either; eleven by the clock and still no one. *Why didn't I leave this life when I had the chance!* Only one thing consoles Emily, that by some alchemy or nearness to the state she longs for, no one bothers or questions her and even the policemen pass her by as if in her little corner of the gate there is nothing but a shadow. Midnight and no one, half-past and she dozes; perhaps three hours later, perhaps four, she is startled awake by the sound of footsteps. She wakes: nothing. She sleeps again and in her dream hears them for the second time, then she wakes to find herself looking into the face of a lady who wears a veil.

"What!" Emily's startled whisper.

The lady gestures vaguely, as if trying to speak.

"What is it?"

"Don't—" and the lady speaks with feeling but, it seems, with difficulty also—"don't go home."

"Home?" echoes Emily, stupefied, and the stranger nods, saying:

"In danger."

"Who?" Emily is horrified.

"He's in danger." Behind her veil her face seems almost to emit a faint light of its own.

"You're one of them," says Emily. "Aren't you?" and when the woman nods, adds desperately, "Then you must save him!"

The lady smiles pitifully; that much of her face can be seen as the light breeze plays with her net veil.

"But you must!" exclaims Emily. "You know how; I don't; you've got to!"

"I don't dare," very softly. Then the veiled woman turns to go, but Emily—quite hysterical now—seizes her hand, saying:

"Who are you? Who are you?"

The lady gestures vaguely and shakes her head.

"Who are you!" repeats Emily with more energy. "You tell me, do you hear?"

Somberly the lady raises her veil and stares at her friend with a tragic, dignified, pitiful gaze. In the darkness her face burns with unnatural and beautiful color.

It is Charlotte.

Dawn comes with a pellucid quickening, glassy and ghostly. Slowly, shapes emerge from darkness and the blue pours back into the world—twilight turned backwards and the natural order reversed. Destruction, which is simple, logical, and easy, finds a kind of mocking parody in the morning's creation. Light has no business coming back, but light does.

Emily reaches the cemetery just as the caldron in

the east overflows, just as the birds (idiots! she thinks) begin a tentative cheeping and chirping. She sits at the gate for a minute to regain her strength, for the night's walking and worry have tried her severely. In front of her the stones lie on graves, almost completely hard and real, waiting for the rising of the sun to finish them off and make complete masterpieces of them. Emily rises and trudges up the hill, slower and slower as the ground rises to its topmost swell, where three hundred years of peaceful Guevaras fertilize the grass and do their best to discredit the one wild shoot that lives on, the only disrespectful member of the family. Weeping a little to herself, Emily lags up the hill, raising her skirts to keep them off the weeds, and murderously hating in her heart the increasing light and the happier celebrating of the birds. She rounds the last hillock of ground and raises her eyes to the Guevaras' eternal mansion, expecting to see nobody again. There is the corner of the building, the low iron gate—

In front of it stands Martin Guevara between her father and Sweet Sweet Will, captived by both arms, his face pale and beautiful between two gold crosses that are just beginning to sparkle in the light of day.

"We are caught," says Guevara, seeing her, directing at her his fixed, white smile.

"You let him go," says Emily—very reasonably.

"You're safe, my Emily!" cries Sweet Will.

"Let him go!" She runs to them, stops, looks at them, perplexed to the bottom of her soul.

"Let him go," she says. "Let him go, let him go!"

Between the two bits of jewelry, Emily's life and hope and only pleasure smiles painfully at her, the color drained out of his face, desperate eyes fixed on the east.

"You don't understand," says Emily, inventing. "He isn't dangerous now. If you let him go, he'll run inside and then you can come back any time during the day and finish him off. I'm sick. You—"

The words die in her throat. All around them, from every tree and hedge, from boughs that have sheltered the graveyard for a hundred years, the birds begin their morning noise. A great hallelujah rises; after all, the birds have nothing to worry about. Numb, with legs like sticks, Emily sees sunlight touch the top of the stone mausoleum, sunlight slide down its face, sunlight reach the level of a standing man—

"I adore you," says Martin to her. With the slow bending over of a drowning man, he doubles up, like a man stuck with a knife in a dream; he doubles up, falls—

And Emily screams; what a scream! as if her soul were being haled out through her throat; and she is running down the other side of the little hill to regions as yet untouched by the sun, crying inwardly: I need help! help! help!— She knows where she can get it. Three hundred feet down the hill in a valley, a wooded protected valley sunk below the touch of the rising sun, there she runs through the trees, past the fence that separates the old graveyard from the new, expensive, cast-iron-and-polished-granite—

There, just inside the door (for they were rich people and Charlotte's mother's sister lived in 'Frisco) lies Emily's good friend, her old friend, with her hat and cloak off and her blonde hair falling over the bier to her knees—Charlotte in a white wrap like a slip. Emily stops in inside the door, confused: Charlotte regards her fixedly.

"There's not much time," says Charlotte.

"Help him!" whispers Emily.

"I can't; he's already gone."

"Please—please—" but Charlotte only rises glidingly on her couch, lifting her beautiful bare shoulders out of the white silk, fixedly regarding her friend with that look that neither time nor age will do anything to dim.

"I won't," says Emily, frightened, "I don't think—" taking a few unwilling steps toward the coffin. "I don't think that now—"

"You only have a moment," says Charlotte. Emily is now standing by her friend and slowly, as if through tired weakness, she slips to her knees.

"Quickly," says Charlotte, scarcely to be heard at all. Looping one arm around her friend's neck, she pulls her face up to hers.

"But not without him"—Emily is half suffocated— "Not without him! Not this way!" She tries to break the grip and cannot. Charlotte smiles and dips her head.

"Not without him," her voice dying away faintly, "Not without him . . . not without . . . without . . ."

Sunlight touches the door, a moment too late.

THE DRAGONBONE FLUTE

LOIS TILTON

LOIS TILTON is an author who has been making a name
for herself in the fantasy and horror fields. Other work
by her appears in *Grails: Quests, Visions and Occurrences;*
Witch Fantastic; and *Enchanted Forests.* She lives in Illinois. "The Dragonbone Flute" is a fantasy dealing with
entirely real emotions, pain and loss, from the point of
view of both man and dragon.

The flute was white as ivory, white as bone. It had been made from a dragon's hollow wing-bone, found one day by a shepherd in a mountainside cave. The bones had lain gleaming in the darkness, the high-arched ribs, the skull with its deep hollow sockets, the razor-edged teeth. Yet it was only one delicate wingtip that he took home to the sod-roofed hut where he lived on the mountain, to spend the long summer evenings patiently boring the fingerholes.

When it was finished he took it outside and blew the first tentative note. The sound was thrillingly clear, high and light. Soon, if he shut his eyes while he played, it almost seemed that he could see dragons soaring, their eyes like jewels, vast wings extended to catch the updraft from the sunwarmed valleys far below.

Summer ended, and when the sky turned gray and the cold wind began to blow down from the peak, the shepherd gathered his animals and went down into the valley. Within days the trails were blocked by snow, and now was the time to sit by the fire in the company of other men. From time to time, when the tavern in the village was full of laughter and dancing, the shepherd would take out his flute and join in with the viol and recorder while the villagers skipped and rollicked to the well-known country tunes. It was a good way to pass the winter evenings and earn a tankard or two of thick brown ale.

But when the snow melted and the new grass came green on the mountain, he gathered up his newly shorn flock to drive it back up to the summer pasture. Now, once again, his songs were of dragons and flight. They seemed to come from the heart of the flute itself, as if the hollow bone retained an echo of the dragon's own voice.

So he sat and played on the mountainside one day when suddenly a black shadow seemed to blot out the sun. As his sheep ran bleating in mindless panic, he looked up to see the vast shape of a dragon plunging down at him, talons extended, tail lashing the sky in a frenzy of rage. Then he heard its voice in his mind, even as he dropped to the ground in a futile effort to evade those claws: *Mlakazar! My mate! Death! Death! Who killed him? Who has his bones?*

The shepherd in his desperate terror cried aloud, "No!" and felt the wind of the dragon's passage engulfing him in its hot, sulphurous scent as he awaited the piercing agony of the talons seizing his flesh. But instead he rolled free, cowering on the ground as the dragon hovered directly overhead, the beating of its wings battering him like a gale. *My mate! I heard the voice of his bones!*

The shepherd in his fear got to his knees, stammering, "I . . . found the bones in a cave. I took only one— this one—to make a flute. I never killed . . . never . . ."

Slowly the dragon lowered itself to the ground, transfixing the trembling man with its gaze, red tongue licking in and out of its mouth. *Yes, this is his, this is his voice. Show me. Show me the rest of the bones.*

He led, the dragon followed, claws scoring the earth of the mountainside to bare stone. The cave was above the grass line, a place the shepherd had found the year before while climbing up to retrieve a strayed lamb. It was then he had spotted the break in the rock and the dim gleam of fleshless bone inside.

The dragon was only barely able to squeeze its bulk through the opening of the cave. The bones lay as the shepherd had found them, as they must have lain for tens of years to be stripped and worn so white. The shepherd felt the cry of the dragon's grief: *Mlakazar!*

He began to plead for his life, "You can see how long ago it must have been. I swear! I meant no harm! I never touched—never took but the one bone. Oh, forgive!"

The dragon lowered its head in sorrow. The shepherd could see now that it was old and a female, her blue-green hide and scales worn. Her eyes were pallid opals, red-veined with age. *Let me hear,* she said at last. *Let me hear the voice of my mate.*

So the shepherd took his flute from his belt and with shaking hands began to play. He played the song of flight, the song of freedom in the air, glorying in the strength of his wings. He played from the flute's heart, not knowing how he did, and beside him the dragon wept huge golden tears.

His voice lives again, she said at last.

"I meant no harm," the shepherd said again, uncertainly. "I was alone up here on the mountain. I thought, a little music, a song or two . . ."

Yes, said the dragon. *I know what it is to be alone.* And after a moment she spread her wings and beat her way into the sky.

The shepherd immediately put down the flute and began to search the mountainside anxiously for his flock, hoping they had not all plunged to their deaths in their panicked rush from descending death. He glanced nervously up at the dragon, soaring about a distant peak, well aware that she could easily swallow a sheep with a single snap of her jaws.

It took three days to gather in the flock, scattered as they had been. And for days after that he did not dare touch the flute for fear of the dragon, that it might return and devour them. Yet from time to time he could see her far-off shape wheeling above him in the sky, bringing back memories of the song of flight, and finally he realized that nothing he did could endanger his sheep or protect them if the dragon wished him harm. So he let the dead dragon's voice live again, and he was no longer alone on the mountain.

But as the summer days grew longer, the presence of the dragon had other consequences. One day an armed man rode up to the high pasture. A squire rode with him, leading a much larger stallion bearing weapons and armor, most conspicuously a lance fully twelve feet long.

The shepherd pulled off his cap as the knight beckoned him over. "Herdsman! Here! What do you know of the drake?"

"Sir?"

"The dragon, lout! I've had word there's a dragon been spotted up in these mountains. Prime trophy! Looking for his lair. Well?"

The shepherd glanced nervously up into the empty sky, then shook his head. "No, Sir. No dragon up here, Sir." As the knight scowled, he added, "I couldn't stay up here with my sheep if there was a dragon on the mountain, Sir. Not with my sheep."

The horseman cursed and turned his glare onto his squire, dismounting. "It's getting late. I'll stay here the night. Go fetch one of those lambs."

The shepherd protested in vain as his lamb was slaughtered and spitted over his own fire. The knight only threw him a coin and ordered him to stop his complaints. In the morning the unwelcome visitors rode on, but the shepherd knew they would not be the last.

That winter, when he led his flock down from the mountain, the villagers pressed him with questions of their own, for they had seen the far-off shape of the dragon soaring high among the peaks. But the shepherd would admit nothing. Only, at last, that nothing had been at the sheep, no dragon, no eagle, no stray pack of wolves. And as they could see for themselves that the flock had not noticeably diminished, the villagers could only shake their heads.

But the shepherd kept mostly to himself throughout that winter, nursing a solitary ale at the side of the fire, and when the patrons of the tavern called for a song from his flute, he shook his head, saying he had lost it on the mountain.

In the spring, he drove his flock out almost before the snow had cleared the trails. Never had the mountain air seemed so fresh and clean, the sunshine so bright. And in the far, far-off distance, a speck of dark flew against the glistening snowcaps, a dragon soaring on outspread wings. His heart lifted at the sight.

She descended almost as soon as he had reached his pasture, with a stiff rustle of leathery wings. *Play, shepherd, play. Let me hear his voice again.* And the shepherd put the flute of bone to his mouth and let the song of flight spill out.

"He was your only mate?" he asked her once.

The dragon shook her scarred, blue-scaled head. *A mate is for life.*

"For life," the shepherd said sadly, thinking of

the churchyard where he had buried his wife so many years ago, before he went up onto the mountain. "Yes, it is the same with some of us."

The dragon was ancient, even for one of her kind. Her leathery wings were scarred, her scales broken and cracked. The shepherd was concerned, for all her immense size, thinking of errant knights and the cruel steel heads of their lances. "This place is dangerous for you," he urged her, but again and again the dragon would return. *Play, shepherd. Let his voice live again.*

Then indeed rumors spread that a dragon had returned to the mountain. Knights and other adventurers would make their way to the high pasture in search of the great head for a trophy, the fabled gold of the hoard. Always the shepherd would show them the flock grazing placidly and unmolested on the tender grass. "I've been grazing this flock up here for half a man's lifetime. Think you that I'd bring my sheep to a dragon's lair?"

So the season passed and the one after. Each spring the shepherd climbed the mountain trails more slowly. The dragon's eyes grew more dim.

Then one spring the sky was empty when the shepherd arrived at the high pasture with his flock. He went to bed that night with a heavy heart, and his flute was silent. But in the morning when he opened the door of his hut she was waiting for him, steaming in the mists. The huge head hung low, and her wings were tattered. *Play, shepherd. Let me hear him one last time.*

He played, and the music of the flute soared higher and lighter than ever. He played until his breath was exhausted, while the dragon's golden tears ran silently from the faded veined opal of her eyes.

When he was finished, she began to creep away with

painful slowness, dragging her ruined wings. The shepherd knew her destination. He followed until she came to the cave where her mate's bones lay. Before she crawled inside, squeezing her bulk through the narrow opening, she turned one last time to face the shepherd. *He was black! Bright black! Mlakazar!*

He waited until sunset colored the mountaintops, but she never emerged again.

The shepherd returned to his solitary existence on the mountain, to his sheep and their new lambs. From time to time he would take out the dragonbone flute and play a few notes, but the sky remained empty.

Then one day in late summer he felt a strange stirring in his heart. He put the flute to his mouth and played the old song of flight, the song of the dragon in his youth and power, soaring on the highest currents of the wind.

At first the shepherd thought he must be dreaming. The sky was full of dragons, wings outstretched, their jewel-tone scales glinting in the sunlight. He blinked, and the flute almost fell from his hands, but the dragons were still there and he could hear their voices in his mind, crying, *Flight! Flight!*

Then, as they dove closer, he saw that these dragons were each no larger than a swan, and he realized they must be newly hatched. *Flight!* they called. *Flight! Flight!* And he played for them again, watching with renewed joy as they swooped and plunged and tumbled in the air. Though he spoke to them, they made no answer, only repeating the same cry.

The next morning, the shepherd once again made the climb to the cave near the mountain's peak. His steps were slower than they had been when he first made this ascent and found a cave full of dry white bones. But this time dragons played above his head.

The immense bulk of a dragon does not decay quickly, even in the summer heat, and the shepherd had to tie a scarf over his face before he could enter the dark, narrow space of the cave. But as soon as his eyes grew accustomed to the light, he was able to make out what he had sought—the precious broken, gold-veined shards of the dragons' eggs, incubated long months in the decomposing warmth of their mother's remains. His heart raced at the first sight of so much wealth, but at last he left the cave as empty-handed as he had come. How could he sell them, even downriver in the marketplace? How could he let the world know of their existence?

Dragons flew over his head as he climbed slowly back down the mountain.

There were twelve of them—gold and green and russet and blue and a solitary jet-brilliant black. Their eyes were bright, their wings supple and unscarred. They grew rapidly in the waning summer days, preying on the smaller beasts of the mountainside. As their wings became stronger they went farther and farther from the cave, until they were flying from peak to peak, higher and higher, until they soared above the most lofty snowcaps.

Yet always they returned to the mountain where they had been born, to the sound of the shepherd's dragonbone flute.

But there came a day in autumn, when the grass was turning coarse and yellow, when the shepherd came upon the carcass of one of his yearling lambs on an outcrop of rock, torn open and half-devoured. The marks of a dragon's talons were clearly visible on the remains.

Despite the shepherd's increased vigilance, several days later another lamb was missing. He grieved, knowing that by the next spring the dragons would be grown strong enough to carry off a mature ram. Now at last he felt the bitter truth of the answer he had always made to the questing knights, that he would not be able to pasture his flock on the mountain if there were dragons laired nearby.

That fall he drove his sheep down to the valley before the first snowflakes flew in the sky. Some of the villagers shook their heads and wondered aloud how many more years the old shepherd would be able to spend all alone up on the mountainside. A few of them suggested that he ought to hire a boy to run after the sheep. To all of them the shepherd made scant response. He sat alone through the winter evenings by the fireside of the tavern, and when people spoke of dancing, none of them seemed to remember the sweet, lively music of the bone flute, lost so many years ago.

Then one evening, as night was coming on, there was a commotion outside the tavern: the stamping of horses and the ring of steel. The innkeeper bustled, shouting for his sons to tend the beasts, his maids to look lively in the kitchen and make up the best bed for the noble knight and his servant.

The customers nearest the door hurried outside, followed quickly by the rest. The shepherd left his seat last of all, dread in his heart. The crowd had gathered thickly around the horses, hindering the tavern's boy in his efforts to lead them into the stable. It was only at the last moment that the shepherd caught a glimpse of what was tied across the largest mount's back, a dragon as large as the horse itself, wings trussed up so they would not drag on the ground, the jewel-tones of its eyes gone dull and its scales still lustrous, gleaming black, the rarest of dragon-colors.

Never again would his wings bear him up into the sky, never again would he experience the pure joy of flight or ever know the long, loyal happiness of a mate.

Soon the knight came into the tavern, followed by the admiring company, where the landlord himself served him his ale. He was a young fellow, fair and flushed with pride, not at all reluctant to boast of his deed in slaying the drake.

"He flew at me with his claws all extended, mouth wide open, hissing—"

"Breathing fire?" one of the serving maids asked eagerly.

"Well," the knight admitted, reluctantly compelled to honesty, "not exactly." He took a deep swallow of his ale. "I couched my lance. The drake came at me, and I spitted him like a charging boar. The point of my lance ran in below his ribs and out between his wings. The force drove my mount to his knees." The knight was on his feet with the excitement of his own tale. "I jumped clear, pulled my sword—"

The crowd exclaimed at the bright ring of steel, stepping back as he pulled his blade free, reenacting the epic battle. "But the drake was already dead. Killed with one blow!"

The shepherd at the back of the room shook his head in sorrow. "Young and foolish, young and foolish," he thought. What had the black dragon known in his short life of knights or lances or swords?

He realized suddenly that a question was being addressed to him. "You, shepherd! You graze your flock on the mountains, is that right?" the knight was asking. "Did you ever see any dragonsign up there? Any sign of a lair?"

The shepherd shook his head again. "Knights came here before, asking me. No, no dragonsign on my mountain. Couldn't bring my sheep up there if there was dragons, now, could I?"

As always, the crowd nodded in acknowledgment of this obvious truth. The shepherd added, "Now, that one I saw tied on the horse. I don't think that one looked the size to take a sheep. Lamb, maybe. Young lamb. Not a sheep, though."

The young knight scowled at this belittling of his deed and shouted loudly to the innkeeper for more ale. In the morning he would be gone with his trophy, but others of his kind would come when they heard of his deed, eager for dragonslaying. One by one the dragons would fall to the lance, the gold and green and russet and blue.

It was a harsh winter that came to the valley that year, filling the passes with snow, so that the village was cut off for weeks from the rest of the world. By the time the snow began to melt, the shepherd had sold his flock, telling the buyer, "Getting too much for me, climbing up the mountain every year. Slowing down. Ache in my joints these days."

He pocketed the gold, little as there was. He might have gotten a better price at the spring fair downriver at the market town, but there wasn't time for that.

He made one last stop before he left the village, at the graveside of his wife. He knelt for a moment on the damp, cold ground, but after so long he hardly knew what to say. "Not like a dragon," he thought, getting stiffly back to his feet. "We forget."

Without his flock, he was only three days climbing up to the hidden cave, even with the half-melted banks of snow blocking his way. From time to time he glanced up, and at last he saw them, the faraway specks that were dragons circling overhead.

At the very back of the fissure in the rock, beyond the carcass of the blue-green dragon, the precious gold-veined broken shells were still untouched. Carefully, he picked them up, the green, the red, the jet, and put them away in his pack. Then, using his knife, he began to cut away a single hollow wingtip bone from the dried and leathery remains.

It was different working this half-raw bone, scraping away the adhering hide, carving out the holes for his mouth and fingers. When it was finished, the flute had a shrill, harsh tone, with a melancholy pitch that hinted of pain and bereavement.

The shepherd put down his tools and stepped outside his hut. Lifting his head to the sky, he put the flute to his mouth and began to play. It was a song of peril and death. Dragons writhed on sharp lances tearing through their vitals. Swords hacked at broken scales, at the delicate bones of their wings, breaking, crippling. No longer able to fly, the dragons twisted, turning in vain on their tormentors, helpless against the steel of their weapons.

Dragons died. Their blood poured out onto the green grass, singeing it brown. Their sightless skulls were impaled on spears as trophies. Their mates circled in the sky, bereft, keening their grief, while their bones slowly bleached and bare and white, to crumble at last into powder and dust.

And constantly as a counterpoint to the song, repeated again and again: Flee! Far away! Far away!

The shepherd played until his lips could not shape another note, until his fingers, with their aching joints, could barely move. When he put down the flute at last, the sky was empty.

Alone, he waited on the mountain, but the dragons did not return.

And when several days had passed and he was sure, he took both flutes and snapped them in half and laid them in the cave with the rest of the dragons' bones.

The path he took down from the mountain led not to the village of his birth but farther downriver to the market town and its spring fair. And beyond to the cities of the plains, where no man could see the snow-capped mountains and the glint of dragons flying against the sun.

THE MAN WHO
LOVED THE SEA

ALAN BRENNERT

ALAN BRENNERT is a Nebula Award–winning author who
has also worked in the television and film industry. He
was a contributing writer, producer, and editor of *The
New Twilight Zone* television series. His work has also
appeared in *The Magazine of Fantasy & Science Fiction*.
He lives in California. "The Man Who Loved the Sea"
asks if it is possible to love something as much as someone. The answer might come as a surprise.

It's a long haul from practically anywhere to Chincoteague: a barrier island off the eastern shore of Virginia,
it's completely inaccessible by train, and the nearest
major airports are hours away—in Baltimore, or Washington. I left Atlanta at eight A.M. Thursday morning,
arrived in D.C. a little after ten, and was on the road by
eleven: across the Chesapeake Bay Bridge, stop-and-go
through a numbing procession of small dull towns,
lunch a burger at Hardee's, then back behind the wheel.
The little Ford Escort weathered the journey better
than I did: by the time I finally crossed Wallops Island
into Chincoteague, I felt hot, tired, irritable—same as
I'd felt twenty years before, when my parents, in the
throes of the marriage spasms which would ultimately
end in divorce, brought me here for my first summer
with Uncle Evan and Aunt Dierdre.

But the minute I started across the Black Narrows
Bridge—the moment I drew my first breath of the
briny air, and saw my first great blue heron loping
casually through the marshland below—my fatigue
and irritation receded like a tide, and the memory of
two glorious summers came back in a rush, etched
brightly onto everything I saw.

I hadn't been here in almost five years, but in many
ways the town didn't look all that different than it had
even twenty years ago. There was still only one stoplight

on Main Street, and the town dock remained sleepy to the point of narcolepsy. Gone were the neighborhood stores known only by their owners' names—Dave Birch's store; Charlie Gold's store—but the storefronts along Main were still small, mom-and-pop operations, not a single tri-level, escalatored shopping mall anywhere to be seen. Further south (or "down the marsh," as they said here) one-story bungalows with screened-in porches fronted the tidal flat; kids drove five-speeds across neatly mowed lawns; out on the channel, motorboats traced foam contrails in the water.

It was so much like the Chincoteague of my youth that for a moment I forgot what brought me here; for a moment, as I pulled into the driveway of the white clapboard house on Margarets Lane, I half-expected to see the tall, rangy figure of Uncle Evan ambling out of the house to greet me.

But it was Aunt Dierdre—heavy-set, middling height, white-haired—who appeared on the front steps as I pulled my travel bag from the trunk, and she was alone.

"Steven? You came—"

Though she didn't intend them to, the words cut deep: *You came.* For too long, I hadn't come. For the five years I'd been married to Rose, I'd been too busy with my own life—had only spoken to Dee and Evan by phone, the occasional holiday call. And now Evan was gone, and it was too late to make up for the lost time between us, to make amends for my thoughtlessness.

Maybe I could make amends to Dierdre, at least. As she approached, I dropped my travel bag and hugged her.

"How you holding up, Aunt Dee?"

I could read the pain in her eyes, but she shrugged in a way she shared with many residents of this fragile island: a stoic acceptance of the sort of calamities—floods, hurricanes, fires—which had always been part of life on Chincoteague. "Better," she said, trying for a smile, "now that you're here. But come on, come in, let me take that." Faster than the eye could follow she'd grabbed my travel bag and was bustling into the house—happy, I suspect, to have someone to look after again.

Both Aunt Dee and Uncle Evan were "Teaguers"—island natives. (Non-natives, even long-time residents who weren't born here, were invariably known as "come-heres" or "come-latelys.") My mother left Chincoteague for college and, after that, Baltimore, but her brother Evan stayed behind, becoming a "waterman"—a fisherman—and marrying his high school sweetheart, Dierdre. They were never able to have children of their own, which could account for why they so readily agreed to play host to a surly, restless ten-year-old city brat.

"You *were* a handful," she admitted, half an hour later, over cake and coffee. "But you settled down soon enough."

I smiled. "Yeah. But only after hijacking Uncle Evan's skiff." By the end of my first week on Chincoteague I'd contracted a near-terminal case of island fever; bored out of my mind, I liberated a small dinghy Evan had been restoring in his back yard, launched it (not without a skinned knee) into the channel, and tried—insane as it may sound, in retrospect—to paddle back to the mainland.

Dierdre laughed, eyes bright for the first time since I'd seen her. "When he found out what you'd done, I thought he was going to shellac your behind, but good. But when he caught up with you and saw you'd made it all the way to Willis Point, he told me, 'Dierdre, the boy may have the makin's of a waterman,' and after that, you could do no wrong, even when you did."

"Maybe I should have listened to him," I said. "There are days when trawling for flounder off Tom's Cove sounds a lot more appealing than putting out a trade magazine."

"Oh no," she said quickly, "it was hard work, Steven, a hard way to make a living. He loved it, but I think you *have* to love it, to keep at it, year in and year out."

I hesitated a moment. "Where . . . was he?" I said, finally broaching the subject we had so far avoided. "When it happened?"

Her eyes clouded over. "Right there," she said, nodding to the old leather recliner in the corner. "He'd had some angina, the month before, but we really had no idea. No warning." She looked down. "I know the Lord has His reasons, but . . . I must admit, I'm hard-pressed to see how He could need Evan more than I do."

I looked at the chair in which he'd spent his last moments, and felt an odd anger, a vague sense of . . . injustice. It must have showed on my face, because Dierdre just nodded sadly. "He should have been out there when it came," she said, glancing toward the waters of the bay. "It would've been awful for me—his boat being late; the search—but even so. He loved the water; loved the sea. That was where he should've passed on . . . not in some ratty old chair in his living room. Out there, in his element."

I didn't want to go see him; didn't want it all to

become real. But of course it was real, whether I wanted it to be or not. And so, too soon, we were in Salyers Funeral Home, and I was gazing down at Evan—at his creased, craggy face; at his big hands, calloused from years of dragging nets and shucking oysters; at his scarecrow-thin body laid out in a simple black suit—and my memories truly became memories, then. Until that moment, I could pretend that I could come back here . . . join him for an afternoon on his boat . . . go wading for clams with him. Now all that belonged irrevocably, and only, to the past.

The satin lining of the casket, the crushed velvet pillow on which his head lay—Evan would have snorted derisively at them. *A little too frou-frou for me,* he would've said—and it was then I remembered something he'd once told me. I turned to Aunt Dierdre. "Didn't Uncle Evan want to be cremated?" I asked. "His ashes scattered across the bay?"

Dierdre looked embarrassed; almost guilty. "I . . . I just couldn't, Steven," she said quietly. "It seems so . . . final. I want a place I can go to, to visit him. He was out there, on the water, for so much of our life together . . . I'd like him near me, now, for as long as I have left." She looked away. "Is that selfish of me?"

I shook my head, and didn't protest.

What would have happened, I wonder, if I had?

The funeral was scheduled for the next day. I made dinner reservations for seven o'clock at the Village Restaurant for Aunt Dee and myself; that left me with an hour or so of free time. Stiff and sore from the long drive, I decided to take a swim on Assateague, another barrier island—and wildlife refuge—due east of Chincoteague.

Both islands are rife with tourists at the height of summer, but this was mid-September, and though the ocean was still warm, the beach was only sparsely populated, particularly this late in the day. I laid my towel and car keys on a sand dune, peeled off my T-shirt, and dove into the water—limbering up with a few kicks, then swimming parallel to the shore for about ten minutes before flipping over on my back and floating there in the waning sun.

As I floated, the sun a red mist beyond my shut eyelids, I felt the slow, languid pace of life here take hold again . . . my thoughts drifting back to the ways I used to pass the time, things I hadn't done in twenty years. 'Signing' for clams—poking a long, two-pronged stick into the tiny keyholes in the sand where innocent shellfish fell to my youthful appetite. Rashly trying to pet the wild ponies which ran free here on Assateague (and narrowly avoiding being kicked in the head by one particularly testy little foal). Bicycling through the refuge, learning to spot and name all manner of animals and birds unknown in the city: heron, ibis, deer, tree frogs, geese . . .

The water gently rocked me back and forth, tiny waves tickling the backs of my legs, elbows, neck. I was wearing a loose-fitting swimsuit; the water flowed through it, seeming almost to caress me with each rolling motion of the surf. I smiled, remembering the times I'd skinny-dipped here as a boy. I lay there, feeling happy and oddly aroused, the touch of the waters feeling almost like that of a human hand—

A hand which now, slowly and gently, began to . . . *stroke* . . . my genitals . . .

Startled, I yelped, kicked out of my floating position, tugged on the waistband of my shorts and peered inside, looking for . . . what?

Of course, there was nothing there. I laughed, embarrassed: Helluva riptide. And in fact the current had carried me, unknowing, about a dozen yards from shore. I paddled back to the beach, toweled off, and went back to Chincoteague for dinner.

The funeral was well-attended; the island, even now, is a tight-knit community, and Evan was particularly well-loved. A few of his fellow watermen spoke of their days together on the island, before the bridge was built connecting it to the mainland—back when boats were more than a livelihood, they were the life's blood of the community. His best friend, Ben Sanders, who owned the Channel Inn, said a few words. The minister read from Psalms. And that was about it.

We buried him in a small cemetery about a quarter-mile down Church Street, and I threw the first handful of dirt onto the coffin, saying good-bye to the uncle I had cared so much for—the uncle who, with his wife, had showed me that men and women *could* love each other, that people could make a safe place for themselves in the world. My marriage to Rose may have ended in divorce, but I took pride in the fact that it was a quick, amicable parting, nothing like the pitched battles my parents engaged in for so long; and I like to think I had Evan and Dierdre in part to thank for that.

When Aunt Dierdre asked me to stay the weekend, I agreed gladly—as much to assuage my guilt over my long absence as to comfort her. When she suggested I take Uncle Evan's boat, the *Sea Breeze,* out onto the channel, I was both surprised and flattered. She knew how much I loved the old tub, and knew as well that I had never piloted her without Evan at my side. I protested (not very strongly, I admit) that it had been at least six years since I'd been at the helm, but she dismissed that with a wave. "Your uncle thought you'd make a good waterman," she said. "That's good enough for me."

The *Sea Breeze* was an old trawler, white paint flaking from its cedar hull, green trim similarly chipping off oak railings. Its deck was scuffed, and mottled with thirty years' accretion of fish oils, but the moment I stepped into the small pilot house and took the wheel in my hands, I might as well have been at the helm of a luxury liner. The old diesel engine wheezed like an asthmatic at first, then settled into a steady (if somewhat tubercular) drone. I cast off, maneuvered the boat away from the town dock, and headed out into the channel.

The channel wasn't too crowded—one or two fishing boats, a half dozen speedboats. I glided past pilings and buoys, veered to port as I approached Chincoteague Point, then guided her slowly into the waters of Tom's Cove.

After about fifteen minutes I cut the engine and let her drift for a while, as I stood by the railing and gazed into the misty distance. Waves slapped gently against the creaking hull, lulling me into remembrance and reverie. I had it in mind, I suppose, that out here, on the water we both shared—the water he introduced me to—I would say my true good-bye to Uncle Evan; but it wasn't meant to be.

As I stood there, all fuzzy-headed and sentimental, I suddenly felt a huge jolt, the *Sea Breeze* shuddering beneath me. Rudely propelled out of my daydreaming, I noticed at once that the gentle rocking of the boat had ceased; it was essentially immobile. And that could only mean one thing. I hurried forward and looked out at what should have been the waters of the cove.

An oval of sand extended outward for a good ten yards ahead of the *Sea Breeze's* bow.

Damn!

I felt mortified. Aground on a sandbar; Uncle Evan would never have allowed this to happen. I told myself that this happened to the best of sailors, particularly here in Chincoteague where sandbars appeared and disappeared like cards in a magician's deck; but I still hoped to hell that wherever Evan was, he couldn't see how his clumsy nephew, first time out of the box, had managed to beach his beloved *Sea Breeze* on a spit of sand.

Luckily I knew what to do. Well, no luck involved, actually—Evan had drummed it into me. I slipped off my sandals and climbed over the side of the boat, onto the sandbar.

Rather than immediately trying to push the boat off—the most common mistake you could make—I started to pace out the sandbar: that is, walk straight away from the boat in every direction until I began to hit deep water, so I knew in which direction to push the boat. I walked twenty paces south; there was a slow dropoff before I found myself up to my waist in water. I backed up, then went twenty feet to the west; a steeper dropoff this time. That might be the best bet. Still, to be sure, I headed twenty paces due east.

Only moments after my feet entered the water, I plummeted straight down. A *very* sheer dropoff.

I bobbed to the surface, started to swim the two feet back to the sandbar—but something stopped me. Almost as though I'd hit a wall, or a reef . . . yet there was nothing in front of me but water. I felt a brief surge of panic, then calmly turned in the water, figuring to swim around to the other side of the sandbar, the part I knew had a slow dropoff.

Something stopped me again.

But this time, it wasn't like a wall. It was like being held back.

Heart pounding, I looked down, terrified I might find a Great White circling below me . . . but there was nothing there.

Nothing . . .

That terrified me more than a shark would have. I flailed my arms, trying to move in any direction at all, but suddenly I could get no purchase at all on the water—couldn't move more than an inch or two in any direction.

Winded, I momentarily stopped treading water . . . and realized it made no difference whether my legs kicked or not. I was being . . . upheld, somehow. And the grip—there was no other word for it—seemed suddenly familiar. It was a gentle grip, firm but not cruel; in fact just the opposite. I could feel the water beneath me swirling and flowing around my legs, like fingers tracing spirals up my calves, my knees, my thighs. Beneath my cut-offs I was wearing only a swim support, and now the water seemed to press against my groin, caressing the bulge of my cock, making little tugs at the cotton fabric. The fingers of water ran up my stomach, teasingly, swirling and tugging at my chest hair, massaging my ribs, my pectorals, my shoulders . . .

My shoulders! I realized with a start that they were under water now. The hands, the water, whatever the hell it was, was *pulling me under*. I screamed for help, fighting wildly now against the force which was dragging me down, the water lapping at my chin, my lips—

I took a deep breath just moments before my head was dragged under the waves. What the hell was happening? Who *are* you, I wanted to scream, why are you doing this to me—

I opened my eyes. The salt stung them, but I saw nothing in front of me; nothing but water. My heart hammered in my chest. I knew I had only thirty, forty seconds before my air ran out; I had to *do* something. But what? How?

I kicked furiously, but remained rooted in place.

I felt something press against my lips. Cold. Wet. Strangely soft.

It was trying to force my mouth open. I resisted with all my strength, but it—whatever the hell *it* was— was stronger. And as my mouth began to open, I suddenly recognized what was pressed against my lips.

Another pair of lips . . .

I started to gag, reflexively fearing the intake of water into my lungs . . . but it never came. I tasted a salt kiss against my open mouth . . . but I could breathe. Almost as though I were somehow drawing the oxygen directly from the water itself.

As soon as I realized I was not going to die . . . as I understood that this force, whatever it was, did not mean to kill me, or even harm me . . . I relaxed a bit. And in that moment of relaxation, I could suddenly appreciate the pleasurable aspects of what was happening to me: the caresses to my body, the gentle eddies of water around my penis . . . and with my fear ebbing, I could even feel myself getting hard. My God, it was true: Given half a chance, men *would* fuck almost anything!

The thought made me laugh, and as my mouth opened further I felt a tongue of water gently dart inside. Salty and a little coarse, in some odd attempt at simulating human flesh, it licked at my own tongue, teased it . . . and I found myself reciprocating. The very perversity of what was happening began to arouse me. I wasn't going to die; I might as well enjoy whatever was happening. Tentatively my tongue explored these strange, liquid lips pressed against mine, cold and wet and somehow thrilling. They tasted of salt and brine and everything I loved about the sea. I was half aware of something inside my shorts, fingers of water gripping the shaft of my penis, moving easily from the base of the shaft to the tip, briefly stroking the foreskin, just long enough to bring me close to orgasm and then back down the shaft again, a gentle squeeze to my testicles, then up again, faster now, back and forth—

I came, and the ocean closed tight and warm around me, and the next thing I knew I was bobbing to the surface, free.

And alone. That much I knew at once.

With nothing holding me back any longer, I swam to the sandbar and lay there a good five minutes, trying to make sense of what had just happened—and failing miserably. It wasn't a delusion, that much I knew; but I could think of no rational explanation for the forces which had taken me (in every sense of the term!). After five minutes, I looked around me and saw that the sandbar had shrunk to half its size, and that the *Sea Breeze* was afloat once more. I took a deep breath and got to my feet.

I clambered back into the boat; its gentle rocking felt soothing, reassuring. I noticed the deck was wet; apparently, while I was gone, a large wave had dumped over the stern, spilling water and seaweed across the deck. It took me a moment before I realized there was something unusual about the seaweed.

Strands of the seaweed were arranged like letters on the oak planks. A strand that looked like a tuning fork was a *y;* a wobbly little circle was an *o;* half that same circle formed a *u.* . . .

I shivered despite the heat, as I took in the entirety of the message which lay at my feet.

It said, *You taste like him.*

I guided the ship back to shore, tied her up at the dock, and got as far away from the water as I possibly could, retreating inland for lunch. I purposely didn't order a drink, as badly as I needed one, trying to keep my jumbled thoughts and emotions in some pathetic approximation of order. My whole world had turned upside down—in more ways than one.

I was terrified to go back out on the water. Afraid not for my life—whatever was out there could easily have killed me, had it desired—but of my own response to what had happened. Afraid of it happening again; afraid of *wanting* it to happen again. If the waters could assume the shapes they had, I wondered, what other forms could they take? Part of me wanted to know, and part of me never wanted to know.

But what really obsessed me was the message on the deck, and all that it implied. I didn't know how to answer the thousand questions that were boiling up in me. I wasn't about to tell anybody what had happened— wasn't about to even allude to it. And the questions I was beginning to ask about Uncle Evan were hardly ones I could put to Aunt Dierdre, even in veiled form.

There was only one person I could think to approach.

The Channel Inn, a quaint little bed-and-breakfast

fronting Main Street, occupied a small but choice plot of land with a fine view of the channel and the marshes beyond. Still spry at seventy-two, Ben Sanders dragged over a white, wood-slatted chaise longue for me to sit in. "Whoops. Hold on," and before I could sit he whisked a rag across the back of the chaise. "Gulls," he spat out. "If I had a nickel for every bird turd I've cleared off these chairs . . . Iced tea?"

"Sure, thanks."

He poured me a tall glass from an old-fashioned pitcher; handed it to me, then settled down in a chair opposite. "Ahh," he sighed, "I can't believe he's gone, can you?"

Ben and Evan had been best friends since they met in grade school, sixty years ago; they had played stick-ball together, wooed girls together, gone fishing together, for the better part of six decades. Now Ben squinted into the distance, toward the channel. "So," he said, "you took the *Sea Breeze* out for a spin today, did you?"

I said that I had.

He shook his head. "It was a fine boat in its time, don't get me wrong, but . . . you must admit, her engines have seen better days." I laughed. "Every Friday morning at eight A.M.," he went on, "Ev would pilot that rickety old scow past my bedroom window, 'cause he knew it drove me crazy. Not Tuesday mornings, not Wednesday mornings, not Sunday mornings. Friday mornings. Eight A.M. For *thirty years*. Ornery old son of a bitch."

He paused. It was quiet on the channel. Ben looked pained.

I waited a moment, then said, "He took the boat out a lot? Even after he'd retired?"

Ben nodded. "Six days out of seven. He may have

stopped fishing for a living, but he just couldn't help himself. He'd go out, maybe catch a few pounds of bluefish, some black drum—give me some for my dining room, and Mrs. Brattle down at the Islander, and take home the rest."

"He fished every day?"

"Well, not every day, I reckon. Sometimes he'd just anchor her off Tom's Cove, or Assateague Beach, and spend the day out there, reading, watching the waves, whatever."

"She never says as much," I said, "but I think it might've been hard on Dierdre, having him away so much of the time."

Ben nodded. "I imagine it was. But he was an odd one, that Evan. Knew him fifty years—we played chess here every Thursday; went bowling every Saturday night; he and Dierdre came over for dinner every other Sunday. And for all that, there was still a part of him Evan kept to himself. Sometimes he'd look into the distance, and I didn't know *what* the hell he was seeing. I'd ask him, 'What's on that fevered little brain of yours, Ev?' and he'd just smile and say something like, 'Isn't the world an amazing place, Ben?' and I'd agree, yeah, the world could be pretty amazing, and that was it. I swear, that was all I'd get out of him. The man could be a goddamned conundrum, at times."

I tried to keep my tone measured. "Do you think he might have been . . . that is, there might have been someone—"

Ben looked at me with suddenly wide eyes—and laughed. "A little something on the side, you mean?" he said, and laughed again. "Hell, I don't see how! Everyone's in each other's pockets on this island. Thing like that would get around." He paused, considering, then went on: "Truth to tell, there were days I wondered the same thing, but . . . he never left the damn island; I *know* it couldn't have been anyone *on* the island; and, most of all . . . I know he loved Dierdre. *Really* loved her. Old men don't stop talking about that kind of thing, Steve, just 'cause they're old. I know how much he cared for Dee."

He looked out onto the channel again; shook his head. "No," he said emphatically, "trust me. If Evan had any mistress, it was the sea."

That night I finally worked up the nerve to return to the ocean. The mosquitoes were fierce, but the beach, thankfully, was deserted; I stood a few feet away from the shoreline, watching the surf roll in, foam spilling up onto the sand and then receding again. I felt like a fool. Already the memory of what had happened seemed more and more like a dream, an illusion. But I had to follow it through.

I stood there a long moment, then called out, my voice muffled by the crashing waves.

"*Who are you? What are you?*"—although I thought I might already know.

The waves crashed to shore, oblivious to my presence. I felt even more like an idiot. But I tried again.

"*What do you want from me?*"

The waves rolled in. Foam washed over the sand, then receded . . . but this time, as the tide ebbed back into the sea, it left behind markings in the sand . . . furrows made as if by fingertips . . . letters. A word. A name.

Evan.

My body shook.

It was a minute before I could speak again. "He's . . . he's dead," I said finally. "You understand? He's gone."

The waves came crashing to shore, nothing un-usual about that, but I shrank back nonetheless. When the water had retreated, it had left behind two more words.

Know this.

My throat was suddenly dry; hoarse. The only thing I could think to ask was, "Why?"

The waves came again, erased the message, and left a new one. Simple, and to the point.

Loved him . . .

My breath caught in my throat. It was true. Everything I'd feared was true. Before I could say anything more—before I could think of what the hell *to* say—the waves had rolled in again, farther than before, swirling around my feet. I felt a light, gentle touch to my foot—not a caress, nothing sexual about it at all—more like a hand, a fingertip, touched in supplication.

When the surf receded, two words lay in the sand, a simple entreaty:

Bring back?

I turned and ran, not even waiting for the tide to erase the plea.

I'm not much of a drinker, but as my car headed up Main Street toward the Chincoteague Inn, I knew it was either stop for a drink or keep on driving—straight back to Atlanta. So, within minutes, I found myself on a barstool in the glass-windowed restaurant, looking out at the harbor—surprised to find, when I glanced at the tumbler in my hands, that I'd downed a seven-and-seven in something like three gulps. Even more surprised when I ordered another.

I guess it said something about me that the most difficult part of all this to accept was not the existence of something unnatural, almost unbelievable, out there in the waters off Assateague—an elemental? a water spirit?—but Uncle Evan's relationship with it. Well, hell, I'd read Joseph Campbell, but no book in the world could have prepared me for the idea that my beloved uncle could have been unfaithful to his wife. It would've been difficult to believe for anyone who'd ever watched the two of them together: even in their sixties, they would touch each other on the back of the hand, on the cheek, with unvarnished affection and understanding. The idea that he could kiss Aunt Dierdre good-bye in the morning, squeeze her hand fondly as he left for work, then go off for a perverted rendezvous with some . . . some *creature* . . . something not even *human* . . . it made me—

It made me furious. I hated him, just then: hated the lie he'd presented to Dee all those years, hated the cruel joke she didn't even know had been played on her, hated the image of him suspended in the water as I had been, in unnatural embrace with a preternatural lover. God *damn* him! How could he *do* this to her? How could he do this to *me?* Everything I believed about men and women, about caring for one another, about honesty and responsibility, I learned from Evan and Dierdre. Certainly not from my own parents. And now—and now—

My anger seemed to sober me up almost as quickly as the bourbon worked on me. I passed on a third drink, got up, and stood by the harbor side a long minute, taking in the air. Suddenly I hated the smell of the sea; hated the sound of the waves lapping against the dock; hated everything about it. I didn't care if I ever saw it again, once I left here.

Bring back?

I shivered and decided to walk the quarter of a mile back to Aunt Dierdre's. I let myself in—she was asleep, upstairs—and eventually I suppose I got to sleep myself, but it was the kind of jittery, superficial slumber in which you dream you're in bed, trying desperately to get to sleep, and you wake up at dawn feeling as though you've gotten no rest at all. The next morning at breakfast I drank three cups of coffee. I looked like hell.

"You look like hell," Aunt Dierdre said. I smiled. Nothing got past Aunt Dee.

Well—almost nothing. "Just a bad night's sleep," I lied. "Did you want to do some shopping today?"

"You go back to bed and get some rest. I'll take care of the shopping."

"I'm *fine*," I said. "Nothing a little coffee can't cure." And so, over her protests, we spent the next hour stocking up on canned goods and household supplies at Parks Market, then browsed the Corner Bookshop and Memory Lane Antiques before having lunch at Don's Seafood—one of the few restaurants on Main Street not directly on the water, much to my relief.

I wasn't very hungry, and my anger had cooled only a little. I felt awkward here with Aunt Dee, feeling somehow complicit in Evan's dirty little secret . . . if not worse: I had had relations with the same *thing* he had. I was more than complicit—I was just as bad as he was.

Dierdre may not have known my thoughts, but she sensed my mood. Quietly she said, "Thinking about Ev?"

Not in any way she could imagine. I nodded.

"Angry at him?" she asked. I looked up, startled.

"For leaving?" she said, and I thought that was as good a way as any to explain my sullen mood, and so I nodded: "Guess so," I lied again.

"Me too, a little," she admitted. "But, Steven . . .

people who love each other always *will* hurt each other. You try not to, but it happens. No help for it. All you can do is forgive. God knows Ev wasn't a perfect husband—remember the time he and Ben went drinking in Franklin City and nearly wrecked the boat coming back?—but I forgave him that, as he forgave me not being a perfect wife. If we could do that, you can forgive him for leaving."

I thought about that. I thought about it a long while. We ate in silence a minute or two, and then I heard myself saying, "Aunt Dee . . . was it really important to Evan that he have his . . . his ashes . . . scattered at sea?"

Dee looked uncomfortable at the subject, and I was sorry to have brought it up again, but I had to know. "I think it was," she said. "But—"

I put a hand on hers. "It's okay," I said gently. "I'm not recriminating you. I just needed to know."

I dropped Aunt Dee at home, and without much pleasure at the prospect, drove back to Assateague and the beach. There were more people there now than last night, so I just stood at the shoreline watching the surf break in the distance, the steady, stately roll of the waves, rising and falling as they'd done for millennia—as they would for millennia to come—and I had an inkling, perhaps, of why Evan wanted to make this his resting place, this place of eternal life and motion, so much bigger and grander than any one human life. I even came to have an inkling, perhaps, of why he had done what else he had.

Loved him.

Yes. Yes, I did.

• • •

I could not quite believe what I was planning to do; it made me queasy just thinking about it. But I had no choice, really. If I felt any kind of debt to Evan—and what I'd gotten from him over the years far outweighed whatever anger I was still feeling—then I owed him this much. And perhaps, this way, I might even make some small amends for those five lost years; time I could never recover, and would always regret. That afternoon I deliberately parked my car a block down Margarets Lane, so when I slipped out of the house a little before one A.M., the ignition start wouldn't wake Aunt Dierdre. I drove through the deathly still streets of Chincoteague, coming—it seemed like hours, though it was only a matter of minutes—to the small cemetery on Church Street . . .

I parked along a deserted stretch of the street, got out and looked around—not without a certain dumbfoundment that I was here, that I was even considering this. The houses across the street were all dark; the only sound for miles was the trilling of a few nightbirds. I popped the trunk . . . took out the large garden shovel I'd hidden there earlier in the day . . . and set off, as stealthily as I could manage, through the empty cemetery. (It was pitch dark, yet I couldn't quite rid myself of the feeling that thousand-watt searchlights were following me all the way.) Finally, after several minutes, I came to the simple granite headstone marked

EVAN McCONNELL
HUSBAND, NEIGHBOR, WATERMAN

I stood there a moment, drawing a deep breath, working up my nerve . . . then, with a sudden spasm of courage, dug the blade into the soft, newly turned ground. I lifted up a big chunk of earth; tossed it aside. I felt as though a threshold had been crossed. No turning back, now. They hadn't seeded the plot with grass just yet, there was no sod to replace; with luck, I would finish in an hour or two, replace the earth, and no one would ever know. Already I dreaded the moment when my blade would strike the metal lid of the coffin; I tried not to think about having to open it, having to reach inside, and about what I would find there. I concentrated on the shovel, on plunging it into the ground, then out, flinging earth to the side; again the blade goes down, another chunk of earth uprooted, and another, and—

"Steven?"

I dropped the shovel, reflexively. I suddenly had a pretty fair inkling of what cardiac arrest felt like.

I turned to discover, to my horror and embarrassment, Aunt Dierdre standing about five feet from the foot of the grave—the grave of her husband, the grave I was desecrating!

I wanted to die. My mouth was dry as sand; I seemed to have forgotten how to form words. "I—I—"

But there was no anger in her face—no surprise, even—just sadness. She took a step toward me and said, with unexpected gentleness, "It's all right. I know what you're trying to do. I know why."

I could only shake my head, helplessly. "No," I said. "No, you don't."

But she just smiled, softly and sadly. "I know more than you think," she said. "I know Evan loved the sea. He wasn't a very religious man, never went to church with me, but . . . there was something about the ocean that moved him, deep inside, ever since he was a boy."

Her gaze drifted to the east; toward the ocean. "If

you love something that much, for that long," she said quietly, "eventually, I suppose . . . it loves you back. . . ."

I was stunned speechless a long moment.

"You . . . you knew?" I said, finally. "He told you?"

She shook her head.

"No," she said, "of course not. Evan would never have hurt me that way. But I could tell. When we were on the boat together . . . at the shore . . . the way the water moved when he was around it . . . I came to feel her, her presence, after a time. But I also knew that she was no threat to what Ev and I had together, so we . . . shared him, in a way."

She looked down, ashamed. "I only got selfish after he died," she said. "Wanted him for myself." She looked up again. "I was wrong."

"No," I said, "you weren't—"

She nodded. "Yes, I was. I'm a good Christian, Steven. And I should've trusted in that." She glanced toward the soft susurrus of the ocean's voice, whispering in the distance.

"Let her have his body," she said. "I'll trust the Lord that when my time comes, his soul will be with me."

I stayed in Chincoteague another three days—long enough for the body to be exhumed and cremated. And on the morning of the third day, Aunt Dierdre and I got up a little before sunrise, drove to Assateague, and stood at the shore's edge, the horizon burnished gold and red, the wind light and dry from the south. Carefully I took the lid off the urn, and poured the first ashes into Dierdre's cupped hands; she looked at them a moment, lowered her lips to her hands, breathed a good-bye onto them, then held out her hands and let the wind take the ashes from her, fanning them across the glassy surface of the sea. I took the next handful, and let the wind take those as well; and within a minute, it was all over. Uncle Evan had returned to the sea.

I stayed with Dee the rest of the day, finally leaving around six P.M. to start the long drive back to Washington. As I drove down Main Street, something made me stop at the town dock for one last look at the *Sea Breeze*, rocking gently in its berth. I noticed from dockside that the deck was wet, although the waters in the harbor seemed calm. I jumped the railing and boarded the old trawler for what was very likely the last time. There was indeed water on the decks—and seaweed as well, strands arranged ever so carefully on the scuffed, oaken deck.

They read: *He loved you too.*

I went back to my car, and in moments I was crossing the Narrows Bridge, the waters of the channel black and bright below me, flowing back endlessly, eternally, to the bosom of the sea.

THE SAME TO
YOU DOUBLED

ROBERT SHECKLEY

ROBERT SHECKLEY is a writer who is constantly pursuing
the unknown in his writing, making his reader rethink
the most ordinary situations. He has written almost
twenty novels, and has collaborated with such authors
as Harry Harrison and the late Roger Zelazny. He was
the fiction editor of *Omni* magazine from 1980 to 1982
and has also written many television and radio plays. A
winner of the Jupiter Award, he lives in Oregon. "The
Same to You Doubled" is a wish-fulfillment story with
the unusual twist he is known for.

I n New York, it never fails, the doorbell rings just when you've plopped down onto the couch for a well-deserved snooze. Now, a person of character would say, "To hell with that, a man's home is his castle and they can slide any telegrams under the door." But if you're like Edelstein, not particularly strong on character, then you think to yourself that maybe it's the blonde from 12C who has come up to borrow a jar of chili powder. Or it could even be some crazy film producer who wants to make a movie based on the letters you've been sending your mother in Santa Monica. (And why not; don't they make movies out of worse material than that?)

Yet this time, Edelstein had really decided not to answer the bell. Lying on the couch, his eyes still closed, he called out, "I don't want any."

"Yes you do," a voice from the other side of the door replied.

"I've got all the encyclopedias, brushes, and water-less cookery I need," Edelstein called back wearily. "Whatever you've got, I've got it already."

"Look," the voice said, "I'm not selling anything. I want to give you something."

Edelstein smiled the thin, sour smile of the New Yorker who knows that if someone made him a gift of a package of genuine, unmarked $20 bills, he'd still somehow end up having to pay for it.

"If it's *free*," Edelstein answered, "then I *definitely* can't afford it."

"But I mean *really* free," the voice said. "I mean free that it won't cost you anything now or ever."

"I'm not interested," Edelstein replied, admiring his firmness of character.

The voice did not answer.

Edelstein called out, "Hey, if you're still there, please go away."

"My dear Mr. Edelstein," the voice said, "cynicism is merely a form of naïveté. Mr. Edelstein, wisdom is discrimination."

"He gives me lectures now," Edelstein said to the wall.

"All right," the voice said, "forget the whole thing, keep your cynicism and your racial prejudice; do I need this kind of trouble?"

"Just a minute," Edelstein answered. "What makes you think I'm prejudiced?"

"Let's not crap around," the voice said. "If I was raising funds for Hadassah or selling Israel bonds, it would have been different. But, obviously, I am what I am, so excuse me for living."

"Not so fast," Edelstein said. "As far as I'm concerned, you're just a voice from the other side of the door. For all I know, you could be Catholic or Seventh-Day Adventist or even Jewish."

"*You knew*," the voice responded.

"Mister, I swear to you—"

"Look," the voice said, "it doesn't matter, I come up against a lot of this kind of thing. Good-bye, Mr. Edelstein."

"Just a minute," Edelstein replied.

He cursed himself for a fool. How often had he

fallen for some huckster's line, ending up, for example, paying $9.98 for an illustrated two-volume *Sexual History of Mankind*, which his friend Manowitz had pointed out he could have bought in any Marboro bookstore for $2.98?

But the voice was right. Edelstein had somehow known that he was dealing with a goy.

And the voice would go away thinking, *The Jews, they think they're better than anyone else.* Further, he would tell this to his bigoted friends at the next meeting of the Elks or the Knights of Columbus, and there it would be, another black eye for the Jews.

"I do have a weak character," Edelstein thought sadly.

He called out, "All right! You can come in! But I warn you from the start, I am not going to buy anything."

He pulled himself to his feet and started toward the door. Then he stopped, for the voice had replied, "Thank you very much," and then a man had walked through the closed, double-locked wooden door.

The man was of medium height, nicely dressed in a gray pinstripe modified Edwardian suit. His cordovan boots were highly polished. He was black, carried a briefcase, and he had stepped through Edelstein's door as if it had been made of Jell-O.

"Just a minute, stop, hold on one minute," Edelstein said. He found that he was clasping both of his hands together and his heart was beating unpleasantly fast.

The man stood perfectly still and at his ease, one yard within the apartment. Edelstein started to breathe again. He said, "Sorry, I just had a brief attack, a kind of hallucination—"

"Want to see me do it again?" the man asked.

"My God, no! So you *did* walk through the door! Oh, God, I think I'm in trouble."

Edelstein went back to the couch and sat down heavily. The man sat down in a nearby chair.

"What is this all about?" Edelstein whispered.

"I do the door thing to save time," the man said. "It usually closes the credulity gap. My name is Charles Sitwell. I am a field man for the Devil."

Edelstein believed him. He tried to think of a prayer, but all he could remember was the one he used to say over bread in the summer camp he had attended when he was a boy. It probably wouldn't help. He also knew the Lord's Prayer, but that wasn't even his religion. Perhaps the salute to the flag . . .

"Don't get all worked up," Sitwell said. "I'm not here after your soul or any old-fashioned crap like that."

"How can I believe you?" Edelstein asked.

"Figure it out for yourself," Sitwell told him. "Consider only the war aspect. Nothing but rebellions and revolutions for the past fifty years or so. For us, that means an unprecedented supply of condemned Americans, Viet Cong, Nigerians, Biafrans, Indonesians, South Africans, Russians, Indians, Pakistanis, and Arabs. Israelis, too, I'm sorry to tell you. Also, we're pulling in more Chinese than usual, and just recently, we've begun to get plenty of action on the South American market. Speaking frankly, Mr. Edelstein, we're overloaded with souls. If another war starts this year, we'll have to declare an amnesty on venial sins."

Edelstein thought it over. "Then you're really not here to take me to hell?"

"Hell, no!" Sitwell said. "I told you, our waiting list is

longer than for Peter Cooper Village; we hardly have any room left in limbo."

"Well . . . Then why are you here?"

Sitwell crossed his legs and leaned forward earnestly. "Mr. Edelstein, you have to understand that hell is very much like U.S. Steel or ITT. We're a big outfit and we're more or less a monopoly. But, like any really big corporation, we are imbued with the ideal of public service and we like to be well thought of."

"Makes sense," Edelstein said.

"But, unlike Ford, we can't very well establish a foundation and start giving out scholarships and work grants. People wouldn't understand. For the same reason, we can't start building model cities or fighting pollution. We can't even throw up a dam in Afghanistan without someone questioning our motives."

"I see where it could be a problem," Edelstein admitted.

"Yet we like to do something. So, from time to time, but especially now, with business so good, we like to distribute a small bonus to a random selection of potential customers."

"Customer? Me?"

"No one is calling you a sinner," Sitwell pointed out. "I said *potential*—which means everybody."

"Oh . . . What kind of bonus?"

"Three wishes," Sitwell said briskly. "That's the traditional form."

"Let me see if I've got this straight," Edelstein said. "I can have any three wishes I want? With no penalty, no secret ifs and buts?"

"There is one but," Sitwell said.

"I knew it," Edelstein said.

"It's simple enough. Whatever you wish for, your worst enemy gets double."

Edelstein thought about that. "So if I asked for a million dollars—"

"Your worst enemy would get two million dollars."

"And if I asked for pneumonia?"

"Your worst enemy would get double pneumonia."

Edelstein pursed his lips and shook his head. "Look, not that I mean to tell you people how to run your business, but I hope you realize that you endanger customer goodwill with a clause like that."

"It's a risk, Mr. Edelstein, but absolutely necessary on a couple of counts," Sitwell said. "You see, the clause is a psychic feedback device that acts to maintain homeostasis."

"Sorry, I'm not following you," Edelstein answered.

"Let me put it this way. The clause acts to reduce the power of the three wishes and, thus, to keep things reasonably normal. A wish is an extremely strong instrument, you know."

"I can imagine," Edelstein said. "Is there a second reason?"

"You should have guessed it already," Sitwell said, baring exceptionally white teeth in an approximation of a smile. "Clauses like that are our trademark. That's how you know it's a genuine hellish product."

"I see, I see," Edelstein said. "Well, I'm going to need some time to think about this."

"The offer is good for thirty days," Sitwell said, standing up. "When you want to make a wish, simply state it—clearly and loudly. I'll tend to the rest."

Sitwell walked to the door. Edelstein said, "There's only one problem I think I should mention."

"What's that?" Sitwell asked.

"Well, it just so happens that I don't have a worst enemy. In fact, I don't have an enemy in the world."

Sitwell laughed hard, then wiped his eyes with a mauve handkerchief. "Edelstein," he said, "you're really too much! Not an enemy in the world! What about your cousin Seymour, who you wouldn't lend five hundred dollars to, to start a dry-cleaning business? Is he a friend all of a sudden?"

"I hadn't thought about Seymour," Edelstein answered.

"And what about Mrs. Abramowitz, who spits at the mention of your name, because you wouldn't marry her Marjorie? What about Tom Cassiday in apartment 1C of this building, who has a complete collection of Goebbels' speeches and dreams every night of killing all of the Jews in the world, beginning with you? . . . Hey, are you all right?"

Edelstein, sitting on the couch, had gone white and his hands were clasped tightly together again.

"I never realized," he said.

"No one realizes," Sitwell said. "Look, take it easy, six or seven enemies is nothing; I can assure you that you're well below average, hatewise."

"Who else?" Edelstein asked, breathing heavily.

"I'm not going to tell you," Sitwell said. "It would be needless aggravation."

"But I have to know who is my worst enemy! Is it Cassiday? Do you think I should buy a gun?"

Sitwell shook his head. "Cassiday is a harmless, half-witted lunatic. He'll never lift a finger, you have my word on that. Your worst enemy is a man named Edward Samuel Manowitz."

"You're sure of that?" Edelstein asked incredulously.

"Completely sure."

"But Manowitz happens to be my best friend."

"Also your worst enemy," Sitwell replied. "Sometimes it works like that. Goodbye, Mr. Edelstein, and good luck with your three wishes."

"Wait!" Edelstein cried. He wanted to ask a million questions; but he was embarrassed and he asked only, "How can it be that hell is so crowded?"

"Because only heaven is infinite," Sitwell told him.

"You know about heaven, too?"

"Of course. It's the parent corporation. But now I really must be getting along. I have an appointment in Poughkeepsie. Good luck, Mr. Edelstein."

Sitwell waved and turned and walked out through the locked solid door.

Edelstein sat perfectly still for five minutes. He thought about Eddie Manowitz. His worst enemy! That was laughable; hell had really gotten its wires crossed on that piece of information. He had known Manowitz for twenty years, saw him nearly every day, played chess and gin rummy with him. They went for walks together, saw movies together, at least one night a week they ate dinner together.

It was true, of course, that Manowitz could sometimes open up a big mouth and overstep the boundaries of good taste.

Sometimes Manowitz could be downright rude.

To be perfectly honest, Manowitz had, on more than one occasion, been insulting.

"But we're *friends*," Edelstein said to himself. "We *are* friends, aren't we?"

There was an easy way to test it, he realized. He

could wish for $1,000,000. That would give Manowitz $2,000,000. But so what? Would he, a wealthy man, care that his best friend was wealthier?

Yes! He would care! He damned well would care! It would eat his life away if a wise guy like Manowitz got rich on Edelstein's wish.

"My God!" Edelstein thought. "An hour ago, I was a poor but contented man. Now I have three wishes and an enemy."

He found that he was twisting his hands together again. He shook his head. This was going to need some thought.

In the next week, Edelstein managed to get a leave of absence from his job and sat day and night with a pen and pad in his hand. At first, he couldn't get his mind off castles. Castles seemed to *go* with wishes. But, on second thought, it was not a simple matter. Taking an average dream castle with a ten-foot-thick stone wall, grounds and the rest, one had to consider the matter of upkeep. There was heating to worry about, the cost of several servants, because anything less would look ridiculous.

So it came at last to a matter of money.

I could keep up a pretty decent castle on $2000 a week, Edelstein thought, jotting figures down rapidly on his pad.

But that would mean that Manowitz would be maintaining two castles on $4000 a week!

By the second week, Edelstein had gotten past castles and was speculating feverishly on the endless possibilities and combinations of travel. Would it be too much to ask for a cruise around the world? Perhaps it would; he wasn't even sure he was up to it. Surely he could accept a summer in Europe? Even a two-week vacation at the Fontainebleau in Miami Beach to rest his nerves.

But Manowitz would get two vacations! If Edelstein stayed at the Fontainebleau, Manowitz would have a penthouse suite at the Key Largo Colony Club. Twice.

It was almost better to stay poor and to keep Manowitz deprived.

Almost, but not quite.

During the final week, Edelstein was getting angry and desperate, even cynical. He said to himself, I'm an idiot, how do I know that there's anything to this? So Sitwell could walk through doors; does that make him a magician? Maybe I've been worried about nothing.

He surprised himself by standing up abruptly and saying, in a loud, firm voice, "I want twenty thousand dollars and I want it right now."

He felt a gentle tug at his right buttock. He pulled out his wallet. Inside it, he found a certified check made out to him for $20,000.

He went down to his bank and cashed the check, trembling, certain that the police would grab him. The manager looked at the check and initialed it. The teller asked him what denominations he wanted it in. Edelstein told the teller to credit it to his account.

As he left the bank, Manowitz came rushing in, an expression of fear, joy and bewilderment on his face.

Edelstein hurried home before Manowitz could speak to him. He had a pain in his stomach for the rest of the day.

Idiot! He had asked for only a lousy $20,000. But Manowitz had gotten $40,000!

A man could die from the aggravation.

Edelstein spent his days alternating between apathy and rage. That pain in the stomach had come back, which meant that he was probably giving himself an ulcer.

It was all so damned unfair! Did he have to push himself into an early grave, worrying about Manowitz?

Yes!

For now he realized that Manowitz was really his enemy and that the thought of enriching his enemy was literally killing him.

He thought about that and then said to himself, Edelstein, listen to me; you can't go on like this, you must get some satisfaction!

But how?

He paced up and down his apartment. The pain was definitely an ulcer; what else could it be?

Then it came to him. Edelstein stopped pacing. His eyes rolled wildly and, seizing paper and pencil, he made some lightning calculations. When he finished, he was flushed, excited—happy for the first time since Sitwell's visit.

He stood up. He shouted, "I want six hundred pounds of chopped chicken liver and I want it at once!"

The caterers began to arrive within five minutes.

Edelstein ate several giant portions of chopped chicken liver, stored two pounds of it in his refrigerator and sold most of the rest to a caterer at half price, making over $700 on the deal. The janitor had to take away seventy-five pounds that had been overlooked. Edelstein had a good laugh at the thought of Manowitz standing in his apartment up to his neck in chopped chicken liver.

His enjoyment was short-lived. He learned that Manowitz had kept ten pounds for himself (the man always had had a gross appetite), presented five pounds to a drab little widow he was trying to make an impression on and sold the rest back to the caterer for one third off, earning over $2000.

I am the world's prize imbecile, Edelstein thought. For a minute's stupid satisfaction, I gave up a wish worth conservatively $100,000,000. And what do I get out of it? Two pounds of chopped chicken liver, a few hundred dollars and the lifelong friendship of my janitor!

He knew he was killing himself from sheer brute aggravation.

He was down to one wish now.

And now it was *crucial* that he spend that final wish wisely. But he had to ask for something that he wanted desperately—something that Manowitz would *not* like at all.

Four weeks had gone by. One day, Edelstein realized glumly that his time was just about up. He had racked his brain, only to confirm his worst suspicions: Manowitz liked everything that he liked. Manowitz liked castles, women, wealth, cars, vacations, wine, music, food. Whatever you named, Manowitz the copycat liked it.

Then he remembered: Manowitz, by some strange quirk of the taste buds, could not abide lox.

But Edelstein didn't like lox, either, not even Nova Scotia.

Edelstein prayed: Dear God, who is in charge of hell and heaven, I have had three wishes and used two miserably. Listen, God, I don't mean to be ungrateful, but I ask you, if a man happens to be granted three wishes, shouldn't he be able to do better for himself than I have done? Shouldn't he be able to have something good happen to him without filling the pockets of Manowitz, his worst enemy, who does nothing but collect double with no effort or pain?

The final hour arrived. Edelstein grew calm, in the manner of a man who had accepted his fate. He realized that his hatred of Manowitz was futile, unworthy of him. With a new and sweet serenity, he said to himself, I am now going to ask for what I, Edelstein, personally want. If Manowitz has to go along for the ride, it simply can't be helped.

Edelstein stood up very straight. He said, "This is my last wish. I've been a bachelor too long. What I want is a woman whom I can marry. She should be about five feet, four inches tall, weigh about 115 pounds, shapely, of course, and with naturally blond hair. She should be intelligent, practical, in love with me, Jewish, of course, but sensual and fun-loving—"

The Edelstein mind suddenly moved into high gear!

"And *especially*," he added, "she should be—I don't know quite how to put this—she should be the *most*, the *maximum*, that I want and can handle, speaking now in a purely sexual sense. You understand what I mean, Sitwell? Delicacy forbids that I should spell it out more specifically than that, but if the matter must be explained to you . . ."

There was a light, somehow *sexual* tapping at the door. Edelstein went to answer it, chuckling to himself. Over twenty thousand dollars, two pounds of chopped chicken liver and now this! Manowitz, he thought, I have you now: Double the most a man wants is something I probably shouldn't have wished on my worst enemy, but I did.

THE DREAMSTONE

C. J. CHERRYH

Another crossover author, C. J. CHERRYH has earned her reputation for gritty, well-reasoned science fiction. She has also written many fantasy novels, using Russian and Celtic folk tales as a basis, as well as creating many original works. She often writes about outsiders and how a character's emotions can conflict with his or her thoughts, creating an internal struggle. She has won the Hugo Award three times, and lives in Oklahoma City. "The Dreamstone" is a dark tale of faeries and man, and of honor lost and regained.

Of all possible paths to travel up out of Caerdale,
that through the deep forest was the least used by
Men. Brigands, outlaws, fugitives who fled mindless
from shadows . . . men with dull, dead eyes and hearts
which could not truly see the wood, souls so attainted
already with the world that they could sense no greater
evil nor greater good than their own—*they* walked that
path; and if by broad morning, so that they had cleared
the black heart of Ealdwood by nightfall, then they
might perchance make it safe away into the new forest
eastward in the hills, there to live and prey on the
game and on each other.

But a runner by night, and that one young and
wild-eyed and bearing neither sword nor blow, but
only a dagger and a gleeman's harp, this was a rare ven-
turer in Ealdwood, and all the deeper shadows chuckled and whispered in startlement.

Eld-born Arafel saw him, and she saw little in this
latter age of earth, wrapped as she was in a passage of
time different from the suns and moons which blink
Men so startling-swift from birth to dying. She heard
the bright notes of the harp which jangled on his
shoulders, which companied his flight and betrayed
him to all with ears to hear, in this world and the other.
She saw his flight and walked into the way to meet
him, out of the soft green light of her moon and into

the colder white of his; and evils which had grown quite bold in the Ealdwood of latter earth suddenly felt the warm breath of spring and drew aside, slinking into dark places where neither moon cast light.

"Boy," she whispered. He startled like a wounded deer, hesitated, searching out the voice. She stepped full into his light and felt the dank wind of Ealdwood on her face. He seemed more solid then, ragged and torn by thorns in his headlong course, although his garments had been of fine linen and the harp at his shoulders had a broidered case.

She had taken little with her out of otherwhere, and yet did take—it was all in the eye which saw. She leaned against the rotting trunk of a dying tree and folded her arms unthreateningly, no hand to the blade she wore, propped one foot against a projecting root, and smiled. He looked on her with no less apprehension for that, seeing, perhaps, a ragged vagabond of a woman in outlaw's habit—or perhaps seeing more, for he did not look to be as blind as some. His hand touched a talisman at his breast and she, smiling still, touched that which hung at her own throat, which had power to answer his.

"Now where would you be going," she asked, "so recklessly through the Ealdwood? To some misdeed? Some mischief?"

"Misfortune," he said, breathless. He yet stared at her as if he thought her no more than moonbeams, and she grinned at that. Then suddenly and far away came a baying of hounds; he would have fled at once, and sprang to do so.

"Stay!" she cried, and stepped into his path a second time, curious what other venturers would come, and on the heels of such as he. "I do doubt they'll come this far. What name do you give, who come disturbing the peace of Eald?"

He was wary, surely knowing the power of names; and perhaps he would not have given his true one and perhaps he would not have stayed at all, but that she fixed him sternly with her eyes and he stammered out: "Fionn."

"Fionn." It was apt, for fair he was, tangled hair and first down of beard. She spoke it softly, like a charm. "Fionn. Come walk with me. I'd see this intrusion before others do. Come, come, have no dread of me; I've no harm in mind."

He did come, carefully, and much loath, heeded and walked after her, held by nothing but her wish. She took the Ealdwood's own slow time, not walking the quicker ways, for there was the taint of iron about him, and she could not take him there.

The thicket which degenerated from the dark heart of the Eald was an unlovely place . . . for the Ealdwood had once been better than it was, and there was yet a ruined fairness there; but these young trees had never been other than what they were. They twisted and tangled their roots among the bones of the crumbling hills, making deceiving and thorny barriers. Unlikely it was that Men could see the ways she found; but she was amazed by the changes the years had wrought—saw the slow work of root and branch and ice and sun, labored hard-breathing and scratched with thorns, but gloried in it, alive to the world. She turned from time to time when she sensed faltering behind her: he caught that look of hers and came on, pallid and fearful, past clinging thickets and over stones, as if he had lost all will or hope of doing otherwise.

The baying of hounds echoed out of Caerdale,

from the deep valley at the very bounds of the forest. She sat down on a rock atop that last slope, where was prospect of all the great vale of the Caerbourne, a dark tree-filled void beneath the moon. A towered heap of stones had risen far across the vale on the hill called Caer Wiell, and it was the work of men: so much did the years do with the world.

The boy dropped down by the stone, the harp upon his shoulders echoing; his head sank on his folded arms and he wiped the sweat and the tangled hair from his brow. The baying, still a moment, began again, and he lifted frightened eyes.

Now he would run, having come as far as he would; fear shattered the spell. She stayed him yet again, a hand on his smooth arm.

"Here's the limit of *my* wood," she said. "And in it, hounds hunt that you could not shake from your heels, no. You'd do well to stay here by me, indeed you would. Is it yours, that harp?"

He nodded.

"Will you play for me?" she asked, which she had desired from the beginning; and the desire of it burned far more vividly than did curiosity about men and dogs: but one would serve the other. He looked at her as though he thought her mad; and yet took the harp from his shoulders and from its case. Dark wood starred and banded with gold, it sounded when he took it into his arms: he held it so, like something protected, and lifted a pale, resentful face.

And bowed his head again and played as she had bidden him, soft touches at the strings that quickly grew bolder, that waked echoes out of the depths of Caerdale and set the hounds to baying madly. The music drowned the voices, filled the air, filled her heart, and she felt now no faltering or tremor of his hands. She listened, and almost forgot which moon shone down on them, for it had been so long, so very long since the last song had been heard in Ealdwood, and that sung soft and elsewhere.

He surely sensed a glamour on him, that the wind blew warmer and the trees sighed with listening. The fear went from his eyes, and though sweat stood on his brow like jewels, it was clear, brave music that he made—suddenly, with a bright ripple of the strings, a defiant song, strange to her ears.

Discord crept in, the hounds' fell voices, taking the music and warping it out of tune. She rose as that sound drew near. The song ceased, and there was the rush and clatter of horses in the thicket below.

Fionn sprang up, the harp laid aside. He snatched at the small dagger at his belt, and she flinched at that, the bitter taint of iron. "No," she wished him, and he did not draw.

Then hounds and riders were on them, a flood of hounds black and slavering and two great horses, bearing men with the smell of iron about them, men glittering terribly in the moonlight. The hounds surged up baying and bugling and as suddenly fell back again, making wide their circle, whining and with lifting of hackles. The riders whipped them, but their horses shied and screamed under the spurs and neither could be driven further.

She stood, one foot braced against the rock, and regarded men and beasts with cold curiosity, for she found them strange, harder and wilder than Men she had known; and strange too was the device on them, that was a wolf's grinning head. She did not recall it— nor care for the manner of them.

Another rider clattered up the shale, shouted and whipped his unwilling horse farther than the others, and at his heels came men with bows. His arm lifted, gestured; the bows arched, at the harper and at her.

"Hold," she said.

The arm did not fall; it slowly lowered. He glared at her, and she stepped lightly up onto the rock so she need not look up so far, to him on his tall horse. The beast shied under him and he spurred it and curbed it cruelly; but he gave no order to his men, as if the cowering hounds and trembling horses finally made him see.

"Away from here," he shouted down at her, a voice to make the earth quake. "Away! or I daresay you need a lesson taught you too." And he drew his great sword and held it toward her, curbing the protesting horse.

"Me, lessons?" She set her hand on the harper's arm. "Is it on his account you set foot here and raise this noise?"

"My harper," the lord said, "and a thief. Witch, step aside. Fire and iron are answer enough for you."

In truth, she had no liking for the sword that threatened or for the iron-headed arrows which could speed at his lightest word. She kept her hand on Fionn's arm nonetheless, for she saw well how he would fare with them. "But he's mine, lord-of-men. I should say that the harper's no joy to you, or you'd not come chasing him from your land. And great joy he is to me, for long and long it is since I've met so pleasant a companion in Ealdwood. Gather the harp, lad, and walk away now; let me talk with this rash man."

"Stay!" the lord shouted; but Fionn snatched the harp into his arms and edged away.

An arrow hissed; the boy flung himself aside with a terrible clangor of the harp, and lost it on the slope and scrambled back for it, his undoing, for now there were more arrows ready, and these better-purposed.

"Do not," she said.

"What's mine is mine." The lord held his horse still, his sword outstretched before his archers, bating the signal; his face was congested with rage and fear. "Harp and harper are mine. And you'll rue it if you think any words of yours weigh with me. I'll have him and you for your impudence."

It seemed wisest then to walk away, and she did so—turned back the next instant, at a distance, at Fionn's side, and only half under his moon. "I ask your name, lord-of-men, if you aren't fearful of my curse."

Thus she mocked him, to make him afraid before his men. "Evald," he said back, no hesitating, with contempt for her. "And yours, witch?"

"Call me what you like, lord. And take warning, that these woods are not for human hunting and your harper is not yours anymore. Go away and be grateful. Men have Caerdale. If it does not please you, shape it until it does. The Ealdwood's not for trespass."

He gnawed at his mustaches and gripped his sword the tighter, but about him the drawn bows had begun to sag and the arrows to aim at the dirt. Fear was in the men's eyes, and the two riders who had come first hung back, free men and less constrained than the archers.

"You have what's mine," he insisted.

"And so I do. Go on, Fionn. Do go, quietly."

"You've what's *mine*," the valley lord shouted. "Are you thief then as well as witch? You owe me a price for it."

She drew in a sharp breath and yet did not waver

in or out of the shadow. "Then do not name too high, lord-of-men. I may hear you, if that will quit us."

His eyes roved harshly about her, full of hate and yet of wariness as well. She felt cold at that look, especially where it centered, above her heart, and her hand stole to that moon-green stone that hung at her throat.

"The stone will be enough," he said. "*That.*"

She drew it off, and held it yet, insubstantial as she, dangling on its chain, for she had the measure of them and it was small. "Go, Fionn," she bade him; and when he lingered yet: "Go!" she shouted. At last he ran, fled, raced away like a mad thing, holding the harp to him.

And when the woods all about were still again, hushed but for the shifting and stamp of the horses and the complaint of the hounds, she let fall the stone. "Be paid," she said, and walked away.

She heard the hooves and turned, felt the insubstantial sword like a stab of ice into her heart. She recoiled elsewhere, bowed with the pain of it that took her breath away. But in time she could stand again, and had taken from the iron no lasting hurt: yet it had been close, and the feel of cold lingered even in the warm winds.

And the boy—she went striding through the shades and shadows in greatest anxiety until she found him, where he huddled hurt and lost within the deepest wood.

"Are you well?" she asked lightly, dropping to her heels beside him. For a moment she feared he might be hurt more than scratches, so tightly he was bowed over the harp; but he lifted his face to her. "You shall stay while you wish," she said, hoping that he would choose to stay long. "You shall harp for me." And when he yet looked fear at her: "You'd not like the new forest. They've no ear for harpers there."

"What is your name, lady?"

"What do you see of me?"

He looked swiftly at the ground, so that she reckoned he could not say the truth without offending her. And she laughed at that.

"Then call me Thistle," she said. "I answer sometimes to that, and it's a name as rough as I. But you'll stay. You'll play for me."

"Yes." He hugged the harp close. "But I'll not go with you. I've no wish to find the years passed in a night and all the world gone old."

"Ah. You know me. But what harm, that years should pass? What care of them or this age? It seems hardly kind to you."

"I am a man," he said, "and it's *my* age."

It was so; she could not force him. One entered otherwhere only by wishing it. He did not; and there was about him and in his heart still the taint of iron.

She settled in the moonlight, and watched beside him; he slept, for all his caution, and waked at last by sunrise, looking about him anxiously lest the trees had grown, and seeming bewildered that she was still there by day. She laughed, knowing her own look by daylight, that was indeed rough as the weed she had named herself, much-tanned and calloused and her clothes in want of patching. She sat plaiting her hair in a single silver braid and smiling sidelong at him, who kept giving her sidelong glances too.

All the earth grew warm. The sun did come here, unclouded on this day. He offered her food, such meager share as he had; she would have none of it, not fond of man-taint, or the flesh of poor forest creatures. She gave him instead of her own, the gift of trees and bees and whatsoever things felt no hurt at sharing.

"It's good," he said, and she smiled at that.

He played for her then, idly and softly, and slept again, for bright day in Ealdwood counseled sleep, when the sun burned warmth through the tangled branches and the air hung still, nothing breathing, least of all the wind. She drowsed too, for the first time since many a tree had grown, for the touch of the mortal sun did that kindness, a benison she had all but forgotten.

But as she slept she dreamed, of a close place of cold stone. In that dark hall she had a man's body, heavy and reeking of wine and ugly memories, such as dark fierceness she would gladly have fled if she might.

Her hand sought the moonstone on its chain and found it at his throat; she offered better dreams and more kindly, and he made bitter mock of them, hating all that he did not comprehend. Then she would have made the hand put the stone off that foul neck; but she had no power to compel, and *he* would not. He possessed what he owned, so fiercely and with such jealousy it cramped the muscles and stifled the breath.

And he hated what he did not have and could not have, that most of all; and the center of it was his harper.

She tried still to reason within this strange, closed mind. It was impossible. The heart was almost without love, and what little it had ever been given it folded in upon itself lest what it possessed escape.

"Why?" she asked that night, when the moon shed light on the Ealdwood and the land was quiet, no ill thing near them, no cloud above them. "Why does he seek you?" Though her dreams had told her, she wanted his answer.

Fionn shrugged, his young eyes for a moment aged; and he gathered against him his harp. "This," he said.

"You said it was yours. He called you thief. What did you steal?"

"It is mine." He touched the strings and brought forth melody. "It hung in his hall so long he thought it his, and the strings were cut and dead." He rippled out a somber note. "It was my father's and his father's before him."

"And in Evald's keeping?"

The fair head bowed over the harp and his hands coaxed sound from it, answerless.

"I've given a price," she said, "to keep him from it and you. Will you not give back an answer?"

The sound burst into softness. "It was my father's. Evald hanged him. Would hang me."

"For what cause?"

Fionn shrugged, and never ceased to play. "For truth. For truth he sang. So Evald hanged him, and hung the harp on his wall for mock of him. I came. I gave him songs he liked. But at winter's end I came down to the hall at night, and mended the old harp, gave it voice and a song he remembered. For that he hunts me."

Then softly he sang, of humankind and wolves, and that song was bitter. She shuddered to hear it, and bade him cease, for mind to mind with her in troubled dreams Evald heard and tossed, and waked starting in sweat.

"Sing more kindly," she said. Fionn did so, while the moon climbed above the trees, and she recalled elder-day songs which the world had not heard in long years, sang them sweetly. Fionn listened and caught up the words in his strings, until the tears ran down his face for joy.

There could be no harm in Ealdwood that hour: the spirits of latter earth that skulked and strove and haunted men fled elsewhere, finding nothing that they knew; and the old shadows slipped away trembling, for they remembered. But now and again the song faltered, for there came a touch of ill and smallness into her heart, a cold piercing as the iron, with thoughts of hate, which she had never held so close.

Then she laughed, breaking the spell, and put it from her, bent herself to teach the harper songs which she herself had almost forgotten, conscious the while that elsewhere, down in Caerbourne vale, on Caer Wiell, a man's body tossed in sweaty dreams which seemed constantly to mock him, with sound of eldritch harping that stirred echoes and sleeping ghosts.

With the dawn she and Fionn rose and walked a time, and shared food, and drank at a cold, clear spring she knew, until the sun's hot eye fell upon them and cast its numbing spell on all the Ealdwood.

Then Fionn slept; but she fought the sleep which came to her, for dreams were in it, her dreams while *he* should wake; nor would they stay at bay, not when her eyes grew heavy and the air thick with urging sleep. The dreams came more and more strongly. The man's strong legs bestrode a great brute horse, and hands plied whip and feet the spurs more than she would, hurting it cruelly. There was noise of hounds and hunt, a coursing of woods and hedges and the bright spurt of blood on dappled hide: he sought blood to wipe out blood, for the harping rang yet in his mind, and she shuddered at the killing her hands did, and at the fear that gathered thickly about him, reflected in his comrades' eyes.

It was better that night, when the waking was hers and her harper's, and sweet songs banished fear; but even yet she grieved for remembering, and at times the cold came on her, so that her hand would steal to her throat where the moon-green stone was not. Her eyes brimmed suddenly with tears: Fionn saw and tried to sing her merry songs instead. They failed, and the music died.

"Teach me another song," he begged of her. "No harper ever had such songs. And will *you* not play for *me*?"

"I have no art," she said, for the last harper of her folk had gone long ago: it was not all truth, for once she had known, but there was no more music in her hands, none since the last had gone and she had willed to stay, loving this place too well in spite of men. "Play," she asked of Fionn, and tried to smile, though the iron closed about her heart and the man raged at the nightmare, waking in sweat, ghost-ridden.

It was that human song Fionn played in his despair, of the man who would be a wolf and the wolf who was no man; while the lord Evald did not sleep again, but sat shivering and wrapped in furs before his hearth, his hand clenched in hate upon the stone which he possessed and would not, though it killed him, let go.

But she sang a song of elder earth, and the harper took up the tune, which sang of earth and shores and water, a journey, the great last journey, at men's coming and the dimming of the world. Fionn wept while he played, and she smiled sadly and at last fell silent, for her heart was gray and cold.

The sun returned at last, but she had no will to eat or rest, only to sit grieving, for she could not find peace. Gladly now she would have fled the shadow-shifting way back into otherwhere, to her own moon and softer sun, and persuaded the harper with her; but there was a portion of her heart in pawn, and she could not even go herself: she was too heavily bound. She fell to mourning bitterly, and pressed her hand often where the stone should rest. He hunted again, did Evald of Caer Wiell. Sleepless, maddened by dreams, he whipped his folk out of the hold as he did his hounds, out to the margin of the Ealdwood, to harry the creatures of woodsedge, having guessed well the source of the harping. He brought fire and axes, vowing to take the old trees one by one until all was dead and bare.

The wood muttered with whisperings and angers; a wall of cloud rolled down from the north on Ealdwood and all deep Caerdale, dimming the sun; a wind sighed in the face of the men, so that no torch was set to wood; but axes rang, that day and the next. The clouds gathered thicker and the wind blew colder, making Ealdwood dim again and dank. She yet managed to smile by night, to hear the harper's songs. But every stroke of the axes made her shudder, and the iron about her heart tightened day by day. The wound in the Ealdwood grew, and he was coming: she knew it well, and there remained at last no song at all, by day or night.

She sat now with her head bowed beneath the clouded moon, and Fionn was powerless to cheer her. He regarded her in deep despair, and touched her hand for comfort. She said no word to that, but gathered her cloak about her and offered to the harper to walk a time, while vile things stirred and muttered in the shadow, whispering malice to the winds, so that often Fionn started and stared and kept close beside her.

Her strength faded, first that she could not keep

the voices away, and then that she could not keep from listening; and at last she sank upon his arm, eased to the cold ground and leaned her head against the bark of a gnarled tree.

"What ails?" he asked, and pried at her clenched and empty fingers, opened the fist which hovered near her throat as if seeking there the answer. "What ails you?"

She shrugged and smiled and shuddered, for the axes had begun again, and she felt the iron like a wound, a great cry going through the wood as it had gone for days; but he was deaf to it, being what he was. "Make a song for me," she asked.

"I have no heart for it."

"Nor have I," she said. A sweat stood on her face, and he wiped at it with his gentle hand and tried to ease her pain.

And again he caught and unclenched the hand which rested, empty, at her throat. "The stone," he said. "Is it *that* you miss?"

She shrugged, and turned her head, for the axes then seemed loud. He looked too—glanced back deaf and puzzled. "'Tis time," she said. "You must be on your way this morning, when there's sun enough. The new forest will hide you after all."

"And leave you? Is that your meaning?"

She smiled, touched his anxious face. "I am paid enough."

"How paid? What did you pay? *What* was it you gave away?"

"Dreams," she said. "Only that. And all of that." Her hands shook terribly, and a blackness came on her heart too miserable to bear: it was hate, and aimed at him and at herself, and all that lived; and it was harder and harder to fend away. "Evil has it. He would do you hurt, and I would dream that too. Harper, it's time to go."

"Why would you give such a thing?" Great tears started from his eyes. "Was it worth such a cost, my harping?"

"Why, well worth it," she said, with such a laugh as she had left to laugh, that shattered all the evil for a moment and left her clean. "I have sung."

He snatched up the harp and ran, breaking branches and tearing flesh in his headlong haste, but not, she realized in horror, not the way he ought—but back again, to Caerdale.

She cried out her dismay and seized at branches to pull herself to her feet; she could in no wise follow. Her limbs which had been quick to run beneath this moon or the other were leaden, and her breath came hard. Brambles caught and held with all but mindful malice, and dark things which had never had power in her presence whispered loudly now, of murder.

And elsewhere the wolf-lord with his men drove at the forest, great ringing blows, the poison of iron. The heavy ironclad body which she sometimes wore seemed hers again, and the moonstone was prisoned within that iron, near a heart that beat with hate.

She tried the more to haste, and could not. She looked helplessly through Evald's narrow eyes and saw—saw the young harper break through the thickets near them. Weapons lifted, bows and axes. Hounds bayed and lunged at leashes.

Fionn came, nothing hesitating, bringing the harp, and himself. "A trade," she heard him say. "The stone for the harp."

There was such hate in Evald's heart, and such fear it was hard to breathe. She felt a pain to the depth of her as Evald's coarse fingers pawed at the stone. She felt his fear, felt his loathing of it. Nothing would be truly let go. But this—this he abhorred, and was fierce in his joy to lose it.

"Come," the lord Evald said, and held the stone, dangling and spinning before him, so that for that moment the hate was far and cold.

Another hand took it then, and very gentle it was, and very full of love. She felt the sudden draught of strength and desperation—sprang up then, to run, to save.

But pain stabbed through her heart, and such an ebbing out of love and grief that she cried aloud, and stumbled, blind, dead in that part of her.

She did not cease to run; and she ran now that shadowway, for the heaviness was gone. Across meadows, under that other moon she sped, and gathered up all that she had left behind, burst out again in the blink of an eye and elsewhere.

Horses shied and dogs barked; for now she did not care to be what suited men's eyes: bright as the moon she broke among them, and in her hand was a sharp blade, to meet with iron.

Harp and harper lay together, sword-riven. She saw the underlings start away and cared nothing for them; but Evald she sought. He cursed at her, drove spurs into his horse and rode at her, sword yet drawn, shivering the winds with a horrid slash of iron. The horse screamed and shied; he cursed and reined the beast, and drove it for her again. But this time the blow was hers, a scratch that made him shriek with rage.

She fled at once. He pursued. It was his nature that he must; and she might have fled otherwise, but she would not. She darted and dodged ahead of the great horse, and it broke the brush and thorns and panted after, hard-ridden.

Shadows gathered, stirring and urgent on this side and on that, who gibbered and rejoiced for the way that they were tending, to the woods' blackest heart, for some of them had been Men; and some had known the wolf's justice, and had come to what they were for his sake. They reached, but durst not touch him, for she would not have it so. Over all, the trees bowed and groaned in the winds and the leaves went flying, thunder above and thunder of hooves below, scattering the shadows.

But suddenly she whirled about and flung back her cloak: the horse shied up and fell, cast Evald sprawling among the wet leaves. The shaken beast scrambled up and evaded his hands and his threats, thundered away on the moist earth, splashing across some hidden stream; and the shadows chuckled. She stepped full back again from otherwhere, and Evald saw her clear, moonbright and silver. He cursed, shifted that great black sword from hand to hand, for his right hand bore a scratch that now must trouble him. He shrieked with hate and slashed.

She laughed and stepped into otherwhere and back again, and fled yet farther, until he stumbled with exhaustion and sobbed and fell, forgetting now his anger, for the whispers came loud.

"Up," she bade him, mocking, and stepped again to here. Thunder rolled upon the wind, and the sound of horses and hounds came at a distance. A joyful malice came into his eyes when he heard it; his face grinned in the lightnings. But she laughed too, and his mirth died as the sound came on them, under them, over them, in earth and heavens.

He cursed then and swung the blade, lunged and

slashed again, and she flinched from the almost-kiss of iron. Again he whirled it, pressing close; the lightning cracked—he shrieked a curse, and, silver-spitted—died.

She did not weep or laugh now; she had known him too well for either. She looked up instead at the clouds, gray wrack scudding before the storm, where other hunters coursed the winds and wild cries wailed—heard hounds baying after something fugitive and wild. She lifted then her fragile sword, salute to lord Death, who had governance over Men, a Huntsman too; and many the old comrades the wolf would find following in his train.

Then the sorrow came on her, and she walked the otherwhere path to the beginning and the end of her course, where harp and harper lay. There was no mending here. The light was gone from his eyes and the wood was shattered.

But in his fingers lay another thing, which gleamed like the summer moon amid his hand.

Clean it was from his keeping, and loved. She gathered it to her. The silver chain went again about her neck and the stone rested where it ought. She bent last and kissed him to his long sleep, fading then to otherwhere.

She dreamed at times then, waking or sleeping; for when she held close the stone and thought of him she heard a fair far music, for a part of his heart was there too, a gift of himself.

She sang sometimes, hearing it, wherever she walked.

That gift, she gave to him.

THE SEVENTH
MANDARIN

JANE YOLEN

World Fantasy Award winner JANE YOLEN has written
well over 150 books for children and adults, and well
over 200 short stories, most of them fantastical. She is
a past president of the Science Fiction and Fantasy
Writers of America as well as a twenty-five-year veteran
of the Board of Directors of the Society of Children's
Book Writers & Illustrators. She lives with her husband
in Hatfield, Massachusetts, and St. Andrews, Scotland.
Sometimes having the courage to speak the truth over-
powers the danger of doing so, as the hero of "The Seventh Mandarin" discovers.

Once in the East, where the wind blows gently on the bells of the temple, there lived a king of the highest degree. He was a good king. And he knew the laws of his land. But of his people he knew nothing at all, for he had never been beyond the high stone walls that surrounded his palace.

All day long the king read about his kingdom in the books and scrolls that were kept in the palace. And all day long he was guarded and guided by the seven mandarins who had lived all their lives, as the king had, within the palace walls.

These mandarins were honorable men. They dressed in silken robes and wore embroidered slippers. They ate from porcelain dishes and drank the most delicate teas.

Now, while it was important that the mandarins guarded and guided their king throughout his days, they had a higher duty still. At night they were the guardians of the king's soul.

It was written in the books and scrolls of the kingdom that each night the king's soul left his body and flew into the sky on the wings of a giant kite. And the king and the seven mandarins believed that what was written in the books and scrolls was true. And so, each mandarin took turns flying the king's kite through the long, dark hours, keeping it high above the terrors of the night.

This kite was a giant dragon. Its tail was of silk with colored tassels. Its body was etched with gold. And when the sun quit that kingdom in the East, the giant kite rose like a serpent in the wind, flown by one of the seven mandarins.

And for uncounted years it was so.

Now, of all the mandarins, the seventh was the youngest. He was also the most simple. While the other mandarins enjoyed feasting and dancing and many rich pleasures, the seventh mandarin loved only three things in all the world. He loved the king, the books and scrolls of the law, and the king's giant kite.

That he loved his king there was no doubt, for the seventh mandarin would not rest until the king rested.

That he loved the books and scrolls there was also no doubt. Not only did the seventh mandarin believe that what was written therein was true. He also believed that what was *not* written was *not* true.

But more than his king and more than the books and scrolls of the law, the seventh mandarin loved the king's kite, the carrier of the king's soul. He could make it dip and soar and crest the currents of air like a falcon trained to his hand.

One night, when it was the turn of the seventh mandarin to fly the king's kite, the sky was black with clouds. A wild wind like no wind before it entered the kingdom.

The seventh mandarin was almost afraid to fly the kite, for he had never seen such a wind. But he knew that he had to send it into the sky. The king's kite *must* fly, or the king's soul would be in danger. And so the seventh mandarin sent the kite aloft.

The minute the giant kite swam into the sky, it began to rage and strain at the string. It twisted and turned and dived and pulled. The wind gnawed and fretted and goaded the kite, ripping at its tender belly and snatching at its silken tail. At last, with a final snap, the precious kite string parted.

Before the seventh mandarin's eyes, the king's kite sailed wildly over the palace spires, over the roofs of the mandarins' mansions, over the high walls that surrounded the courtyards, and out of sight.

"Come back, come back, O Magnificent Wind Bird," cried the seventh mandarin. "Come back with the king's soul, and I will tip your tail with gold and melt silver onto your wings."

But the kite did not come back.

The seventh mandarin ran down the steps. He put his cape about his face so that no one would know him. He ran through the echoing corridors. He ran past the mandarins' mansions and through the gates of the high palace walls. Then he ran where he had never been before—past the neat houses of the merchants, past the tiny homes of the workers, past the canals that held the peddlers' boats, past the ramshackle, falling-down huts and hovels of the poor.

At last, in the distance, hovering about the hills that marked the edge of the kingdom, the seventh mandarin saw something flutter like a wounded bird in the sky. And though the wind pushed and pulled at his cape and at last tore it from his back, the seventh mandarin did not stop. He ran and ran until he came to the foot of the mountain.

There he found the king's kite. But what a terrible sight met his eyes. The wings of the dragon were dirty and torn. Its tail was shredded and bare. The links of its body were broken apart.

It would never fly again.

The seventh mandarin did not know what to do. He was afraid to return to the palace. It was not that he feared for his own life. He feared for the life of his king. For if the king's soul had flown on the wings of the kite, the king was surely dead.

Yet, much as he was afraid to return, the seventh mandarin was more afraid not to. And so he gathered the king's kite in his arms and began the long, slow journey back.

He carried the king's kite past the canals and the ramshackle, falling-down huts and hovels of the poor. And as he passed with the broken kite in his arms, it came to him that he had never read of such things in the books and scrolls of the kingdom. Yet the cries and groans he heard were not made by the wind.

At last, as the first light of the new day touched the gates of the high palace walls, the seventh mandarin entered the courtyard. He climbed the stairs to his chamber and placed the battered, broken kite on his couch.

Then he sat down and waited to hear of the death of the king.

Scarcely an hour went by before all seven of the mandarins were summoned to the king's chamber. The king lay on his golden bed. His face was pale and still. His hands lay like two withered leaves by his side.

Surely, thought the seventh mandarin, I have killed my king. And he began to weep.

But slowly the king opened his eyes.

"I dreamed a dream last night," he said, his voice low and filled with pain. "I dreamed that in my kingdom there are ramshackle hovels and huts that are falling down."

"It is not so," said the six mandarins, for they had

never been beyond the high palace walls and so had never seen such things.

Only the seventh mandarin was silent.

"I dreamed that in my kingdom," continued the king, "there are people who sigh and moan—people who cry and groan when the night is dark and deep."

"It is not so," said the six mandarins, for they had never read of such things in the books and scrolls.

The seventh mandarin was silent.

"If it is not so," said the king, slowly raising his hand to his head, "then how have I dreamed it? For is it not written that the dream is the eye of the soul? And if my soul was flying on the wings of my kite and these things are not so, then how did my dream see all this?"

The six mandarins were silent.

Then the seventh mandarin spoke. He was afraid, but he spoke. And he said, "O King, I saw these same things last night, and I did not dream!"

The six mandarins looked at the seventh mandarin in astonishment.

But the seventh mandarin continued. "The wind was a wild, mad beast. It ripped your kite from my hands. And the kite flew like an angel in the night to these same huts and hovels of which you dreamed. And there are many who moan and sigh, who groan and cry beyond the high palace walls. There are many—although it is not written in any of the books or scrolls of the kingdom."

Then the seventh mandarin bowed his head and waited for his doom. For it was death to fail the king. And it was death to damage his kite. And it was death to say that what was *not* written in the books and scrolls was so.

Then the king spoke, his voice low and crackling

like the pages of an ancient book. "For three reasons that you already know, you deserve to die."

The other mandarins looked at one another and nodded.

"But," said the king, sitting up in his golden bed, "for discovering the truth and not fearing to reveal it, you deserve to live." And he signaled the seventh mandarin to stand at his right hand.

That very night, the king and his seven mandarins made their way to the mountain at the edge of the kingdom. There they buried the king's kite with honors.

And the next morning, when the kingdom awoke, the people found that the high walls surrounding the palace had been leveled to the ground.

As for the king, he never again relied solely upon the laws of the land, but instead rode daily with his mandarins through the kingdom. He met with his people and heard their pleas. He listened and looked as well as read.

The mandarins never again had to fly the king's kite as a duty. Instead, once a year, at a great feast, they sent a giant dragon kite into the sky to remind themselves and their king of the folly of believing only what is written.

And the king, with the seventh mandarin always by his side, ruled a land of good and plenty until he came to the end of his days.

THE MONTAVARDE CAMERA

AVRAM DAVIDSON

Avram Davidson (1923–1993), like many of the authors included here, wrote in several genres during his lifetime. Getting his start in speculative fiction in the 1950s, he wrote several classic stories such as "All the Seas with Oysters," and "The Golem." At the urging of the editor for *Ellery Queen's Mystery Magazine*, he turned to writing mysteries, and won the Ellery Queen as well as the Edgar Allan Poe Award. When he began writing novels, he went back to the form that he started in, science fiction and fantasy. Notable works include *The Phoenix and the Mirror* and *The Island Under the Earth*. In "The Montavarde Camera," he combines science and magic with dangerous results.

M r. Azel's shop was set in between a glazier's establishment and a woolen draper's; three short
steps led down to it. The shopfront was narrow; a
stranger hurrying by would not even notice it, for the
grimy brick walling of the glazier's was part of a separate building, and extended farther out.

Three short steps down, and there was a little
areaway before the door, and it was always clean,
somehow. The slattern wind blew bits of straw and
paper scraps in circles up and down the street, leaving
its discarded playthings scattered all about, but not in
the areaway in front of the shop door. Just above the
height of a man's eye there was a rod fastened to the
inside of the door, and from it descended, in neat folds,
a red velveteen curtain. The shop's window, to the door's
left, was veiled in the same way. In old-fashioned let-
tering the gold-leaf figures of the street number stood
alone on the glass pane.

There was no slot for letters, no name or sign,
nothing displayed on door or window. The shop was a
blank, it made no impression on the eye, conveyed no
message to brain. If a few of the many people scurrying
by noticed it at all, it was only to assume it was empty.

No cats took advantage of this quiet backwater to
doze in the sun, although at least two of them always
reclined under the projecting window of the draper.

On this particular day the pair were jolted out of their calm by the running feet of Mr. Lucius Collins, who was chasing his hat. It was a high-crowned bowler, a neat and altogether proper hat, and as he chased it indignantly Mr. Collins puffed and breathed through his mouth—a small, full, red-lipped mouth, grazed on either side by a pair of well-trimmed, sandy, mutton chop whiskers.

Outrageous! Mr. Collins thought, his stout little legs pumping furiously. *Humiliating!* And no one to be blamed for it, either, not even the Government, or the Boers, or Mrs. Collins, she of the sniffles and rabbity face. *Shameful!* The gold seals on his watchchain jingled and clashed together and beat against the stomach it confined, and the wind carried the hat at a rapid clip along the street.

Just as the wind had passed the draper's, it abruptly abandoned the object of its game, and the forsaken bowler fell with a thud in front of the next shop. It rolled down the first, the second, and the third step, and leaned wearily against the door.

Mr. Collins trotted awkwardly down the steps and knelt down to seize the hat. His head remained where it was, as did his hands and knees. About a foot of uncurtained glass extended from the lower border of the red velveteen to the wooden doorframe, and through this Mr. Lucius Collins looked. It almost seemed that he gaped.

Inside the shop, looking down at Mr. Collins's round and red face, was a small, slender gentleman, who leaned against a showcase as if he were (the thought flitted through Mr. Collins's mind) posing for his photograph. The mild amusement evident on his thin features brought to Mr. Collins anew the realization that his position was, at best, undignified. He took up his hat, arose, brushed the errant bowler with his sleeve, dusted his knees, and entered the shop. Somewhere in the back a bell tinkled as he did so.

A red rug covered the floor and muffled his footsteps. The place was small, but well furnished, in the solid style more fashionable in past days. Nothing was shabby or worn, yet nothing was new. A gas jet with mantle projected from a paneled wall whose dark wood had the gleam of much polishing, but the burner was not lit, although the shop was rather dark. Several chairs upholstered in leather were set at intervals around the shop. There was no counter, and no shelves, and only the one showcase. *It* was empty, and only a well-brushed Ascot top hat rested on it.

Mr. Collins did not wish the slender little gentleman to receive the impression that he, Lucius, made a practice of squatting down and peering beneath curtained shop windows.

"Are you the proprietor?" he asked. The gentleman, still smiling, said that he was. It was a dry smile, and its owner was a dry-looking person. His was a long nose set in a long face. His chin was cleft.

The gentleman's slender legs were clad in rather baggy trousers, but it was obvious that they were the aftermath of the period when baggy trousers were the fashion, and were not the result of any carelessness in attire. The cloth was of a design halfway between plaid and checkered, and a pair of sharply pointed and very glossy shoes were on his small feet. A gray waistcoat, crossed by a light gold watchchain, a rather short frock coat, and a wing collar with a black cravat completed his dress. No particular period was stamped on his clothes, but one felt that in his prime—whenever that had been—this slender little gentleman had been a dandy, in a dry, smiling sort of way.

From his nose to his chin two deep lines were etched, and there were laughter wrinkles about the corners of his eyes. His hair was brown and rather sparse, cut in the conventional fashion. Its only unusual feature was that the little gentleman had on his forehead, after the manner of the late Lord Beaconsfield, a ringlet of the type commonly known as a "spit curl." And his nicely appointed little shop contained, as far as Mr. Collins could see, absolutely no merchandise at all.

"The wind, you know, it—ah, blew my hat off and carried it away. Dropped it at your door, so to speak."

Mr. Collins spoke awkwardly, aware that the man seemed still to be somewhat amused, and believed that this was due to his own precipitate entry. In order to cover his embarrassment and justify his continued presence inside, he asked in a rush, "What is it exactly that you sell here?" and waved his arm at the unstocked room.

"What is it you wish to buy?" the man asked.

Mr. Collins flushed again, and gaped again, and fumbled about for an answer.

"Why what I meant was: in what line *are* you? You have nothing displayed whatsoever, you know. Not a thing. How is one to know what sort of stock you have, if you don't put it about where it can be seen?" As he spoke, Mr. Collins felt his self-possession returning, and went on with increased confidence to say: "Now, just for example, my own particular avocation is photography. But if you have nothing displayed to show you sell anything in that line, I daresay I would pass by here every day and never think to stop in."

The proprietor's smile increased slightly, and his eyebrows arched up to his curl.

"But it so happens that I, too, am interested in photography, and although I have no display or sign to beguile you, in you came. I do not care for advertising. It is, I think, vulgar. My equipment is not for your tuppeny-tintype customer, nor will I pander to his tastes."

"Your equipment?" Mr. Collins again surveyed the place. "Where is it?" A most unusual studio—if studio it was—or shop, he thought; but he was impressed by what he considered a commendable attitude on the part of the slender gentleman—a standard so elevated that he refused to lower it by the most universally accepted customs of commerce.

The proprietor pointed to the most shadowy corner of the shop. There, in the semidarkness between the showcase and the wall, a large camera of archaic design stood upon a tripod. Mr. Collins approached it with interest, and began to examine it in the failing light.

Made out of some unfamiliar type of hardwood, with its lens piece gleaming a richer gold than ordinary brass, the old camera was in every respect a museum piece; yet, despite its age, it seemed to be in good working order. Mr. Collins ran his hand over the smooth surface; as he did so, he felt a rough spot on the back. It was evidently someone's name, he discovered, burned or carved into the wood, but now impossible to read in the thickening dusk. He turned to the proprietor.

"It is rather dark back here."

"Of course. I beg your pardon; I was forgetting. It is something remarkable, isn't it? There is no such workmanship nowadays. Years of effort that took, you know." As he spoke, he lit the jet and turned up the gas. The soft, yellow light of the flame filled the shop, hissing quietly to itself. More and more shops now had electric lights; this one, certainly, never would.

Mr. Collins reverently bowed his head and peered at the writing. In a flourishing old-fashioned script, someone long ago had engraved the name of *Gaston Montavarde*. Mr. Collins looked up in amazement.

"Montavarde's camera? Here?"

"Here, before you. Montavarde worked five years on his experimental models before he made the one you see now. At that time he was still—so the books tell you—the pupil of Daguerre. But to those who knew him, the pupil far excelled the master; just as Daguerre himself far excelled Niepce. If Montavarde had not died just as he was nearing mastery of the technique he sought, his work would be world famous. As it is, appreciation of Montavarde's style and importance is largely confined to the few—of whom I count myself one. You, sir, I am pleased to note, are one of the others. One of the few others." Here the slender gentleman gave a slight bow. Mr. Collins was extremely flattered, not so much by the bow—all shopkeepers bowed—but by the implied compliment to his knowledge.

In point of fact, he knew very little of Montavarde, his life, or his work. Who does? He was familiar, as are all students of photography, with Montavarde's study of a street scene in Paris during the 1848 Revolution. *Barricades in the Morning,* which shows a ruined embattlement and the still bodies of its defenders, is perhaps the first war photograph ever taken; it is usually, and wrongly, called a Daguerrotype. Perhaps not more than six or eight, altogether, of Montavarde's pictures are known to the general public, and all are famous for that peculiar luminous quality that seems to come from some unknown source within the scene. Collins was also aware that several more Montavardes in the possession of collectors of the esoteric and erotic could not be published or displayed. One of the most famous of these is the so-called *La Messe Noire*.

The renegade priest of Lyons, Duval, who was in the habit of conducting the Black Mass of the Demonolaters, used for some years as his "altar" the naked body of the famous courtesan, La Manchette. It was this scene that Montavarde was reputed to have photographed. Like many popular women of her type, La Manchette might have eventually retired to grow roses and live to a great age, had she not been murdered by one of her numerous lovers. Montavarde's photographs of the guillotine (*The Widow*) before and after the execution, had been banned by the French censor under Louis Napoleon as a matter of public policy.

All this is a digression, of course. These asides are mentioned because they were known to Mr. Lucius Collins, and largely explained his awe and reverence on seeing the—presumably—same camera which had photographed these scenes.

"How did you get this?" he asked, not troubling to suppress or conceal his eagerness.

"For more than thirty years," explained the proprietor, "it was the property of a North American. He came to London, met with financial reverses and pawned his equipment. He did not know, one assumes, that it was *the* Montavarde camera. Nor did he redeem. I had little or no competition at the auction. Later I heard he had gone back to America, or done away with himself, some said; but no matter: the camera was a *bon marché*. I never expected to see it again. I sold it soon after, but the payments were not kept up, and so here it is."

On hearing that the camera could be purchased, Mr. Collins began to treat for its sale (though he knew he could really not afford to buy) and would not take no for an answer. In short, an agreement was drawn up, whereby he was to pay a certain sum down, and something each month for eight months.

"Shall I make out the check in pounds or in guineas?" he asked.

"Guineas, of course. I do not consider myself a tradesman." The slender gentleman smiled and fingered his watchchain as Mr. Collins drew out his checkbook.

"What name am I to write, sir? I do not—"

"My name, sir, is Azel. The initials, A. A. Ah, just so. Can you manage the camera by yourself? Then I bid you a good evening, Mr. Collins. You have made a rare acquisition, indeed. Allow me to open the door."

Mr. Collins brought his purchase home in a four-wheeler, and spent the rest of the evening dusting and polishing. Mrs. Collins, a wispy, weedy little figure, who wore her hair in what she imagined was the manner of the Princess of Wales—Mrs. Collins had a cold, as usual. She agreed that the camera *was* in excellent condition, but, with a snuffle, she pointed out that he had spent far too much money on it. In her younger days, as one of the Misses Wilkins, she had done quite a good bit of amateur photography herself, but she had given it up because it cost far too much money.

She repeated her remarks some evenings later when her brother, the Reverend Wycliffe Wilkins, made his weekly call.

"Mind you," said Mr. Collins to his brother-in-law, "I don't know just what process the inventor used in developing his plates, but I did the best I could, and I don't think it's half bad. See here. This is the only thing I've done so far. One of those old Tudor houses in Great Cumberland Street. They say it was one of the old plague houses. Pity it's got to be torn down to make way for that new road. I thought I'd beat the wreckers to it."

"Very neatly done, I'm sure," said his brother-in-law. "I don't know much about photography myself. But evidently you haven't heard about this particular house. No? Happened yesterday. My cook was out marketing, and just as she came up to the corner, the house collapsed in a pile of dust. Shoddy workmanship somewhere; I mean, the house couldn't have been more than three hundred years old. Of course, there was no one in it, but still, it gave the cook quite a turn. I suppose there's no harm in your having this camera, but, as for me, considering its associations, I wouldn't have it in the house. Naked women, indeed!—saving your presence, Mary."

"Oh, come now," said Mr. Collins. "Montavarde was an artist."

"Many artists have been pious, decent people, Lucius. There can be no compromise between good and evil." Mrs. Collins snuffled her agreement. Mr. Collins pursed his little mouth and said no more until his good humor was restored by the maid's coming in with the tea tray.

"I suppose, then, Wycliffe, you wouldn't think of letting me take your picture."

"Well, I don't know why ever not," Mrs. Collins protested. "After the amount of money Lucius spent on the camera, we ought to make *some* use out of it, I think. Lucius will take your likeness whenever it's convenient. He has a great deal of free time. Raspberry jam or gooseberry, Wycliffe?"

Mr. Collins photographed his brother-in-law in the vicarage garden—alone, and then with his curate, the Reverend Osias Gomm. Both clerical gentlemen were very active in the temperance movement, and this added a note of irony to the tragic events of the following day. It was the carriage of Stout, the brewer; there was no doubt about that. The horses had shied at a scrap of paper. The witnesses (six of them) had described seeing the two clergymen start across the street, deep in conversation. They described how the carriage came flying around the corner.

"They never knew wot 'it 'em," the witnesses agreed. Mrs. Collins said that was the only thing that comforted her. She said nothing, of course, about the estate (three thousand pounds in six percent bonds), but she did mention the picture.

"How bright it is, Lucius," she said. "Almost shining."

After the funeral she felt free to talk about the financial affairs of her late brother, and until the estate was close to being settled, Mr. Collins had no time for photography. He did keep up the monthly payments on the camera, however, although he found them rather a drain. After all, it had not been *his* income which had just been increased 180 pounds per annum.

It was almost November before Mrs. Collins would consent to have a fire laid. The inheritance of her brother's share of their patrimony had not changed her habits for what her husband, if no one else, would have considered the better. Although he still transferred the same amount each quarter from his personal account to the household funds, there was less and less to show for it each week. Meat appeared on the table less often, and it was much more likely to be a piece of the neck than a cut off the joint. The tea grew dustier and the pieces of butter shrank in size, and more than once Mr. Collins had asked for another bit of cake at tea and been told (truthfully, as he learned by prowling around the kitchen late at night) that there wasn't another bit of cake in the house. (Perhaps it was his going to sleep on an empty—and hence, nervous, stomach—that caused the odd dreams which began about this time: confused scenes he could never remember, come daylight, and a voice—flat, resonant—repeating over and over, *"The life is in the light . . . the life is in the light."*)

He had, of course, protested, and it had, of course, done him no good at all. Mrs. Collins, with a snuffle, spoke of increased prices, the unsteady condition of World Affairs, and the necessity of Setting Something Aside For the Future, because, she said, who knows?

So, at any rate, here it was November, and a nice sea-coal fire in the grate, with Mr. Collins sitting by it in his favorite chair, reading the newspaper (there had formerly been two, but Mrs. Collins had stopped one of them in the interests of domestic economy). There were a number of interesting bits in the paper that evening, and occasionally Mr. Collins would read one of them aloud. Mrs. Collins was unraveling some wool with an eye toward reknitting it.

"Dear me!" said Mr. Collins.

"What is that, Lucius?"

"'Unusual Pronouncement By the Bishop of Lyons.'" He looked over at his wife. "Shall I read it to you?"

"Do."

His Grace the Bishop of Lyons had found it necessary to warn all the faithful against a most horrible series of crimes that had recently been perpetrated in the City and See of Lyons. It was a sign of the infamy and decadence of the age that not once but six times in the course of the past year, consecrated wafers had been stolen from churches and rectories in the City and See of Lyons. The purpose of these thefts could only indicate one thing, and it behooved all of the faithful, and so forth. There was little doubt (wrote the Paris correspondent of Mr. Collins's newspaper) that the bishop referred to the curious ceremony generally called the Black Mass, which, it would appear, was still being performed in parts of France; and not merely, as might be assumed, among the more uneducated elements of the population.

"Dear me!" said Mr. Collins.

"Ah, those French!" said Mrs. Collins. "Wasn't it Lyons—wasn't that the place that this unpleasant person came from? The camera man?"

"Montavarde?" Mr. Collins looked up in surprise. "Perhaps. I don't know. What makes you think so?"

"Didn't poor Wycliffe say so on that last night he was here?"

"Did he? I don't remember."

"He must have. Else how could I know?"

This was a question which required no answer, but it aroused other questions in Mrs. Collins's mind. That night he had the dream again, and he recalled it very clearly on awakening. There was a woman, a foreign woman . . . though how he knew she was foreign, he could not say. It was not her voice, for she never spoke, only gestured: horrid, wanton gestures, too! Nor was it in her clothes, for she wore none. And she had something in her hand, about the size of a florin, curiously marked, and she offered it to him. When he went to take it, she snatched it back, laughing, and thrust it into her red, red mouth. And all the while the voice—inflectionless, echoing—repeated over and again, *"The light is in the life . . . the light is in the life."* It seemed, somehow, a familiar voice.

The next day found him at his bookdealer's, the establishment of little Mr. Pettigew, the well-known antiquary, known among younger and envious members of the trade as "the well-known antiquity." There, under pretense of browsing, Mr. Collins read as much as he could on demonolatry in general, and the Black Mass in particular. It was most interesting, but, as the books all dated from the previous century, there was no mention of either Duval or Montavarde. Mr. Collins tipped his hat to the bookdealer (it was the same bowler) and left the shop.

He bought an *Illustrated London News* at a tobacconist's, got a seat on top of the omnibus, and prepared to enjoy the ride home. It was a bright day despite the time of year, one of the brightest Guy Fawkes's Days that Mr. Collins could remember.

The *Illustrated,* he noted, was showing more and more photographs as time went on, and fewer drawings. Progress, progress, thought Mr. Collins, looking with approval and affection at a picture of the Duke of York and his sons, the little princes, all in Highland costume. Then he turned the page, and saw something which almost caused him to drop the paper. It was a picture of a dreadnought, but it was the style and not the subject that fixed his attention to the page.

"The above photograph," read the caption, "of the

ill-fated American battleship, the *U.S.S. Maine,* was taken shortly before it left on its last voyage for Havana. Those familiar with photography will be at once attracted by the peculiar luminosity of the photograph, which is reminiscent of the work of the Frenchman, Montavarde. The *Maine* was built at—" Mr. Collins read no further. He began to think, began to follow a train of thought alien to his mind. Shying away from any wild and outrageous fantasies, Mr. Collins began to enumerate as best he could all the photographs known to him to have been taken by the Montavarde camera.

Barricades in the Morning proved nothing, and neither did *The Widow;* no living person appeared in either. On the other hand, consider the matter of La Manchette, the subject of Montavarde's picture *La Messe Noire;* consider the old house in Great Cumberland Street, and the Reverends Wilkins and Gomm. Consider also the battleship *Maine.*

After considering all this, Mr. Collins found himself at his stop. He went directly home, took the camera in his arms, and descended with it to the basement.

Was there some quality in the camera which absorbed the life of its subjects? Some means whereby that life was transmuted into light, a light impressed upon the photograph, leaving the subjects to die?

Mr. Collins took an ax and began to destroy the camera. The wood was intensely hard, and he removed his coat before falling to work again. Try as he might, Mr. Collins could not dent the camera, box, brass or lens. He stopped at last, sweat pouring down his face, and heard his wife's voice calling to him. What*ever* was he doing?

"I'm breaking up a box for kindling wood," he shouted back. And then, even as she warned him not to use too much wood, that the wood had to last them another fortnight, that wood had gone up—even as she chattered away, Mr. Collins had another idea. He carried the camera up to the fire and thrust it in. He heaped on the coals, he threw in kerosene at the cost of his eyebrows, and he plied the bellows.

Half an hour's effort saw the camera not only unconsumed, but unscorched. He finally removed it from the fire in despair, and stood there, hot and disheveled, not knowing what to do. All doubts that he had felt earlier were now removed. Previously he had been uncertain as to the significance of Montavarde's presence with his dreadful camera at the Rites of Lucifer, at the foul ritual conducted by the renegade priest Duval. It was *not* merely as a spectator that the cameraman had attended these blasphemous parodies. The spitting on the crucifix, the receiving of the witch mar, the signing of the compact with his own blood, the ceremonial stabbing of the stolen Host while awaiting the awful moment when the priest or priestess of the unholy sect declared manifest in his or her own body the presence of the Evil One—surely Montavarde had *done* all these things, and not just seen them.

Mr. Collins felt that he needed some air. He put on his hat and coat and went down to the street. The breeze cooled his hot face and calmed his thoughts. Several children came down the street toward him, lighting firecrackers and tossing them into the air.

> *"Remember, remember, the 5th of*
> *November*
> *Was gunpowder, treason, and plot"*

the children began to chant as they came up to him.

They were wheeling a tatterdemalion old bath chair, and in it was a scarecrow of a Guy Fawkes, clad in old clothes; just as Mr. Collins had done as a boy.

"I see no reason why gunpowder treason
Should ever be forgot"

ended the traditional phrases, and then the outstretched, expectant grimy paws, and a general cry of "Remember the Guy, sir! Remember the Guy!" Mr. Collins distributed some money to the eager group, even though he could see that his wife, who had come down and was now looking out of the first floor window, was shaking her head at him and pursing her lips, pantomiming that he wasn't to give them a farthing. He looked away and glanced at the Guy.

Its torn trousers were of a plaid design, its scuffed shoes were sharply pointed. A greasy gray waistcoat, a ragged sort of frock coat, a drooping and dirty wing collar, and a battered Ascot top hat completed its dress. The costume seemed unpleasantly familiar to Mr. Collins, but he could not quite place it. Just then a gust of wind blew off the old topper and revealed the Guy's head. It was made of one of those carven coconuts that visitors from southern countries sometimes bring back, and its carven features were a horrible parody of the face of the slender gentleman who had sold the camera.

The children went on their way while Mr. Collins remained standing, his mind a maze of strange thoughts, and Mrs. Collins frowned down at him from the window. She seemed to be busy with something; her hands moved. It seemed to him that an age passed as he stood there, hand in pocket, thinking of the long-dead Montavarde (How did he die? "Untimely" was the word invariably used) who had purchased, at a price unknown and scarcely to be guessed at, unsurpassable skill in building and using his camera. What should one do? One might place the camera in a large sack, or encase it in concrete, and throw it in the Thames.

Or one might keep it hidden in a safe place that one knew of.

He turned to his house and looked up at Mrs. Collins, there at the window. (What *had* she been busied with?) It seemed to him that she had never looked so much like a rabbit before, and it also occurred to him how much he disliked rabbits and always had, since he was a boy. That, after all, was not so very long ago. He was still a comparatively young man. Many attractive women might still find him attractive too.

Should he submit, like some vegetable, while his wife nibbled, nibbled away at him forever? No. The way had been shown him; he had fought, but that sort of victory was plainly not to be his. So be it; he would follow the way which had been open to him since the moment he took the camera. And he would use it again, this time with full knowledge.

He started up the steps, and had just reached the top one when a searing pain stabbed him in the chest, and the sun went out. His hat fell off as he dropped. It rolled down the first, the second, and the third step. Mrs. Collins began to scream. It occurred to him, even in that moment of dark agony, how singularly unconvincing those screams sounded.

For some reason the end did not come at once.

"I'm not completely satisfied with that likeness I took of you just before you were stricken," Mrs. Collins said. "Of course, it *was* the first time I had used a camera since we were married. And the picture, even while you look at it, seems to be growing brighter."

Logically, Mr. Collins thought; for at the same time he was growing weaker. Well, it did not matter.

"Your affairs *are* in order, aren't they, Lucius?" Her eyes, as she gazed at him, were bright, birdlike. A bird, of course, is not human. He made no reply. "Yes, to be sure they are. I made certain. Except for this unpleasant Mr. Azel asking me for money he claims is still owing on the camera. Well, I shan't pay it. I have all I can do to keep myself. But I mean to show him. He can have his old camera back, and much good may it do him. I took my mother's ring and I scratched the nasty lens up completely with the diamond."

Her voice was growing weaker now. "It's a tradition in our family, you know. It's an old diamond, an heirloom; it has been in our family ever so long, and they say that it was once set in a jeweled monstrance that stood upon the high altar at Canterbury before the days of good King Harry.

"*That* will teach that Mr. A. A. Azel a good lesson."

SHOTTLE BOP

BOP

THEODORE STURGEON

Theodore Sturgeon (1918–1985) influenced many authors with his penetrating insight into the psychology of human behavior applied to science fiction and fantasy. Better known for his many short stories than his novels, he had the ability to distill novel-length ideas into clear crisp stories. He was the guest of honor at the twentieth World Science Fiction Convention, and was awarded the Life Achievement Award by the World Fantasy Association in 1985. In "Shottle Bop," he applied his incredible talent to a variation on the classic ghost story.

I'd never seen the place before, and I lived just down the block and around the corner. I'll even give you the address, if you like. "The Shottle Bop," between Twentieth and Twenty-first Streets, on Tenth Avenue in New York City. You can find it if you go there looking for it. Might even be worth your while, too.

But you'd better not.

"The Shottle Bop." It got me. It was a small shop with a weather-beaten sign swung from a wrought crane, creaking dismally in the late fall wind. I walked past it, thinking of the engagement ring in my pocket and how it had just been handed back to me by Audrey, and my mind was far removed from such things as shottle bops. I was thinking that Audrey might have used a gentler term than "useless" in describing me; and her neatly turned remark about my being a "constitutional psychopathic incompetent" was as uncalled-for as it was spectacular. She must have read it somewhere, balanced as it was by "And I wouldn't marry you if you were the last man on earth!" which is a notably worn cliché.

"Shottle Bop!" I muttered, and then paused, wondering where I had picked up such oddly rhythmic syllables with which to express myself. I'd seen it on that sign, of course, and it had caught my eye. "And what," I asked myself, "might be a Shottle Bop?" Myself replied promptly, "Dunno. Toddle back and have a look." So toddle I did, back along the east side of Tenth, wondering what manner of man might be running such an establishment in pursuance of what kind of business. I was enlightened on the second point by a sign in the window, all but obscured by the dust and ashes of apparent centuries, which read:

WE SELL BOTTLES

There was another line of smaller print there. I rubbed at the crusted glass with my sleeve and finally was able to make out:

WITH THINGS IN THEM.

Just like that:

WE SELL BOTTLES
WITH THINGS IN THEM.

Well of course I went in. Sometimes very delightful things come in bottles, and the way I was feeling, I could stand a little delighting.

"Close it!" shrilled a voice, as I pushed through the door. The voice came from a shimmering egg adrift in the air behind the counter, low-down. Peering over, I saw that it was not an egg at all, but the bald pate of an old man who was clutching the edge of the counter, his scrawny body streaming away in the slight draft from the open door, as if he were made of bubbles. A mite startled, I kicked the door with my heel. He immediately fell on his face, and then scrambled smiling to his feet.

"Ah, it's good to see you again," he rasped.

I think his vocal cords were dusty, too. Everything else here was. As the door swung to, I felt as if I were inside a great dusty brain that had just closed its eyes. Oh yes, there was light enough. But it wasn't the lamp light and it wasn't daylight. It was like—like light reflected from the cheeks of pale people. Can't say I enjoyed it much.

"What do you mean, 'again'?" I asked irritably. "You never saw me before."

"I saw you when you came in and I fell down and got up and saw you again," he quibbled, and beamed. "What can I do for you?"

"Oh," I said. "Well, I saw your sign. What have you got in a bottle that I might like?"

"What do you want?"

"What've you got?"

He broke into a piping chant—I remember it yet, word for word.

> For half a buck, a vial of luck
> Or a bottle of nifty breaks
> Or a flask of joy, or Myrna Loy
> For luncheon with sirloin steaks.
>
> Pour out a mug from this old jug,
> And you'll never get wet in rains.
> I've bottles of grins and racetrack wins
> And lotions to ease your pains.
>
> Here's bottles of imps and wet-pack shrimps
> From a sea unknown to man,
> And an elixir to banish fear,
> And the sap from the pipes of Pan.

> *With the powdered horn of a unicorn*
> *You can win yourself a mate;*
> *With the rich hobnob; or get a job—*
> *It's yours at a lowered rate.*

"Now wait right there!" I snapped. "You mean you actually sell dragon's blood and ink from the pen of Friar Bacon and all such mumbo-jum?"

He nodded rapidly and smiled all over his improbable face.

I went on—"The genuine article?"

He kept on nodding.

I regarded him for a moment. "You mean to stand there with your teeth in your mouth and your bare face hanging out and tell me that in this day and age, in this city and in broad daylight, you sell such trash and then expect me—me, an enlightened intellectual—"

"You are very stupid and twice as bombastic," he said quietly.

I glowered at him and reached for the doorknob— and there I froze. And I mean froze. For the old man whipped out an ancient bulb-type atomizer and squeezed a couple of whiffs at me as I turned away; and so help me, *I couldn't move!* I could cuss, though, and boy, did I.

The proprietor hopped over the counter and ran over to me. He must have been standing on a box back there, for now I could see he was barely three feet tall. He grabbed my coat tails, ran up my back and slid down my arm, which was extended doorward. He sat down on my wrist and swung his feet and laughed up at me. As far as I could feel, he weighed absolutely nothing.

When I had run out of profanity—I pride myself on never repeating a phrase of invective—he said,

"Does that prove anything to you, my cocky and unintelligent friend? That was the essential oil from the hair of the Gorgon's head. And until I give you an antidote, you'll stand there from now till a week text Neusday!"

"Get me out of this," I roared, "or I smack you so hard you lose your brains through the pores in your feet!"

He giggled.

I tried to tear loose again and couldn't. It was as if all my epidermis had turned to high-carbon steel. I began cussing again, but quit in despair.

"You think altogether too much of yourself," said the proprietor of the Shottle Bop. "Look at you! Why, I wouldn't hire you to wash my windows. You expect to marry a girl who is accustomed to the least of animal comfort, and then you get miffed because she turns you down. Why does she turn you down? Because you won't get a job. You're a no-good. You're a bum. He, he! And you have the nerve to walk around telling people where to get off. Now if I were in your position I would ask politely to be released, and then I would see if anyone in this shop would be good enough to sell you a bottle full of something that might help out."

Now I never apologize to anybody, and I never back down, and I never take any guff from mere tradesmen. But this was different. I'd never been petrified before, nor had my nose rubbed in so many galling truths. I relented. "OK, OK; let me break away then. I'll buy something."

"Your tone is sullen," he said complacently, dropping lightly to the floor and holding his atomizer at the ready. "You'll have to say 'Please. Pretty please.' "

"Pretty please," I said, almost choking with humiliation.

He went back of the counter and returned with a paper of powder which he had me sniff. In a couple of seconds I began to sweat, and my limbs lost their rigidity so quickly that it almost threw me. I'd have been flat on my back if the man hadn't caught me and solicitously led me to a chair. As strength dribbled back into my shocked tissues, it occurred to me that I might like to flatten this hobgoblin for pulling a trick like that. But a strange something stopped me—strange because I'd never had the experience before. It was simply the idea that once I got outside I'd agree with him for having such a low opinion of me.

He wasn't worrying. Rubbing his hands briskly, he turned to his shelves. "Now let's see . . . what would be best for you, I wonder? Hm-m-m. Success is something you couldn't justify. Money? You don't know how to spend it. A good job? You're not fitted for one." He turned gentle eyes on me and shook his head. "A sad case. *Tsk, tsk.*" I crawled. "A perfect mate? Nup. You're too stupid to recognize perfection, too conceited to appreciate it. I don't think that I can— Wait!"

He whipped four or five bottles and jars off the dozens of shelves behind him and disappeared somewhere in the dark recesses of the store. Immediately there came sounds of violent activity—clinkings and little crashes; stirrings and then the rapid susurrant grating of a mortar and pestle; then the slushy sound of liquid being added to a dry ingredient during stirring; and at length, after quite a silence, the glugging of a bottle being filled through a filtering funnel. The proprietor reappeared triumphantly bearing a four-ounce bottle without a label.

"This will do it!" he beamed.

"That will do what?"

"Why, cure you!"

"Cure—" My pompous attitude, as Audrey called it, had returned while he was mixing. "What do you mean cure? I haven't got anything!"

"My dear little boy," he said offensively, "you most certainly have. Are you happy? Have you ever been happy? No. Well, I'm going to fix all that up. That is, I'll give you the start you need. Like any other cure, it requires your cooperation.

"You're in a bad way, young fellow. You have what is known in the profession as retrogressive metempsychosis of the ego in its most malignant form. You are a constitutional unemployable; a downright sociophagus. I don't like you. Nobody likes you."

Feeling a little bit on the receiving end of a blitz, I stammered, "W-what do you aim to do?"

He extended the bottle. "Go home. Get into a room by yourself—the smaller the better. Drink this down, right out of the bottle. Stand by for developments. That's all."

"But—what will it do to me?"

"It will do nothing *to* you. It will do a great deal *for* you. It can do as much for you as you want it to. But mind me, now. As long as you use what it gives you for your self-improvement, you will thrive. Use it for self-gratification, as a basis for boasting, or for revenge, and you will suffer in the extreme. Remember that, now."

"But what is it? How—"

"I am selling you a talent. You have none now. When you discover what kind of a talent it is, it will be up to you to use it to your advantage. Now go away. I still don't like you."

"What do I owe you?" I muttered, completely snowed under by this time.

"The bottle carries its own price. You won't pay anything unless you fail to follow my directions. Now will you go, or must I uncork a bottle of jinn—and I don't mean London Dry?"

"I'll go," I said. I'd seen something swirling in the depths of a ten-gallon carboy at one end of the counter, and I didn't like it a bit. "Good-bye."

"Bood-gy," he returned.

I went out and I headed down Tenth Avenue and I turned east up Twentieth Street and I never looked back. And for many reasons I wish now that I had, for there was, without doubt, something very strange about that Shottle Bop.

I didn't simmer down until I got home; but once I had a cup of black Italian coffee under my belt I felt better. I was skeptical about it at last. I was actually inclined to scoff. But somehow I didn't want to scoff too loudly. I looked at the bottle a little scornfully, and there was a certain something about the glass of it that seemed to be staring back at me. I sniffed and threw it up behind some old hats on top of the closet, and then sat down to unlax. I used to love to unlax. I'd put my feet on the doorknob and slide down in the upholstery until I was sitting on my shoulder blades, and as the old saying has it, "Sometimes I sets and thinks, and sometimes I just sets." The former is easy enough, and is what even an accomplished loafer has to go through before he reaches the latter and more blissful state. It takes years of practice to relax sufficiently to be able to "just set." I'd learned it years ago.

But just as I was about to slip into the vegetable status, I was annoyed by something. I tried to ignore it. I manifested a superhuman display of lack of curiosity, but the annoyance persisted. A light pressure on my elbow, where it draped over the arm of the chair. I was put in the unpleasant predicament of having to concentrate on what it was; and realizing that concentration on anything was the least desirable thing there could be. I gave up finally, and with a deep sigh, opened my eyes and had a look.

It was the bottle.

I screwed up my eyes and then looked again, but it was still there. The closet door was open as I had left it, and its shelf almost directly above me. Must have fallen out. Feeling that if the damn thing were on the floor it couldn't fall any farther, I shoved it off the arm of the chair with my elbow.

It bounced. It bounced with such astonishing accuracy that it wound up in exactly the same spot it had started from—on the arm of the easy-chair, by my elbow. Startled, I shoved it violently. This time I pushed it hard enough to send it against the wall, from which it rebounded to the shelf under my small table, and thence back to the chair arm—and this time it perched cozily against my shoulder. Jarred by the bouncing, the stopper hopped out of the bottle mouth and rolled into my lap; and there I sat, breathing the bitter-sweet fumes of its contents, feeling frightened and silly as hell.

I grabbed the bottle and sniffed. I'd smelled that somewhere before—where was it? Uh—oh, yes; that mascara the Chinese honkytonk girls use in Frisco. The liquid was dark—smoky black. I tasted it cautiously. It wasn't bad. If it wasn't alcoholic, then the old man in the shop had found a darn good substitute for alcohol. At the second sip I liked it and at the third I really enjoyed it and there wasn't any fourth because by then the little bottle was a dead marine. That was about the time I remembered the name of the black ingredient with the funny smell. Kohl. It is an herb the Orientals use to make it possible to see supernatural beings. Silly superstition!

And then the liquid I'd just put away, lying warm and comfortable in my stomach, began to fizz. Then I think it began to swell. I tried to get up and couldn't. The room seemed to come apart and throw itself at me piecemeal, and I passed out.

Don't you ever wake up the way I did. For your own sake, be careful about things like that. Don't swim up out of a sodden sleep and look around you and see all those things fluttering and drifting and flying and creeping and crawling around you—puffy things dripping blood, and filmy, legless creatures, and little bits and snatches of pasty human anatomy. It was awful. There was a human hand afloat in the air an inch away from my nose; and at my startled gasp it drifted away from me, fingers fluttering in the disturbed air from my breath. Something veined and bulbous popped out from under my chair and rolled across the floor. I heard a faint clicking, and looked up into a gnashing set of jaws without any face attached. I think I broke down and cried a little. I know I passed out again.

The next time I awoke—must have been hours later, because it was broad daylight and my clock and watch had both stopped—things were a little better. Oh, yes, there were a few of the horrors around. But somehow they didn't bother me much now. I was practically convinced that I was nuts; now that I had the conviction, why worry about it? I dunno; it must have been one of the ingredients in the bottle that had calmed me down so. I was curious and excited, and that's about all. I looked around me and I was almost pleased.

The walls were green! The drab wallpaper had turned to something breathtakingly beautiful. They were covered with what seemed to be moss; but never moss like that grew for human eyes to see before. It was long and thick, and it had a slight perpetual movement—not that of a breeze, but of growth. Fascinated, I moved over and looked closely. Growing indeed, with all the quick magic of spore and cyst and root and growth again to spore; and the swift magic of it was only a part of the magical whole, for never was there such a green. I put out my hand to touch and stroke it, but I felt only the wallpaper. But when I closed my fingers on it, I could feel that light touch of it in the palm of my hand, the weight of twenty sunbeams, the soft resilience of jet-darkness in a closed place. The sensation was a delicate ecstasy, and never have I been happier than I was at that moment.

Around the baseboards were little snowy toadstools, and the floor was grassy. Up the hinged side of the closet door climbed a mass of flowering vines, and their petals were hued in tones indescribable. I felt as if I had been blind until now, and deaf, too; for now I could hear the whispering of scarlet, gauzy insects among the leaves and the constant murmur of growth. All around me was a new and lovely world, so delicate that the wind of my movements tore petals from the flowers, so real and natural that it defied its own impossibility. Awestruck, I turned and turned, running from wall to wall, looking under my old furniture, into my old books; and everywhere I looked I found newer and more beautiful things to wonder at. It was while I was flat on my stomach looking up at the bed springs, where a colony of jewellike lizards had nested, that I first heard the sobbing.

It was young and plaintive, and had no right to be in my room where everything was so happy. I stood up and looked around, and there in the corner crouched the translucent figure of a little girl. She was leaning back against the wall. Her thin legs were crossed in front of her, and she held the leg of a tattered toy elephant dejectedly in one hand and cried into the other. Her hair was long and dark, and it poured and tumbled over her face and shoulders.

I said, "What's the matter, kiddo?" I hate to hear a child cry like that.

She cut herself off in the middle of a sob and shook the hair out of her eyes, looking up and past me, all fright and olive skin and big, filled violet eyes. "Oh!" she squeaked.

I repeated, "What's the matter? Why are you crying?"

She hugged the elephant to her breast defensively, and whimpered, "W-where are you?"

Surprised, I said, "Right here in front of you, child. Can't you see me?"

She shook her head. "I'm scared. Who are you?"

"I'm not going to hurt you. I heard you crying, and I wanted to see if I could help you. Can't you see me at all?"

"No," she whispered. "Are you an angel?"

I guffawed. "By no means!" I stepped closer and put my hand on her shoulder. The hand went right through her and she winced and shrank away, uttering a little wordless cry. "I'm sorry," I said quickly. "I didn't mean . . . you can't see me at all? I can see you."

She shook her head again. "I think you're a ghost," she said.

"Do tell!" I said. "And what are you?"

"I'm Ginny," she said. "I have to stay here, and I have no one to play with." She blinked, and there was a suspicion of further tears.

"Where did you come from?" I asked.

"I came here with my mother," she said. "We lived in lots of other rooming houses. Mother cleaned floors in office buildings. But this is where I got so sick. I was sick a long time. Then one day I got off the bed and come over here but then when I looked back I was still on the bed. It was awful funny. Some men came and put the 'me' that was on the bed onto a stretcher-thing and took it—me—out. After a while Mummy left, too. She cried for a long time before she left, and when I called to her she couldn't hear me. She never came back, and I just got to stay here."

"Why?"

"Oh, I got to. I—don't know why. I just—got to."

"What do you do here?"

"I just stay here and think about things. Once a lady lived here, had a little girl just like me. We used to play together until the lady watched us one day. She carried on somethin' awful. She said her little girl was possessed. The girl kept callin' me, 'Ginny! Ginny! Tell Mamma you're here!'; an' I tried, but the lady couldn't see me. Then the lady got scared an' picked up her little girl an' cried, an' so I was sorry. I ran over here an' hid, an' after a while the other little girl forgot about me, I guess. They moved," she finished with pathetic finality.

I was touched. "What will become of you, Ginny?"

"I dunno," she said, and her voice was troubled. "I

guess I'll just stay here and wait for Mummy to come back. I been here a long time. I guess I deserve it, too."

"Why, child?"

She looked guiltily at her shoes. "I couldn' stand feelin' so awful bad when I was sick. I got up out of bed before it was time. I shoulda stayed where I was. This is what I get for quittin'. But Mummy'll be back; just you see."

"Sure she will," I muttered. My throat felt tight. "You take it easy, kid. Any time you want someone to talk to, you just pipe up. I'll talk to you any time I'm around."

She smiled, and it was a pretty thing to see. What a raw deal for a kid! I grabbed my hat and went out.

Outside things were the same as in the room to me. The hallways, the dusty stair carpets wore new garments of brilliant, nearly intangible foliage. They were no longer dark, for each leaf had its own pale and different light. Once in a while I saw things not quite so pretty. There was a giggling thing that scuttled back and forth on the third floor landing. It was a little indistinct, but it looked a great deal like Barrel-head Brogan, a shanty-Irish bum who'd returned from a warehouse robbery a year or so ago, only to shoot himself accidentally with his own gun. I wasn't sorry.

Down on the first floor, on the bottom step, I saw two youngsters sitting. The girl had her head on the boy's shoulder, and he had his arms around her, and I could see the banister through them. I stopped to listen. Their voices were faint, and seemed to come from a long way away.

He said, "There's one way out."

She said, "Don't talk that way, Tommy!"

"What else can we do? I've loved you for three

years, and we still can't get married. No money, no hope—no nothing. Sue, if we did it, I just *know* we'd always be together. Always and always—"

After a long time she said, "All right, Tommy. You get a gun, like you said." She suddenly pulled him even closer. "Oh, Tommy, are you sure we'll always be together just like this?"

"Always," he whispered, and kissed her. "Just like this."

Then there was a long silence, while neither moved. Suddenly they were as I had first seen them, and he said:

"There's only one way out."

And she said, "Don't talk that way, Tommy!"

And he said, "What else can we do? I've loved you for three years—" It went on like that, over and over and over.

I felt lousy. I went on out into the street.

It began to filter through to me what had happened. The man in the shop had called it a "talent." I couldn't be crazy, could I? I didn't *feel* crazy. The draught from the bottle had opened my eyes on a new world. What was this world?

It was a thing peopled by ghosts. There they were—story-book ghosts, and regular haunts, and poor damned souls—all the fixings of a storied supernatural, all the things we have heard about and loudly disbelieved and secretly wonder about. So what? What had it all to do with me?

As the days slid by, I wondered less about my new, strange surroundings, and gave more and more thought to that question. I had bought—or been given—a talent. I could see ghosts. I could see all parts of a ghostly world, even the vegetation that grew in it. That was perfectly reasonable—the trees and birds and fungi and flowers. A ghost world is a world as we know it, and a world as we know it must have vegetation. Yes, I could see them. But they couldn't see me!

OK; what could I get out of it? I couldn't talk about it or write about it because I wouldn't be believed; and besides, I had this thing exclusive, as far as I knew; why cut a lot of other people in on it?

On what, though?

No, unless I could get a steer from somewhere, there was no percentage in it for me that I could see. And then, about six days after I took that eye-opener, I remember the one place where I might get that steer.

The Shottle Bop!

I was on Sixth Avenue at the time, trying to find something in a five-and-dimie that Ginny might like. She couldn't touch anything I brought her but she enjoyed things she could look at—picture books and such. By getting her a little book on photographs of trains since the "De Witt Clinton," and asking her which of them was like ones she had seen, I found out approximately how long it was she'd been there. Nearly eighteen years. Anyway, I got my bright idea and headed for Tenth Avenue and the Shottle Bop. I'd ask that old man—he'd tell me. And when I got to Twenty-first Street, I stopped and stared. Facing me was a blank wall. The whole side of the block was void of people. There was no sign of a shop.

I stood there for a full two minutes not even daring to think. Then I walked downtown toward Twentieth, and then uptown to Twenty-first. Then I did it again. No shop. I wound up without my question answered— what was I going to do with this "talent"?

• • •

I was talking to Ginny one afternoon about this and that when a human leg, from the knee down, complete and puffy, drifted between us. I recoiled in horror, but Ginny pushed it gently with one hand. It bent under the touch, and started toward the window, which was open a little at the bottom. The leg floated toward the crack and was sucked through like a cloud of cigarette smoke, reforming again on the other side. It bumbled against the pane for a moment and then ballooned away.

"My gosh!" I breathed. "What *was* that?"

Ginny laughed. "Oh, just one of the Things that's all 'e time flying around. Did it scare you? I used to be scared, but I saw so many of them that I don't care any more, so's they don't light on me."

"But what in the name of all that's disgusting are they?"

"Parts." Ginny was all childish *savoir-faire*.

"Parts of what?"

"People, silly. It's some kind of a game, *I* think. You see, if someone gets hurt and loses something—a finger or an ear or something, why, the ear—the *inside* part of it, I mean, like me being the inside of the 'me' they carried out of here—it goes back to where the person who owned it lived last. Then it goes back to the place before that, and so on. It doesn't go very fast. Then when something happens to a whole person, the 'inside' part comes looking for the rest of itself. It picks up bit after bit—Look!" she put out a filmy forefinger and thumb and nipped a flake of gossamer out of the air.

I leaned over and looked closely; it was a small section of semitransparent human skin, ridged and whorled.

"Somebody must have cut his finger," said Ginny matter-of-factly, "while he was living in this room.

When something happens to um—you see! He'll be back for it!"

"Good heavens!" I said. "Does this happen to everyone?"

"I dunno. Some people have to stay where they are—like me. But I guess if you haven't done nothing to deserve bein' kept in one place, you have to come all around pickin' up what you lost."

I'd thought of more pleasant things in my time.

For several days I'd noticed a gray ghost hovering up and down the block. He was always on the street, never inside. He whimpered constantly. He was—or had been—a little inoffensive man of the bowler hat and starched collar type. He paid no attention to me—none of them did, for I was apparently invisible to them. But I saw him so often that pretty soon I realized that I'd miss him if he went away. I decided I'd chat with him the next time I saw him.

I left the house one morning and stood around for a few minutes in front of the brownstone steps. Sure enough, pressing through the flotsam of my new, weird coexistent world, came the slim figure of the wraith I had noticed, his rabbit face screwed up, his eyes deep and sad, and his swallowtail coat and striped waistcoat immaculate. I stepped up behind him and said, "Hi!"

He started violently and would have run away, I'm sure, if he'd known where my voice was coming from.

"Take it easy, pal," I said. "I won't hurt you."

"Who are you?"

"You wouldn't know if I told you," I said. "Now stop shivering and tell me about yourself."

He mopped his ghostly face with a ghostly hand-kerchief, and then began fumbling nervously with a gold toothpick. "My word," he said. "No one's talked to me for years. I'm not quite myself, you see."

"I see," I said. "Well, take it easy. I just happen to've noticed you wandering around here lately. I got curious. You looking for somebody?"

"Oh, no," he said. Now that he had a chance to talk about his troubles, he forgot to be afraid of this mysterious voice from nowhere that had accosted him. "I'm looking for my home."

"Hm-m-m," I said. "Been looking for a long time?"

"Oh, yes." His nose twitched. "I left for work one morning a long time ago, and when I got off the ferry at Battery Place I stopped for a moment to watch the work on that newfangled elevated railroad they were building down there. All of a sudden there was a loud noise—my goodness! It was terrible—and the next thing I knew I was standing back from the curb and looking at a man who looked just like me! A girder had fallen, and—my word!" He mopped his face again. "Since then I have been looking and looking. I can't seem to find anyone who knows where I might have lived, and I don't understand all the things I see floating around me, and I never thought I'd see the day when grass would grow on lower Broadway—oh, it's terrible." He began to cry.

I felt sorry for him. I could easily see what had happened. The shock was so great that even his ghost had amnesia! Poor little egg—until he was whole, he could find no rest. The thing interested me. Would a ghost react to the usual cures for amnesia? If so, then what would happen to him?

"You say you got off a ferry boat?"

"Yes."

"Then you must have lived on the Island . . . Staten Island, over there across the bay!"

"You really think so?" He stared through me, puzzled and hopeful.

"Why sure! Say, how'd you like me to take you over there? Maybe we can find your house."

"Oh, that would be splendid! But—oh, my, what will my wife say?"

I grinned. "She might want to know where you've been. Anyway, she'll be glad to see you back, I imagine. Come on; let's get going!"

I gave him a shove in the direction of the subways and strolled along behind him. Once in a while I got a stare from a passer-by for walking with one hand out in front of me and talking into thin air. It didn't bother me very much. My companion, though, was very self-conscious about it, for the inhabitants of his world screeched and giggled when they saw him doing practically the same thing. Of all the humans, only I was invisible to them, and the little ghost in the bowler hat blushed from embarrassment until I thought he'd burst.

We hopped a subway—it was a new experience for him, I gathered—and went down to South Ferry. The subway system in New York is a very unpleasant place to one gifted as I was. Everything that enjoys lurking in the dark hangs out there, and there is quite a crop of dismembered human remains. After this day I took the bus.

We got a ferry without waiting. The little gray ghost got a real kick out of the trip. He asked me about the ships in the harbor and their flags, and marveled at the dearth of sailing vessels. He *tsk, tsked* at the Statue of

Liberty; the last time he had seen it, he said, was while it still had its original brassy gold color, before it got its patina. By this I placed him in the late '70s; he must have been looking for his home for over sixty years!

We landed at the Island, and from there I gave him his head. At the top of Fort Hill he suddenly said, "My name is John Quigg. I live at 45 Fourth Avenue!" I've never seen anyone quite so delighted as he was by the discovery. And from then on it was easy. He turned left again, straight down for two blocks and again right. I noticed—he didn't—that the street was marked "Winter Avenue." I remembered vaguely that the streets in this section had been numbered years ago.

He trotted briskly up the hill and then suddenly stopped and turned vaguely. "I say, are you still with me?"

"Still here," I said.

"I'm all right now. I can't tell you how much I appreciate this. Is there anything I could do for you?"

I considered. "Hardly. We're of different times, you know. Things change."

He looked, a little pathetically, at the new apartment house on the corner and nodded. "I think I know what happened to me," he said softly. "But I guess it's all right . . . I made a will, and the kids were grown." He sighed. "But if it hadn't been for you I'd still be wandering around Manhattan. Let's see—ah; come with me!"

He suddenly broke into a run. I followed as quickly as I could. Almost at the top of the hill was a huge old shingled house, with silly cupola and a complete lack of paint. It was dirty and it was tumble-down, and at the sight of it the little fellow's face twisted sadly. He gulped and turned through a gap in the hedge and down beside the house. Casting about in the long grass, he spotted a boulder sunk deep into the turf.

"This is it," he said. "Just you dig under that. There is no mention of it in my will, except a small fund to keep paying the box rent. Yes, a safety-deposit box, and the key and an authority are under that stone. I hid it"—he giggled—"from my wife one night, and never did get a chance to tell her. You can have whatever's any good to you." He turned to the house, squared his shoulders, and marched in the side door, which banged open for him in a convenient gust of wind. I listened for a moment and then smiled at the tirade that burst forth. Old Quigg was catching real hell from his wife, who'd sat waiting for over sixty years for him! It was a bitter stream of invective, but—well, she must have loved him. She couldn't leave the place until she was complete, if Ginny's theory was correct, and she wasn't really complete until her husband came home! It tickled me. They'd be all right now!

I found an old pinchbar in the drive and attacked the ground around the stone. It took quite a while and made my hands bleed, but after a while I pried the stone up and was able to scrabble around under it. Sure enough, there was an oiled silk pouch under there. I caught it up and carefully unwrapped the strings around it. Inside was a key and a letter addressed to a New York bank, designating only "Bearer" and authorizing the use of the key. I laughed aloud. Little old meek and mild John Quigg, I'd bet, had set aside some "mad money." With a layout like that, a man could take a powder without leaving a single sign. The son-of-a-gun! I would never know just what it was he had up his sleeve, but I'll bet there was a woman in the case. Even fixed up with his will! Ah, well—I should kick!

It didn't take me long to get over to the bank. I had a little trouble getting into the vaults, because it took quite a while to look up the box in the old records. But I finally cleared the red tape, and found myself the proud possessor of just under eight thousand bucks in small bills—and not a yellowback among 'em!

Well, from then on I was pretty well set. What did I do? Well, first I bought clothes, and then, I started out to cut ice for myself. I clubbed around a bit and got to know a lot of people, and the more I knew the more I realized what a lot of superstitious dopes they were. I couldn't blame anyone for skirting a ladder under which crouched a genuine basilisk, of course, but what the heck—not one in a thousand have beasts under them! Anyway, my question was answered. I dropped two grand on an elegant office with drapes and dim indirect lighting, and I got me a phone installed and a little quiet sign on the door—Psychic Consultant. And, boy, I did all right.

My customers were mostly upper crust, because I came high. It was generally no trouble to get contact with people's dead relatives, which was usually what they wanted. Most ghosts are crazy to get in contact with this world anyway. That's one of the reasons that almost anyone can become a medium of sorts if he tries hard enough; Lord knows that it doesn't take much to contact the average ghost. Some, of course, were not available. If a man leads a pretty square life, and kicks off leaving no loose ends, he gets clear. I never did find out where these clear spirits went to. All I knew was that they weren't to be contacted. But the vast majority of people have to go back and tie up those loose ends after they die—righting a little wrong here, helping someone they've hindered, cleaning up a bit of dirty work. That's where luck itself comes from, I do believe. You don't get something for nothing.

If you get a nice break, it's been arranged that way by someone who did you dirt in the past, or someone who did wrong to your father or your grandfather or your great-uncle Julius. Everything evens up in the long run, and until it does, some poor damned soul is wandering around the earth trying to do something about it. Half of humanity is walking around crabbing about its tough breaks. If you and you and you only knew what dozens of powers were begging for the chance to help you if you'll let them! And if you let them, you'll help clear up the mess they've made of their lives here, and free them to go wherever it is they go when they've cleaned up. Next time you're in a jam, go away somewhere by yourself and open your mind to these folks. They'll cut in and guide you all right, if you can drop your smugness and your mistaken confidence in your own judgment.

I had a couple of ghostly stooges to run errands for me. One of them, an ex-murderer by the name of One-eye Rachuba, was the fastest spook ever I saw, when it came to locating a wanted ancestor; and then there was Professor Grafe, a frog-faced teacher of social science who'd embezzled from a charity fund and fallen into the Hudson trying to make a getaway. He could trace the most devious genealogies in mere seconds, and deduce the most likely whereabouts of the ghost of a missing relative. The pair of them were all the office force I could use, and although every time they helped out one of my clients they came closer to freedom for themselves, they were both so entangled with their own sloppy lives that I was sure of their services for years.

But do you think I'd be satisfied to stay where I was making money hand over fist without really working for it? Oh, no. Not me. No, I had to big-time. I had to brood over the events of the last few months, and I had to get dramatic about that screwball Audrey, who really wasn't worth my trouble. It wasn't enough that I'd prove Audrey wrong when she said I'd never amount to anything. And I wasn't happy when I thought about the gang. I had to show them up.

I even remembered what the little man in the Shottle Bop had said to me about using my "talent" for bragging or for revenge. I figured I had the edge on everyone, everything. Cocky, I was. Why, I could send one of my ghostly stooges out any time and find out exactly what anyone had been doing three hours ago come Michaelmas. With the shade of the professor at my shoulder, I could back-track on any far-fetched statement and give immediate and logical reasons for back-tracking. No one had anything on me, and I could out-talk, out-maneuver, and out-smart anyone on earth. I was really quite a fellow. I began to think, "What's the use of my doing as well as this when the gang on the West Side don't know anything about it?" and "Man, would that half-wit Happy Sam burn up if he saw me drifting down Broadway in my new six-thousand-dollar roadster!" and "To think I used to waste my time and tears on a dope like Audrey!" In other words, I was tripping up on an inferiority complex. I acted like a veridam fool, which I was. I went over to the West Side.

It was a chilly, late winter night. I'd taken a lot of trouble to dress myself and my car so we'd be bright and shining and would knock some eyes out. Pity I couldn't brighten my brains up a little.

I drove up in front of Casey's pool room, being careful to do it too fast, and concentrating on shrieks from the tires and a shuddering twenty-four-cylinder roar from the engine before I cut the switch. I didn't hurry to get out of the car, either. Just leaned back and lit a fifty-cent cigar, and then tipped my hat over one ear and touched the horn button, causing it to play "Tuxedo Junction" for forty-eight seconds. Then I looked over toward the pool hall.

Well, for a minute I thought that I shouldn't have come, if that was the effect my return to the fold was going to have. And from then on I forgot about everything except how to get out of here.

There were two figures slouched in the glowing doorway of the pool room. It was up a small side street, so short that the city had depended on the place, an old institution, to supply the street lighting. Looking carefully, I made out one of the silhouetted figures as Happy Sam, and the other was Fred Bellew. They just looked out at me; they didn't move; they didn't say anything, and when I said, "Hiya, small fry—remember me?" I noticed that along the darkened walls flanking the bright doorway were ranked the whole crowd of them—the whole gang. It was a shock; it was a little too casually perfect. I didn't like it.

"Hi," said Fred quietly. I knew he wouldn't like the big-timing. I didn't expect any of them to like it, of course, but Fred's dislike sprang from distaste, and the others from resentment, and for the first time I felt a little cheap. I climbed out over the door of the roadster and let them have a gander at my fine feathers.

Sam snorted and said, "Jellybean!" very clearly. Someone else giggled, and from the darkness beside the building came a high-pitched, "Woo-woo!"

I walked up to Sam and grinned at him. I didn't feel like grinning. "I ain't seen you in so long I almost forgot what a heel you were," I said. "How you making?"

"I'm doing all right," he said, and added offensively, "I'm still *working* for a living."

The murmur that ran through the crowd told me that the really smart thing to do was to get back into that shiny new automobile and hoot along out of there. I stayed.

"Wise, huh?" I said weakly.

They'd been drinking, I realized—all of them. I was suddenly in a spot. Sam put his hands in his pockets and looked at me down his nose. He was the only short man that ever could do that to me. After a thick silence he said:

"Better get back to yer crystal balls, phony. We like guys that sweat. We even like guys that have rackets, if they run them because they're smarter or tougher than the next one. But luck and gab ain't enough. Scram."

I looked around helplessly. I was getting what I'd begged for. What had I expected, anyway? Had I thought that these boys would crowd around and shake my hand off for acting this way?

They hardly moved, but they were all around me suddenly. If I couldn't think of something quickly, I was going to be mobbed. And when those mugs started mobbing a man, they did it up just fine. I drew a deep breath.

"I'm not asking for anything from you, Sam. Nothing; that means advice; see?"

"You're gettin' it?" he flared. "You and your seeanses. We heard about you. Hanging up widdow-women for fifty bucks a throw to talk to their 'dear departed'! P-sykik investigator! What a line! Go on; beat it!"

I had a leg to stand on now. "A phony, huh? Why I'll bet I could put a haunt on you that would make that hair of yours stand up on end, if you have guts enough to go where I tell you to."

"You'll bet? That's a laugh. Listen at that, gang." He laughed, then turned to me and talked through one side of his mouth. "All right, you wanted it. Come on, rich guy; you're called. Fred'll hold stakes. How about ten of your lousy bucks for every one of mine? Here, Fred—hold this sawbuck."

"I'll give you twenty to one," I said half hysterically. "And I'll take you to a place where you'll run up against the homeliest, plumb-meanest old haunt you ever heard of."

The crowd roared. Sam laughed with them, but didn't try to back out. With any of that gang, a bet was a bet. He'd taken me up, and he'd set odds, and he was bound. I just nodded and put two century notes into Fred Bellew's hand. Fred and Sam climbed into the car, and just as we started, Sam leaned out and waved.

"See you in hell, fellas," he said. "I'm goin' to raise me a ghost, and one of us is going to scare the other one to death!"

I honked my horn to drown out the whooping and hollering from the sidewalk and got out of there. I turned up the parkway and headed out of town.

"Where to?" Fred asked after a while.

"Stick around," I said, not knowing.

There must be some place not far from here where I could find an honest-to-God haunt, I thought, one that would make Sam back-track and set me up with the boys again. I opened the compartment in the dashboard and let Ikey out. Ikey was a little twisted imp who'd got his tail caught in between two sheets of steel when they were assembling the car, and had to stay there until it was junked.

"Hey, Ike," I whispered. He looked up, the gleam of the compartment light shining redly in his bright little eyes. "Whistle for the professor, will you? I don't want to yell for him because those mugs in the back seat will hear me. They can't hear you."

"OK, boss," he said; and putting his fingers to his lips, he gave vent to a blood-curdling, howling scream.

That was the prof's call-letters, as it were. The old man flew ahead of the car, circled around and slid in beside me through the window, which I'd opened a crack for him.

"My goodness," he panted, "I wish you wouldn't summon me to a location which is traveling with this high degree of celerity. It was all I could do to catch up with you."

"Don't give me that, professor," I whispered. "You can catch a stratoliner if you want to. Say, I have a guy in the back who wants to get a real scare from a ghost. Know of any around here?"

The professor put on his ghostly pince-nez. "Why, yes. Remember my telling you about the Wolfmeyer place?"

"Golly—he's bad."

"He'll serve your purpose admirably. But don't ask me to go there with you. None of us ever associates with Wolfmeyer. And for Heaven's sake, be careful."

"I guess I can handle him. Where is it?"

He gave me explicit directions, bade me good night and left. I was a little surprised; the professor traveled around with me a great deal, and I'd never seen him refuse a chance to see some new scenery. I shrugged it off and went my way. I guess I just didn't know any better.

I headed out of town and into the country to a certain old farmhouse. Wolfmeyer, a Pennsylvania Dutchman, had hung himself there. He had been, and was, a bad egg. Instead of being a nice guy about it all, he was the rebel type. He knew perfectly well that unless he did plenty of good to make up for the evil, he'd be stuck where he was for the rest of eternity. That didn't seem to bother him at all. He got surly and became a really bad spook. Eight people had died in that house since the old man rotted off his own rope. Three of them were tenants who had rented the place, and three were hobos, and two were psychic investigators. They'd all hung themselves. That's the way Wolfmeyer worked. I think he really enjoyed haunting. He certainly was thorough about it anyway.

I didn't want to do any real harm to Happy Sam. I just wanted to teach him a lesson. And look what happened!

We reached the place just before midnight. No one had said much, except that I told Fred and Sam about Wolfmeyer, and pretty well what was to be expected from him. They did a good deal of laughing about it, so I just shut up and drove. The next item of conversation was Fred's, when he made the terms of the bet. To win, Sam was to stay in the house until dawn. He wasn't to call for help and he wasn't to leave. He had to bring in a coil of rope, tie a noose in one end and string the other up on "Wolfmeyer's Beam"—the great oaken beam on which the old man had hung himself, and eight others after him. This was an added temptation to Wolfmeyer to work on Happy Sam, and was my idea. I was to go in with Sam, to watch him in case the thing became too dangerous. Fred was to stay in the car a hundred yards down the road and wait.

I parked the car at the agreed distance and Sam and I got out. Sam had my tow rope over his shoulder, already noosed. Fred had quieted down considerably, and his face was dead serious.

"I don't think I like this," he said, looking up the road at the house. It hunched back from the highway, and looked like a malign being deep in thought.

I said, "Well, Sam? Want to pay up now and call it quits?"

He followed Fred's gaze. It sure was a dreary-looking place, and his liquor had fizzed away. He thought a minute, then shrugged and grinned. I had to admire the rat. "Hell, I'll go through with it. Can't bluff me with scenery, phony."

Surprisingly, Fred piped up, "I don't think he's a phony, Sam."

The resistance made Sam stubborn, though I could see by his face that he knew better. "Come on, phony," he said and swung up the road.

We climbed into the house by way of a cellar door that slanted up to a window on the first floor. I hauled out a flashlight and lit the way to the beam. It was only one of many that delighted in turning the sound of one's footsteps into laughing whispers that ran round and round the rooms and halls and would not die. Under the famous beam the dusty floor was dark-stained.

I gave Sam a hand in fixing the rope, and then clicked off the light. It must have been tough on him then. I didn't mind, because I knew I could see anything before it got to me, and even then, no ghost could see me. Not only that, for me the walls and floors and ceilings were lit with the phosphorescent many-hued glow of the ever-present ghost plants. For its eerie effect I wished Sam could see the ghost-molds feeding greedily on the stain under the beam.

Sam was already breathing heavily, but I knew it would take more than just darkness and silence to get his goat. He'd have to be alone, and then he'd have to have a visitor or so.

"So long, kid," I said, slapping him on the shoulder, and I turned and walked out of the room.

I let him hear me go out of the house and then I crept silently back. It was without doubt the most deserted place I have ever seen. Even ghosts kept away from it, excepting, of course, Wolfmeyer's. There was just the luxurious vegetation, invisible to all but me, and the deep silence rippled by Sam's breath. After ten minutes or so I knew for certain that Happy Sam had more guts than I'd ever have credited him with. He had to be scared. He couldn't—or wouldn't—scare himself.

I crouched down against the walls of an adjoining room and made myself comfortable. I figured Wolfmeyer would be along pretty soon. I hoped earnestly that I could stop the thing before it got too far. No use in making this anymore than a good lesson for a wiseacre. I was feeling pretty smug about it all, and I was totally unprepared for what happened.

I was looking toward the doorway opposite when I realized that for some minutes there had been the palest of pale glows there. It brightened as I watched; brightened and flickered gently. It was green, the green of things moldy and rotting away; and with it came a subtly harrowing stench. It was the smell of flesh so very dead that it had ceased to be really odorous. It was utterly horrible, and I was honestly scared out of my wits. It was some moments before the comforting thought of my invulnerability came back to me, and

I shrank lower and closer to the wall and watched.

And Wolfmeyer came in.

His was the ghost of an old, old man. He wore a flowing, filthy robe, and his bare forearms thrust out in front of him were stringy and strong. His head, with its tangled hair and beard, quivered on a broken, ruined neck like the blade of a knife just thrown into soft wood. Each slow step as he crossed the room set his head to quivering again. His eyes were alight; red they were, with deep green flames buried in them. His canine teeth had lengthened into yellow, blunt tusks, and they were like pillars supporting his crooked grin. The putrescent green glow was a horrid halo about him. He was a bright and evil thing.

He passed me completely unconscious of my presence and paused at the door of the room where Sam waited by the rope. He stood just outside it, his claws extended, the quivering of his head slowly dying. He stared in at Sam, and suddenly opened his mouth and howled. It was a quiet, deadly sound, one that might have come from the throat of a distant dog, but, though I couldn't see into the other room, I knew that Sam had jerked his head around and was staring at the ghost. Wolfmeyer raised his arms a trifle, seemed to totter a bit, and then moved into the room.

I snapped myself out of the crawling terror that gripped me and scrambled to my feet. If I didn't move fast—

Tiptoeing swiftly to the door, I stopped just long enough to see Wolfmeyer beating his arms about erratically over his head, a movement that made his robe flutter and his whole figure pulsate in the green light; just long enough to see Sam on his feet, wide-eyed, staggering back and back toward the rope. He clutched his throat and opened his mouth and made no sound, and his head tilted, his neck bent, his twisted face gaped at the ceiling as he clumped backward away from the ghost and into the ready noose. And then I leaned over Wolfmeyer's shoulder, put my lips to his ear, and said:

"*Boo!*"

I almost laughed. Wolfmeyer gave a little squeak, jumped about ten feet, and, without stopping to look around, high-tailed out of the room so fast that he was just a blur. That was one scared old spook!

At the same time Happy Sam straightened, his face relaxed and relieved, and sat down with a bump under the noose. That was as close a thing as ever I want to see. He sat there, his face soaking wet with cold sweat, his hands between his knees, staring limply at his feet.

"That'll show you!" I exulted, and walked over to him. "Pay up, scum, and you may starve for that week's pay!" He didn't move. I guess he was plenty shocked.

"Come on!" I said. "Pull yourself together, man! Haven't you seen enough? That old fellow will be back any second now. On your feet!"

He didn't move.

"Sam!"

He didn't move.

"*Sam!*" I clutched at his shoulder. He pitched over sideways and lay still. He was quite dead.

I didn't do anything and for a while I didn't say anything. Then I said hopelessly, as I knelt there, "Aw, Sam, Sam—cut it out, fella."

After a minute I rose slowly and started for the door. I'd taken three steps when I stopped. Something was happening! I rubbed my hand over my eyes. Yes, it is—it was getting dark! The vague luminescence of the vines and flowers of the ghost world was getting dimmer, fading, fading—

But that had never happened before!

No difference. I told myself desperately, it's happening now, all right. *I got to get out of here!*

See? You see. It was the stuff—the damn stuff from the Shottle Bop. It was wearing off! When Sam died it . . . it stopped working on me! Was this what I had to pay for the bottle? Was this what was to happen if I used it for revenge?

The light was almost gone—and now it was gone. I couldn't see a thing in the room but one of the doors. Why could I see the doorway? What was that pale-green light that set off its dusty frame?

Wolfmeyer! *I got to get out of here!*

I couldn't see ghosts any more. Ghosts could see me now. I ran. I darted across the dark room and smashed into the wall on the other side. I reeled back from it, blood spouting from between the fingers I slapped to my face. I ran again. Another wall clubbed me. Where was that other door? I ran again, and again struck a wall. I screamed and ran again. I tripped over Sam's body. My head went through the noose. It whipped down on my windpipe, and my neck broke with an agonizing crunch. I floundered there for half a minute, and then dangled.

Dead as hell, I was. Wolfmeyer, he laughed and laughed.

Fred found me and Sam in the morning. He took our bodies away in the car. Now I've got to stay here and haunt this damn old house. Me and Wolfmeyer.

THE KING
OF THE ELVES

PHILIP K. DICK

PHILIP K. DICK (1928–1982) wrote novels and stories which examined "reality" in all of its myriad forms, letting his protagonists, along with his readers, try to sort out what was real and what wasn't. His novel *The Man in the High Castle* won the Hugo Award in 1962, and he also received the John W. Campbell Memorial Award. His work has also inspired films, most notably the Ridley Scott–directed *Blade Runner*. In "The King of the Elves," an old man finds out that fate has one more adventure waiting for him, from a most unlikely place.

It was raining and getting dark. Sheets of water blew along the row of pumps at the edge of the filling station; the trees across the highway bent against the wind.

Shadrach Jones stood just inside the doorway of the little building, leaning against an oil drum. The door was open and gusts of rain blew in onto the wood floor. It was late; the sun had set, and the air was turning cold. Shadrach reached into his coat and brought out a cigar. He bit the end off it and lit it carefully, turning away from the door. In the gloom, the cigar burst into life, warm and glowing. Shadrach took a deep draw. He buttoned his coat around him and stepped out onto the pavement.

"Darn," he said. "What a night!" Rain buffeted him, wind blew at him. He looked up and down the highway, squinting. There were no cars in sight. He shook his head, locked up the gasoline pumps.

He went back into the building and pulled the door shut behind him. He opened the cash register and counted the money he'd taken in during the day. It was not much.

Not much, but enough for one old man. Enough to buy him tobacco and firewood and magazines, so that he could be comfortable as he waited for the occasional cars to come by. Not very many cars came along the highway any more. The highway had begun to fall into disrepair; there were many cracks in its dry, rough surface, and most cars preferred to take the big state highway that ran beyond the hills. There was nothing in Derryville to attract them, to make them turn toward it. Derryville was a small town, too small to bring in any of the major industries, too small to be very important to anyone. Sometimes hours went by without—

Shadrach tensed. His fingers closed over the money. From outside came a sound, the melodic ring of the signal wire stretched along the pavement.

Dinggg!

Shadrach dropped the money into the till and pushed the drawer closed. He stood up slowly and walked toward the door, listening. At the door, he snapped off the light and waited in the darkness, staring out.

He could see no car there. The rain was pouring down, swirling with the wind; clouds of mist moved along the road. And something was standing beside the pumps.

He opened the door and stepped out. At first, his eyes could make nothing out. Then the old man swallowed uneasily.

Two tiny figures stood in the rain, holding a kind of platform between them. Once, they might have been gaily dressed in bright garments, but now their clothes hung limp and sodden, dripping in the rain. They glanced halfheartedly at Shadrach. Water streaked their tiny faces, great drops of water. Their robes blew about them with the wind, lashing and swirling.

On the platform, something stirred. A small head

turned wearily, peering at Shadrach. In the dim light, a rain-streaked helmet glinted dully.

"Who are you?" Shadrach said.

The figure on the platform raised itself up. "I'm the King of the Elves and I'm wet."

Shadrach stared in astonishment.

"That's right," one of the bearers said. "We're all wet."

A small group of elves came straggling up, gathering around their king. They huddled together forlornly, silently.

"The King of the Elves," Shadrach repeated. "Well, I'll be darned."

Could it be true? They were very small, all right, and their dripping clothes were strange and oddly colored.

But *Elves*?

"I'll be darned. Well, whatever you are, you shouldn't be out on a night like this."

"Of course not," the king murmured. "No fault of our own. No fault . . ." His voice trailed off into a choking cough. The Elf soldiers peered anxiously at the platform.

"Maybe you better bring him inside," Shadrach said. "My place is up the road. He shouldn't be out in the rain."

"Do you think we like being out on a night like this?" one of the bearers muttered. "Which way is it? Direct us."

Shadrach pointed up the road. "Over there. Just follow me. I'll get a fire going."

He went down the road, feeling his way onto the first of the flat stone steps that he and Phineas Judd had laid during the summer. At the top of the steps, he looked back. The platform was coming slowly along, swaying a little from side to side. Behind it, the Elf soldiers picked their way, a tiny column of silent dripping creatures, unhappy and cold.

"I'll get the fire started," Shadrach said. He hurried them into the house.

Wearily, the Elf King lay back against the pillow. After sipping hot chocolate, he had relaxed and his heavy breathing sounded suspiciously like a snore.

Shadrach shifted in discomfort.

"I'm sorry," the Elf King said suddenly, opening his eyes. He rubbed his forehead. "I must have drifted off. Where was I?"

"You should retire, Your Majesty," one of the soldiers said sleepily. "It is late and these are hard times."

"True," the Elf King said, nodding. "Very true." He looked up at the towering figure of Shadrach, standing before the fireplace, a glass of beer in his hand. "Mortal, we thank you for your hospitality. Normally, we do not impose on human beings."

"It's those Trolls," another of the soldiers said, curled up on a cushion of the couch.

"Right," another soldier agreed. He sat up, groping for his sword. "Those reeking Trolls, digging and croaking—"

"You see," the Elf King went on, "as our party was crossing from the Great Low Steps toward the Castle, where it lies in the hollow of the Towering Mountains—"

"You mean Sugar Ridge," Shadrach supplied helpfully.

"The Towering Mountains. Slowly we made our way. A rain storm came up. We became confused. All at once a group of Trolls appeared, crashing through the underbrush. We left the woods and sought safety on the Endless Path—"

"The highway. Route Twenty."

"So that is why we're here." The Elf King paused a moment. "Harder and harder it rained. The wind blew around us, cold and bitter. For an endless time we toiled along. We had no idea where we were going or what would become of us."

The Elf King looked up at Shadrach. "We knew only this: Behind us, the Trolls were coming, creeping through the woods, marching through the rain, crushing everything before them."

He put his hand to his mouth and coughed, bending forward. All the Elves waited anxiously until he was done. He straightened up.

"It was kind of you to allow us to come inside. We will not trouble you for long. It is not the custom of the Elves—"

Again he coughed, covering his face with his hand. The Elves drew toward him apprehensively. At last the king stirred. He sighed.

"What's the matter?" Shadrach asked. He went over and took the cup of chocolate from the fragile hand. The Elf King lay back, his eyes shut.

"He has to rest," one of the soldiers said. "Where's your room? The sleeping room."

"Upstairs," Shadrach said. "I'll show you where."

Late that night, Shadrach sat by himself in the dark, deserted living room, deep in meditation. The Elves were asleep above him, upstairs in the bedroom, the Elf King in the bed, the others curled up together on the rug.

The house was silent. Outside, the rain poured down endlessly, blowing against the house. Shadrach could hear the tree branches slapping in the wind. He clasped and unclasped his hands. What a strange business it was—all these Elves, with their old, sick king, their piping voices. How anxious and peevish they were!

But pathetic, too; so small and wet, with water dripping down from them, and all their gay robes limp and soggy.

The Trolls—what were they like? Unpleasant and not very clean. Something about digging, breaking and pushing through the woods . . .

Suddenly, Shadrach laughed in embarrassment. What was the matter with him, believing all this? He put his cigar out angrily, his ears red. What was going on? What kind of joke was this?

Elves? Shadrach grunted in indignation. Elves in Derryville? In the middle of Colorado? Maybe there were Elves in Europe. Maybe in Ireland. He had heard of that. But here? Upstairs in his own house, sleeping in his own bed?

"I've heard just about enough of this," he said. "I'm not an idiot, you know."

He turned toward the stairs, feeling for the banister in the gloom. He began to climb.

Above him, a light went on abruptly. A door opened.

Two Elves came slowly out onto the landing. They looked down at him. Shadrach halted halfway up the stairs. Something on their faces made him stop.

"What's the matter?" he asked hesitantly.

They did not answer. The house was turning cold, cold and dark, with the chill of the rain outside and the chill of the unknown inside.

"What is it?" he said again. "What's the matter?"

"The king is dead," one of the Elves said. "He died a few moments ago."

Shadrach stared up, wide-eyed. "He did? But—"

"He was very old and very tired." The Elves turned away, going back into the room, slowly and quietly shutting the door.

Shadrach stood, his fingers on the banister, hard, lean fingers, strong and thin.

He nodded his head blankly.

"I see," he said to the closed door. "He's dead."

The Elf soldiers stood around him in a solemn circle. The living room was bright with sunlight, the cold white glare of early morning.

"But wait," Shadrach said. He plucked at his necktie. "I have to get to the filling station. Can't you talk to me when I come home?"

The faces of the Elf soldiers were serious and concerned.

"Listen," one of them said. "Please hear us out. It is very important to us."

Shadrach looked past them. Through the window he saw the highway, steaming in the heat of day, and down a little way was the gas station, glittering brightly. And even as he watched, a car came up to it and honked thinly, impatiently. When nobody came out of the station, the car drove off again down the road.

"We beg you," a soldier said.

Shadrach looked down at the ring around him, the anxious faces, scored with concern and trouble. Strangely, he had always thought of Elves as carefree beings, flitting without worry or sense—

"Go ahead," he said. "I'm listening." He went over to the big chair and sat down. The Elves came up around him. They conversed among themselves for a moment, whispering, murmuring distantly. Then they turned toward Shadrach.

The old man waited, his arms folded.

"We cannot be without a king," one of the soldiers said. "We could not survive. Not these days."

"The Trolls," another added. "They multiply very fast. They are terrible beasts. They're heavy and ponderous, crude, bad-smelling—"

"The odor of them is awful. They come up from the dark wet places, under the earth, where the blind, groping plants feed in silence, far below the surface, far from the sun."

"Well, you ought to elect a king, then," Shadrach suggested. "I don't see any problem there."

"We do not elect the King of the Elves," a soldier said. "The old king must name his successor."

"Oh," Shadrach replied. "Well, there's nothing wrong with that method."

"As our old king lay dying, a few distant words came forth from his lips," a soldier said. "We bent closer, frightened and unhappy, listening."

"Important, all right," agreed Shadrach. "Not something you'd want to miss."

"He spoke the name of him who will lead us."

"Good. You caught it, then. Well, where's the difficulty?"

"The name he spoke was—was your name."

Shadrach stared. *Mine?*

"The dying king said: 'Make him, the towering mortal, your king. Many things will come if he leads the Elves into battle against the Trolls. I see the rising once again of the Elf Empire, as it was in the old days, as it was before—' "

"Me!" Shadrach leaped up. "Me? King of the Elves?"

Shadrach walked about the room, his hands in his pockets. "Me, Shadrach Jones, King of the Elves." He grinned a little. "I sure never thought of it before."

He went to the mirror over the fireplace and studied himself. He saw his thin, graying hair, his bright eyes, dark skin, his big Adam's apple.

"King of the Elves," he said. "King of the Elves. Wait till Phineas Judd hears about this. Wait till I tell him!"

Phineas Judd would certainly be surprised!

Above the filling station, the sun shown, high in the clear blue sky.

Phineas Judd sat playing with the accelerator of his old Ford truck. The motor raced and slowed. Phineas reached over and turned the ignition key off, then rolled the window all the way down.

"What did you say?" he asked. He took off his glasses and began to polish them, steel rims between slender, deft fingers that were patient from years of practice. He restored his glasses to his nose and smoothed what remained of his hair into place.

"What was it, Shadrach?" he said. "Let's hear that again."

"I'm King of the Elves," Shadrach repeated. He changed position, bringing his other foot up on the runningboard. "Who would have thought it? Me, Shadrach Jones, King of the Elves."

Phineas gazed at him. "How long have you been— King of the Elves, Shadrach?"

"Since the night before last."

"I see. The night before last." Phineas nodded. "I see. And what, may I ask, occurred the night before last?"

"The Elves came to my house. When the old Elf king died, he told them that—"

A truck came rumbling up and the driver leaped out. "Water!" he said. "Where the hell is the hose?"

Shadrach turned reluctantly. "I'll get it." He turned back to Phineas. "Maybe I can talk to you tonight when you come back from town. I want to tell you the rest. It's very interesting."

"Sure," Phineas said, starting up his little truck. "Sure, Shadrach. I'm very interested to hear."

He drove off down the road.

Later in the day, Dan Green ran his flivver up to the filling station.

"Hey, Shadrach," he called. "Come over here! I want to ask you something."

Shadrach came out of the little house, holding a waste-rag in his hand.

"What is it?"

"Come here." Dan leaned out the window, a wide grin on his face, splitting his face from ear to ear. "Let me ask you something, will you?"

"Sure."

"Is it true? Are you really the King of the Elves?"

Shadrach flushed a little. "I guess I am," he admitted, looking away. "That's what I am, all right."

Dan's grin faded. "Hey, you trying to kid me? What's the gag?"

Shadrach became angry. "What do you mean? Sure, I'm the King of the Elves. And anyone who says I'm not—"

"All right, Shadrach," Dan said, starting up the

flivver quickly. "Don't get mad. I was just wondering."

Shadrach looked very strange.

"All right," Dan said. "You don't hear me arguing, do you?"

By the end of the day, everyone around knew about Shadrach and how he had suddenly become King of the Elves. Pop Richey, who ran the Lucky Store in Derryville, claimed Shadrach was doing it to drum up trade for the filling station.

"He's a smart old fellow," Pop said. "Not very many cars go along there any more. He knows what he's doing."

"I don't know," Dan Green disagreed. "You should hear him. I think he really believes it."

"King of the Elves?" They all began to laugh. "Wonder what he'll say next."

Phineas Judd pondered. "I've known Shadrach for years. I can't figure it out." He frowned, his face wrinkled and disapproving. "I don't like it."

Dan looked at him. "Then you think he believes it?"

"Sure," Phineas said. "Maybe I'm wrong, but I really think he does."

"But how could he believe it?" Pop asked. "Shadrach is no fool. He's been in business for a long time. He must be getting something out of it, the way I see it. But what, if it isn't to build up the filling station?"

"Why, don't you know what he's getting?" Dan said, grinning. His gold tooth shone.

"What?" Pop demanded.

"He's got a whole kingdom to himself, that's what—to do with like he wants. How would you like that, Pop? Wouldn't you like to be King of the Elves and not have to run this old store anymore?"

"There isn't anything wrong with my store," Pop said. "I ain't ashamed to run it. Better than being a clothing salesman."

Dan flushed. "Nothing wrong with that, either." He looked at Phineas. "Isn't that right? Nothing wrong with selling clothes, is there, Phineas?"

Phineas was staring down at the floor. He glanced up. "What? What was that?"

"What you thinking about?" Pop wanted to know. "You look worried."

"I'm worried about Shadrach," Phineas said. "He's getting old. Sitting out there by himself all the time, in the cold weather, with the rain water running over the floor—it blows something awful in the winter, along the highway—"

"Then you *do* think he believes it?" Dan persisted. "You *don't* think he's getting something out of it?"

Phineas shook his head absently and did not answer.

The laughter died down. They all looked at one another.

That night, as Shadrach was locking up the filling station, a small figure came toward him from the darkness.

"Hey!" Shadrach called out. "Who are you?"

An Elf soldier came into the light, blinking. He was dressed in a little gray robe, buckled at the waist with a band of silver. On his feet were little leather boots. He carried a short sword at his side.

"I have a serious message for you," the Elf said. "Now, where did I put it?"

He searched his robe while Shadrach waited. The Elf brought out a tiny scroll and unfastened it, breaking the wax expertly. He handed it to Shadrach.

"What's it say?" Shadrach asked. He bent over, his eyes close to the vellum. "I don't have my glasses with me. Can't quite make out these little letters."

"The Trolls are moving. They've heard that the old king is dead, and they're rising, in all the hills and valleys around. They will try to break the Elf Kingdom into fragments, scatter the Elves—"

"I see," Shadrach said. "Before your new king can really get started."

"That's right." The Elf soldier nodded. "This is a crucial moment for the Elves. For centuries, our existence has been precarious. There are so many Trolls, and Elves are very frail and often take sick—"

"Well, what should I do? Are there any suggestions?"

"You're supposed to meet with us under the Great Oak tonight. We'll take you into the Elf Kingdom, and you and your staff will plan and map the defense of the Kingdom."

"What?" Shadrach looked uncomfortable. "But I haven't eaten dinner. And my gas station—tomorrow is Saturday, and a lot of cars—"

"But you are King of the Elves," the soldier said.

Shadrach put his hand to his chin and rubbed it slowly.

"That's right," he replied. "I am, ain't I?"

The Elf soldier bowed.

"I wish I'd known this sort of thing was going to happen," Shadrach said. "I didn't suppose being King of the Elves—"

He broke off, hoping for an interruption. The Elf soldier watched him calmly, without expression.

"Maybe you ought to have someone else as your king," Shadrach decided. "I don't know very much about war and things like that, fighting and all that sort of business." He paused, shrugged his shoulders. "It's nothing I've ever mixed in. They don't have wars here in Colorado. I mean they don't have wars between human beings."

Still the Elf soldier remained silent.

"Why was I picked?" Shadrach went on helplessly, twisting his hands. "I don't know anything about it. What made him go and pick me? Why didn't he pick somebody else?"

"He trusted you," the Elf said. "You brought him inside your house, out of the rain. He knew that you expected nothing for it, that there was nothing you wanted. He had known few who gave and asked nothing back."

"Oh." Shadrach thought it over. At last he looked up. "But what about my gas station? And my house? And what will they say, Dan Green and Pop down at the store—"

The Elf soldier moved away, out of the light. "I have to go. It's getting late, and at night the Trolls come out. I don't want to be too far away from the others."

"Sure," Shadrach said.

"The Trolls are afraid of nothing, now that the old king is dead. They forage everywhere. No one is safe."

"Where did you say the meeting is to be? And what time?"

"At the Great Oak. When the moon sets tonight, just as it leaves the sky."

"I'll be there, I guess," Shadrach said. "I suppose you're right. The King of the Elves can't afford to let his kingdom down when it needs him most."

He looked around, but the Elf soldier was already gone.

Shadrach walked up the highway, his mind full of doubts and wonderings. When he came to the first of the flat stone steps, he stopped.

"And the old oak tree is on Phineas's farm! What'll Phineas say?"

But he was the Elf King and the Trolls were moving in the hills. Shadrach stood listening to the rustle of the wind as it moved through the trees beyond the highway, and along the far slopes and hills.

Trolls? Were there really Trolls there, rising up, bold and confident in the darkness of the night, afraid of nothing, afraid of no one?

And this business of being Elf King . . .

Shadrach went on up the steps, his lips pressed tight. When he reached the top of the stone steps, the last rays of sunlight had already faded. It was night.

Phineas Judd stared out the window. He swore and shook his head. Then he went quickly to the door and ran out onto the porch. In the cold moonlight a dim figure was walking slowly across the lower field, coming toward the house along the cow trail.

"Shadrach!" Phineas cried. "What's wrong? What are you doing out this time of night?"

Shadrach stopped and put his fists stubbornly on his hips.

"You go back home," Phineas said. "What's got into you?"

"I'm sorry, Phineas," Shadrach answered. "I'm sorry I have to go over your land. But I have to meet somebody at the old oak tree."

"At this time of night?"

Shadrach bowed his head.

"What's the matter with you, Shadrach? Who in the world you going to meet in the middle of the night on my farm?"

"I have to meet with the Elves. We're going to plan out the war with the Trolls."

"Well, I'll be damned," Phineas Judd said. He went back inside the house and slammed the door. For a long time he stood thinking. Then he went back out on the porch again. "What did you say you were doing? You don't have to tell me, of course, but I just—"

"I have to meet the Elves at the old oak tree. We must have a general council of war against the Trolls."

"Yes, indeed. The Trolls. Have to watch for the Trolls all the time."

"Trolls are everywhere," Shadrach stated, nodding his head. "I never realized it before. You can't forget them or ignore them. They never forget you. They're always planning, watching you—"

Phineas gaped at him, speechless.

"Oh, by the way," Shadrach said. "I may be gone for some time. It depends on how long this business is going to take. I haven't had much experience in fighting Trolls, so I'm not sure. But I wonder if you'd mind looking after the gas station for me, about twice a day, maybe once in the morning and once at night, to make sure no one's broken in or anything like that."

"You're going away?" Phineas came quickly down the stairs. "What's all this about Trolls? Why are you going?"

Shadrach patiently repeated what he had said.

"But what for?"

"Because I'm the Elf King. I have to lead them."

There was silence. "I see," Phineas said, at last. "That's right, you *did* mention it before, didn't you? But, Shadrach, why don't you come inside for a while and you can tell me about the Trolls and drink some coffee and—"

"Coffee?" Shadrach looked up at the pale moon above him, the moon and the bleak sky. The world was still and dead and the night was very cold and the moon would not be setting for some time.

Shadrach shivered.

"It's a cold night," Phineas urged. "Too cold to be out. Come on in—"

"I guess I have a little time," Shadrach admitted. "A cup of coffee wouldn't do any harm. But I can't stay very long . . ."

Shadrach stretched his legs out and sighed. "This coffee sure tastes good, Phineas."

Phineas sipped a little and put his cup down. The living room was quiet and warm. It was a very neat little living room with solemn pictures on the walls, gray uninteresting pictures that minded their own business. In the corner was a small reed organ with sheet music carefully arranged on top of it.

Shadrach noticed the organ and smiled. "You still play, Phineas?"

"Not much any more. The bellows don't work right. One of them won't come back up."

"I suppose I could fix it sometime. If I'm around, I mean."

"That would be fine," Phineas said. "I was thinking of asking you."

"Remember how you used to play 'Vilia' and Dan

Green came up with that lady who worked for Pop during the summer? The one who wanted to open a pottery shop?"

"I sure do," Phineas said.

Presently, Shadrach set down his coffee cup and shifted in his chair.

"You want more coffee?" Phineas asked quickly. He stood up. "A little more?"

"Maybe a little. But I have to be going pretty soon."

"It's a bad night to be outside."

Shadrach looked through the window. It was darker; the moon had almost gone down. The fields were stark. Shadrach shivered. "I wouldn't disagree with you," he said.

Phineas turned eagerly. "Look, Shadrach. You go on home where it's warm. You can come out and fight Trolls some other night. There'll always be Trolls. You said so yourself. Plenty of time to do that later, when the weather's better. When it's not so cold."

Shadrach rubbed his forehead wearily. "You know, it all seems like some sort of a crazy dream. When did I start talking about Elves and Trolls? When did it all begin?" His voice trailed off. "Thank you for the coffee." He got slowly to his feet. "It warmed me up a lot. And I appreciated the talk. Like old times, you and me sitting here the way we used to."

"Are you going?" Phineas hesitated. *"Home?"*

"I think I better. It's late."

Phineas got quickly to his feet. He led Shadrach to the door, one arm around his shoulder.

"All right, Shadrach, you go on home. Take a good hot bath before you go to bed. It'll fix you up. And maybe just a little snort of brandy to warm the blood."

Phineas opened the front door and they went slowly down the porch steps, onto the cold, dark ground.

"Yes, I guess I'll be going," Shadrach said. "Good night—"

"You go on home." Phineas patted him on the arm. "You run along home and take a good hot bath. And then go straight to bed."

"That's a good idea. Thank you, Phineas. I appreciate your kindness." Shadrach looked down at Phineas's hand on his arm. He had not been that close to Phineas for years.

Shadrach contemplated the hand. He wrinkled his brow, puzzled.

Phineas's hand was huge and rough and his arms were short. His fingers were blunt, his nails broken and cracked. Almost black, or so it seemed in the moonlight.

Shadrach looked up at Phineas. "Strange," he murmured.

"What's strange, Shadrach?"

In the moonlight, Phineas's face seemed oddly heavy and brutal. Shadrach had never noticed before how the jaw bulged, what a great protruding jaw it was. The skin was yellow and coarse, like parchment. Behind the glasses, the eyes were like two stones, cold and lifeless. The ears were immense, the hair stringy and matted.

Odd that he had never noticed before. But he had never seen Phineas in the moonlight.

Shadrach stepped away, studying his old friend. From a few feet off, Phineas Judd seemed unusually short and squat. His legs were slightly bowed. His feet were enormous. And there was something else—

"What is it?" Phineas demanded, beginning to grow suspicious. "Is there something wrong?"

Something was completely wrong. And he had never noticed it, not in all the years they had been friends. All around Phineas Judd was an odor, a faint, pungent stench of rot, of decaying flesh, damp and moldy.

Shadrach glanced slowly about him. "Something wrong?" he echoed. "No, I wouldn't say that."

By the side of the house was an old rain barrel, half fallen apart. Shadrach walked over to it.

"No, Phineas. I wouldn't exactly say there's something wrong."

"What are you doing?"

"Me?" Shadrach took hold of one of the barrel staves and pulled it loose. He walked back to Phineas, carrying the barrel stave carefully. "I'm King of the Elves. Who—or what—are you?"

Phineas roared and attacked with his great murderous shovel hands.

Shadrach smashed him over the head with the barrel stave. Phineas bellowed with rage and pain.

At the shattering sound, there was a clatter and from underneath the house came a furious horde of bounding, leaping creatures, dark bent-over things, their bodies heavy and squat, their feet and heads immense. Shadrach took one look at the flood of dark creatures pouring out from Phineas's basement. He knew what they were.

"Help!" Shadrach shouted. "Trolls! Help!"

The Trolls were all around him, grabbing hold of him, tugging at him, climbing up him, pummeling his face and body.

Shadrach fell to with the barrel stave, swung again and again, kicking Trolls with his feet, whacking them with the barrel stave. There seemed to be hundreds of them. More and more poured out from under Phineas's house, a surging black tide of pot-shaped creatures, their great eyes and teeth gleaming in the moonlight.

"Help!" Shadrach cried again, more feebly now. He was getting winded. His heart labored painfully. A Troll bit his wrist, clinging to his arm. Shadrach flung it away, pulling loose from the horde clutching his trouser legs, the barrel stave rising and falling.

One of the Trolls caught hold of the stave. A whole group of them helped, wrenching furiously, trying to pull it away. Shadrach hung on desperately. Trolls were all over him, on his shoulders, clinging to his coat, riding his arms, his legs, pulling his hair—

He heard a high-pitched clarion call from a long way off, the sound of some distant golden trumpet, echoing in the hills.

The Trolls suddenly stopped attacking. One of them dropped off Shadrach's neck. Another let go of his arm.

The call came again, this time more loudly.

"Elves!" a Troll rasped. He turned and moved toward the sound, grinding his teeth and spitting with fury.

"Elves!"

The Trolls swarmed forward, a growing wave of gnashing teeth and nails, pushing furiously toward the Elf columns. The Elves broke formation and joined battle, shouting with wild joy in their shrill, piping voices. The tide of Trolls rushed against them, Troll against Elf, shovel nails against golden sword, biting jaw against dagger.

"Kill the Elves!"

"Death to the Trolls!"

"Onward!"

"Forward!"

Shadrach fought desperately with the Trolls that were still clinging to him. He was exhausted, panting and gasping for breath. Blindly, he whacked on and on, kicking and jumping, throwing Trolls away from him, through the air and across the ground.

How long the battle raged, Shadrach never knew. He was lost in a sea of dark bodies, round and evil-smelling, clinging to him, tearing, biting, fastened to his nose and hair and fingers. He fought silently, grimly.

All around him, the Elf legions clashed with the Troll horde, little groups of struggling warriors on all sides.

Suddenly Shadrach stopped fighting. He raised his head, looking uncertainly around him. Nothing moved. Everything was silent. The fighting had ceased.

A few Trolls still clung to his arms and legs. Shadrach whacked one with the barrel stave. It howled and dropped to the ground. He staggered back, struggling with the last troll, who hung tenaciously to his arm.

"Now you!" Shadrach gasped. He pried the Troll loose and flung it into the air. The Troll fell to the ground and scuttled off into the night.

There was nothing more. No Troll moved anywhere. All was silent across the bleak moon-swept fields.

Shadrach sank down on a stone. His chest rose and fell painfully. Red specks swam before his eyes. Weakly, he got out his pocket handkerchief and wiped his neck and face. He closed his eyes, shaking his head from side to side.

When he opened his eyes again, the Elves were coming toward him, gathering their legion together again. The Elves were disheveled and bruised. Their golden armor was gashed and torn. Their helmets were bent or missing. Most of their scarlet plumes were gone. Those that still remained were drooping and broken.

But the battle was over. The war was won. The Troll hordes had been put to flight.

Shadrach got slowly to his feet. The Elf warriors stood around him in a circle, gazing up at him with silent respect. One of them helped steady him as he put his handkerchief away in his pocket.

"Thank you," Shadrach murmured. "Thank you very much."

"The Trolls have been defeated," an Elf stated, still awed by what had happened.

Shadrach gazed around at the Elves. There were many of them, more than he had ever seen before. All the Elves had turned out for the battle. They were grim-faced, stern with the seriousness of the moment, weary from the terrible struggle.

"Yes, they're gone, all right," Shadrach said. He was beginning to get his breath. "That was a close call. I'm glad you fellows came when you did. I was just about finished, fighting them all by myself."

"All alone, the King of the Elves held off the entire Troll army," an Elf announced shrilly.

"Eh?" Shadrach said, taken aback. Then he smiled. "That's true, I *did* fight them alone for a while. I *did* hold off the Trolls all by myself. The whole darn Troll army."

"There is more," an Elf said.

Shadrach blinked. "More?"

"Look over here, O King, mightiest of all the Elves. This way. To the right."

The Elves led Shadrach over.

"What is it?" Shadrach murmured, seeing nothing at first. He gazed down, trying to pierce the darkness. "Could we have a torch over here?"

Some Elves brought little pine torches.

There, on the frozen ground, lay Phineas Judd, on his back. His eyes were blank and staring, his mouth half open. He did not move. His body was cold and stiff.

"He is dead," an Elf said solemnly.

Shadrach gulped in sudden alarm. Cold sweat stood out abruptly on his forehead. "My gosh! My old friend! What have I done?"

"You have slain the Great Troll."

Shadrach paused.

"I *what*?"

"You have slain the Great Troll, leader of all the Trolls."

"This has never happened before," another Elf exclaimed excitedly. "The Great Troll has lived for centuries. Nobody imagined he could die. This is our most historic moment."

All the Elves gazed down at the silent form with awe, awe mixed with more than a little fear.

"Oh, go on!" Shadrach said. "That's just Phineas Judd."

But as he spoke, a chill moved up his spine. He remembered what he had seen a little while before, as he stood close by Phineas, as the dying moonlight crossed his old friend's face.

"Look." One of the Elves bent over and unfastened Phineas's blue-serge vest. He pushed the coat and vest aside. "See?"

Shadrach bent down to look.

He gasped.

Underneath Phineas Judd's blue-serge vest was a suit of mail, an encrusted mesh of ancient, rusting iron, fastened tightly around the squat body. On the mail stood an engraved insignia, dark and time-worn, embedded with dirt and rust. A moldering half-obliterated emblem. The emblem of a crossed owl leg and toadstool.

The emblem of the Great Troll.

"Golly," Shadrach said. "And *I* killed him."

For a long time he gazed silently down. Then, slowly, realization began to grow in him. He straightened up, a smile forming on his face.

"What is it, O King?" an Elf piped.

"I just thought of something," Shadrach said. "I just realized that—that since the Great Troll is dead and the Troll army has been put to flight—"

He broke off. All the Elves were waiting.

"I thought maybe I—that is, maybe if you don't need me any more—"

The Elves listened respectfully. "What is it, Mighty King? Go on."

"I thought maybe now I could go back to the filling station and not be king any more." Shadrach glanced hopefully around at them. "Do you think so? With the war over and all. With him dead. What do you say?"

For a time, the Elves were silent. They gazed unhappily down at the ground. None of them said anything. At last they began moving away, collecting their banners and pennants.

"Yes, you may go back," an Elf said quietly. "The war is over. The Trolls have been defeated. You may return to your filling station, if that is what you want."

A flood of relief swept over Shadrach. He straightened up, grinning from ear to ear. "Thanks! That's fine. That's really fine. That's the best news I've heard in my life."

He moved away from the Elves, rubbing his hands together and blowing on them.

"Thanks an awful lot." He grinned around at the silent Elves. "Well, I guess I'll be running along, then. It's late. Late and cold. It's been a hard night. I'll—I'll see you around."

The Elves nodded silently.

"Fine. Well, good night." Shadrach turned and started along the path. He stopped for a moment, waving back at the Elves. "It was quite a battle, wasn't it? We really licked them." He hurried on along the path. Once again he stopped, looking back and waving. "Sure glad I could help out. Well, good night!"

One or two of the Elves waved, but none of them said anything.

Shadrach Jones walked slowly toward his place. He could see it from the rise, the highway that few cars traveled, the filling station falling to ruin, the house that might not last as long as himself, and not enough money coming in to repair them or buy a better location.

He turned around and went back.

The Elves were still gathered there in the silence of the night. They had not moved away.

"I was hoping you hadn't gone," Shadrach said, relieved.

"And we were hoping you would not leave," said a soldier.

Shadrach kicked a stone. It bounced through the tight silence and stopped. The Elves were still watching him.

"Leave?" Shadrach asked. "And me King of the Elves?"

"Then you will remain our king?" an Elf cried.

"It's a hard thing for a man of my age to change. To stop selling gasoline and suddenly be a king. It scared me for a while. But it doesn't any more."

"You will? You *will*?"

"Sure," said Shadrach Jones.

The little circle of Elf torches closed in joyously. In their light, he saw a platform like the one that had carried the old King of the Elves. But this one was much larger, big enough to hold a man, and dozens of the soldiers waited with proud shoulders under the shafts.

A soldier gave him a happy bow. "For you, Sire."

Shadrach climbed aboard. It was less comfortable than walking, but he knew this was how they wanted to take him to the Kingdom of the Elves.

SALVE, REGINA

❧

MELANIE RAWN

Known for the *Dragon Prince* and *Dragon Star* trilogies, MELANIE RAWN has earned a reputation for far-ranging fantasy novels which reinvent the tropes of the genre with new life and ambition. She was a teacher and editor before turning to fiction writing full-time. Her most recent novel is the second in the Exiles trilogy, *The Mageborn Traitor*. The clash of religion and mythology has widespread effects in the cultures where it has happened. "Salve, Regina" takes a close look at what happens when one person is at the center of that conflict.

Her bones were numb with kneeling on cold stone. On the cobbled floor beside the beds of her fevered children; on the broken pebbles beside the graves of her parents and her sister and her sister's sons and her friends and her own dear husband; on the rough flags of the Church, before the altar and the candles—she knelt and tended and wept and prayed all this long winter until her bones were numb.

The priest stood upright beside the deathbeds, beside the graves, before the altar, intoning the sacred incomprehensible words of the Faith. He called to Christ for surcease of famine and disease, for deliverance from poisoned water and dying cattle and withered soil. He stood upright amid the Holy Relics and the Holy Water, the candles, and the chalice her own dear husband had fashioned with worshiping hands and Monseigneur le Baron's gift of silver.

Excepting the priest's, all heads in the village bowed heavy with repentance for sins committed and sins imagined and sins unknown. The miller's wife flogged herself bloody; she died four days later, so it was obvious she had not repented enough. The baker's weakling newborn daughter did not cry out when Holy Water drenched her brow; she died the next morning, so it was obvious that her silence meant the Devil had not flown out of her at Baptism. All that winter there were ashes and offerings, vows and Masses. The dying confessed, were shriven, tasted Wine and Wafer one last time. The living begged God the Father and Christ the Son to save them, have pity, reveal to them their sins so that they might mend their ways so the horror would cease.

The horror continued.

Worse than cold and hunger, worse even than her husband's death, her children did not know her. Their small bodies burned with Hell's own fires (and why, for surely such little ones had no sins upon their sweet young souls). Her own body was numb, and her heart and mind as well, the endless horror burning away all that she was.

Only last summer she had been plump and pretty, her husband the envy of the village for her pink cheeks and sunlight hair and bright laughter. Only last summer she had quickened with her sixth child that this winter had been born too soon and lived too briefly even to be baptized. Now she was gaunt and hollow, gray and empty. There would be no more children, and the five that were left her would soon be no more if she could not give them fresh water and nourishing food and certain cure for the fever.

She knew no medicine. There was no food. The water in the village well was fouled, and she dared not use it even to soothe the heat from her children's skin, for who knew but that it did not soak fever demons into their bodies? But water there must be—somewhere, somewhere, clean and pure. Water obsessed her. She remembered its coolness that slaked thirst and washed small hands and faces clean for Sunday Mass. She remembered how her children waved pink fists when Holy Water drenched their brows and consecrated them to Christ (but for that last baby, born too soon, whose soul would forever wander—and why, for surely there could be no sin on a newborn child).

She had no medicine and no food—but surely somewhere, somewhere, there must be water.

She bade her husband's sister, whose husband the cobbler was dead, to come sit with the children while she was gone, for the promise of sweet water to drink when she returned. She took up her cloak and two wooden buckets with fraying rope handles, and walked. Past the village well, past the Church, past the graveyard, past the dying apple orchard and the unplowed fields. She felt her cold numb bones come back to aching life, but when her heart and her mind threatened to awaken like her body, she said the word *water* over and over and over again, a talisman like a Holy Relic against fear and thought and pain.

Water, water, water.

And then, deep in the forest, she could smell it. Not trapped in stone, like the water in the village well, or plate-smooth like the water in the font, but wild and free and swift-running over rock and moss.

Water.

She was deep in the forest, and did she allow herself to think, she would know she was hopelessly lost. Did she allow herself to feel, she would be terrified. But she smelled water, and walked deeper into the forest, where no daughter of the True Faith should ever go alone, for within lurked forbidden caves and mysterious groves and strange standing stones no man could pull down, stones that at each turning of the year were said to rise up and dance by white wicked moonlight.

And then she heard water, its soft laughter so like her children's laughter of only last summer that she cried out and ran. No root or vine or fallen log tripped her on her way, no bush or bramble or branch waylaid her. She came to a broad stream of clear, laughing water. Soft moss cushioned its banks like the fat pillows on Madame la Baronne's chair. Bright flowers nodded above its ripples like Madame's daughters in their lovely gowns. Old oaks and graceful willows whispered just like Madame's ladies gossiping around the great hearth that always blazed with fire. She had seen these splendid things, for she had been in Madame's service before her marriage. But all the comforts and colors of the distant Chateâu were as nothing to the sumptuous miracle of water.

The moss gave gently beneath her aching bones as she fell on her knees to drink. *Water, fresh water, such as she had not tasted in months—* She scooped handful after handful into her mouth, over her face, tore off her dirty scarf and cap and unpinned her hair to rinse the winter's sickness and grief away.

When her emptiness was filled and her hair spread wet and clean down her back, she lifted her eyes to the white-gold sunlight and murmured a prayer of thanksgiving—not to God the Father or Christ the Son, but to the Blessed Mother whose compassion was surely responsible for this miracle of water.

And a woman's voice answered her.

"You are most welcome, daughter."

The woman's voice was low and gentle and warm, like a breeze returned from last summer. She turned, still on her knees, to behold a woman standing beside an ancient oak. Neither young nor old, dark nor fair, smiling nor solemn—and yet all these things at the same time. Her beauty was of face and form, but also of spirit that gleamed in her eyes that were all the colors of the forest: earth-brown, willow-green, sun-gold. She wore simple robes of white, gathered at waist and shoulder. Around her throat coiled a necklace of gold, and at her wrists wrapped matching bracelets.

All the numbness and all the pain were gone. Covering her face with her hands, she bowed low to the Blessed Mother.

"What is your name, my dear?"

For all the water, her mouth was suddenly parched dry. She swallowed hard, bit her lips, and with her face still hidden in her hands she stammered, "Berthilde, Lady."

"Ah! Bright One—doubtless for your lovely golden hair. This is one of my Names, also." There was a smile in the warm soft voice. "I have so many!"

The words tumbled from Berthilde's lips in spontaneous joy, for here was the Lady for whom they were meant: "Queen of Heaven, Mother of God, Mystic Rose, Seat of Wisdom, Blessed Virgin, Lady of Light, Health of the Sick—" She caught her breath and dared peek from between her fingers. She *was* smiling now, with great sweetness and even a little humor.

"Lady of the Mountains, the Beasts, the Forest, the Lake," she said, nodding. "Quite a list! Add to these the Names Gaia, Isis, Hera, Ashtoreth, Brigid, Inanna, Britomartis, Car, and a thousand others that would mean even less to you, Bright One."

Her hands fell shaking to her knees and suddenly she was afraid. "Lady," she whispered, "never have I heard such sounds, not even when the priest speaks the Holy Mass."

"They are Names only. Those who know me know who I am." Pausing, she shook her head. "The priest does not."

"But—surely he serves you!"

"Not he. Few in this land serve me now."

Berthilde hung her head with shame. "We have sinned, Lady, I know this. Else why would there be this blight upon our land, and this sickness that kills even the strongest among us? We are unworthy of the sacrifice made by your Holy Son—we have not followed God's Laws—"

"On the contrary," the Lady replied, brows arching, "you have followed them all too well."

"I am only a woman, I do not understand such things—but I beg you, Sweet Lady, help my children! Free them from the fever that is killing them and all our village!"

"This is why you have come here, daughter. Such will be *your* doing. Bring water to your children, and to your village, and to the cattle starving in your byres and the fouled well and the weary earth of your fields. Take this water, pure and clean, and give back thanks for it."

"I do thank you, Most Blessed Lady—"

"But *not* like that!" she exclaimed. "Groveling with your face in the dirt displeases me. Stand upright! Lift up your hands to the warmth of the sun!" Berthilde did as bidden; the Lady smiled. "Much better. Now you show your gratitude with joy, not fear. Take the water, Bright One, and return as often as you have need. The water and I will always be here."

Berthilde dipped her two buckets deep into the stream. As she turned to say her thanks again, she was alone but for the sighing of the summer-memory breeze in the willows and the dance of sunshine on the water.

She walked swiftly, light of step and heart for sureness that soon her children would be well, the grass would grow, the orchard would bloom, the crops would flourish, the cattle would fatten and give sweet milk. These first two buckets would be for her children, then the sickest of the village and, of course, the priest. After that, the rest of the people and then the animals and the land itself would drink, and be healed.

Still, as she passed the withering apple trees, she could not but stop, and set down her buckets, and cup in her hands water for one tree that was special to her. Beneath its branches, heavy with spring leaves and white blossoms and the promise of sweet fruit, her husband had kissed her for the first time. She sprinkled the dry earth at its roots with water, and stood back. She waited, holding her breath.

The apple tree quivered, seeming to shake off the blight and the cold. Tender green shoots appeared. She cried out in wonder and snatched up the buckets, hurrying home anxious to watch the miracle occur to her children.

Yet caution slowed her steps as she neared the village. Last moondark, the tanner, trudging the long miles home from the Château, was set upon by cloaked men who stole the flour that had paid him for repairing Monseigneur's favorite saddle. If people saw this fresh water, would she, too, crawl to her doorstep bruised and bloodied—and lacking something even more precious than flour for a single loaf?

She could not risk it. She was sorry to be suspicious of anyone, but she must think of her children first, and the bloom of health that would replace the hectic fever in their cheeks. So she took the long way around the village so that none would see her. None did, and she crossed her own threshold at last.

The children were alone. Their father's sister had not stayed as she promised. Berthilde was angry for a moment, then shrugged, for it did not matter. Swiftly she took a cup—their wedding cup, made by her husband of good pewter polished to silver's gleam—from the shelf above the cold dead hearth and dipped it into the water.

Margot first, she was the youngest. Madeleine. Arnaud. Anne. Jean. Standing beside their small beds, she lifted her weary hands and gave wordless thanks to the Queen of Heaven as their breathing eased and their burning skin cooled.

Anne stirred, opened her eyes, and whispered, "Maman?"

Berthilde wept and laughed and hugged her children to her breast. After a time, when they had fallen into healing sleep, she picked up the buckets and started for the blacksmith's home; he was ill, and his family were close to death, they should have the water first.

The smithy was beyond the Church. As she neared the gray stone sanctuary, she knew she must give the water first of all to the priest. He was God's Voice in the village, a sincere and holy man, not like his long-dead predecessor who had always reeked of ale. Père Jerome went to every house every day, to comfort and hear confession and give the Last Rites. He would be wiser than she about whose need was greatest.

Accordingly, she carried the buckets up the three steps (symbolizing the Holy Trinity) and under the lintel with its carved wooden Virgin huddled beneath the eaves. As she passed below the Lady's sight, she looked up. Although this stiff, sorrowing face was nothing like the warm loveliness of the woman she had seen in the forest, she fancied she saw a smile curve the corners of those lips.

The priest was at the altar, but in a pose Berthilde had never seen before: prostrate on the floor, arms flung out, fists clenched and face hidden against cold stones. Shocked, she stood mute at the back of the nave, listening as he cried out and beat his fists on the flags for anguish.

"No," she heard herself say, and set down the buckets, and hurried to him. She bent, touched his shoulder. "Oh, no, you must not, Père Jerome! You must put away your despair, we are saved!"

He scrambled to his feet, a tall, thin, ascetic man in brown cassock and rope cincture with a fine ivory cross on a leather thong around his neck. He dashed tears from his face and stared down at Berthilde.

"Saved? When only today three more have sickened, and two others have died? What else is there but despair when there are too many bodies for the ground to receive?"

"There will be no more deaths." She tugged him by the arm to the back of the nave, and showed him the water. "I found it—no, I was led to it by the Blessed Lady, and I *saw* her, Père Jerome, I saw her and she spoke to me and—"

"You—" He choked on the rest, and stood back from her. "Berthilde, where did you find this water?"

"I will tell you everything, but first you must drink. You are not well, I can see the fever beginning in your face. Drink, Père Jerome. Please."

He cupped a handful of water, sniffed it warily, but did not drink. "Tell me where you have found fresh water in this blighted land, and then I will decide whether or not to drink."

So she told him of the forest, of the stream, of the Blessed Lady, of the water, of the apple tree. All the while the precious water dribbled between his fingers onto the stones. His dark eyes grew darker, and grim. At last, when she was finished, he crossed himself and murmured many of the Holy Words she did not understand.

Fixing her with a stern, worried gaze, he said, "Berthilde, there are things I wish to make clear in my mind. Questions I wish you to answer. Will you do this?"

"Of course, Père Jerome!"

"This woman you say you saw. Was she wearing a blue mantle?"

"No. She was dressed all in glowing white—finer even than Madame la Baronne's finest clothes."

"Was there a light about her? A nimbus?"

"I do not understand this word, Père Jerome."

"A halo, as you saw around Christ in the Château's chapel window."

"No. But the sun shone warmly around her, as if in her presence it was always spring."

"Did she carry a book? Or a lily, perhaps?"

"No, but she wore a necklace and bracelets of gold, all twined around itself."

"Did she speak with reverence of the Lord God and His Son Jesus Christ, and say that she had Their blessing to show you this water?"

"N-no," she said more slowly now. "But she did speak of God's Holy Law."

"And what did she say?"

"That—that we had followed it only too well. And that few in this land serve her now, or know her for who she truly is."

"You say she spoke many strange names to you.

What were these names she used of herself?"

"I do not recall them, Père Jerome. I am only a simple, ignorant woman. I have no learning—" She hesitated, trying to remember the sounds, then said shyly, "She *did* say that my name means Bright One, and that this was one of her own Names as well."

"Was one of them"—and here his voice fell to a hush—"Ashtoreth?"

"Yes! Ashtoreth—and a word like my daughter's name, Anne—"

The priest crossed himself several times and spoke very rapidly in the Holy Tongue. Then he took Berthilde by the shoulders and gazed with awesome intensity into her eyes.

"You have been cozened, seduced by frightful powers of evil. I give thanks to Almighty God that He has sent you here to His Holy Church before your simplicity could lead you into direst peril of your immortal soul."

Berthilde's heart thudded with terror. "Père Jerome," she breathed, "what have I done?"

"It is true that you are ignorant, thus easy prey. This is my fault for not instructing you more strictly." He bowed his head, the small circle of his tonsure pale and naked at the crown of his head. "What priest, becoming shepherd of so gentle a flock, would believe his sheep capable of any but small everyday sins—let alone of being led so far astray? I spoke no harsh warnings, I saw no need. And I was wrong." Looking at her once more, he went on, "I repent of my sin and will remedy your ignorance. It was not the Blessed Virgin you saw, but a spawn of Satan."

"No!" she blurted. "She was not, she could not have been—"

"I tell you that it was. Had you truly seen the Mother of God, she would have worn a blue mantle, for blue is her color. Her head would be surrounded by a blaze of light, for she is the Queen of Heaven. She would have held a book, as she did when the Archangel Gabriel came to her, or the lily he gave her as symbol of her blessedness among all women. She would have told you that of her compassion she had pleaded with God and Christ to let her help you by giving you water. Instead—"

She trembled, not daring to breathe.

"She wore glowing white, as bright as the star Lucifer was before he fell into the Pit. Did she not say that Bright One was one of her own names? And the necklace and bracelets of gold—were they not like snakes twisting about her throat and arms? The names she called herself—oh, Berthilde, the name Ashtoreth is a word damned and damned again in the Holy Bible! As for the seeming miracle of the apple tree—do you not recall that it was this very fruit in the hand of a woman that led to banishment from Eden? You did not see the Blessed Virgin, you did not hear the words of the Mother of God! You saw and heard the Devil!"

Reeling with fear and confusion, she cried out. "But—but she was so beautiful, so kind—she smiled at me—"

"And do you believe that Satan cannot assume any shape he pleases, to trick and betray foolish women? How much wicked pleasure you gave, kneeling at the Evil One's feet instead of to God!"

"She bade me *not* to kneel, but to lift up my hands in joyful thanks—"

"Which only proves that she was *not* Holy Mary! Before her, all people and especially all women should go down on their knees, for she alone among you is without sin!"

"No, Père Jerome—please, no—"

"You have consorted with the very author of all our misery! When we turn our hearts from God, who is waiting to seize us? To torment us? To make of our lives on earth a foretaste of the Hell that awaits us for all eternity?"

Struggling, the air clogging in her throat, she protested, "But—but my children—they are well now, they sleep peacefully and without fever—the water cured them—"

"The water is accursed," he intoned, and with his bare foot kicked both buckets over onto the stone floor. Crossing himself, he said, "It cannot harm consecrated ground."

Berthilde moaned. "It will save us—the people, the animals, the crops—it saved the apple tree—"

"The tree must be cut down, for any fruit of it is accursed. You and your children, having drunk of the water, are accursed until confessions are made and penances given. Perhaps even an exorcism is needed." He fixed her with dark eyes that burned. "Kneel, and give thanks that Almighty God has brought you to His Church in order to save your soul."

Berthilde shook like a willow in the wind. Her knees quivered—but she did not fall upon them. She could not.

"On your knees, and beseech the Lord to forgive your sin!"

She could not.

Through the thin worn leather of her shoes she felt the water, pooling in tiny lakes on the rough-hewn stones, soaking into the skin of her feet. She remembered how clean it had tasted on her lips, how bright it had felt on her face and in her hair.

It was not evil. It had not come from the Devil. It had revived the apple tree, *her* apple tree. It had cured her children.

She did not feel accursed. And she could not kneel.

She ran, out the door beneath the stiff unsmiling wooden statue and down the three steps, across the churchyard and through the village. She ran past the apple tree and the blighted fields, and deep into the forest.

The Lady was waiting for her.

"Your children are well now."

Wordless, Berthilde nodded.

"Then why are you distraught? Like me, you are a mother, and the first joy of a mother's heart is to know her children safe and well."

"Lady—" Breath caught in her throat. "Lady, the priest—"

The lovely face changed subtly. "Ah. Yes. The priest. Tell me, Berthilde."

"He says—he says you are evil, that the water is accursed, that you caused our land to sicken—"

Suddenly all warmth and sunlight vanished. The golden necklace seemed to writhe about the Lady's throat, the bracelets twisting about her wrists. Berthilde stumbled back from her terrible wrath.

"I?" she exclaimed. "Have I plowed the land until it bleeds, and never given back to it a single drop of the blood that poured from its flesh? Have I slaughtered trees for the burning, for clearing more land to feel cold and soulless teeth of iron? Have I fouled the sacred wells? Have I done any of these things? Have I?"

Wind shuddered in the old oaks, whirled across the water. Yet as quickly as it came, it departed, and with it the Lady's anger. The gold stilled around her neck and arms, and with wise, sad eyes she gazed at Berthilde.

"And yet this priest does me homage, though he knows it not. Had my other Names not been forgotten and denied, perhaps even priests would understand who I truly am."

Berthilde asked humbly, "Please—I am too ignorant to understand, but I would at least truly know you so that I may truly serve you."

"I am the Mother of the Sacred King who is slain. I am She of Eternal Sorrow, for my beloved Son must die so that the earth and all else may live. All life begins and ends in me. All peoples are my children. I am She who gives life, and She to whom all life returns to be reborn. I am the Maiden, the Mother, and the Old Woman of Wise Blood, the Trinity, the faces of the Moon."

She felt her arms lift, her hands open, not to ward off these words but to gather them to herself as the truth she knew they must be.

"My Breath spoke the Sound that began the world. The difference between me and the priests' god is that I will never speak the Sound that ends it."

In an awed whisper, Berthilde heard herself say, "For—for a mother's joy is to see her children safe and well. . . ."

The Lady nodded. "You see, you do understand. Go now, daughter, and be a mother to your children. You have been a Maiden, as I am, and served me with your dancing and your laughter. Now you are a Mother, as I am, and you may best serve me by tending your children. Women who are old, as I am, serve me in yet another way. Go now, daughter, and serve me by keeping your children safe and well."

She never saw her children again.

When she returned to the village, past sere fields and her apple tree, the priest seized her with his own hands, for no one else would touch her. The blacksmith, though hollow-eyed and reeling with fever, had yet made iron shackles for her wrists and her ankles. What little kindling was left after the long cold winter was piled up in the square, and someone brought the fresh green wood of the slaughtered apple tree, and at eventide she was burned as a witch and heretic.

The smoke rose, stinking of scorched human flesh and greenwood, to blacken the sky. And the horror continued, and the blight, and the grief. More in the village sickened, and more died. But not the priest.

For when Berthilde fled, in a moment of weakness—*water, fresh water, such as he had not tasted in months*—he fell to his knees and touched his hand to the pooling water. The droplets on his fingertips were almost near enough his lips to taste when he realized the temptation to which he had nearly succumbed. He prayed for a long while, and at last, his Faith assuring him that all the Devil's handiwork had vanished, once more he touched the water and let it touch his lips. It was as sweet and clean and wondrous as Berthilde had promised. Of all the village, the priest alone did not sicken, and in due course this evidence of purity and holiness made him bishop, archbishop, and cardinal.

One Sunday many years later, as he lifted his hands in exaltation before a cathedral altar, a vision appeared before him. The woman was neither young nor old, dark nor fair, smiling nor solemn—and yet all these things at the same time. Her beauty was of face and form, but also of spirit that gleamed in her eyes. She wore a mantle of blue. One hand held a book; the other, a lily. About her head was a nimbus like golden sunlight, as if in her presence it was always spring. About her throat coiled a necklace of gold, and at her wrists wrapped matching bracelets.

His heart thudded in his chest at sight of her. She gave him a wise, sad smile, murmuring, "And do you know me now, priest?"

With his hands raised and trembling, his voice rang through Notre Dame de Paris:

> *"Salve, regina, mater misericordiae,*
> *Vita, dulcedo et spes nostra, salve!"*

"I suppose that must do," she said.

> *"Hail Holy Queen, Mother of Mercy, our Life,*
> *our Sweetness and our Hope, hail!"*

THE ONES WHO WALK AWAY FROM OMELAS

URSULA K. LE GUIN

URSULA K. LE GUIN is considered one of the most influential authors in the science fiction and fantasy field. Her Earthsea novels have been favorably compared to Tolkien's work for their intricate detailing of a fantasy world. Like Tolkien, Le Guin makes her worlds come alive though the use of language, and accomplishes this end as well as he did. Her work in the field has been critically acclaimed as well, garnering her four Nebula Awards, five Hugo Awards, three Jupiter Awards, and the Gandalf Award. She has taught writing courses all around the world, and currently lives in Portland, Oregon. "The Ones Who Walk Away From Omelas" poses a simple question, and poses her own elegantly terrible answer. The question is this: "What is the price of happiness?"

With a clamor of bells that set the swallows soaring, the Festival of Summer came to the city Omelas, bright-towered by the sea. The rigging of the boats in harbor sparkled with flags. In the streets between houses with red roofs and painted walls, between old moss-grown gardens and under avenues of trees, past great parks and public buildings, processions moved. Some were decorous: old people in long stiff robes of mauve and gray, grave master workmen, quiet, merry women carrying their babies and chatting as they walked. In other streets the music beat faster, a shimmering of gong and tambourine, and the people went dancing, the procession was a dance. Children dodged in and out, their high calls rising like the swallows' crossing flights over the music and the singing. All the processions wound towards the north side of the city, where on the great water-meadow called the Green Fields boys and girls, naked in the bright air, with mud-stained feet and ankles and long, lithe arms, exercised their restive horses before the race. The horses wore no gear at all but a halter without bit. Their manes were braided with streamers of silver, gold, and green. They flared their nostrils and pranced and boasted to one another; they were vastly excited, the horse being the only animal who has adopted our ceremonies as his own. Far off to the north and west the mountains stood up half encircling Omelas on her bay. The air of morning was so clear that the snow still crowning the Eighteen Peaks burned with white-gold fire across the miles of sunlit air, under the dark blue of the sky. There was just enough wind to make the banners that marked the racecourse snap and flutter now and then. In the silence of the broad green meadows one could hear the music winding through the city streets, farther and nearer and ever approaching, a cheerful faint sweetness of the air that from time to time trembled and gathered together and broke out into the great joyous clanging of the bells.

Joyous! How is one to tell about joy! How describe the citizens of Omelas?

They were not simple folk, you see, though they were happy. But we do not say the words of cheer much any more. All smiles have become archaic. Given a description such as this one tends to make certain assumptions. Given a description such as this one tends to look next for the King, mounted on a splendid stallion and surrounded by his noble knights, or perhaps in a golden litter borne by great-muscled slaves. They were not barbarians. I do not know the rules and laws of their society, but I suspect that they were singularly few. As they did without monarchy and slavery, so they also got on without the stock exchange, the advertisement, the secret police, and the bomb. Yet I repeat that these were not simple folk, not dulcet shepherds, noble savages, bland utopians. They were not less complex than us. The trouble is that we have a bad habit, encouraged by pedants and sophisticates, of considering happiness as something rather stupid. Only pain is intellectual, only evil interesting. This is the treason of the artist: a refusal to admit the banality of evil and the terrible boredom of pain. If you can't lick 'em, join 'em. If it hurts, repeat it. But to praise despair is to condemn delight, to embrace violence is to lose hold of everything else. We have almost lost hold; we can no longer describe a happy man, nor make any celebration of joy. How can I tell you about the people of Omelas? They were not naïve and happy children—though their children were, in fact, happy. They were mature, intelligent, passionate adults whose lives were not wretched. O miracle! But I wish I could describe it better. I wish I could convince you. Omelas sounds in my words like a city in a fairy tale, long ago and far away, once upon a time. Perhaps it would be best if you imagined it as your own fancy bids, assuming it will rise to the occasion, for certainty I cannot suit you all. For instance, how about technology? I think that there would be no cars or helicopters in and above the streets; this follows from the fact that the people of Omelas are happy people. Happiness is based on a just discrimination of what is necessary, what is neither necessary nor destructive, and what is destructive. In the middle category, however—that of the unnecessary but undestructive, that of comfort, luxury, exuberance, etc.—they could perfectly well have central heating, subway trains, washing machines, and all kinds of marvelous devices not yet invented here, floating lightsources, fuelless power, a cure for the common cold. Or they could have none of that: it doesn't matter. As you like it. I incline to think that people from towns up and down the coast have been coming in to Omelas during the last days before the Festival on very fast little trains and double-decked trams, and that the train station of Omelas is actually the handsomest building in town, though plainer than the magnificent Farmers' Market. But even granted trains, I fear that Omelas so far strikes some of you as goody-goody. Smiles, bells, parades, horses, bleh. If so, please add an orgy. If an orgy would help, don't hesitate. Let us not, however, have temples from which issue beautiful nude priests and priestesses already half in ecstasy and ready to copulate with any man or woman, lover or stranger, who desires union with the deep godhead of the blood, although that was my first idea. But really it would be better not to have any temples in Omelas—at least, not manned temples. Religion yes, clergy no. Surely the beautiful nudes can just wander about, offering themselves like divine souf- flés to the hunger of the needy and the rapture of the flesh. Let them join the processions. Let tambourines be struck above the copulations, and the glory of desire be proclaimed upon the gongs, and (a not unimportant point) let the offspring of these delightful rituals be beloved and looked after by all. One thing I know there is none of in Omelas is guilt. But what else should there be? I thought at first there were no drugs, but that is puritanical. For those who like it, the faint insistent sweetness of *drooz* may perfume the ways of the city, *drooz* which first brings a great lightness and brilliance to the mind and limbs, and then after some hours a dreamy languor, and wonderful visions at last of the very arcana and inmost secrets of the Universe, as well as exciting the pleasure of sex beyond all belief; and it is not habit-forming. For more modest tastes I think there ought to be beer. What else, what else belongs in the joy- ous city? The sense of victory, surely, the celebration of courage. But as we did without clergy, let us do without soldiers. The joy built upon successful slaughter is not the right kind of joy; it will not do; it is fearful and it is trivial. A boundless and generous contentment, a mag- nanimous triumph felt not against some outer enemy but in communion with the finest and fairest in the souls of all men everywhere and the splendor of the world's summer: this what swells the hearts of the people of Omelas, and the victory they celebrate is that of life. I really don't think many of them need to take *drooz*.

Most of the processions have reached the Green Fields by now. A marvelous smell of cooking goes forth from the red and blue tents of the provisioners. The faces of small children are amiably sticky; in the benign gray beard of a man a couple of crumbs of rich pastry are entangled. The youths and girls have mounted their horses and are beginning to group around the starting line of the course. An old woman, small, fat, and laughing, is passing out flowers from a basket, and tall young men wear her flowers in their shining hair. A child of nine or ten sits at the edge of the crowd, alone, playing on a wooden flute. People pause to listen, and they smile, but they do not speak to him, for he never ceases playing and never sees them, his dark eyes wholly rapt in the sweet, thin magic of the tune.

He finishes, and slowly lowers his hands holding the wooden flute.

As if that little private silence were the signal, all at once a trumpet sounds from the pavilion near the starting line: imperious, melancholy, piercing. The horses rear on their slender legs, and some of them neigh in answer. Sober-faced, the young riders stroke the horses' necks and soothe them, whispering, "Quiet, quiet, there my beauty, my hope. . . ." They begin to form in rank along the starting line. The crowds along the racecourse are like a field of grass and flowers in the wind. The Festival of Summer has begun.

Do you believe? Do you accept the festival, the

city, the joy? No? Then let me describe one more thing.

In a basement under one of the beautiful public buildings of Omelas, or perhaps in the cellar of one of its spacious private homes, there is a room. It has one locked door, and no window. A little light seeps in dustily between cracks in the boards, secondhand from a cobwebbed window somewhere across the cellar. In one corner of the little room a couple of mops, with stiff, clotted, foul-smelling heads, stand near a rusty bucket. The floor is dirt, a little damp to the touch, as cellar dirt usually is. The room is about three paces long and two wide: a mere broom closet or disused tool room. In the room a child is sitting. It could be a boy or a girl. It looks about six, but actually is nearly ten. It is feebleminded. Perhaps it was born defective, or perhaps it has become imbecile through fear, malnutrition, and neglect. It picks its nose and occasionally fumbles vaguely with its toes or genitals, as it sits hunched in the corner farthest from the bucket and the two mops. It is afraid of the mops. It finds them horrible. It shuts its eyes, but it knows the mops are still standing there; and the door is locked; and nobody will come. The door is always locked; and nobody ever comes, except that sometimes—the child has no understanding of time or interval—sometimes the door rattles terribly and opens, and a person, or several people, are there. One of them may come in and kick the child to make it stand up. The others never come close, but peer in at it with frightened, disgusted eyes. The food bowl and the water jug are hastily filled, the door is locked, the eyes disappear. The people at the door never say anything, but the child, who has not always lived in the tool room, and can remember sunlight and its mother's voice, sometimes speaks. "I will be good," it says. "Please let me out. I will be good!" They never answer. The child used to scream for help at night, and cry a good deal, but now it only makes a kind of whining, "Eh-haa, eh-haa," and it speaks less and less often. It is so thin there are no calves to its legs; its belly protrudes; it lives on a half-bowl of corn meal and grease a day. It is naked. Its buttocks and thighs are a mass of festered sores, as it sits in its own excrement continually.

They all know it is there, all the people of Omelas. Some of them have come to see it, others are content merely to know it is there. They all know that it has to be there. Some of them understand why, and some do not, but they all understand that their happiness, the beauty of their city, the tenderness of their friendships, the health of their children, the wisdom of their scholars, the skill of their makers, even the abundance of their harvest and the kindly weathers of their skies, depend wholly on this child's abominable misery.

This is usually explained to children when they are between eight and twelve, whenever they seem capable of understanding; and most of those who come to see the child are young people, though often enough an adult comes, or comes back, to see the child. No matter how well the matter has been explained to them, these young spectators are always shocked and sickened at the sight. They feel disgust, which they had thought themselves superior to. They feel anger, outrage, impotence, despite all the explanations. They would like to do something for the child. But there is nothing they can do. If the child were brought up into the sunlight out of that vile place, if it were cleaned and fed and comforted, that would be a good thing, indeed; but if it were done, in that day and hour all the prosperity and beauty and delight of Omelas would wither and be destroyed. Those are the terms. To exchange all the goodness and grace of every life in Omelas for that single, small improvement: to throw away the happiness of thousands for the chance of the happiness of one: that would be to let guilt within the walls indeed.

The terms are strict and absolute; there may not even be a kind word spoken to the child.

Often the young people go home in tears, or in a tearless rage, when they have seen the child and faced this terrible paradox. They may brood over it for weeks or years. But as time goes on they begin to realize that even if the child could be released, it would not get much good of its freedom: a little vague pleasure of warmth and food, no doubt, but little more. It is too degraded and imbecile to know any real joy. It has been afraid too long ever to be free of fear. Its habits are too uncouth for it to respond to humane treatment. Indeed, after so long it would probably be wretched without walls about it to protect it, and darkness for its eyes, and its own excrement to sit in. Their tears at the bitter injustice dry when they begin to perceive the terrible justice of reality, and to accept it. Yet it is their tears and anger, the trying of their generosity and the acceptance of their helplessness, which are perhaps the true source of the splendor of their lives. Theirs is no vapid, irresponsible happiness. They know that they, like the child, are not free. They know compassion. It is the existence of the child, and their knowledge of its existence, that makes possible the nobility of their architecture, the poignancy of their music, the profundity of their science. It is because of the child that they are so gentle with children. They know that if the wretched ones were not there sniveling in the dark, the other one, the flute-player, could make no joyful music as the young riders line up in their beauty for the race in the sunlight of the first morning of summer.

Now do you believe in them? Are they not more credible? But there is one more thing to tell, and this is quite incredible.

At times one of the adolescent girls or boys who go to see the child does not go home to weep or rage, does not, in fact, go home at all. Sometimes also a man or woman much older falls silent for a day or two, and then leaves home. These people go out into the street, and walk down the street alone. They keep walking, and walk straight out of the city of Omelas, through the beautiful gates. They keep walking across the farm-lands of Omelas. Each one goes alone, youth or girl, man or woman. Night falls; the traveler must pass down village streets, between the houses with yellow-lit windows, and on out into the darkness of the fields. Each alone, they go west or north, towards the moun-tains. They go on. They leave Omelas, they walk ahead into the darkness, and they do not come back. The place they go towards is a place even less imaginable to most of us than the city of happiness. I cannot describe it at all. It is possible that it does not exist. But they seem to know where they are going, the ones who walk away from Omelas.

DEDRAK'S QUEST

❦

TRACY HICKMAN

TRACY HICKMAN is a partner with Margaret Weis in the world bestselling fantasy writing collaboration that has created more than a dozen *New York Times* bestsellers. He started out in the Research and Development department at TSR and helped design the Dragonlance expanson of the original Dungeons & Dragons game. When no writer could be found for a planned series of companion novels to the game, he and Margaret decided to create them . . . and the rest in history. Together they've written many novels in five different series, The Dragonlance Saga, The Darksword Trilogy, The Death Gate Cycle, Rose of the Prophet, and the Starshield series. He also has written a number of solo novels. He writes very few short stories, but this time provides a unique and original perspective on a dragon culture.

For the fifth time, Dedrak Kurbin Flamishar, the Minister of Peace for the Tsultak Empire, raked the third row of horns on his massive head against the stones of the archway. It made a tremendous noise but relieved the dragon considerably. Just the previous day, he had a new set of ornamental chains fitted; they looped through titanium bands on each of the first five rows of horns. He was not yet used to them, and the third row was irritating him.

Dedrak hoped that the noise did not disturb the musings of the council convened just beyond the massive doors before him. The truth was that Dedrak was upset by far more than annoying accessories to his outfit. The Tsultak Council had called him from a deep sleep to join them in their crisis and offer his advice. As to just what that crisis was—well, the young dragon that had been sent to fetch him was of far lower status than Dedrak and, therefore, had no idea as to why he had been sent for or just what crisis was taking place. Dedrak, whose curiosity was one of his primary faults, left at once.

The Minister of Peace thus found himself poorly dressed as he paced about the antechamber waiting for the Council to call him. His ruffled shirt had been so hastily donned that his right wing had torn it, and he had to fasten the front twice since he had misaligned the holes and buttons the first time. Dedrak looked down at himself for the umpteenth time. The deep blue doublet, he decided, covered the torn shirt nicely. The kilt that splayed around his hindquarters and tail was one he had worn the previous day, and it was badly wrinkled. Still, it was one of his better kilts—perhaps the Council would not notice.

The bolt on the other side of the door drew back. Dedrak reared up under the tall, frescoed ceiling and adjusted his cravat and ceremonial sash. Two puffs of smoke to clear his nostrils, and Dedrak moved into the Hall of Nine.

The dragons of the Tsultak Council lay on their huge fainting couches. Each was set in its magnificently detailed alcove high above the polished floor where Dedrak now quietly walked. Above them loomed the great dome of the dragons' citadel, which looked out on the rim of the volcano in which they lived. Beyond that, the stars glittered in the night sky.

Dedrak folded his foreclaws under him, resting his head on the polished marble floor beneath him with his eyes averted. It was prescribed by the New Code—as was nearly every other aspect of the lives of the Tsultak dragons. "Lord Master of the K'dei and Arch-empiris of the Majestik Sphere—may the celestial spheres shine forever on his magnificence and wisdom. All praise to his righteous reign and blessing upon his clutch and brood. I, Dedrak Kurbin Flamishar, Minister of Peace to the Tsultak Empiris and descendant of the Flamishars of Kharanishai come at thy word and offer my service to the Empiris and her clans."

"Your services are needed in a time of great exigency, Minister of Peace," the salmon-colored dragon spoke from her alcove off Dedrak's right wing. Dedrak, having been addressed, was now allowed to look up. He knew the speaker's name to be Tukairana, one of the youngest of the Nine Ke'dal and very attractive. Her canine teeth were particularly large and sharp. Dedrak always thought that she dressed well. "The Empiris is in grave danger."

"Indeed?" Dedrak said cautiously.

"Not since the Tsultak left their dying world and crossed the great blackness have we faced such a threat," Snishankh, the rus-colored dragon intoned deeply from his alcove to Flamishar's left. "Clans from our outlying conquests have petitioned us regarding a terrible evil that assaults them. Warrens being destroyed completely. Entire clans vanishing."

The cobalt dragon thundered from her alcove next to Tukairana. Dedrak remembered her name as Tsonksulka.

"It is said that the humans have returned!"

"Humans?" Dedrak snorted a puff of smoke. "With all respect to the Council—may honor be theirs forever and their names trumpeted with glory through all the halls of time—humans are . . . are . . ."

"Legends," agreed Snishankh. "Stories for hatchlings!"

"Stories or not," Tukairana hissed, "these reports were easy enough to dismiss when they came from our distant outposts. Yet now these very legends seem to be somewhat closer to our home. A human has been spotted on E'knar."

"With my humble deference to the most esteemed and justly honored Tukairana," Dedrak rolled his head in the dragon negative even as he completed the formal declaration, "—blessed be her clutch and brood for generations—you cannot possibly believe these gnome tales! Even if humans once existed in some ancient past, there have been no sightings of a human for over two millennia. I am inclined to believe that they never existed at all."

"I would not suggest such a conclusion to the Provost of E'knar. On that planet—by the Provost's own words—this monster even demanded that the clan offer one of their own young females as a sacrifice," Tukairana rumbled, her quiet voice shaking the stones in the hall. "Clutchless young dragons, if the reports are to be believed!"

"Clutchless!" Dedrak replied in surprise.

"Indeed," Tukairana continued, her speech patterns heated, "although I cannot upon my very life understand what the significance of that would be."

"These reports cannot be dismissed lightly," Tsonksulka stated flatly. "This monster exists, and it is making its way to Tsultaki itself. We are the K'dei, and our will is the will of the Tsultak clans, bonded to uphold the sanctity of our race and preserve the legacy of our ancestors. When last humans were known among us, dragons were nearly destroyed in epic genocide. The K'dei calls for a champion for a holy quest to find and destroy the evil human in his lair. What say you, Dedrak Kurbin Flamishar, Minister of Peace? Are you the champion we seek?"

Dedrak smiled even as he folded his right claw under his chest and bowed down toward the floor. "I would seek out this mythic human creature and, if such a monster is to be discovered, destroy him for the honor of the K'dei and the protection of our clans in the Majestik."

Dedrak returned to his own warren, carefully removed his sash and doublet, and handed them to a dozen of his own E'knari slaves. The E'knari were a diminutive race—smaller even than humans if the legends were true, Dedrak thought to himself. They had been an early conquest of the space-going Tsultak dragons during the Age of the Expanse and the days of the Great Fleet. When the Tsultak first encountered the E'knari, there was a time of confusion where some of the dragon seers of the Mystic Circle thought that the gnomish creatures might actually be human, but such theories were quickly proven groundless. Since that time, the captive E'knari served their dragon masters well, if not always with the most enthusiastic of hearts. There was even some talk among the younger dragons in the various academies and lyceums that the E'knari should be freed from their status as slaves and made lower-caste citizens of the Majestik. Such talk was radical and, at least in Dedrak's eyes, to be expected of the inexperienced young. "One hundred years old, and already they think they know everything," Dedrak muttered to himself.

The E'knari stumbled off under the weight of the dragon's clothing. Each was careful to keep the cloth clear of the floor as they struggled with it into the closet nearby.

Dedrak waited until the E'knari had completed their work and left through the huge doors leading to his central chamber. Once the circular chamber was deserted, Dedrak lifted up his right wing and craned his head around to inspect the damage he had done to his favorite shirt.

"Torn clear down," he huffed with a short burst of flame from his nostrils. "What a shame!"

It was still too early in the morning for his household to be up. His wives would still be resting in their own private warrens adjacent to his own. His young brood tended to rise early, but even their cavorting would not take place for several hours yet. Dedrak knew that he should get some rest, but sleep somehow seemed far off just yet. There were things to be done in preparation for his newly assigned quest. A cascade of thoughts, plans, and preparations tumbled through his head.

"A ship, of course," he muttered to himself. Dedrak always preferred to think aloud—a weakness which, he thought, might lead to his downfall one day. Still, he was careful to do so only in his own chambers. "I shall need a ship if I am to go to E'knar. Battle armor as well. I've the old ceremonial armor, but that is certainly too heavy and cumbersome for this task."

The great dragon warrior snorted billows of smoke to himself. "This task, indeed! Chasing across the stars after a human! Hah!"

"You find amusement in the night, my lord?"

Dedrak turned toward the intrusive voice behind him; a voice he knew well indeed. "Cachakra, my love. I trust I have not disturbed your rest!"

"My rest is not in question, my lord," returned the deep voice of Dedrak's first wife. "It is your own lack of sleep that troubles me. What pressing issues trouble your mind this night? What news of the Council keeps your thoughts from blissful rest?"

Dedrak smiled to himself. Cachakra was a female of high breeding, and her clan lineage was high indeed. In the days before the New Code, dragons were monogamous. The destruction of their home world brought the New Code and with it a different way of life. Harems were expected—indeed, demanded—of those who could afford them. This insured many clutches and the repopulating of the stars with dragonkind. No matter how noble the ideals, however, this new social arrangement brought with it numerous headaches, not the least of which was the organization of the harem itself. First wife was a position that was earned as a right of combat, and thus one that tended to shift from time to time. The politics of interstellar diplomacy paled compared to those that often took place within a single-family clan. Cunning, diplomacy, raw strength, and a touch of ruthlessness were required basics for a successful First Wife. Cachakra, Dedrak reflected, was a master of all these skills and more.

"I am to leave on a quest from the Council," Dedrak said simply. "They have asked that I hunt a monster on behalf of all the clans."

"Monster, indeed!" Cachakra replied, entering the chamber fully. She wore a quilted nightcoat that was cut just below her wing joints. Beyond that, a flowing kilt of a suggestively diaphanous fabric barely hid her ample flanks. Her claws were bare on the marble floor.

Dedrak could feel his blood run a little hotter just at the sight of her.

"My poor lair-mate," Cachakra crooned. "Sent into the night on some fool's errand. You'll just have to tell them that you cannot possibly go at this time. They shall have to find someone else."

"Cachakra, my love," Dedrak lolled his head from side to side to signify his disbelief. "The Council has ordained it: it is done! My claws are bound in his matter! I am the Minister of Peace, you know. It is my sworn duty to the clan to undertake this very sort of quest!"

"What sort of quest?" Cachakra's eyes narrowed suspiciously.

"I am to hunt a human."

"Human?" Cachakra giggled. "You cannot be serious!"

"That is the mandate of the council," Dedrak replied as gravely as he could muster.

"But what am I supposed to do?" his first wife whined. "It's my month starting in the next ten-day!" Cachakra turned her wide flanks toward him suggestively.

Dedrak shook his head. The time he spent with his various wives was something of a sensitive issue with the First Wife. Betrikai, third wife, had produced a surprisingly large number of clutches. Most of his clan had seen this fact as a blessing, but Cachakra seemed to have taken offense at Betrikai's good fortune, feeling it somehow reflected on her own abilities. So overzealous was Cachakra with Dedrak during their next time together—in a rotating order established by the First Wife herself—that she had dislocated his shoulder. Her flaming breath had inadvertently destroyed several reams of official papers. Worst of all, she had also left a bite mark on his neck. Decency required him to wear a high-collared shirt and large cravat just to cover up the mark while he was in public. That was eight months ago, and Dedrak could not see any signs of her enthusiasm or ego abating in the slightest as her rotation approached.

Now, he thought, would be an excellent time to be away from home for a few weeks . . . or months.

"Cachakra, nothing would please me more than to spend my entire month with you." Dedrak lied as smoothly as he could. "But the orders of the Council are most specific and urgent. This human—should he exist—could prove a real threat to the clans. Our entire family enjoys the benefits of my position—its wealth, power, and privilege—and if the council requires that I actually do something from time to time, then so be it. I must do my job, or we all say farewell to these warrens, and I look for other work."

Cachakra gave him a look that could have turned his flaming breath to ice.

"I'm glad that you understand," he said. "It is my wish that you have all the harem and my brood assembled in the morning for the leave-taking. I shall return as soon as my task is complete."

"If that is your wish, my lord," pouted Cachakra with a sudden gleam in her eyes, "then it shall be done. Meanwhile, as my lord is restless this night, perhaps you would indulge me a little in advance of the proscribed schedule?"

Dedrak stammered as his first wife turned toward him. She tore her nightcoat from her shoulders and leaped toward him.

Dedrak only hoped she would not hurt him too badly. No, he thought, a few weeks away from home might just be the thing he needed.

The dragonship drifted down through the atmosphere of E'knar. Dedrak bobbed his head with satisfaction as the great sails of the ship were rotated upward. Each held a glowing mystic bubble. The conjuring dragons that lined the main deck in front of Dedrak constantly renewed these globes of light with their murmured incantations. It was one of many ways to travel the stars, Dedrak knew, and just happened to be the one that worked in this particular region. Other places required things called hyperdrives or force-projectors or ether-enducers. As

Minister of Peace, his actual knowledge of any of these details was limited. His job was to administer justice and wage war for the clans when necessary. The technical aspects of interstellar travel were beyond his purview.

So, too, Dedrak thought humorously to himself, were wild chases after legendary characters from nursery stories.

Dedrak suddenly winced with a renewed pain in his right shoulder.

Dedrak turned and, with a slight limp, made his way down a spiraling ramp to his quarters at the aftmost part of the dragonship. The ship would take nearly another hour to come to the dock at Zeklak—the last outpost to have reported seeing a human. He could afford the time to return to his cabin.

Dedrak carefully unbuttoned his traveling coat and slipped it off over his wings. The cabin was cramped compared to the warrens to which he was accustomed—merely twenty feet tall and only sixty feet at its greatest length. Such were the rigors of shipboard life, he reminded himself. Space was at a premium. Dedrak draped the coat over the side of a low table before him and glanced again at the sheaf of papers that were spread across its surface.

Legends, the dragon reminded himself.

He reflected on what those papers had told him about humans. They had not been known among the Tsultak Imperium in over two thousand years. Some of the legends claim it to be closer to three thousand, although the difference was lost on Dedrak. All of the legends from that time centered around some mythic creature called L'kan of the Star-sunderer, who was the greatest and most dread of humankind. His magic and power were undisputed and terrible. Worlds were destroyed through the use of his Star-sunderer—a human device of such awful power that not even the collected clans could stand before it. This thing called "sword" mastered the dragons and nearly silenced their songs for all time among the stars.

So the legends said.

Dedrak sniffed.

"Nonsense," he sniffed once more. "Little creatures without wings flying among the stars? No taller than the length of my talons and capable of bringing entire warrens to their knees? I'm chasing phantoms of smoke!"

Dedrak picked up his coat and turned to hang it on the wallpeg. As he did so, the great suit of gleaming dragon-armor that awaited him caught his eye. Its metallic scales were polished to a brilliant shine. The great headpiece, molded specifically for his skull, sparkled with over a hundred inlaid gems. The barding for his flanks and the breastplate were magnificently tooled in gold, titanium, and silver over the strongest forged steel. The tailpiece alone was encrusted with over a thousand diamonds. The claw extensions were of a metal alloy that held its edge for over a hundred years of battle use.

Dedrak sighed. It was time to put on the heavy armor and prepare for the hunt.

What would humans want from dragons anyway, he wondered?

Dedrak lumbered up on the ship's deck, the planks creaking under his weight. He was in full battle armor, its plates gleaming painfully into the crew's eyes under the E'knari sun. Dedrak looked forward to the respect that his armor always engendered among other dragons of the clan. If only the blasted suit were not so cumbersome and heavy, he thought. Yet as he stepped onto the deck, not a single dragon aboard turned to look at him. Each was craning his neck wide over the port side railing of the main deck.

No one paid attention to his entrance.

Rage threatened to boil up within him at their lack of respect but was quickly replaced by cold reason. Few things could account for such a lack of protocol.

Something must be dreadfully wrong.

Dedrak lumbered forward toward the captain—an ancient dragon named Djekar. The thunderous shaking of Dedrak's movements on deck brought the captain to turn toward the Minister of Peace.

"By all the Stars," Djekar hissed, his lips curling back in fear. "In all my ages, I have never seen the like!"

Dedrak pushed passed the captain to look over the railing for himself.

The ship drifted slowly over the trees toward the massive landing dock jutting out from the rockface before them. Various warrens could be seen in the vertical cliff face and, at first observation everything seemed in order, if a bit quiet.

Then he saw it.

Several dragon carcasses were hanging bloodily from the warrens of the cliff face. Dedrak's gaze drifted downward, following the bloody trail.

In the clearing drifting slowly beneath them lay a scene of carnage. At first, Dedrak's mind refused to accept what his eyes told him was true. Yet the more he observed, the more real the scene became, until the linking chains of his armor shook terribly under outrage building within him.

Dead dragons. Murdered. Flayed. Burned. Exploded. Drawn and quartered. Every dragon was stripped of its clothing and left obscenely naked. Entire claws were missing, as was every single head. Every conceivable way to violate the sacred bodies of the Tsultak clans lay displayed openly under the E'knar sun.

"Warriors to the deck!" the captain cried.

"What?" Dedrak responded slowly, his mind still dulled by the butchery drifting below the ship's hull.

"The E'knari shall pay for this insult!" Captain Djekar trumpeted loudly. "An attack upon our rightful colony! They shall feel the sting of our hot breath before the day is out! The deaths of our clan shall be avenged a thousandfold!"

Dedrak turned on Djekar. "You shall not, Captain! I am the Minister of Peace for the Empiris. No investigation has been conducted here, nor have the required rituals been completed! It is proscribed by the New Code!"

"New Code?" Djekar snapped back, his nostrils flaring. "This is the frontier, Flamishar! What is the New Code to this atrocity? Where was the New Code when the blood of our kin was being spilt in unspeakable savagery? The New Code . . . it has no place here!"

Dedrak lunged forward, the weight of his armor adding to his momentum as his body struck the ship captain. Djekar was pressed bodily backward against the huge main mast of the ship. The captain opened his leathery wings, but it was too late. Dedrak's own wings already were pushing forward, his forearm pressing the long neck of the dragon captain against the mast. The Minister's tail whipped quickly around, despite the weight of the tail armor, its sharp end pointing directly at a gap between the captain's throat scales.

"The New Code is everything," Dedrak intoned with a snarl. "We are a clan of honor and virtue,

Djekar! Without the New Code, our songs would no longer be sung among the stars—we would have died as a race long ago. We do not abandon the New Code whenever our bloodlust demands it of us! Do we understand one another, Captain?"

"Yes," hissed Djekar. "I hear your words and do obey, lord Minister of Peace."

"You know the penalty for questioning the New Code, Djekar?"

"Yes," Djekar hissed more quietly. "I do, my lord Minister of Peace."

"Then consider yourself fortunate that I failed to hear you clearly when last you spoke in haste. I would not desecrate ground so hallowed as that which is before us by adding to it the body of a traitor to our Empiris."

Dedrak released the captain and turned scornfully away from him.

"The New Code separates us from the evil that has been done to us, Djekar," Dedrak intoned somberly. "Now, make landing at the port that I might track down those who have offended our race and bring them to justice—as prescribed by the Code!"

The fitted stone cracked under him as Dedrak leaped onto the pier that jutted from the cliff face. Djekar's ship cleared away from the platform at once and sailed off in the general direction of E'kritanush, the traditional capital of E'knar. Had this been a case of open warfare, then the entire complement would have accompanied him on this journey, but the New Code was quite clear on this subject. This was a Quest for Honor. As such, it was to be conducted singly until it was deemed that the attack was perpetrated by an opposing clan or government rather than an individual. Djekar had specific instructions to keep his craft on station should the situation become clear and assistance be required.

The very real possibility that such assistance would be needed was growing by the moment. Zeklak had been an outpost settlement on E'knar, but it had been well defended, and the dragons of the region were not accustomed to strangers. That so many of his clansmen had been destroyed so swiftly frightened Dedrak. He had his battle armor and was perhaps the most prepared of the dragon warriors of his time. Still, in this moment, as he looked down from the docking platform to the dreadful scene below, he could not help but wonder whether he was up to this task.

In that moment, Dedrak knew fear. It was the fear of the doomed, for he felt himself trapped between the New Code and the despair of facing a horrendous foe. In that moment, the lark of adventure and escape from the machinations of his harem seemed distant and small. His business had become deadly.

He could face the unknown with honor and die, or he could abandon the New Code and live a life not worth the living.

Dedrak stepped down the wide stairs leading to the blood-soaked clearing below. He knew that there was no choice after all. The New Code was what separated him from the butchery before him. It was what made him better than the animals that had committed this sacrilege. He would defend it to his death.

Methodically he examined each of the corpses—or what remained of them. It was grim work but necessary to complete his investigation. He discovered a clutch of broken dragon eggs. The remains of several unborn dragons lay among the shells. The sight sickened him, but he continued, cataloging a list of sins whose outrages would soon surpass anything the New Code addressed.

He was prepared, however, to deal with it. Because he was Minister of Peace, it was his province to mete out vengeance and justice as proscribed by the New Code. By the time he reached the base of the clearing, it was a duty he was well prepared to execute.

Something caught Dedrak's gaze at the base of the clearing just at the tree line. The grasses there had been trampled thoroughly, and the blood seemed to be tracked in that same direction. Dedrak moved forward carefully, craning his great head down closer to the ground. In places the grasses had been churned into mud.

Tracks!

Dedrak looked more closely at the tracks. The prints were unlike any creature he had ever seen. They had a minute stride of less than a talon's length. Longer than an E'knari to be sure, but the E'knari always were without shoes on their own world. These tracks had a strange but uniform pattern impressed into the mud. By their depth he also judged them to be quite heavy.

"By the Stars," Dedrak murmured. "Humans!"

Dedrak slid through the dense foliage. The humans had not bothered to disguise their tracks. Dedrak took this as a sign of their arrogance. No predator would leave so common a trail unless it was contemptuously sure of its supremacy over its prey. Once more, fear tugged at Dedrak's heart as he continued to advance.

Dedrak tracked his prey to a deep gorge. The E'knari sun could not penetrate its depths. Dense foliage carpeted the floor of the chasm, no doubt hiding the terrible humans that now lurked there.

Dedrak said a prayer to his ancestors and spread his wings. With a minor incantation, the magic of his armor was activated, and the dragon soared as gently and as quietly as a feather down toward the base of the deep ravine.

Dedrak quickly picked up the trail once more and drifted quietly through the dense and dark foliage. Quite abruptly, the dense woods that had surrounded him gave way to another scene of carnage. The tree trunks about him had been splintered with their limbs laid flat and twisted on the ground.

"Some terrible battle was fought here," Dedrak murmured to himself as he floated over a massive fallen tree and was suddenly brought up short.

In the center of all the destruction, half buried in the ground, lay a huge metallic egg. It was apparently cracked. A wide, ragged gap ran from the crater up one side and nearly to the top of its curve. The destruction radiated out in all directions from the egg, and the trail had led him directly to this spot.

Dedrak let out a long, thin breath of smoke as he whispered quietly to himself. "A human egg! Each of their eggs must carry a vast brood—like a clutch of many in a single shell. What a discovery! I could easily be awarded the Star of Nine for this—should I live that long."

The danger of what he was attempting suddenly occurred to him. He was not back in his own warren yet. Dedrak checked his armor and snorted a few times as he stoked his own internal flames in preparation of his approach. When the fire in his belly seemed hot enough and his mystical armor was prepared, he

extended his claws and drifted silently toward the rup-
tured human egg.

The ravine was silent. Dedrak drifted closer.

Something was moving within the darkness of the
egg's broken shell.

A sharp sound of metal rang out.

Dedrak shook but kept his resolve, his claw extensions held forward and at the ready. At last, the massive
dragon came to the cracked shell itself. Something indeed
was moving within the shell. Dedrak's heart was racing,
and he felt a little lightheaded. The truth was that he was
really too young to be the Minister of Defense. His clan
had arranged the appointment with the majority of the
Council of Nine as a political move. He had participated
in many battles and was an accomplished warrior and
statesman, yet never had he come up against anything
like this before. Thoughts of the horrors that might lurk
just yards away ran rampant through his mind. Yet still he
moved closer, as if in some nightmare from which he
could not awaken, driven by the Code and by his duty.

Resolve suddenly took hold of him. Dedrak grasped
the ragged edge of the metal egg and tore it aside.

A black-clad human looked back at him from
under a metal beam that pinned it. Seeing the fierce
armor of the mammoth dragon ripping the metal aside
not three feet from where he lay, the human cried out
in fear and alarm.

Dedrak, shocked with horror at seeing the human
screaming at him fiercely not a claw's breadth away,
reared back, trumpeted loudly once . . . and fainted.

Dedrak came to his senses.

It was late afternoon, and he was still in the clearing.

There was a human standing a few yards in front of where his head lay on the ground.

"Feeling better?" the human said.

Dedrak instantly leaped to his feet. He sucked in a massive breath with which to defend himself, his claw extensions flashing suddenly in the evening light. He was prepared to strike. The human before took a defensive stance, his hands rising before him with globes of blue light suddenly appearing in his palms.

Dedrak, Minister of Peace for all the clans, spread his wings even as his eyes narrowed. Here was an uncertain target, one whose capabilities were only known in legend and story. Dedrak's head wove around on his long neck, trying to examine the human from various sides while also presenting a moving target to his foe.

"Look, dragon, I only wanted to thank you!"

"Thank me!" Dedrak roared. "You who are unworthy to speak to me dare to offer me thanks for anything? You who have murdered my kinsmen and offended the very life and honor of all the Tsultak dragons across all space and time? I am the Minister of Peace to the Tsultak Majestik. I answer only to the Lord Master of the K'dei and Arch-empiris of the Majestik Sphere—may the celestial spheres shine forever on his magnificence and wisdom, all praise to his righteous reign and blessing upon his clutch and brood. You, hideous creature, shall surrender yourself to the justice of my wrath that your clan shall answer for your crimes life for life and blood for blood! Your crimes are beyond counting in the annals of the . . . of the . . ."

Curiosity. It was one of Dedrak's worst faults.

The dragon's eyes suddenly narrowed. "How is it that I understand your words, human?"

"Ah," the black figure before him continued to move under the dragon's gaze. "It's something of a gift, you might say—from me to you. I just thought it might help us understand one another a little better."

"You have nothing you could possibly surrender to me except your life, worthless creature," Dedrak responded, suddenly coming back to his sense of duty and the New Code. "Your crimes against the Majestik are unprecedented. Surrender or die!"

"Those are my only options?" the human asked quickly.

"In the name of the K'dei, I hereby pronounce death sentence upon . . ."

"I surrender!"

Dedrak stopped in mid-sentence and stared. "What did you say?"

"I said I surrender," the human said, louder than before.

"Liar!" Dedrak roared. "It is well known that all humans are cunning liars and twisters of the truth!"

The black-cloaked human circled around warily, trying to find some advantage. "What if I told you I was lying when I said I surrendered?"

"Aha!" Dedrak sneered. "Just as I thought!"

"But then I would be lying about the fact that I had lied," the human shouted back. "Wouldn't that mean that I actually had surrendered?"

Dedrak froze, his eyes narrowing. "Humans! Cunning indeed! Slick words and an oiled tongue. Your legends precede you, evil monster!"

"As do your own legends, great Minister of Peace," the human returned cautiously. "I know your cause is just. Your clans have been greatly offended by the horrors that have taken place. My organization—my clan—is not a part of what has happened here. Yet there are those humans who are committing these unthinkable atrocities. I have been sent to investigate, just as you have, to stop these . . ."

"Liar!" Dedrak trumpeted and his voice shook the trees the entire length of the valley.

"I do not lie," the human responded firmly. "I am your prisoner. We both want to know exactly what is happening here. I tell you now that, if you kill me, you will never put a stop to what is happening to your clans. However, if you do as I ask, I believe that you will be allowed to mete out the justice that your Code requires."

"Humans lie," Dedrak said firmly.

"That is often so," the human replied. "Trust comes hard—but we must start somewhere. I put myself at your mercy."

In that moment, the black-robed human straightened and dropped his hands to his sides. The glowing magic in his hands vanished in a slight thunderclap.

Dedrak moved swiftly, his coiled neck suddenly straightened as he head lunged with incredible speed directly at the head of the standing human. His mind raced as he moved. Strike while you still can! Never trust a human! His jaws gaped open. His needle-like teeth gleamed in the evening sun.

Trust comes hard—but we must start somewhere!

His jaw slammed shut, his incisors clicking noisily less than a talon's width from the face of the human. The black robed figure was sweating profusely but had not moved. Dedrak snorted puffs of hot smoke from his nostrils to both sides of the diminutive figure that was shaking slightly just beyond the end of his nose.

"You are under sentence of death, and I will execute you when I choose to do so . . . but what do you have in mind?" Dedrak rumbled with a low voice that shook the stones beneath the feet of the human.

"A short trip and a little subterfuge on our part should fulfill your quest," the human said as he once more found his voice.

"I will not lie," Dedrak responded.

"I don't want you to lie," the human said after taking a deep breath. "I just want you to keep silent and listen."

The human paused for a moment.

"As a matter of fact," the human said, baring its teeth slightly, "I want you to promise me that you won't kill me until—let's say, until the dawn of this world rises again on your scales."

"And if I should make such a ridiculous promise?" Dedrak snorted.

"Then I promise that you'll have that justice that you are looking for—and that you will more than have fulfilled your glorious quest before that same sun rises. It's my promise to you. Now, will you promise as much to me?"

Dedrak looked at the human. *Trust comes hard.*

"Promise me that you will submit to the justice that the Code requires at the moment of that selfsame dawn," Dedrak's deep voice rumbled once more.

"I so promise—on my honor as a Vestis and on the Nine Oracles of the Omnet."

Dedrak narrowed his eyes once more. "Is such a promise sacred to your kind?"

The human looked over the great snout of the dragon with its small, bright eyes. "It is most sacred to my kind."

"Then I promise not to destroy you until the sun of E'knar rises on my scales once more."

The human considered for a moment, then spoke again. "Promise me also that you will not speak again to any human during that same time—unless I speak to you first."

"This goes beyond tolerance!" Dedrak trumpeted. "Humans have always bargained for their lives with lies! I should kill you where you stand!"

"But you will not," the human countered. "I am the key to your discovering the truth. Kill me, and the truth dies with me. Kill the truth, and many more of your clan will fall before the horrors you have already witnessed!

"I have given my word twice," the human pressed once more. "Promise me this one thing more, and both truth and your clan will triumph!"

Dedrak's words were quiet but clearly audible. "Very well, I so promise."

"On your honor and your Code?" the human demanded smoothly.

We must start somewhere.

"Yes," Dedrak sighed. "On my honor and on the New Code."

Dedrak floated quietly through the trees, his human prisoner moving with surprising silence through the bush below. The human wore a red suit that covered his entire body, and some sort of helmet—also completely red—which hid his face from Dedrak's piercing gaze. Dedrak had been suspicious of it at first, until the human had allowed Dedrak to burn, chew, claw, and otherwise mutilate several similar costumes. Each appeared to be rather poorly made—so far as Dedrak could determine—and offered little or no protection against various natural weapons, let alone his enhanced battle armor. Dedrak had witnessed all of this in silence. He noted curiously that his prisoner had not spoken to him since the dragon had sworn the curious oath. Yet Dedrak also knew that he needed the truth. This one tiny creature did not seem capable of the terrible destruction he had witnessed earlier. No, the truth lay somewhere else.

The trail that Dedrak had followed earlier continued beyond the metallic egg. It was this trail that his prisoner picked up below. Together they wound their quiet way down the valley toward a great confluence of three canyons.

There were several small fires burning around the confluence. Their smoke drifted lazily upward to curl into a thin layer at the top of the canyon's vertical walls. *It obscures the stars,* Dedrak thought to himself.

A glowing dome could be seen in the center of a large clearing directly before Dedrak. The great dragon squinted in the darkness, trying to see the outlines of the thing toward which he drifted slowly. Perhaps if he gained a little altitude he could get a better look, he thought. Dedrak spread his wings slightly, pulling his head higher as his magically enhanced armor began to raise him up.

Suddenly, the armor became dead weight. Dedrak fought down a rush of panic. The mystic spells had failed! He was too low, too slow, and too heavy suddenly to stay aloft. Instinctively, his wings began to beat furiously, but the armored bracers that lined the leading edge of his wings hampered them. He began to tumble down through the trees, snapping branches and trunks even as he continued to struggle with the activation gems in his armor plating. He hit the ground with a terrible thud, plowing a long furrow through the brush. Dedrak came to rest on his right side against a rock outcropping, the breath pushed out of him from the impact.

Wheezing, Dedrak turned his head. Several humans, all clad in the same red outfit as his prisoner, were walking toward him from the woods.

His prisoner, however, was waving at the newcomers and shouting. "Nice shooting, men! I think you may have taken the prize for this hunt!"

Dedrak tried to strike at the deceiver, but he found that he could not move.

"Who goes there?" came the cry from the approaching figures.

"I'm Luf Darmen," Dedrak's former prisoner replied. "I'm the scout that brought you this beast, and I demand a full share for my trouble!"

One of the newly arrived humans lifted up his helmet visor and inspected the jewel-encrusted armor of the dragon with obvious lust. "It's been a long day, but I'm looking forward to taking this one apart!"

"You and me both, brother! Strip his armor while he's still stunned—all of it, mind you! Don't kill him, though! This one's old and feeble—mute and fireless as well. I think we might take him back alive!"

"As you wish, Luf Darmen," the grinning human smiled in reply. "You've done well!"

Luf Darmen, the dragon thought, as he lay paralyzed on the ground, *if I am still living when the sun rises, you will die squealing between my teeth.*

Naked, a humiliated Dedrak was lifted by magical rods carried by each of the evil humans. By this means he was floated into the center of their hideous encampment. The glowing dome he had seen earlier proved to be a much larger version of the metallic egg in which he had found Luf Darmen. Several smaller, similar eggs were set around the edge of the clearing. No, Dedrak realized, they are not eggs. These are the ships of the humans. This is how they cross the stars.

Before him strode Luf Darmen—the human who had betrayed him and brought him to the very center of those who sought to destroy his kind. Darmen led the procession to the base of the largest ship and then stopped. The bearers stopped as well and, indicating with their glowing rods, lowered Dedrak to the ground of the clearing.

The entire procession had attracted quite a crowd. Hundreds of humans began to gather around the clearing. A few still wore their opaque red helmets, but the vast majority of them had removed both their helmets and their red outer garments. Dedrak was suddenly struck at how different the humans were from one another. Light hides and dark hides in all imaginable shades. Hair colors spanning rainbows in lengths ranging from long braids to none at all. Thin, wide, tall, short: all were undeniably human and yet so very different one from another. Dedrak, when he had considered the possibility of their existence at all, had thought that there might be some means of telling the males from the females. It had never occurred to him that such a vast variety of types might make such distinctions difficult for the untrained eye.

A ramp extended from the large ship before them, light spilling from its interior. A single, wide human descended and stood facing Luf Darmen. The wide human, without saying a word, then walked around Dedrak, inspecting his naked scales before coming full circle and addressing Luf directly.

"Nice prize!" he said flatly.

"Yes, Maris Phlyn, it is a great treasure indeed," Luf responded as he removed his helmet, just a claw's length from Dedrak's maw.

Maris's face fell into a frown. "You aren't Luf Darmen!"

"I am Vestis Khyne Enderly of the Inquisition."

A gasp rose from the assemblages at the sight of his face. Several weapons were trained on Khyne Enderly with deadly earnest.

"Maris Phlyn, you are under arrest for the murder of the Dragons of the Tsultak Majestik. You will surrender yourselves to their representatives for trial according to their laws."

Maris snorted. "Or what?"

Enderly said simply, "I will do my duty."

"I, too, will do my duty," Maris said with a laugh. "Have you any idea how many mystical societies across the stars want even the most insignificant part of a dragon?"

"It's still murder. There isn't a legitimate government among the stars that would sanction what you're doing here! Humans are not all the same," Khyne said, his voice carrying a little farther than before. "The vast majority of humanity deplores what you are doing here!"

Dedrak shifted his head so that he could hear well. He realized that Khyne was actually speaking for his benefit.

"And I'm supposed to care?" Maris giggled. "Oh, you are funny, Enderly. I'm going to miss watching your news reports. The fact is that your story dies here with you! I don't need to please the masses as you do! Trade in dragon meat, dragon scales, dragon eyes, dragon tails—it might be illegal, but there are enough people willing to pay anything to obtain them that legality might not be high on my list of priorities."

"Humanity considers you a criminal and a murderer," Enderly shouted.

"Murderer? Of what?" Maris yelled back in red-faced rage, pointing to Dedrak as he spoke. "That?"

"You know," Khyne said idly as he folded his arms across his chest and gazed up. "Your mystic dampening technology is pretty impressive." Khyne turned slowly to face Dedrak as he spoke. His hands were cupped before his chest. "By the way, you seem to do well against panicked dragons with long range weapons and against armored dragons with your dampening projectors. That is because the Tsultak have chosen to try living civilized lives. Yet beneath the veneer of their clothes and their magical armor, their Code and their manners, there still beat the hearts of dragons, warriors, and predators."

Dedrak's great eyes stared into the eyes of the human standing before him.

"You're a dead man, Enderly," Maris intoned.

"I was just wondering," the Vestis responded, "how you and your gang would fare if you were stripped of your all your smug technology to face a naked warrior dragon who wanted to exact pain for pain done to his clan?"

Dedrak shook within his glowing restraints. His eyes were locked with Enderly's as he inhaled a great breath.

The Vestis turned suddenly, a brilliant blue flash bursting from his hands. The star flew from his hands and slammed against the dome of Maris's ship. The dome exploded, and the lights that had illuminated the clearing quietly died. Muzzle flashes punctuated the darkness from the weapons around the clearing, but few found their mark. Those that did bounced off the dragon's scales, whose magic had suddenly returned.

The darkness was complete and, in the sudden absence of light, it was also blinding. Humans stumbled about in the darkness. Several of them called out for light.

Dedrak granted their wish. Searing flame erupted from his nostrils.

The dawn rose over the E'knar wilderness. Billowing flames roiled out of the canyon below Dedrak. Justice had been done. The human infestation had been cleansed.

All, that was, but one.

Khyne Enderly stood next to Dedrak, his soot-streaked face examining the destruction below.

Enderly sighed. "The dawn has risen. The light has hit your scales, Minister. Does your Code require that you kill me now?"

"No," Dedrak smiled. "I may defer that judgment to the Council of Nine. The truth is that I look forward to bringing you before the Council. No one has brought a mythological creature back before the Nine before. Some may be concerned—but not all of us will be your enemy. Not all dragons think alike. Do not judge us so harshly."

Khyne smiled. "And I hope you'll extend me the same courtesy."

"Perhaps," Dedrak rumbled. "Besides, I should bring a present to placate my first wife. A pet, perhaps . . ."

Khyne could not tell whether the dragon was smiling.

COPYRIGHTS

MARGARET WEIS is the *New York Times* bestselling co-creator, with Tracy Hickman, of the World of Dragonlance, which now covers two trilogies, Dragonlance Chronicles and Dragonlance Legends, four books of short stories, and numerous novels. Other series, also written with Tracy Hickman, include the Death Gate Cycle and the epic science fiction series Star of the Guardian. Her most recent series is the action/adventure series featuring an intergalactic mercenary company, Mag Force 7, written with her husband, Don Perrin. Margaret and Don live in a converted barn near Lake Geneva, Wisconsin.

TRACY HICKMAN is the co-creator of the world bestselling Dragonlance books, the most recent novel being *The Dragons of Summer Flame,* co-written with Margaret Weis. He has also collaboratedwith Margaret Weis on several other novel series, including Death Gate Cycle and Starshield, Book 1: *Sentinels*. His latest book is a stand-alone novel entitled *The Immortals*. He lives in Flagstaff, Arizona.